PLAYBOY'S CHRISTMAS LIST

BY
CAROL MARINELLI

THE ARMY DOC'S BABY BOMBSHELL

BY
SUE MacKAY

MILLS
BOON

12778224

Carol Marinelli recently filled in a form asking for her job title. Thrilled to be able to put down her answer, she put 'writer'. Then it asked what Carol did for relaxation and she put down the truth—'writing'. The third question asked for her hobbies. Well, not wanting to look obsessed, she crossed her fingers and answered 'swimming'—but, given that the chlorine in the pool does terrible things to her highlights, I'm sure you can guess the real answer!

Sue MacKay lives with her husband in New Zealand's beautiful Marlborough Sounds, with the water at her doorstep and the birds and the trees at her back door. It is the perfect setting to indulge her passions of entertaining friends by cooking them sumptuous meals, drinking fabulous wine, going for hill walks or kayaking around the bay—and, of course, writing stories.

PLAYBOY ON HER CHRISTMAS LIST

BY
CAROL MARINELLI

Published in Great Britain 2016
By Mills & Boon, an imprint of HarperCollins*Publishers*
1 London Bridge Street, London, SE1 9GF

© 2016 Carol Marinelli

ISBN: 978-0-263-91528-0

Our policy is to use papers that are natural, renewable and recyclable
products and made from wood grown in sustainable forests.
The logging and manufacturing processes conform to the legal
environmental regulations of the country of origin.

Printed and bound in Spain
by CPI, Barcelona

Dear Reader,

I hope you enjoy reading about Daniel and Holly as much as I did writing about them.

For me, Christmas is such a special time, and I enjoy every moment of the build-up and all the tradition that surrounds it. I know, though, that Christmas can be a difficult time for a lot of people. My hero, Daniel, just wants Christmas to be over and done with, and he has no interest in all the festivities. Certainly the last thing he wants is romance. I love writing *opposites attract* stories, and my heroine, Holly, not only adores Christmas, she is head over heels in love with Daniel too!

This is my first story set in The Primary Hospital in London—a busy, modern teaching hospital—and I am looking forward to writing many more.

Happy reading,

Carol x

Books by Carol Marinelli

Mills & Boon Medical Romance

Desert Prince Docs
Seduced by the Sheikh Surgeon

The Hollywood Hills Clinic
Seduced by the Heart Surgeon

Baby Twins to Bind Them
Just One Night?
The Baby of Their Dreams
The Socialite's Secret

Mills & Boon Modern Romance

The Billionaire's Legacy
Di Sione's Innocent Conquest

The Sheikh's Baby Scandal

Visit the Author Profile page at
millsandboon.co.uk for more titles.

**Praise for
Carol Marinelli**

'It had me in tears at the beginning, and then again
at the end, and I could hardly put it down. A brilliant
emotional read by Carol Marinelli!'

—*Goodreads* on
The Baby of Their Dreams

CHAPTER ONE

'HOLLY, PUT THE decorations back. I've already told you that there are quite enough already. This is the emergency department, *not* the children's ward.'

Holly, dressed in baggy scrubs and weighted down with tinsel and glittery silver snowmen, jumped when she heard Kay's strong Irish accent and realised that the nurse unit manager was sitting at the nurses' station.

Caught!

Holly had also thought that locum registrar Daniel Chandler was on his supper break but, no, he was drinking a coffee at the desk. Holly's blush spread like spilled red wine across her chest as she stood, dripping glitter, and was scolded in front of the very suave Daniel.

'I thought that you'd gone home,' Holly admitted to Kay.

'I know that you did,' Kay tartly responded, but then she let out a long sigh. 'I'm staying back to try and sort out the Christmas roster.'

'But it's already done.' Holly frowned. The last thing she wanted were any alterations to the roster—her plans to be with her family over the festive break had been made weeks ago. But Kay had other ideas and proceeded to tell Holly the reasons that things might have to change.

'Yes, but since then I've had two members of staff go

on extended sick leave. Thank goodness for Nora, she's offered to work Christmas night but things are *very* tight. Now, put the tinsel back where it belongs, please and, when you've done that, tie up your hair.'

'It's already tied up.'

'No, Holly, it's not.'

Holly's long, curly brown hair always started the shift in a neat ponytail and then proceeded to work its way out of its confines, curl by wild curl.

As Holly slunk back to the storeroom Daniel found himself smiling.

He'd only been doing locum shifts at The Primary for a couple of months but it was enough to know that Holly Jacobs took her Christmas decorations very seriously. She had been waiting all afternoon for Kay, who was supposed to have finished at four, to go home so that Holly could, as she put it, 'Christmas the place up'.

The Primary Hospital was a modern, busy, North London teaching hospital. It was very different in character from the prestigious Royal, where Daniel had started as a medical student and worked his way up to Accident and Emergency Registrar.

Working at The Primary was a step down, his father, an esteemed professor of surgery, would say. Certainly, renowned Professor Marcus Chandler could never fathom why his son was doing locum shifts at various hospitals around London when he could have any hours he chose at the Royal.

For Daniel, though, working at The Primary felt, if not a step up, then a step in the right direction. When he had commenced his first shift here Kay had rolled her eyes at the prospect of giving a tour to yet another temporary doctor but had soon realised Daniel was very good at his job.

More importantly, Daniel was really enjoying his work. Here there was no reputation to uphold; instead, he was slowly making his own.

And it had been noticed.

'You know there's a consultant's position coming up,' Kay said. She stared at the computer as she spoke.

'I do,' Daniel responded, and confirmed that he had been approached. 'I've already told Mr Edwards that I'm not interested.'

'Are we not good enough for you, Daniel?'

'There was a consultant's position at the Royal when I left,' Daniel pointed out. 'I wasn't interested then either.'

'You're a mystery,' Kay said, and gave a soft laugh then brushed from the desk some glitter dust that Holly had left in her wake. 'Holly would have glitter everywhere,' she tutted. 'It's an emergency department, not Santa's Grotto. People don't need festivities waved in their face when they come here. This time of year is often hard enough for our patients. I'm already over Christmas and it's only the second of December.'

'You're preaching to the converted,' Daniel agreed.

'Are you not a fan of Christmas?' Kay asked.

'Nope.'

'Nor me,' Kay agreed. 'It brings out the worst in everyone. You should see this place on Christmas night.' She got back to the staring at the computer screen, though she carried on chatting with Daniel. 'Are you going to the emergency department Christmas party tonight?'

'Nope.'

Kay laughed at his truculent response but then she frowned. 'How come you're still here? I thought you were just doing a few locums until your friend got married. The wedding was last week, wasn't it?'

'It was.' Daniel nodded and carried on writing.

He had finished up his role at the Royal at the end of September and had just been killing time until his best friend Rupert's wedding had taken place. Soon he would be taking a year off. First he would hit the ski slopes in Switzerland and then…well, he'd see what happened when it happened.

'Why didn't you just start your travels and fly back for the wedding?' Kay asked.

'Oh, no…' Daniel shook his head. 'Once I'm gone, I'm gone for good.'

'That sounds profound!' Holly was back, minus tinsel and snowmen. Her hair had been scraped back into an even tighter ponytail but was now dotted with glitter. She had a worried expression aimed at Kay because she really *needed* Christmas off this year.

Holly knew that, if the roster had to be changed, she didn't really have a leg to stand on—around this time last year her mother had been diagnosed with breast cancer. Then, despite Holly being rostered to work Christmas and New Year, Kay had been wonderful, giving Holly ten days off so that she could have some family time.

The trouble was, a cancer diagnosis didn't follow a specified timeline with a neat conclusion to signal the end.

The last year had been a fraught one, with Holly taking her little red car up and down the motorway every chance she could and wrestling the off duty around her mother's treatment. Esther had recently had to have a second round of chemotherapy, and while the news was a whole lot better Esther really wanted her family home for Christmas.

And lately, what Esther wanted, Esther got!

Holly blew out a tense breath. She loved her family dearly but things had been a bit difficult lately, to say the least.

While she hoped that Kay would understand when she came to make the necessary changes Holly needed to be sure. 'Kay, could I have a word?'

'If it's about the Christmas roster, the answer is no. Your request has been noted. And, yes,' she added. 'I do know it's also your birthday.'

'Were you a Christmas baby, Holly?' Daniel asked.

'Why do you think I'm called Holly?'

'Because you're so prickly.'

It was a small joke—Holly was the *least* prickly person. She was happy and sunny and that they could tease each other about such things without having to explain they were joking, well, it was sort of where they were at.

'So,' Daniel asked, 'do you miss out on your birthday?'

'No.' Holly shook her head. 'My parents always make sure that both are celebrated.'

'Of course they do, Polly.'

She got the Pollyanna insinuation and gave him a sweet smile. 'Better than cynical. So,' she asked, returning to the conversation she had walked in on the tail end of, 'why didn't you just fly home for the wedding?'

'There was the stag night to organise,' Daniel explained. 'Actually, there were two of them.'

'You could have just flown back for a couple of weeks.' Holly repeated Kay's assumption but Daniel shook his head.

'Rupert had a highly strung bride-to-be who was worried that I'd be a no-show if I left the country. She was actually right to be concerned—as I said, when I'm gone, I'm gone.'

Holly didn't like that.

Daniel had worked quite a few shifts now and she was getting used to having him around.

Or rather she was starting to get used to the feeling that an egg beater had been set at full whisk in the middle of her chest.

Daniel was, for want of a better word, gorgeous.

Yes, yes, he was tall and had thick black hair and a scent that had her toes curl, he had *all* of that but it was his eyes that had first sent Holly's world spinning.

Absolute navy.

It was as if the artist had meant to get back and add silvery flecks and little dots of aqua but had forgotten to. Yet he was no unfinished masterpiece. Those eyes were just this delicious navy rimmed with a halo of black and, at first look, Holly had been unable to stop staring. She had wanted to apologise, to explain she was looking for said silver specks and dots of aqua, but instead she had stared.

And so had he.

At green eyes that had appeared startled.

'Is everything okay?' he had checked.

'I have an abdo pain…' Holly had attempted to explain that she had a patient she would like him to see in Cubicle Four but she had been so flustered that it had come out all wrong. 'And vomiting.'

'Then go and lie down and let me take a look at you.'

His voice was snobby, his humour *hers,* and she had been tempted, almost, to call his bluff and do just that. Instead she had smiled. 'I'll see you in Cubicle Four.'

Holly's abdo pain had turned out to be a twenty-year-old with query appendicitis. Daniel had walked in to where Holly had been holding a bowl for the patient and he had given her a tiny smile to insinuate he had rather hoped she had been lying in wait for him.

'Pity,' he'd said.

Yet a little flirt, though huge to Holly, was just a walk in the park for him. He was suave and from what she gathered he dated a lot, and, in truth, neither was the other's type.

Except…

'What was the wedding like?' Holly asked. She was curious to know more about the reason for delaying his trip.

'Like all weddings are,' Daniel said, as Holly jumped up and sat on the bench beside where he was trying to write his notes. 'Long.'

'What did the bride wear?' she asked.

'From memory, a dress,' Daniel said. 'Possibly it was white.'

'I love winter weddings,' Holly sighed. 'Especially if it's snowing.'

'The church was freezing,' Daniel told her, and from his voice it was clear that he had a rather less dreamy take on things. 'And then it poured with rain for the photos.'

'Who was your plus one?' Kay asked, without turning her head from the computer screen.

'I never take a plus one to a wedding.' Daniel shook his head. 'Well, I haven't for a long time. I learnt the hard way that if you bring a date she assumes that it must mean you're serious. Anyway, I was the best man for this one so all that was expected from me in that department was to get off with the chief bridesmaid.'

'And did you?' Kay asked.

'That would be telling,' Daniel said. 'And I never do.'

He looked at Holly then—just an itsy-bitsy look that told her she'd be in very discreet hands.

God, he was forward!

Yet she smiled at the tiny flirt behind Kay's back.

'Anyway,' Daniel continued, 'I wanted to do the right thing by Rupert. He was very good to me when...' He didn't finish, or rather he just didn't continue with what he had started to say. 'He's a very good friend.'

'So how come you weren't out on the first flight after the wedding?' Kay pushed.

'Just...' He gave a small shrug and it was there that the conversation ended.

Daniel simply didn't answer—he did that a lot.

He might be forward with his flirting but when a conversation veered too close to personal he simply halted it.

Daniel got back to his notes and, interlude over, Kay carried on staring at the off duty, but finally she gave in.

'I'm going home,' Kay said, and closed up the screen. 'Daniel, shall we see you again?'

'I don't think so,' he answered.

Locums came and locums went but Kay gave him a smile that told Daniel he would be missed. 'Well, safe travels,' she said, and then turned to Holly. 'I'll see you tonight at the pub. The night staff should be coming in a little bit early so that the late staff can get to the party at a reasonable time. How are you getting there?'

'Taxi,' Holly said. 'Anna, Laura and I are sharing. Do you want to come with us, Daniel? There's room for one more.'

'I'm not going.'

He offered no reason and thankfully he didn't look up as he spoke because, despite her best efforts, Holly knew her shoulders had briefly slumped, but quickly she righted herself.

Actually, it was good news that he wasn't coming tonight.

The way Holly felt she was at high risk of doing something very stupid where Daniel Chandler was concerned.

Stupid as well as pointless, given that this was his last shift and that very soon he'd be heading off overseas.

Daniel, she had heard, was very into casual one-night stands. Whereas she was the complete opposite.

With one possible exception.

Him.

Oh, it would be bliss to be bad.

Sometimes, all joking and flirting aside, she felt him looking at her and there was a tension between them that Holly was almost convinced wasn't one-sided. Of course, Daniel was a natural-born flirt, but it wasn't just that, there was something in his eyes that could flip her stomach like a pancake...

Egg analogy again, Holly thought to herself, and decided that she must be hungry.

'I'm going to go for my supper break while it's quiet. I'll see you later, Kay.'

'You shall,' Kay said. 'Oh, wait. I got you a present.' She smiled at Daniel. 'I got you one too.'

Kay was big on presents.

Silly things, happy things, she passed on what had made her smile. Her charity wasn't just for the staff, though—there were regular fundraisers held throughout the year on behalf of the homeless.

Kay took the displaced seriously.

She took an overfull bag from beneath the bench and handed them both a slim card from a choice of many.

'An Advent calendar!' Holly beamed.

'I got them at the discount store,' Kay said, clearly delighted with her purchase. 'There's one for everyone.'

'There's chocolate in here,' Daniel said, opening up one of the little windows.

'Of course there is. Have you never had an Advent calendar?' Kay checked.

'Actually, no.'

'It's December the second so you get to eat two,' she told him, 'but after that it's just one a day.'

Daniel gave Holly a sideways smile that told her all twenty-five would be eaten the very moment Kay had gone and Holly smiled back as she shook her head. 'One a day,' she warned him.

'I'm lousy at self-restraint.'

Ouch.

Sometimes, in fact a little too often, he threw out those lines and usually Holly could shrug them off, but it had been getting harder and harder to of late.

'Well, I've got excellent self-control,' Holly replied, and watched the slight questioning rise of one eyebrow.

They were talking about chocolate, Holly told herself.

At least where chocolate was concerned she had self-control.

Where Daniel was concerned it was melting just as fast. It was a good job that he was leaving, Holly decided.

She had a king-size crush on him and she wasn't used to them, well, not for a very long time. At twenty-eight, Holly had rather thought that the days of wild dreams and fixating on someone's every word were long since gone.

They weren't.

Kay was just about to go when Laura, the nurse in charge this evening, came in swiftly.

'Holly—Resus,' she said. 'We've got a cardiac arrest coming in. Fifty-five-year-old male collapsed at home.'

Holly nodded and, supper forgotten, she jumped down from the bench and Daniel got down from his stool to go and prepare for the incoming patient.

'I'll just stay and see if I'm needed...' Kay offered. And Holly was expecting Laura to, as she usually did, point out that they'd be fine and could more than cope but instead Laura gave Kay a worried look.

'Can I have a quick word, Kay?' she asked.

As Laura pulled Kay aside Holly put out an arrest call to alert the medical team to come to Emergency and then started to set up for the incoming patient. Until the team arrived Daniel would be in charge but from working with him she knew that he could more than cope with anything that presented.

'What's going on?' Daniel asked, as he taped some syringes to the vial of medication he'd just pulled up in anticipation of the patient's arrival. He nodded in the direction of Laura and Kay, who were still huddled together and talking.

'I'm not sure.' Holly frowned. 'But something is.'

The alert meant that they had everything ready for the patient, going on the information they had, but just as a blue light flashed in the high windows above, Kay came over and offered more.

'Holly,' Kay said, and her voice was serious as she pulled on a plastic apron to indicate she would be participating in the resuscitation. 'The patient is Nora's husband.'

Holly swallowed. Nora Hewitt was second in charge to Kay and everyone adored her. More importantly, Paul, Nora's husband, was the good man behind a great woman. He was often at the department, picking up Nora or bringing in the lunch she had forgotten and had left sitting in the fridge at home. He always had a friendly word for everyone and should have been at the emergency department Christmas party tonight with his wife.

Instead, he was being raced into Resus on the very edge of death.

There were the sounds of sobs and tears coming from outside, though Holly could tell that it wasn't Nora.

'The daughter is *very* upset,' the paramedic informed them.

'Anna—' Kay called for assistance '—can you stay with the family?'

'Where's the team?' Holly asked in an urgent tone, desperate for them to appear so that Paul could be given the very best chance.

'We'll be fine,' Daniel said in his composed deep voice and Holly glanced over at him.

He was at the head of the resuscitation bed that the paramedics were moving Paul onto and Daniel was his usual mixture of aloof and calm.

It was everything that was needed now.

CHAPTER TWO

'ON MY COUNT,' Daniel said, and Paul was transferred from the ambulance stretcher onto the solid resuscitation bed.

Everyone was a touch flustered. All the staff knew Nora, including the paramedics, and so this was incredibly personal.

But not to Daniel.

He checked the placement of the breathing tube and looked at the monitor once Paul had been transferred to the emergency department equipment. He asked Kay to recommence massage and called for the necessary drugs and did all this as he listened to the handover.

Apparently things had been rather chaotic back at the house. Paul's daughter and her boyfriend had become agitated and distressed and had got somewhat in the way.

'He was in the bathroom when he collapsed.'

'Was someone with him?'

'It was hard to get a clear history.'

Daniel nodded as Holly handed him the drug he had asked for but, aware that everyone was tense and there was the potential for mistakes to be made, he checked and double-checked everything.

Paul was still in an arrhythmia and not responding to drugs, and though he had been shocked several times both at home and en route they had been unable to revert him to a normal rhythm. Daniel delivered more of the same and then called for the defibrillator to be charged and asked for fresh pads to be placed on Paul's chest.

Holly could see that her hands were shaking as she did as asked.

'Is anybody getting a fuller history from the family?' Daniel checked.

'I've sent Anna in to speak with Nora,' Kay said. 'I don't think he has any previous history, though.'

'I want to hear what Nora says.' Daniel was firm. This was no time for hearsay and Kay nodded as for now they worked on.

The emergency team started to arrive and gradually took over. Daniel had it all under control so that they were able to get a full handover as he worked on. Kay was massaging Paul's chest and her face was red and sweating.

'Can you take over, Holly?' she asked.

Holly did so. She was slight and really had to put in an effort to deliver effective massage. She glanced up at the clock and then back to Paul. There had been absolutely no response since he had collapsed back at home.

'Step back,' Mr Dawson, the cardiologist, ordered, and Holly climbed from the bed and once she was safely standing back another shock was delivered.

'So he collapsed at five?' Mr Dawson checked the timeline of events.

It was now five forty-five…

Holly could smell burning from the repeated shocks to his body and she looked over at Kay, who looked up at the clock.

'Was he found collapsed?' Mr Dawson checked.

'We're just waiting to have that verified,' Daniel said. The paramedics had been very thorough in their treatment and had done well but there were still some gaps in the history.

Anna came in then. 'There's no previous history and he's on no medication. Paul was standing in the bathroom, chatting to Nora, when he developed chest pain. Nora sat him on the floor and called for an ambulance. She gave him some aspirin and stayed with him, and a couple of moments later he arrested and she commenced resuscitation straight away.'

It had been a witnessed arrest, which was incredibly relevant, especially given Nora's skills. It was now evident that he'd had effective cardiac massage delivered from the very start.

Not that it seemed to be counting for much.

'Resume massage,' Mr Dawson ordered, and Holly was about to climb back on the bed when Daniel halted her.

'Hold on a moment.' He had his fingers in Paul's groin to feel for a femoral pulse. 'He's got a pulse.'

And then, better than any music, better than any other sound in the world really, the monitor started to deliver bleeps.

Two at first, followed by a long pause, then a run of three and then sinus rhythm kicked in and there was the beep-beep-beep of a rapid heart rate and suddenly there was hope.

It was tainted, though.

Paul had been down for some considerable time. The cardiologists were going through his ECG tracings and deciding whether to take him straight up to ICU or directly to the catheter lab to see exactly what had occurred. The hope was that they could dissolve the blockage and open up the blocked vessels in Paul's heart and minimise damage to the heart muscle.

'I'll go up with him,' Kay said, as she gathered up the necessary equipment for the urgent transfer. 'Daniel, can you go and speak with Nora and explain that Mr Dawson is busy with Paul but he'll be in to get the consent…' Her voice trailed off. 'You know the drill.'

'I do.'

'I forget how experienced you are.'

'That's fine,' Daniel responded with ease, but then he asserted himself—not just with Kay but also with the cardiologist who would like Paul up in the lab, preferably ten minutes ago. 'First of all, though, we need to bring in his wife.'

'Time is of the essence,' Mr Dawson said.

'I'm sure she'll understand that.'

Nora must have been getting ready for the party and chatting to Paul as she did so, with no idea as to what was about to come. One of her eyes was made up with glittery eye shadow and the other was not.

Seeing someone so visibly shaken who was always so together and strong, but doing her best to hold it together, had Holly on the edge of tears.

'He's going to go up very soon,' Holly told Nora quietly, once Mr Dawson had obtained her consent and explained that they'd be moving him to the catheter lab. Holly watched as Nora took one of Paul's hands and held it in both of hers as if trying to warm it.

'He was telling me he'd just hidden my Christmas present.' Nora looked at Paul as she spoke. 'Please, don't leave me,' she asked him, and then, looking at Holly, said, 'I knew the day I met him that he was the one. He took a couple of weeks to get used to the idea…'

Holly didn't know what to say.

What was there to say to add to a love that had lasted for more than thirty years?

And so instead of saying the right thing, Holly found herself wearing her nervous smile.

Thankfully, Nora knew her well enough not to take offence.

'I just need a minute alone with him,' Nora said.

Holly nodded as Anna popped her head around the curtain. 'Nora, your daughter wants to come in.'

'No.' Nora was firm. 'She's too upset and she'd just distress him.'

Kay nodded her head and called for Holly to come the other side of the curtain, leaving Nora with Paul and the anaesthetist. Holly had turned up the volume on the monitors so that the staff could move in quickly if there was any change.

And they listened as Nora told her husband she loved him and to stay strong and that she'd be waiting for him once the procedure was done, and she did it all in a voice that did not waver, just in case Paul could hear.

Holly knew that voice only too well.

She could remember her mother going in for surgery and, because Holly was the only remotely medical person in the family, all questions had been aimed at her. All decisions had been run by Holly too and it had felt overwhelming. Her father had asked her to come with them up to Theatre. When he had started to break down it had been Holly who had stepped in. Holly had concentrated on keeping her smile in place while trying to ignore the fact that her mother was so very weak and frail from the chemotherapy and doing her best not to reveal that she wasn't terrified for her.

'What do you think?' Kay asked Daniel, and Holly looked at his grim face.

'They're giving him every chance.' His response was noncommittal but for Holly it said enough—he didn't think things looked good.

The quiet start had turned into a very busy shift and it didn't relent.

Holly felt all shaken but there was no time to sit down and reflect on what had happened. There was no pause button in Emergency, especially when you needed one.

Just as Paul left, another critically ill patient came in.

Kay handed Paul over to the care of the catheter lab staff but, given she was officially off duty, remained with Nora in the waiting room there. Holly was so busy that she had forgotten completely she was going out tonight and frowned when she saw that it was eight and that the night staff were starting to arrive.

'What are you doing here?' Holly asked.

'So you can leave early for the Christmas party.' Gloria grinned and then saw Holly's serious face. 'What is it?'

And there was no point in not telling the arriving staff—one look at the admissions board and they would see the truth for themselves.

'Nora's husband was brought in...'

As she brought the night staff up to speed Holly admitted that she had changed her mind about going to the party tonight, but Kay had other ideas. She had popped down to Emergency for that very reason, in fact, and called Holly round to her office.

'I need you to give the landlord the cash we've been collecting,' Kay said. They'd all been putting into the collection for a few weeks. 'Holly, I know the last thing you feel like is partying but word is already getting out about Paul. Nora's daughter has put it up on social media and honestly...' Kay let out a long sigh. 'Nora wants the party to go ahead. She thinks if it's called off now it means that we've given up on Paul.'

Holly nodded. 'How is he doing?'

'He's over on Intensive Care. He's in an induced coma and really we shan't know for a few days. Oh, I don't know, Holly, I don't have a very good feeling about it. He was down for a long time.'

'Less than an hour,' Holly pointed out.

'I know but...'

Kay looked as if she was about to cry and Holly had no idea what to say so she offered the only thing she knew might help. 'Do you want a cup of tea?'

Kay laughed the simplicity of Holly's solution and then she let out a little sob. 'I do,' she admitted. 'A quick one and then I'll head back up there. Have one with me?'

Holly brought in a tray as Kay got the envelope from the safe.

'I'd better not lose it,' Holly said, peering inside.

'You'd better not!' Kay barked, and then closed her eyes and leant back in her chair. 'It's nice to relax for five minutes.'

'Did you call Eamon and let him know?' Holly asked, referring to Kay's husband.

'I did. He's going to come and get me when I'm ready but I think I should stay awhile. Poor Nora. Honestly, that family of hers...' Kay rolled her eyes. 'Do you know? Her daughter asked what was going to happen for dinner! Does she not know how a bloody vending machine works? Fancy bothering her mother with that?'

'And fancy bothering you with this,' Daniel said, as he knocked on the half-open door.

'What do you want?' Kay asked. But as Daniel came in, though he gave Kay a smile, he then looked at Holly as he spoke.

'All the night staff are here but Laura is having no luck getting a taxi. The wait is an hour at best. I said that I could drop you all off at the end of my shift, which is right about now.'

'Then you'd better get ready,' Kay said, moving to stand. 'And I'd better get back up to Nora.'

'Finish your tea,' Holly suggested, and thought of the times she had sat with her own family, waiting for news, and how utterly exhausting it was. 'Have a few moments to yourself.'

'I might just do that,' Kay agreed. 'You're not on tomorrow, are you?'

'No, I'm off now till Monday, but I'll call in the morning and see how Paul's doing and—' Her voice halted abruptly as Holly stopped herself from saying what she had been about to—fancy bothering Kay with a stupid thing like the off duty while Paul was so sick, but Nora had been the one practically keeping the off duty running over the Christmas break.

It could wait, Holly knew that, and felt guilty for even considering raising it now.

So instead of worrying about tomorrow, or the next, or the next, she went into the changing room and had the quickest shower ever. There was just time for a dart under the jets and a quick soap and rinse then she dried herself and pulled on her little black dress.

'That's nice,' Anna said as Holly came out. Anna was hogging the one tiny mirror and applying eyeliner, while looking stunning in a very slinky, very red dress. 'You *always* look good in that.'

It was such a backhanded compliment that Holly actually stopped in her tracks for a second, before sitting down on the bench and pulling out her make-up bag.

'Thanks.' Holly smiled, pretending she had missed the rather bitchy comment. Oh, she was in no mood for make-up but it was certainly needed! As well as that the steam, even from a very brief shower, had made her curly hair even more so.

'Daniel's waiting,' Anna said rather pointedly as she turned from the mirror, all ready, just as Holly got her mascara out. 'We don't really have much time.'

'Daniel can wait for five minutes,' Holly answered. She hadn't asked him to play taxi driver and, more to the point, she wouldn't have minded the long wait for a taxi just to be able to get ready and allow for some time to jolt herself out of her morose mood. 'Or you guys can go on without me and I'll see you there.'

'No need for that. I'll go and wait with Daniel,' Anna said.

'Sure.'

'I'll see if I can persuade him to stay for a drink. After all, it is effectively his leaving do.'

'It's been Daniel's leaving do since October,' Holly said. There was a knot of disquiet in her stomach, though, at the thought she might not see him again but Anna merely shrugged.

'Then I might just have to kiss him goodbye!'

Holly, whether she liked Anna or not, was genuinely curious. 'Doesn't it bother you that he'll be gone soon?'

'Any one of us could be gone soon.' Anna shrugged. 'If working here doesn't prove that, then I don't know what will. I intend to enjoy every moment.'

And Anna was off. Teetering out on skinny legs and high heels and leaving that thought hanging in the air as heavily as her perfume.

Finally Holly had a moment alone.

She leant her head against the wall and closed her eyes and thought not just of Nora and Paul but of her own parents.

This time last year had been fraught, with Holly accompanying her mother to appointments and dashing to be there on her days off to offer support.

Tomorrow, after she'd done some shopping, Holly would be back on the motorway and again headed for home.

One year on it felt as if not much had changed. And in a year where there had been a rather marked absence of fun, in the latter months Daniel had somehow brightened her days.

She was, very possibly, never going to see him again, and that *wasn't* the reason for the sudden threat of tears, Holly told herself. No, it had been an emotional shift and it was coming to the end of a difficult year.

That was why she was suddenly teary.

It had nothing to do with lost opportunities.

Had there even been any? Holly pondered as she sat there and thought back over their time. Yes, there had certainly been a few occasions where a little flirt could have maybe spilled into more.

But to what end?

Maybe she needed a more generous dose of Anna's thinking instead of her usual caution where men were concerned.

Or maybe, Holly conceded as she put on her coat and walked out of the changing room, she was just looking for an excuse to misbehave.

She made her way through the department.

There was Daniel looking all sexy in black jeans and

a really thin jumper that almost looked silky and the fabric was so thin that she could see his nipples.

Talk about *Think Like a Man*.

'Are you coming after all?' Holly asked, seeing that he looked dressed for, well, anything.

'No. Why?'

'Because you've changed.'

'I've changed because I'm a locum,' Daniel pointed out. 'If I didn't throw my scrubs in the linen skip at the end of my shift I'd have quite a collection at my flat by now from the various hospitals I've worked at.'

As they walked past the nurses' station he retrieved his Advent calendar. 'Do you want yours?' he said.

'Yes.' Holly said, and smiled at Gloria. 'I don't trust the night staff a bit.'

She added it to her bag, which she would lock up with her coat at the pub.

Really, she would far prefer to be on her way home than heading off to a party, especially one that Daniel wasn't attending.

They walked out of the hospital and towards his car. It was one of those cold, damp nights and Holly was glad she hadn't made any attempt to tame her hair.

So was Daniel.

He was used to seeing it tied back and wrestling its way out of confinement, but now it fell in a dark cloud past her shoulders and some curls fell forward as she stopped for a moment and checked inside her bag.

He had seen her out of uniform before—arriving at work in jeans—but he had never seen Holly dressed up before and he found himself wanting to know what she wore under that coat.

They fell into step as they walked towards the car

and it was Anna who asked the question that was on Holly's mind.

'When do you fly?'

'I haven't booked it yet,' Daniel answered. 'Probably next week.'

'Where are you going first?'

'Switzerland.'

He aimed his keys at a black car, which lit up, and then everyone loaded their bags into the boot and then piled in, Laura and Holly in the back, Anna in the front, and suddenly Daniel knew that one of the reasons he wasn't indulging in a little *après ski* right about now was Holly.

Several hospitals had called, asking him to work, and the answer had been no. It was only when a shift had come up in the emergency department at The Primary that he had accepted a shift.

And now, as everyone climbed into his car and Anna got in the front, it felt wrong—as if Holly should be the one in his front passenger seat.

Holly felt the same.

It was odd and it was with absolutely no reason, yet Holly found that she resented the way Anna had jumped in the front. Holly sat behind Anna and when Daniel turned his head to reverse out, for a moment their eyes met. Holly was tempted to wind down the window because it had suddenly become very warm in the car and the heater had barely gone on.

Daniel moved the car out of the parking spot and then drove to the barrier and swiped his ID card. There he glanced in the rear-view mirror, not to check for traffic, more to see if her eyes were waiting.

They were.

All too often she averted her gaze, failing to complete what they started.

Not tonight.

Holly hoped it was dark enough that he couldn't see she was blushing and then a car tooted behind them.

'Daniel,' Anna prompted, because although the barrier was up the car hadn't moved.

'Sorry,' Daniel said. 'I was miles away.'

In bed with Holly!

'Everyone's asking about Paul,' Laura said, going through the messages on her phone. 'What do we say?'

'As little as possible,' Daniel suggested.

They were on the main road now and he glanced back into the mirror but Holly was now looking out of the window, watching the world go by and lost in thoughts of her own,

She liked Daniel far, far too much, Holly knew.

There was nothing wrong with liking someone except she wasn't wired like Anna. For Holly it would be foolish at best to get involved with a man who was days away from leaving the country.

Except she already was.

In her head Holly was already involved and yet she had not a single memory to draw from.

Was it time to change that?

'We're here.' Laura nudged her and Holly wiped the steamed-up window and looked out at the pub—a regular venue for Emergency dos. They often hired a room at the back and a lot of good times had been had there.

'Come in for one,' Anna said to Daniel, and Holly felt her skin prickle because Anna could flirt for England and she was seriously flirting now.

'I'm driving.'

Holly's eyes went to the mirror and again met his. Both of them knew that she would usually have looked away or been halfway out of the car by now.

'Come on,' Anna pushed, oblivious to the current coming from behind. 'You might enjoy yourself.'

'You know, I think I might,' Daniel said.

And so, instead of them climbing out, Daniel drove to the car park at the rear. It was packed but he found a space and soon they were all walking to the pub.

All except Holly, who was still by the car and going through her bag.

'What are you doing?' Daniel asked her because since they'd left Emergency he had seen her go through her bag many times.

'Compulsively checking that I've still got the envelope that Kay gave me.' Holly said. 'I have to pay the landlord…'

They went in the main entrance and there was the lovely pub scent but mixed with the woody smell of a fire in the entrance, and Holly felt her cheeks go pink for no other reason than it was lovely and warm.

The women all handed over their coats and their hands were all stamped so that they could get in and out of the function room. As Laura and Anna went through Holly asked where she should put the bar money.

'You'll need to see Desmond,' she was told, and was pointed in the right direction. 'He's in the lounge bar.'

'Thanks.'

'I'll come with you,' Daniel offered, and Holly nodded.

It had been well worth coming in, Daniel decided, for under Holly's coat she was wearing a black velvet dress, or rather it was raven. As he walked behind her Daniel noted the deep blue hue shimmering on the curves of her hips. Holly's legs were dressed in very sheer stockings and her heels were high, and as he moved forward to hold open the door, Daniel resisted placing his hand on the small of her back to guide her in.

Holly already felt as if he had, for her spine felt warm and her bottom too big, just from the burn of his gaze.

Desmond wasn't there, but they waited at the bar while one of the staff tracked him down.

It was a lovely old pub and there was a pine Christmas tree that was beautifully decorated and its scent filled the room.

'Christmassy enough for you?' Daniel asked.

'It's lovely.' Holly smiled but it was a bit of a forced one.

'Are you not in the mood for a party?' Daniel said, toying with the idea of suggesting they skip it when Holly nodded.

'I feel awful.'

'He might be okay.'

'No, I feel awful because...' She shook her head.

And then, for Daniel, something rather untoward happened—instead of wondering how quickly they could dispense with the small talk and get in the car and back to his, he actually wanted to hear what Holly had to say and *then* get back to the essentials.

'Tell me.'

'No,' Holly said, but then her guilty conscience demanded full disclosure. 'You know Kay was saying how, when they were waiting outside the catheter lab, Nora's daughter asked her what was for dinner...'

Daniel laughed a black laugh, it was nothing he hadn't seen with relatives.

'I'm as bad,' Holly said.

'Why, did you demand that Nora feed you?'

'No.' Holly smiled but then it changed. 'I almost asked Kay what would happen to the off duty for Christmas.' It had worried at her all evening. 'I mean, Paul's lying there half-dead, and I'm stressing over the off duty.'

'I'm quite sure Kay is.'

'I doubt it,' Holly sighed. 'Nora and she are best friends.'

'Off the record?' Daniel said, and Holly nodded.

'Kay's words to me just before she headed off to the catheter lab, and I quote, "How the feck am I going to sort out the roster now?"'

'Really?' Holly laughed.

'Really.' Daniel nodded. 'And I bet Nora, if Paul is now stable, is worrying about the million and one things that you women seem to worry about at this time of year.'

'That's very sexist.'

'Just an observation.'

'A wrong one.'

'I can only go by what I've seen. My father never did a thing for Christmas, I aim to be far away from it…' He thought for a moment. 'My uncle leaves it all to my aunt…'

Desmond came along then and he took the money and wrote out a receipt, which Holly put in her purse for Kay. 'What can I get you?' he offered. 'On the house, before you go in to that mad lot.'

Oh.

'I'll just have a soda water, thanks.' Daniel said.

'Well, he's a cheap date.' Desmond smiled at Holly. 'What can I get you?'

'I'd love a Scotch, please.'

She really, really would.

Holly wasn't a big drinker at the best of times but a lovely Scotch felt about right and Daniel motioned to a table near an open fire and the tree and they took a seat there.

'Maybe I am in the mood for Christmas after all.' Holly smiled, sitting back in the chair and relaxing to the lovely crackle of the fire and inhaling the scent of her drink.

'I want one,' Daniel admitted.

'Tough.' Holly smiled and then took a sip, enjoying the burn of the liquor. 'I don't really like spirits but my dad loves Scotch so I always keep a bottle at home and every now and then I have one.'

'Well, that's good to know.'

'What?'

He smiled and she realised he was perhaps inviting himself to her home for a drink.

Or had she been inviting him?

Hmm.

Holly still didn't know where this might lead, but it was just so nice to be out in the real world with him and without buzzers and patients and others around. And it was definitely nice to squeeze in five minutes' pause after work before they headed into the party.

'Do you get on with your parents?' he asked.

'Very much so.'

'They live…?' Daniel frowned. He wasn't sure, though he knew that it was some distance that she often travelled to get home.

'Up north,' Holly said, and then told him the village where her family lived.

'So how come you're in London?'

'Because I get on so well with my family.' Holly smiled. 'I trained up there and it was all too easy to just live at home… I knew I needed a change.'

'Yet you're still home a lot?'

'My mum hasn't been very well.' Holly said, and decided the night had already been grim enough without going further into it. 'What about you? Are your family in London?'

She didn't know him at all, Daniel realised.

Holly could have no idea just how refreshing that was. Even before he had started medicine there had been a constant stream of 'Marcus Chandler's son'. His father had been head boy at the boarding school Daniel had attended and his record was just as impressive at med school and beyond. Even Kay had made a few comments and had asked if he was any relation to the esteemed Professor Chandler.

Holly had no idea as to that side of his life.

'Yes.' Daniel answered the question as to whether his family was in London very simply.

'Do you get on?'

'Nope,' Daniel said.

'Why?'

'Because my father is an arrogant git,' he said, and then looked at her Scotch. 'Given that I'm on soda water tonight, I shan't be sharing.'

Holly laughed. 'What about your mother?'

'She's dead.'

Well, that wiped the smile from her face.

'He married again. I've got a sister...'

Daniel refused to call Maddie a half-sister.

'Do you get on with her?'

'I do when I see her. And that reminds me, I must get her a Christmas present before I head off.'

Holly's phone buzzed, indicating an incoming text, and she glanced down and saw that it was Anna, asking where they had disappeared to.

'Has our absence been noted?' Daniel asked.

'It has.'

The pleasant interlude was over but it had been nice,

Holly thought as she drained her drink and then stood. It had been a tiny but very welcome pause before she pushed out a smile and faced the masses.

He knew it was pointless suggesting that they didn't go through.

Holly took her Christmas party as seriously as her decorations.

'Time to be positive…' Holly said, though she didn't really feel it. 'It *is* Christmas and if ever there was a time for miracles…'

'Please,' Daniel scorned, pouring a bucket of iced water on that. 'There's no such thing as Christmas miracles.'

'Are you always so negative?' Holly asked as they headed towards the function room.

'Always.'

The doors swung open and there were a few shouts of 'Holly!' but there were a lot more shouts of Daniel's name! Clearly a lot of women were very glad to see him.

Anna, of course, leapt to his side and handed him an elaborate-looking cocktail.

'I'm driving,' he pointed out again.

'It a virgin.' Anna smiled. 'I had it prepared just for you.'

Oh, please. Holly thought she might spit at the suggestive tone, but she refused to be rattled by Anna. Instead, she put on her smile and chatted with friends.

It was a difficult night. Everyone wanted first-hand information and Holly knew that wasn't her place to give it. It was up to Nora what she wanted to share and for now Nora wanted upbeat and so that's what Holly did her best to be, but by ten she was done.

She looked over and Anna and Daniel were locked in conversation.

Or rather Anna was conversing and Daniel was locked, given the slight eye roll that he gave her.

Holly smiled but it was a regretful one because she simply didn't know how to run wild. How to go over there and be all sparkling and witty and flirt…

Except, as it turned out, she didn't have to go over there to flirt. Holly quickly realised that standing in the middle of the room and blatantly staring at the object of your desire seemed to work rather well too!

Yikes.

She hadn't meant that!

Holly watched as he said something to Anna and Holly realised he was excusing himself and about to make his way over.

It was time for a quick getaway.

'You're not going already?' Trevor, one of the male nurses, asked.

'I am.' Holly kept up that smile. 'I'm hitting the shops tomorrow and then…' She didn't finish. An absolute novice in the field of sexual adventure, she found her coat and headed outside.

'Leaving?'

She turned and there was Daniel.

'Yes.'

'Do you want a lift?'

'I've just called for a taxi,' Holly lied.

'It's no problem.'

'I live miles away.'

'I'll save you the fare, then.'

'No, thanks.'

Why? Holly asked herself. Why was she saying no? Because she *couldn't* say no to him.

'Come on.'

He jangled his keys and Holly nodded. Really, it was

just a colleague giving her a lift home and it would be bliss not to have to make small talk with a taxi driver or sit in the back as he chatted on his phone.

Liar, liar.

They got in his car, and this time she was in the front.

That's better, both thought but didn't say.

'Address?' he asked, and she gave it to him.

Daniel typed it into his phone and that took care of that, and then he started the engine.

'Head north,' his phone said.

'I hate that,' Daniel admitted. 'I have no idea which way north is. I need a compass in the middle of my steering wheel.'

'She means turn left,' Holly said.

'Thank you.'

'Are you all packed?' Holly made a feeble attempt at small talk and he nodded.

'Sort of. I'm trying to rent out my flat. Apparently December isn't an ideal time to find tenants.'

'So it that why your plans keep changing?'

'In part.'

'Well, you might just as well stick around for Christmas…'

'I doubt it. I might even fly out then, it's just another day.'

'You don't mean that.'

'I do,' Daniel said, and he gave her a smile. 'We're polar opposites.' And then he stared ahead at the road and it did not need stating—that opposites attracted.

Both already knew.

CHAPTER THREE

SHE SHOULD HAVE said goodbye to him back at the pub.

Then there might have been a hope that, should they meet up in the future, all they would be were ex-colleagues who had flirted a little on occasion.

Back at the pub she could have wished him well for his trip and, yes, of course she could do the same when he pulled up at her flat.

Holly didn't want to, though.

How did it even work? Holly thought. She was way too far out of her comfort zone. Did she offer him a drink, or did she leave it to him to suggest coming in?

And what about the morning?

Holly wished that she didn't overthink things, she wished she could be more like Anna and just worry about the day, or rather the night, at hand.

She wanted the traffic lights to turn red, for a pause, to turn and tell him that the flirty version of Holly he had met at times wasn't the real one. That the woman who had laughed at the suggestive tone in his voice when he'd told her she'd be in discreet hands, did not, prior to his arrival on her part of the planet, exist.

Yet the lights all stayed green and afforded swift passage.

And anyway, Daniel knew all that.

While he was driving he was trying to convince himself that this wasn't any different from what he was used to and that Holly could more than handle a hook-up. And he was also trying to convince himself that he didn't care in the way he actually did.

He couldn't afford to care. It wasn't an emotion he sought, and he was leaving after all.

His phone told him that the destination was on his left and he slid the car into a parking space outside her flat and his conscience won—Daniel didn't want to risk hurting her.

'You'd better go in,' Daniel said.

And so this was it.

'Thanks for the lift.'

'No problem.'

'It's been nice working with you,' Holly said. 'I'm going to miss your sulking face.'

'I'll miss your smiling one.'

And this really was it.

There was a charge in the air that should signal thunder but instead Daniel turned and looked ahead.

Holly reached to open the door and he did nothing to halt her so she got out.

They were both congratulating themselves on how adult and sensible they had been.

Now she could breathe, except, despite the cool and the drizzle, the night felt as humid as if it was summer.

Holly looked at the path to her door and she was six, maybe seven steps away from saving herself from a rather big mistake, except she wanted so badly to turn around and to follow desire rather than walk away.

Just once.

It was her choice as to what happened next, Holly knew.

Could she keep it light, without revealing how deeply she felt?

Daniel was just about to hit 'Home' as his destination when she tapped on the window.

'What?' he asked as it slid down. His voice was surly. He didn't want to do this a second time, especially as now that she was bending down there was the pearly white of her breasts at eye level.

And she looked at him and, no, she would not be so cheesy as to ask him in for a drink and then somehow, whoops, they'd up in bed.

She wanted a kiss, Daniel knew, but he was also rather certain she wanted a whole lot more than that. Not just sex, but the part of himself he refused to give.

'What?' he said again, and then his face broke into a smile, as, very unexpectedly, Holly, sweet Holly, showed another side of her.

'Are you going to *make* me invite you in?'

'Yes.'

'You're not even going to try and persuade me with a kiss?' Holly checked.

'You want me or you don't.' Daniel shrugged. 'There's no question that I want you. But, Holly, do you get that—?'

She knew what was coming and she didn't need the warning—he had made his position perfectly clear—so she interrupted him. 'I don't need the speech.'

She just needed this.

Holly had thought his hand was moving to open the door but instead it came out of the window and to her head and pulled her face down to his.

He kissed her hard, even though she was the one standing. The stubble of his unshaven jaw was rough on her face and his tongue was straight in.

He pulled her in tight so that her upper abdomen hurt from the pressure of the open window and it was a warning, she knew, of the passion to come.

Even now she could pull back and straighten, say goodnight and walk off, but Holly was through with being cautious.

In a second she would be falling through the open window for all the neighbours to see and sucked into the dark vacuum of his car.

Holly simply didn't care.

Her bag dropped to the pavement and he then released her.

Holly stared back at him, breathless, her lipstick smeared across her face, and all it made him want to do was to kiss her again.

But this was a street.

Holly bent and retrieved her bag and then walked off towards her flat. There was a roaring sound in her ears and her heart seemed to be leaping up near her throat.

Daniel closed up the car and was soon following her to the flats.

She turned the key in the main door to the flats and clipped up the concrete steps.

She could hear his heavy footsteps coming up the steps behind her as she turned and Holly almost broke into a run.

Daniel actually did!

He had thought her cute, sweet and gorgeous these past months and had done all he could not to think of her outright as sexy.

Except she was, and seriously so.

Those heavy footsteps chasing her were thrilling and caught up with her just as she was getting her key into the door of her own flat. Holly was breathless with excitement and the rush and power of him grabbing for her almost toppled Holly as they burst in through the door.

The hall was in darkness; he could just make out some Christmas-tree lights in a room down the hall but there was no time to get to the lounge.

Daniel had no patience now.

Holly had never known anything like it. Never, in her almost twenty-nine years, had she had that simply-have-to-have-you feeling.

And Daniel *had* to have her.

Every obstacle he dealt with.

He hitched her lovely raven dress up.

Stockings?

No problem, he expertly removed them and then her knickers too.

And when he wanted a better view of her breasts he lowered her zipper at the back, just enough to free them.

Holly looked down at her exposed breasts, and then at her stockings and knickers lying on the hallway floor—she felt slutty and sexy. She liked it. So much so that she was pulling at his thin jumper just to reveal his stomach, and then running a hand up the heavy jeans-clad thighs, getting closer to the lovely bit in the middle. She dealt with the brass button deftly, though she broke a nail on the zipper, and then freed him. He was clearly as keen and eager as she, and Holly was so utterly ready for him she nearly forgot about condoms.

To Holly's mind there was nothing sexy about condoms, but he changed that in an instant, for he pulled out his wallet, found one, tossed the wallet to the floor and tore the foil with his teeth.

'Put it on,' Daniel told her, and he started to squeeze and play with her breasts as she did just that.

She rolled it down slowly, which was quite a feat,

given the way his fingers were exploring her, and she felt the jerk of impatience in her hand.

Then he said the two little words that tonight she was desperate to hear.

'Get on.'

Gladly she did.

He bent his knees just enough that he could thrust into her and Holly's shoulders hit the wall. She arched back at the consuming pleasure as he stabbed inside her.

Totally consumed and controlled by him, Holly was close to coming as Daniel lifted her legs even further; she wrapped them around his hips.

'I've been wanting you all night.' He told her as she wrapped her legs tighter, wiggling herself down further so he could push deeper. 'I wanted you on sight.'

They stared at each other as he banged her into wall, kissing her with raw passion and digging his fingers into her bottom, holding her firm. Heat flooded her centre and she moved her mouth away. 'I'm going to come...'

Her voice divulged her own surprise. Not just because she usually took for ever, more because of the intensity that hit.

Daniel felt her gather and pull tight around him as he plunged one last time before letting go deep inside her.

He lowered her down and she stood a moment on legs that felt she was getting over a bout of the flu they were so weak.

They followed the Christmas-tree lights to what he assumed was the lounge.

Maybe he'd get that Scotch after all, Daniel thought.

Instead, they collapsed onto her bed.

'Holly?'

The room had stopped spinning and they lay on their

backs on the bed when Daniel started to take in his sur-
roundings. 'Why is there a Christmas tree in your bedroom?'

'My neighbours are a bit noisy,' Holly explained. 'And
so I tend to spend more time in here.'

'Oh.'

'And it seemed a shame to have a Christmas tree in a
room that I don't spend much time in.'

They were half-undressed already so it took only a
moment to throw off the rest of their clothes and to get
into bed.

They lay talking, about nothing much as well as a lot.

And it turned out their paths had almost crossed.

'I went for an interview at the Royal when I was looking at moving to London.' She thought back to that time
and her nervousness as she'd entered the huge Victorian
building.

It was funny to think now that he might have been
inside.

'How long ago?'

'I was twenty-one,' Holly said. 'So eight, nearly nine
years ago. Were you there then?'

He nodded. 'Did you get the job?'

'Yes,' Holly said. 'But I got offered the job at The Primary in the same week and I chose to go there. I didn't
like how they rotated the staff at the Royal. Too many
night shifts.'

'Don't you like nights?'

'Not really,' Holly said. 'I don't sleep very well during the day.'

'I could have had you when you were twenty-one.'
Daniel mused, liking that idea.

'No, you couldn't have.' Holly smiled at his arrogant assumption. 'I was seeing someone then. I nearly got engaged.'

And he lay there, not liking that idea.

'We might have ended up having an affair,' Daniel said, determined to have had her at twenty-one in his head.

'No,' she said. 'We wouldn't have.'

And he lay there wondering why the hell he was sulking over an event that had never even taken place some eight or nine years ago!

'Why did you break up?'

'He got offered a job in America,' Holly said. 'I didn't want to go and he did. We were too young, I guess.'

They were heading into territory that Daniel generally avoided so they started chatting about work.

'I don't do well with grieving relatives,' Holly announced.

'Yes, you do.' He frowned because the few times he'd been with Holly while breaking bad news she'd always been fine.

If a little quiet.

'Oh, I'm better than I was,' Holly agreed. 'I have this nervous smile...'

And Daniel found that he was smiling as she spoke.

'I didn't know that I had it, well, I sort of did but then Kay had to take me to one side...'

'You smile at bad news?' Daniel checked.

'No, but I smile when I'm nervous. You should see me in my school photos and when I go for an interview and things...'

And there it was again.

This wanting to look at old photos.

To hear more.

To know more.

It was everything he was trying to resist.

* * *

Freezing.

Daniel woke to the cold air and warm bed and rolled into Holly.

God, she felt good.

Her soft bottom was against him and as his hand went over hers he kissed her bare shoulder and then his mouth moved up her neck.

Last night had been amazing.

Now he wanted more.

And so did Holly.

His hand lifted her hair and his kiss was heavy on her neck as light fingers circled her stomach.

But then he stopped.

Daniel actually stopped in mid-kiss because fast sexy sex was one thing, but the way he wanted her now could only serve to confuse Holly.

Arrogant assumption perhaps but he knew she liked him, seriously liked him, and he liked her enough not to want to give mixed messages.

And so how did you end things nicely?

Usually he didn't give it too much thought, for he generally played to a far tougher crowd.

Holly closed her eyes at the abrupt end to his kiss on her shoulder. They were both in that lovely turned-on morning feeling and she wanted to turn her face to his mouth, to kiss him slowly and make love.

Yes, that.

She wanted the hand that had been slowly stroking her stomach to resume its perusal and move lower yet it didn't.

Too intimate for you, Daniel? she wanted to say, though didn't, but she did get her own back a little because she slowly stretched and yawned, just so he could *feel* what he was missing, and then rolled over to face him and smiled.

Yes, she was nice but, oh, she could be wicked.

'It's so nice to have a weekend off.' Holly smiled and chatted as if she hadn't even noticed his erection.

'I've got every weekend off now.' Daniel smiled back as she gave him a small kick to let him know how unfair that was.

She was back to looking into those amazing eyes but from her pillow this time. 'Are you registering to practise overseas?' Holly asked.

'It's an option, I guess.' He couldn't tell her his plans because the truth was he didn't really have any. 'I just want to take a year and work things out.'

'Fair enough,' Holly said, but her slight frown told him that she didn't really get it. They truly were opposites, not just that he had made so few plans but also that he could afford to take a year off. Shouldn't he have worked this all out some time ago?

'I'll make coffee…' Daniel offered.

'I'll go,' Holly said. 'The machine's tricky.'

'I'm sure I can work it out.'

She lay there and wondered how this would end. Awkwardness was creeping in and she didn't know how to put on a brave smile when he left.

And then she heard her front door open and then quietly close.

'Bastard,' Holly breathed.

But then a moment or so later she heard the door open again and lay back on the pillows, recanting her curse as she realised he must have left the door on the latch so he could get back in.

Holly knew she was way out of her comfort zone here, so much so that she had actually thought he might just walk off without so much as a goodbye. Instead, though, he walked in with two mugs of coffee *and* two Advent calendars that he must have retrieved from the car. He put the drinks on the bedside tables and dropped the calendars on the bed.

'Holly, why don't you have any food in your fridge?'

'There are eggs.'

'But no bread,' he pointed out. 'I heard the neighbours, or rather I could hear breakfast television and her shouting for him to get up...'

'I told you,' Holly said. 'It's worse during the week. She must call to him about fifteen times before he surfaces. Sometimes I want to go round there and pull the duvet off him myself!'

And he would rather like to pull the duvet from her but instead he just climbed in.

She reached for the floor and handed out cushions so that they could sit up in comfort.

Her bedroom really was rather lovely. Even aside from the Christmas tree! There were books and a pile of DVDs lining shelves and a television on a chest of drawers. There was her computer and phone and, really, apart from the occasional trip to the bathroom or kitchen he could absolutely see why she might not want to leave. 'You could bring the coffee maker in here,' Daniel suggested.

'I did think of that...' Holly nodded '...but then I'd need a little fridge too...'

'And then you'd get bedsores,' Daniel said, and was about to make a little joke about having to roll her every couple of hours, but he knew where that would lead.

'I'd better go soon.'

'Good,' Holly said, 'because I've got a lot to do.'

She picked up her Advent calendar and started to peel off the Cellophane as Daniel tackled his.

'I can't believe you've never had one of these.'

'I might have when I was really little,' Daniel said. 'I honestly can't remember.'

For all his inexperience he found the number one before Holly did and was soon pulling out a small circle of dark chocolate from behind the little cardboard window.

'I doubt it's very good,' Holly warned as she too found hers. 'Given that Kay bought a job lot. Still, it's the thought...' Her voice trailed off as she popped it in her mouth. It was the darkest, sweetest and most melt-in-the-mouth chocolate she had ever tasted, and Daniel clearly felt the same since he was already opening door number two.

'Oh, my!' Holly said.

'Wait till you taste December the second,' Daniel warned. 'It's some orange liqueur...'

'I think I'm going to come!' Holly said as she rolled it around her tongue.

'Well, lucky for you, it's December the third now, so you can have another.'

The third was behind a little door with a gingerbread man on it and the chocolate was a coffee and cream.

'They get better and better,' Daniel said.

The chocolate was so seriously superb that Holly was very much considering breaking her own rule and just eating all twenty-five in one go.

'If that's the beginning of the month,' Daniel said, 'then what's behind those double doors...?' He turned the calendar over and read the fine print. 'It's from Belgium.'

'So what's it doing in the discount store?'

'We should go and buy up all that's left.' Daniel suggested.

'I'll have to find out which one she went to.'

Hot coffee soon washed down the chocolate but instead of Daniel heading for home and Holly to the shops they were back on their sides and facing each other.

'I'm starving,' Daniel said.

'There's a baker's across the street, they do really nice pastries.'

'Go on, then,' he said, but she shook her head.

'You go.'

And for someone who had been about to leave, Daniel was considering not just heading to the bakers on his way home but returning to her bed with a box of pastries.

'We could just go and get breakfast.' Daniel suggested the name of a very nice department store and as she licked her lips at the suggestion he waited for that ping of regret for prolonging things to descend in his chest, but it wasn't there. His only regret was that he might be leading her on, and yet, he reasoned, it was just breakfast.

'Sounds good,' Holly said. 'It has to be a quick breakfast, though…' She glanced at the time. 'I want to do some Christmas shopping.'

'And me.'

Daniel did, as he hadn't got anything for Maddie. She was already terribly disappointed that he wouldn't be there for Christmas and he hoped that it might be tempered by a lovely gift.

But what to get a five-year-old who has everything?

And whatever it was he would have to have it delivered. There was no way he was rocking up for Christmas dinner after the disaster of last year.

As he borrowed Holly's shower, Daniel told himself that the expedition he'd suggested was a terrible idea.

From sex to shopping?

And Holly was thinking the same, though along different lines, because as Daniel showered his phone rang and she looked at the screen and saw the name 'Maddie'.

Whoever Maddie was she was impatient, because she rang three times in the space of five minutes.

Holly tried not to mind.

Yet she did.

When he came out of the shower it was to the sight of Holly sitting on the bed and pulling on boots.

'I wish I'd done this before I put on my jeans,' Holly said and to Daniel it seemed there was nothing more on her mind than breakfast.

He picked up the phone and gave a small eye roll when he saw that there were a few missed calls from Maddie.

There often were!

He had a listen to check there wasn't a problem.

There wasn't.

'Hello, I've got your ticket for the nativity play.'

Next message. 'I'm an angel.'

And so on.

What on earth should he get her for Christmas?

'Let's go,' Holly said, trying to keep the edge from her voice as he blatantly listened to his messages. 'I think the café opens at ten.'

They arrived at a quarter past, which, as it turned out, was perfect timing because everyone who had been queuing for the café to open were pretty much served.

'I'll have the full English breakfast…' Daniel didn't even need to look at the menu.

'Well, I'm going to have mince pies and cream and a strong coffee.'

The fruit mix in the pie was warm and spicy and the cream sweet and it was the perfect breakfast really, although it had little to do with the food.

Despite their brief misgivings about their breakfast date, conversation was surprisingly easy.

Usually for Daniel the conversation ran out at first

kiss, or certainly by the time his head had hit the pillow, but Holly's company was just as pleasant this morning as it had been last night.

'Who do you have to buy for?' Holly asked as Daniel slathered brown sauce on his mushrooms.

'My sister.'

'Who else?'

'No one else. You?'

'Everyone!' Holly sighed and then took out her phone. 'But first I'm going to call work.'

'About Paul or the Christmas roster?'

'Stop!' Holly blushed. 'Don't you dare repeat that to anyone.'

'I never repeat pillow talk.'

'It was said in your car.'

'Yes, but by then you'd already made up your mind that you'd be hauling me into your lair.'

'No,' Holly said as she made the call, and having asked the switchboard operator to put her through to Kay she smiled at him. 'That was a last-minute decision.'

'I'm glad you made it.'

So too was she, Holly thought as she returned to her phone call.

'Kay, it's Holly.'

'He's stable, no real change, but that's good.' Kay got straight to it. 'No arrhythmias overnight but they'll keep him intubated for a couple of days.'

'How's Nora?'

'Exhausted. She's just gone home for a sleep. How was the party?'

'It was good,' Holly said. 'Everyone was concerned about Paul, of course, but I think it went well.'

'I heard that you left early.'

'Well, I wasn't exactly in the mood...you know that.'

'I also heard Daniel didn't just drop you girls off but came in for a drink.'

'He did.'

'Hold on a moment.' Holly sat there and she heard Kay closing her office door and Holly sat holding her breath, wondering if their leaving together had been noted.

She didn't have to worry, Holly soon realised as Kay spoke on. 'Anna was all over him, apparently?'

'I didn't notice.'

'Get out of here,' Kay scoffed. She knew Holly was always up to date with goings-on, although Kay prided herself on being The One Who Knew. 'So, who did he leave with?'

Holly sat there, watching as Daniel mopped up the egg with a thick bit of buttery toast, and she should be relieved, really, that Kay didn't for a second think it might be with her.

'I don't think he was with anyone,' Holly said, and her voice came out a little too high.

Daniel looked up when he heard her strained voice and saw her very red cheeks and he could guess what was being asked so he mouthed a suggestion.

'Do you want me to speak to her?'

Holly laughed at the thought of Kay's shocked expression if she handed Daniel the phone but shook her head and looked away, hunching her shoulders so she could talk without seeing the object of her sins.

'Oh.' Kay sounded deflated at the lack of gossip but when Kay spoke on so too did Holly. 'I'm going to have to take a long hard look at the roster, Holly.'

'I know.'

'And you know that I'll try to accommodate everyone but I do have to be fair. There are mums with little ones who need their mum to be there at Christmas, but you know that I'll try to do my best for all my staff.'

'I do appreciate it.'

Holly hung up and as she did so Daniel gave her a thin smile. 'Off duty?'

She nodded.

'See, I told you it wouldn't take long. The real world always surfaces.'

And it was surfacing now because as she glanced at the time Holly knew if she had wanted to do her shopping and get to her parents' by dinnertime, then she needed to get going.

They finished up their food and wandered out, but instead of parting ways they looked at the floor plan.

'What does your sister like?' Holly asked.

'Elephants.'

'Oh.'

He didn't explain that Maddie was five.

In truth, Daniel was very touchy about the fact his sister could very well be his daughter. In fact, when they were out together they were always mistaken as such.

They joined the swarms of people all looking for the perfect gift that would make another happy.

There was no such thing, Daniel knew.

Holly swallowed when he held up a necklace with an ugly-looking elephant hanging on the chain, Of course she assumed Daniel's sister was close to his age, and she found that she was wearing her nervous smile, which she quickly righted and then made a suggestion.

'Why don't you adopt an elephant for her?'

Daniel rolled his eyes.

'If I loved elephants,' Holly said, 'it would be the perfect gift.'

And then she found *her* perfect gift!

It was beach glass, all wired and knotted together into the most fantastic necklace and earrings.

'I should get this for Adam,' Holly said, 'though it's a bit pricey.'

'Adam?'

'My brother.'

'Right,' Daniel said, to show he had no problem with all of that. 'Right! It's very nice.'

'The necklace would be for me, Daniel.' Holly smiled at his attempt to be PC. 'After too many disasters we now buy what we really want for ourselves and wrap it, though it's from the other.'

'I see.'

He didn't.

Daniel knew very little of family traditions and the little things that others seemed to do so seamlessly to make Christmas Day special.

But then, in the middle of a department store and completely out of the blue, he remembered something. He had woken up and there was this lumpy sock at the end of his bed and there was some fruit in it but also a tiny miniature of a castle. A castle he knew because they had been on holiday there that summer.

The holiday wasn't really a memory, more that the castle he had held in his palm that morning was, for he had looked at it in the gift shop.

His mum must have done that, Daniel realised. She must have bought it then and saved it for Christmas. Certainly it wouldn't have been his father.

He just stood in the busy department store, remembering something from a long time ago.

Something precious.

'Why are they queuing?' Holly nudged him and pulled him from introspection.

She had put down the necklace and looked up to see a long line forming towards the back of the store.

'Because they've got nothing better to do.' Daniel shrugged. 'Maybe it's to see Santa.'

'But they're mainly adults,' Holly pointed out.

'Maybe it's an adult-rated Santa,' he suggested, but Holly didn't smile at his joke. 'You don't approve?'

'I refuse to buy into your constant downgrading of the magic of Christmas. I want to know what they're queuing for,' Holly said, and they made their way over to see what was going on.

No, it wasn't Santa and neither was it an adult Santa. It was really rather amazing. They clearly weren't the only ones who thought so because and if the queue was big, so too was the crowd gathered at the end of the line, watching what was being made.

A little elf, okay, a person dressed up as a little elf, was typing on a miniature keyboard. Further down the line a tiny stamp-sized letter was printed. There another elf was placing the tiny letters in equally small envelopes.

It took a moment to work out that the letters were being placed within hand-blown Christmas-tree decorations.

They both stood and watched the glassblower and time really did run away that morning because it was simply fascinating to watch.

Once made and cooled another group of elves then decorated the glass bauble and added a silver chain to hang it from the tree and then it was placed in a gorgeous box that was tied with a heavy silver bow.

'What a beautiful gift,' Holly said, although Daniel, though interested, was too practical to be convinced.

'I don't get it,' Daniel admitted. 'You'd have to break the glass to read the letter.'

'That's the whole point,' Holly said. 'You don't break the glass. Or maybe you do…'

They were debating this when someone called his name.

'Daniel!'

They both turned and walking towards them was a rather beautiful woman around Holly's age but light years ahead in style. She had long straight honey-brown hair that fell immaculately and she looked as if she had just stepped out of a make-up salon, though it was subtly done, of course. She wore neat grey trousers and boots and had on a thin coat and she was one of those people who couldn't spill something on themselves if they tried.

Her cheeks were pink, though, and starting to fire up like a sunset as Daniel said her name.

'Hi, Amelia.' He responded to her greeting with a rather terse nod. 'How are you?'

'Busy,' she admitted, and held up a couple of shopping bags. 'I'm just trying to get a few things…'

'I see.'

It was all rather tense and uncomfortable and when Amelia looked over at Holly, clearly expecting to be introduced, Daniel said nothing.

How did you? Daniel wondered. Did he turn to Holly and say, *Oh, Holly this is my stepmother.*

He hadn't seen her in almost a year.

Not since last Christmas Day, when Amelia had had rather too much drink and had told Daniel that, though the money was nice, the marriage wasn't great. He had woken from a doze on the sofa to be told by Amelia that she was tired of sleeping with an older man and wanted the younger version—his son, namely Daniel.

And no one would ever have to know.

Daniel had got up, got his jacket and gone home, and hadn't seen Mommy Dearest since.

'So what are you up to?' Amelia asked.

'Not much.'

Those two words crushed Holly.

He could have said Christmas shopping, Holly thought, or that they had just been and had breakfast. No, she didn't want him to go into detail but to stand beside her and tell this woman 'Not much' had Holly's confidence shrink as if salt had been poured over it.

She stood there, wearing that stupid, nervous smile as they carried on talking while she was, at best, ignored.

'So what are you doing over Christmas?' Amelia asked him.

Avoiding you and my father, Daniel was tempted to answer, but his voice was its usual mixture of boredom and disinterest.

'I'm not sure,' Daniel said. 'Working or skiing.'

'I could have guessed it would be one of the two.' She gave a tight smile. 'I'd better get on.'

'Sure,' Daniel said.

Amelia walked off and now it was Holly and Daniel who stood in strained silence but the fun of watching the glassblower do his work had now left them.

Daniel glanced over his shoulder to make sure Amelia had gone.

Holly saw that he did and misinterpreted it as Daniel craning his neck for one lingering look and suddenly she didn't want to be here any more. She just did not want to stand beside a man whose mind was elsewhere. A man who couldn't even be bothered to introduce her and described their morning as 'Not much'. A man who listened to his voice messages from another woman straight after getting out of her bed.

He had come with a warning and, a little late perhaps, Holly chose to heed it.

It was time to put her big girl's blouse on and remember just what it was that she had agreed to—a one-night stand and then they parted ways.

This wasn't a date, no matter how much Holly wanted to convince herself of that. Neither was it the start of something. She'd agreed to abide by Daniel Chandler's standards last night, which meant they should have been over with several hours ago.

She made it now.

'I'm going to head off,' Holly said. 'I've got a lot to get and then I'm heading off to my parents'.'

'Sure.'

'Thanks for breakfast.' Holly smiled.

'You're welcome.'

There was a very good chance that she'd never see him again, Holly knew that. *And so how did you end it?* she wondered. *Did you say, Have a nice life? Did you kiss the other on the cheek when you went your separate ways? Or did you just give a sort of half-wave and then walk off?*

Holly chose the latter.

CHAPTER FOUR

HOME.

Holly had rung ahead to say she'd be late and just before seven she exited the motorway and saw the lights of her village in the distance.

There was no sense of relief at being at her parents', though. In truth, it had been ages since she'd had a full weekend off and it would have been nice to catch up with some friends. Or rather, given the turn of events, it would have been nice to spend a night in alone and watch a movie and dwell on what had happened with Daniel. Still, her mum wanted some help getting things ready for Christmas and so instead of being morose Holly waved to her mum as she got out of the car and smiled brightly as she headed up the path.

Inside, the tree was up and the decorations were all out, so her father had clearly been busy. Her mother went back into the kitchen to finish off making dinner and Holly went in to give her a hand.

'We waited for you,' Esther said.

'I told you not to,' Holly replied, because she'd told them to go ahead and eat.

The sound of the electric knife filled the room for a moment but when it went silent Holly knew that she ought to give her mother fair warning so she spoke. 'Mum, there might be a change to the off duty over Christmas.'

'I thought it had all been done.' Esther turned and then looked at the calendar on the fridge. 'You're off from the twenty-third till the twenty-eighth.'

'I was supposed to be but a couple of people have gone off sick and…' Holly didn't really want to tell her mum about Paul. Everything seemed to upset Esther these days and they all tended to tiptoe a little around her. 'Well, Kay's just not able to cover the department.'

'Your brother's going to be in Mongolia next year,' Esther said. 'I've got everyone coming…'

'I know all that,' Holly said. 'And I'll do all I can to be here but I had last Christmas and New Year off and we have to take turns. There are mums with little children and—'

'Holly, I'm a mother and I *want* my family together this Christmas. Surely, given the year we've all had, that's not too much to ask?'

'I don't do the off duty, Mum,' Holly pointed out, but she could see that her mother was upset. So too was Holly. It had been a difficult enough day, without having to justify that she was needed at work, but Esther wouldn't let it go.

'Holly, they can't just expect you to change your plans at the last minute…'

You do, Holly was tempted to point out, but she didn't want to row.

Actually, she did.

Once they had been able to bicker, once Holly had been able to have a proper conversation with her mum, and she missed those times. 'I'm going to take my bag upstairs.'

She did just that and back in her old bedroom Holly sat for a moment on her old bed and took in a deep breath.

Pollyanna indeed!

She wanted to go back down and speak her mind, which was that she was tired of walking on eggshells around her mother.

Holly was, in fact, tired.

Not just from a late night and long drive but from a very difficult year. Right now she had problems of her own. Okay, not major ones, but she was wrestling with last night and wondering if she might never even see Daniel again, but there just wasn't a place for that now. Her mother had no idea what was going on in Holly's life and lately never thought to ask.

She looked up as there was a knock on the door and saw that it was her father. 'Your mum said that you might not be able to get Christmas off.'

'It looks that way.'

'Holly, I know they were good to last year but you know what Christmas means to your mum. Is there any way—?'

'Dad, the charge nurse who was supposed to be working over Christmas had her husband go into cardiac arrest in front of her last night.'

'Oh.'

'Yes, "oh". I want to be with my family at Christmas but so too does everyone else and Mum sending you up here to talk to me doesn't change that. Everyone's Christmas is important.'

Apart from the rather jumpy start it was a nice weekend. Holly went shopping with her mum and actually got rather a lot done, including ordering the turkey, but as pleasant as it had been, Holly arrived back at work more tired for her days off than when she had left.

There was no word from Daniel.

She hadn't expected flowers or a phone call, or a follow-up date.

But she *had* hoped.

And those hopes had been dashed.

What part of 'one-night stand' don't you get, Holly? she asked herself.

The 'one night' part.

How could something that had been so good simply end?

CHAPTER FIVE

HOLLY KNEW SHE shouldn't take her coffee back to bed.

It was five-thirty and she started work at seven so really she should be hitting the shower, but instead she allowed herself one small luxury that was becoming a habit of late.

Not just for Holly.

The whole emergency department were *thrilled* with their Advent calendars.

It was the fifteenth of December, which meant that so far fourteen chocolaty delights had been eaten.

They had ranged from raspberry to mulled wine, from salted caramel to sticky toffee, and each was a masterpiece.

Every morning the staff all compared their treat.

Holly found the window that said fifteen and peeled back the little door and there it was—a little ball of chocolate with red and green dotted through it and dusted in icing sugar, and with a flurry of relish she popped into her mouth.

It was awful!

So awful that despite three chews waiting for the taste sensation to hit she ended up spitting it out into a tissue. It was glacé cherries and this sickly-sweet chocolate. It was so bad that, had that been the first day's chocolate, none of the rest would have been opened and the calendar would have found its way straight to the bin.

Grumbling, removing the taste with a mug of coffee, Holly headed for the shower and then took the underground to work.

She caught sight of her reflection in the window and saw just how drab she looked, especially given that it was so close to Christmas.

It wasn't just her.

The department was rather gloomy.

Paul had at first rallied and been moved from Intensive Care to the coronary care unit, but just two days ago he had thrown off another clot and collapsed again. Now he was back on ICU on a ventilator.

It wasn't just that, though.

Now that Daniel wasn't around the days seemed longer and the run-up to Christmas, which Holly usually loved, felt just a little less, well, Christmassy.

Even the very thorough Kay was falling behind in her plans.

'Holly, can you sort out the Secret Santa?' Kay said as Holly took off her coat.

The underground had been packed, her boots had let in the rain and Holly's mood was a touch frazzled, possibly down to the fact she had her period, but she'd kill anyone who suggested it might be that.

'Nora usually does it…' Kay sighed.

'Sure,' Holly agreed.

'I'm going to have a cup of tea before we start.'

That sounded like a good idea to Holly.

'Hey,' Trevor said as Kay and Holly walked in with large mugs of tea. 'Did you have your chocolate this morning?'

Holly pulled a face and nodded.

'I still feel a bit sick,' Anna moaned.

'I think,' Holly said, 'that for the fifteenth one, the master chocolatier went on his break and left the work-experience kid in charge.'

They all laughed and then she startled because she recognised Daniel's. Turning, she saw that he was sitting behind where she stood. He was eating toast and drinking tea and Holly's heart told her to be wary.

This had the potential to really hurt!

'I thought you'd left,' Kay said.

'So did I,' Daniel admitted. 'But try telling that to Admin. They called me this morning at six and asked me to come in. I'm only here till midday, though.'

Holly ignored him.

It had been twelve days since she had last seen him.

The Twelve Days of Absence, Holly now named them, and if he expected her to be smiling and peppy and, oh, so pleased to see him then he was mistaken. Instead, she drank her tea as she sorted out the Secret Santa.

'What are you doing?' he asked Holly, who had taken a seat and written out a list and was now tearing it up.

'Secret Santa.' Holly said, but didn't look up, when usually she'd answer with a smile.

She didn't know how to be around Daniel. They'd been friends who flirted before, now they were…what?

Ex-lovers.

Or was that too grand a word to describe them?

Not for Holly.

She had no idea as to his feelings, if any, for her, no idea where she stood in the scheme of things.

Probably nowhere.

But Holly wanted to find out.

The morning flew by and all were kept busy, especially as Kay took herself off to the office to wrestle with the dreaded off duty. The Christmas roster was the most awaited one of the entire year. Kay had tried to put it off as Nora had assured her she'd be back, but with Paul's further deterioration it was now clear that wouldn't be the case.

To have to change it at the last minute was not a decision that Kay had taken lightly.

And to forge the Secret Santa was not something Holly took lightly either. She just had to know how Daniel felt.

She slipped into the changing room and wrote 'Holly Jacobs', 'Holly Jacobs', 'Holly Jacobs' out about twenty times and screwed them up into little balls.

The original names she took out and placed carefully in the pocket of her scrubs and then added the duplicate copies of her own name to the envelope. Then she went out and found him checking results on a computer as Kay held out a form for him to sign.

'Pick a name,' Holly said, and waved the envelope under his nose.

'I shan't be here for Christmas,' Daniel told her, 'so there's no point in taking one.'

'Everyone takes a name,' Holly said. 'It's all about getting into the Christmas spirit.'

Daniel rolled his navy eyes, which indicated what he thought of that, and got back to the computer screen.

'Take a name, Daniel,' Kay said. 'You can drop it off on your way to the airport if you don't work again. If you can't manage that then I always have extras given half the staff are off for Christmas. It's just a bit of fun.'

Daniel didn't do fun.

Well, he did, but it was a rather more sophisticated type of fun he indulged in.

Not stupid Christmas-present swaps where people sulked if they didn't get what they wanted or you forgot, but for the sake of peace he put in his hand and pulled out a name.

Holly Jacobs.

Of course it was.

He looked at her vivid green eyes and mop of dark curls that were, as always, coming loose.

'You're not allowed to say who you got,' Holly told him. 'Just stick within the price limit and put it under the tree. Usually we check when the name we have is working. So, say you had…' she plucked a name out of thin air '… Trevor, well, he finishes up on—'

'I get the drift,' Daniel interrupted.

'Good.'

Daniel got up from his stool and stalked off and Holly gave a little satisfied smile.

Now she'd finally know—if he got her something truly awful, or forgot completely, then she'd have to simply accept that he cared not a jot for her and it had just been a one-night stand. Maybe then she could turn off the fairy lights that were perpetually twinkling in her head when he was around.

'I'll take a name,' Kay said, and reached out her hand.

Oh!

For all her plotting and scheming, Holly hadn't thought of that. Kay was about to reach in and she had to come up with something fast.

Very fast! Because walking towards her was Anna, and she hadn't taken a name yet either.

Holly suddenly had visions of twenty gifts all with her name under the tree and it would look a bit suspicious, especially as she was the one organising the thing.

'Are you okay?' Kay checked, as Holly whipped the envelope away.

'No!' Holly said, and did the only thing she could think of.

She fled!

And one lie led to another, it truly did, because she had no choice but to dash off to the staff loos and close the door behind her.

'Holly...' Kay followed her in and stood on the other side of the door. 'What's wrong?'

'I just feel a bit...sick.' Oh, she was the worst liar but at least Kay couldn't see her blush as she quickly changed the names over. 'A bit dizzy.'

She finally came out and Kay looked at her with narrowed eyes.

'Do you need to go home?'

'No.'

'Thank goodness for that. Go and get a cup of tea and sit down.'

Oh, please don't be nice, Holly thought, but she did as she was told and took a seat back in the staffroom.

Daniel appeared ten minutes later.

'Kay said that you weren't feeling very well.'

'I'm fine.'

He grinned.

'What?'

'She's decided that you're pregnant.'

'Oh, God!' Holly groaned.

'You're not, are you?'

Daniel's grin had, she noted, disappeared.

'No.'

'You're sure? I mean, I know we were careful...'

'Shh...' Holly looked around to be sure there was no one near. 'There's nothing to worry about.'

'Well, if there was something to worry about...'

'There isn't.'

There wasn't.

'I've got my period.'

'Is that why you're in such a filthy mood?' Daniel asked.

'Nope, that would be the company,' Holly said. 'Don't worry, Daniel, there are no repercussions for you to worry about!' Holly gave him a tight smile and got up from her chair. 'I'd better get back to work.'

Daniel stood as she brushed past him and he knew that Holly was wrong, there were repercussions from that night. Their friendship had changed. Gone was the easygoing banter and the little flirts and gone too was the lie that once they'd slept together he'd be over her, as was usually the case.

Oh, he could blame it on being half-asleep that he'd said yes when Admin had rung this morning to ask him to work, but it was more than that. And he could insist to himself that he was still in England because he had found out that neither his father nor Amelia could make Maddie's nativity play this afternoon and so had decided to stick around for that.

He took out the bunched-up piece of paper from his pocket and read her name.

Holly Jacobs.

Yes, there were repercussions.

CHAPTER SIX

INDEED, KAY HAD pegged Holly as pregnant!

Before Holly could even make it back to the department, Kay had called her into the office for a little talk.

'I've worked with a lot of young women in my time and generally when they're dizzy and throwing up...' She went into her pocket and pulled out a pregnancy test. 'It's better to face things.'

'Kay, please.'

'You can talk to me, Holly...'

'I know that I can,' Holly said. 'But I'm not pregnant.' As Kay held out the test, Holly refused to take it.

'You're not yourself, Holly!'

'Kay, I've got my period...'

'Well, it's the mother of a period, then, because it's lasted for two weeks. You've been awful,' Kay said, and Holly gave a reluctant smile. 'You can talk to me.'

Holly looked at Kay and she was touched by Kay's forthrightness and concern and, yes, she could talk to her. In some ways it would be a relief to tell someone how jumbled up she was feeling. Once she had been able to talk to her mother but those days seemed a long way off right now.

And so she told Kay the truth, well, a small part of it. 'I didn't feel sick or faint. I just had to come up with something. I didn't want you and Anna to take a name because I fudged the Secret Santa.'

'You what?' Kay frowned.

'It was only my name written down,' Holly explained.

'So that Daniel would choose you?' Kay said, smiling as realisation dawned. 'That's very ingenious. We'll have to see what he gets you.'

'Nothing, I expect.' Holly shrugged and Kay saw the sparkle of tears in her eyes.

'I don't think Daniel's very into Christmas.'

And Holly didn't think Daniel was very into her either.

'He's leaving, Holly,' Kay pointed out. 'He's made it very clear that he'll soon be off.'

Holly nodded. 'I wish he'd gone already.'

'No, you don't.'

Kay was right. This morning when she'd seen him, though cross and confused, she'd felt her heart simply leap at the sight of him. And now she had to start back at the beginning of getting over him when the last days had been hell.

She didn't just like Daniel, it felt like a whole lot more.

More than she'd ever liked anyone in her entire life.

Oh, she was trying so hard not to use the love word, even to herself.

Surely it couldn't be that?

'Be careful,' Kay suggested, and Holly nodded, even if it was a bit late for that. 'Now,' Kay added, 'while I can be terribly indiscreet I don't break confidences, so you don't have to worry about that. Daniel's lovely to chat to but I know his type—all he wants is inside your knickers, not your mind.' She saw Holly's pinched face and while she was delivering gloomy verdicts she decided to just get it over with. 'I've finished the Christmas roster. I'd better put it up.'

Holly knew that her cheeks had turned pink.

'Do you want a sneak preview?' Kay asked, and when Holly nodded she turned the computer screen around and Holly took a look.

She had been given a half-day on Christmas Eve, which meant that she finished at midday and was due back for a night shift on Christmas night, though she was off for New Year's Eve.

'I did my best,' Kay said.

Kay really had done, because at least there was a chance for Holly to make it home and spend the best part of Christmas with her family. Certainly Kay hadn't been gentle on herself—she was working all of it, just as she had last year and the year before that.

'Don't you ever want Christmas off?' Holly asked.

'Not really. Eamon used to get weary of me working it every year,' Kay admitted, 'but he's got used to it now. Next year I'm taking it off, though.'

She smiled that gorgeous Irish smile and Holly smiled back.

Kay's daughter, Louise, was due to give birth in the new year and Kay would be a first-time grandmother.

'I'm not missing that baby's first Christmas for the world,' Kay said as they walked through to the department.

The off duty had been posted and Holly stood back, chatting with Kay, as all the staff clustered around the computers.

'Louise might have the baby on Christmas Day,' Holly commented.

'God, I hope not,' Kay said, 'for the baby's sake. They never get a real birthday…'

'Yes, they do,' Holly said, and would have argued more

strongly but she suddenly remembered the Christmas that everyone in her immediate family would rather forget.

Because they'd forgotten her birthday.

Why today did everything make her want to cry?

'Holly!'

She looked over and saw that a patient was being wheeled in by Karen, a cheery paramedic.

The lady looked to be in her seventies and was very well dressed in a lovely woollen coat and scarf but she was sitting in the wheelchair, holding her arm, which was wrapped in a sling.

'This is Iris Morrison…'

It was a familiar injury at this time of the year. People were busy and the streets were slippery and when Iris had fallen she had put out her hand to save herself and had, it appeared, broken her wrist.

She was taken into a cubicle and Holly had a look at the wrist. It was causing Iris a lot of pain and she was also very pale, which meant Holly didn't really want her sitting for ages in a chair, so she decided to put her on a trolley.

The handover was brief. Iris was fit and well and was more cross with herself than anything.

'I haven't got time for a broken wrist,' she sighed when the paramedics had left.

'I think you're going to have to make time.' Holly smiled. It was terribly warm in the department and Iris's coat would have to come off for the X-ray, but Holly decided to do that after Iris had been given something for pain.

She told Iris she would be back in a moment and saw Daniel looking at *another* wrist X-ray.

'I've got a seventy-two-year-old lady…'

'I saw,' Daniel said.

'Can she have something for pain before I undress her?'

He nodded and took the patient card from Holly and then followed her in.

'Good morning, Mrs Morrison, I'm Dr Chandler.'

'Chandler?' Iris frowned and then looked up at navy eyes. 'I used to work for a Marcus Chandler, I'm guessing from those eyes that you must be Daniel!'

'That's correct.' Daniel gave her a smile. 'I'm sorry, I don't...'

'You were about five years old,' Iris said, 'so I don't expect you to remember. We've never actually met. I was your father's secretary for a year. He was a very impressive surgeon.'

'And you're a very tactful woman,' Daniel said, because his father was a very difficult man and he doubted any secretary of his had many nice words to say about him.

Iris laughed but then winced as Daniel gently examined her wrist. 'You don't need me to tell you it's broken?'

'No.'

'I'll get you something for the pain and then we'll get that coat off and get you straight round—'

'Actually,' Holly said, 'there's rather a wait for X-Ray.'

'I'll see if I can get you squeezed in,' Daniel said to Iris, and she gave a delighted smile at the upgrade.

Soon the coat was off and because of the strong painkillers she had been given, Holly went to X-Ray with her.

Of course he had managed to squeeze Iris in because, from the way the radiographer was batting her eyelashes, she was another fan of Daniel's.

The entire female population was, it would seem.

'Gorgeous-looking young man, isn't he?' Iris smiled as they waited.

'He knows it,' Holly said.

'Well, he seems nice with it, though, not like his father. Oh, that man!' She rolled her eyes to indicate just how difficult Daniel's father had been. 'Such a fantastic surgeon but he was the coldest man I have ever come across. I tried to be nice, given that his wife had died, I mean I guessed it must be hard to be left with a five-year-old…'

Holly swallowed.

The thought of losing her mother had rocked Holly's world for more than a year and she was twenty-eight. Holly just sat there for a moment and tried to imagine a world without her mother in it from the age of five.

She couldn't.

And neither could Daniel imagine a world with a happy family in it.

They sort of danced around each other for the best part of the morning. Iris got a plaster on her wrist and was picked up by her daughter. Holly got caught up with a patient who needed to be closely watched as they waited for him to be admitted to the psychiatric unit.

At midday Daniel came out of the changing room to head for home and saw Holly sitting by the patient's trolley. She was reading a magazine while the patient slept.

'Still no bed for him?' Daniel checked.

'Another hour.'

She barely glanced up and Daniel, who was always so certain where woman were concerned, was less so now.

He didn't know what he wanted, and even if he did, he wasn't sure that an offer to catch up would be welcomed by Holly.

She didn't look happy, when Holly always had, and Daniel was sure he had contributed to that.

'Daniel?' Kay was walking past. 'I've just been speaking with Mr Edwards and he said to ask you if there's any chance you could stay on till five.'

'Sorry.' Daniel shook his head. 'I've already got plans.'

'What plans?' Kay busied herself with his business. 'A date?'

'You could say that,' Daniel answered without thinking, as Holly did all she could to stop her top lip from curling like the family Labrador's when someone reached for his bone.

'Have a nice Christmas, Holly,' Daniel said.

'I shall.'

She would!

Holly had spent way too long daydreaming about him.

When her shift ended and Holly raced to the department store where she'd been with Daniel a few weeks before, she found herself watching the glassblower for a little while.

Thanks to her own meddling, she had Daniel to buy a gift for.

Yes, while she would have loved to queue up and buy him a hand-blown Christmas decoration and have the elves write a letter, she had no idea what she'd have them write.

And it was far too expensive.

And it would be embarrassing to reveal just how much he meant to her.

Anyway, he probably wouldn't be back to claim his Secret Santa present, let alone deposit hers.

And so instead of pouring her heart out in a tiny letter that would never be read she headed to the men's floor and tried to decide on a more appropriate present for him.

Yes, she exceeded the strict Secret Santa budget, but not by a ridiculous amount. Holly bought him a lip balm for when he went skiing. It was a very nice lip balm, in fact, and as close to his lips as she'd allow herself to get again.

It was a nice little gift—personal but not too personal, and useful as well.

It wasn't a gift from the heart—Daniel had made it very clear that her heart was something he didn't want.

CHAPTER SEVEN

Daniel headed straight from work to Maddie's school but his mind was on Holly.

She was nothing like his usual type yet he had liked her on sight and that feeling had not just remained, it had grown.

The more he knew her the more he wanted to know, and for someone who did his best not to get too involved it was the oddest feeling.

It was also a very new feeling and one he'd done his best not to properly examine.

He knew that she liked him. And that wasn't arrogance speaking, that was concern. After all, Daniel knew his own reputation.

Then he got out of the car and knew that it was time to focus on Maddie. He was cross with both his father and Amelia for not being here today.

His mother had always made the effort to be there for stuff like that, Daniel thought, and as he did so he suddenly halted.

All these years later memories seemed to be coming in and he felt floored anew by each and every one of them. As he took his seat in the audience he remembered standing on a stage with a towel on his head and his father's tie, and looking out and seeing his mother nod and smile to him.

And so he did the same for Maddie as she came out.

She was dressed as an angel and had a silver tinsel halo and didn't stay in character at all because she smiled and waved to him when she was supposed to be being serious.

Daniel smiled and waved back.

It was actually rather good!

Joseph's front teeth were missing and there was a worrying moment when he nearly dropped baby Jesus and he and Maddie shared a little *yikes* look but apart from that it went well.

'Which one's yours?' a woman beside him asked and nodded towards the stage.

'The loud angel,' Daniel answered, so glad with his decision to delay his trip just so that Maddie could have a family member in the crowd.

Afterwards, in the playground, she ran to him.

'You were fantastic!' Daniel told her.

'I know.' Maddie beamed. 'Did you see when Thomas nearly dropped the baby?'

'I did.'

'Where are we going?' she asked with all the confidence of a sister who knew she would be getting an extra treat from her brother.

'I thought we might go to the movies.'

'Really?'

'Yes.' He told her what they would be seeing but instead of her eyes lighting up they were suddenly worried.

'I wanted to dress up when I saw that!'

'I thought that you might,' Daniel said, and handed her a bag he had brought with him. It was her princess costume that he had picked up from Jessica, the nanny, on his way back from work.

He waited as Maddie dashed off to the facilities and came out a few minutes later in all her finery and wearing a tiara, with her friends all oohing and ahhing as she paraded about.

'I love it when you pick me up from school.' Maddie said as he took out the booster seat from the boot of his car.

'I enjoy it too.'

He did.

'Why don't you do it more often?' Maddie asked as she jumped onto the booster seat, which Jessica had also given him, and strapped herself in.

Daniel didn't answer.

It wasn't picking Maddie up from school that was the problem, it was dropping her off and avoiding being asked in.

Maddie didn't notice his silence. As they drove off she did the royal wave to her friends from the back of the car.

'If you marry a prince do you *definitely* become a princess?' Maddie asked.

'Not necessarily,' Daniel said. 'You might become a duchess or a countess...'

'What's the point, then?' Maddie sighed.

Oh, she was her mother's daughter, but, unlike Amelia, Maddie made him laugh.

She was so cute and had the same navy eyes as he had and, for a five-year-old, was very good company.

'How is school?' Daniel asked as he drove.

'I love it,' Maddie said. 'How is your work at the other hospital?'

'I love it too,' Daniel said.

He did.

He'd *liked* working at his old hospital. He had been through medical school there, had worked his way through the ranks and had a strong network of friends. Yet for some reason working at The Primary felt right.

It wasn't about Holly, he wasn't that shallow. It was maybe that at The Primary he wasn't Marcus Chandler's son. There were no expectations. If anything, given that he was a locum there was the expectation he'd need his hand held and then an element of surprise when he shone.

Back to focusing on Maddie!

Except, even as Daniel parked his car, he rather wished Holly was here, for he had no idea what to do. He knew this wasn't going to be a quiet evening at the movies but there was an endless stream of little girls all dressed the same as Maddie and the queue for tickets was incredibly long.

For a moment he considered taking out his phone and booking on line—the nice seats where you had food brought to you—but he knew that wasn't the treat his little sister needed. Instead, they chatted with several other families as they waited to buy their tickets.

'How old is she?' a woman asked.

'Five.'

'Are you giving her mum a rest?'

Daniel gave a noncommittal nod—it was clear that again the woman thought that Maddie was his child and he certainly wasn't about to enlighten a stranger, or tell her that giving Amelia a rest was far from being the reason he was here.

'Is it nice to be out with your dad?' The woman smiled at Maddie.

'I don't get to go out with my dad very often!' Maddie pouted and the woman gave Daniel a cool stare and then turned away, no doubt assuming it was an access visit.

'Maddie,' he warned.

'Well, it's true. Me and Daddy hardly ever go out, he's always working. And when we do…' She blew out a breath that sent her fringe flying into her tiara. 'I hate it when he takes me to his club, it's so boring.'

Daniel said nothing but he thought of the long afternoons he had spent at that bloody club, sitting with a colouring book and pencils as the adults carried on outside.

He had hated it too.

Still, they were a world away from a stuffy club this afternoon. Instead, it was all about a bucket of popcorn and two large icy drinks and just a couple of hours checking out of the world.

The place was bedlam.

Children were cheering and singing along to the film.

One little boy was so overexcited and overfed that he vomited.

'Should you say you're a doctor?' Maddie checked.

'I don't think his mum needs a doctor to work out what's wrong.'

Maddie smiled and got back to enjoying the movie.

It was fun, it was light-hearted and it was exactly what big brother and little sister needed. All too soon though it was over and they were headed for home.

After a few hours of easy conversation as they sat in a line of traffic making its slow way out of the car park, suddenly Maddie was quiet.

'Are you tired?' Daniel asked looking in the rear-view mirror, where she stared ahead.

'No,' Maddie answered. And then, as only five-year-olds could, she asked a question. 'Why aren't you going to be there at Christmas?'

Daniel took a moment to answer. 'I'm going away on a trip, it's been planned for a long time.'

'But it's only ten more sleeps until Christmas…'

'Maddie!' His tone told her to be quiet and he sounded like his father so he changed tack. 'I don't know exactly when I'm leaving.'

But it wasn't just Christmas that was troubling her. 'I don't want you to go.'

She broke into noisy sobs and Daniel stared ahead, not really knowing how he felt himself, let alone what to say. He could point out that it was just for a year. But a year was for ever when you were five years old.

He wasn't about to change his plans because his little sister kicked up. He was thirty-two, for God's sake, he was hardly going to stick around because his father had decided to attempt to parent…

Only it wasn't about his father.

'I hardly see you any more,' Maddie said.

'We've been out tonight,' Daniel pointed out.

'Only because you're saying goodbye. I don't see you so much any more.'

Daniel hadn't seen much of Maddie for the first couple of years of her life.

He and his father had barely been speaking when Maddie had been born. Daniel didn't really approve of his father taking such a very young bride. In turn his father was furious that Daniel had decided he didn't want to be a surgeon. When Maddison had been born, he had been pretty much told to stay back and that Amelia and Maddison were his father's family now.

At first it had suited him fine. Daniel wasn't exactly into babies and he'd just dropped off a birthday present or stood at the christening and things. But then Maddison the baby had become Maddie the two-year-old, with a smile and a cheeky personality that had soon endeared her to him.

And she was his family now.

Daniel didn't want to be some distant figure so he had started to factor her more into his life.

Till last Christmas when Amelia had come on to him.

Daniel's intention had been to be as far away as humanly possible this Christmas, to just stay out of his father's life, only it wasn't proving that easy.

'Look,' he said as the car pulled up at the picture-perfect house. 'I don't know what my plans are yet. I've got a lot of things going on now, Maddie. Grown-up stuff.'

'I hate grown-up stuff.'

'So do I.'

He really did.

'Please can I see you for Christmas?'

Daniel wanted to be able to just say no. To go home and hop on the internet and choose a flight and hotel. He looked over at what had once been his family home and though there were few happy memories of his time there, it didn't have to be that way for Maddie.

No, he would not stay for long but, yes, he could drop in and make a five-year-old happy on Christmas Day.

'I'll come around on Christmas Day to bring your present.'

Maddie gave a little squeal and smile and then climbed down from her seat, which Daniel collected, along with her school uniform.

Jessica came to the door and Daniel explained they'd had a good time, but that Maddie had just got a bit teary on the way home.

'She doesn't want you to leave.' Jessica nodded.

'Well, I'll be there for a little while on Christmas Day.'

Jessica opened her mouth to say something and then changed her mind and just gave him a smile. 'That's good,' she said.

Both knew that he was just delaying the inevitable—
Maddie was going to be very upset when it really came
time for him to leave.

His phone buzzed as he got back into the car and it
was the agency he had signed up with, offering him various shifts. He was about to decline and point out that he
had finished up.

Yet, given to what he'd agreed to for Maddie, he was
here for at least another week.

'Are you available to work Christmas Eve, nine a.m.
until till four p.m., in Outpatients at The Primary Hospital?'

'No,' Daniel said.

'Well, there's a night shift on New Year's Eve at the
Royal.'

'No, thank you!' His response was a little sarcastic.
There was no way that he'd work a night on New Year's
Eve, and especially not at the Royal, he had seen in way
too many there. He was about to explain that he was no
longer available when she offered him one more shift.

'Well, you can't blame me for trying. What about
Christmas Eve in Emergency at The Primary?'

And maybe this shift was the one he had been holding
out for and perhaps the reason he hadn't taken himself
completely off the books.

'What time?' Daniel asked.

'Seven a.m. until four.'

Holly would be on that morning, Daniel knew.

But even though she sprang to mind first, it wasn't
just Holly that drew him back to The Primary. He liked
the department and vibe there. He thought of Mr Edwards and Kay who had come to see him a valued part
of the team, and he wanted to know how Nora's husband
was going.

There were worse places to spend Christmas Eve, Daniel reasoned.

One more shift and he could find out all that had been going on and see how Holly was doing and hopefully he could manage a much better goodbye than the tense, stilted farewell they had achieved today.

'I'll take it,' Daniel agreed.

And so, if he was to be working on Christmas Eve, it meant that he needed to shop and so on the Saturday before Christmas, possibly the busiest shopping day of the year, he found himself back in the department store he had been to with Holly.

If he was going to stick to the Secret Santa budget then here really wasn't the place.

Except he knew what to get Holly, and so Daniel spent three very long hours thinking of what to put in a tiny letter.

But where to start?

Given he was standing here weeks after the event, yes, it had been more than a one-night stand.

And yet he was leaving.

It was getting harder and harder to do that.

There was family, namely Maddie, who needed him, a potential consultant's position at The Primary, which he was coming to love.

And there was Holly.

Yet there was so much more that he needed to sort out. His whole life had been spent failing to live up to his father's expectations, and falling off the chosen path.

Daniel knew he needed to sort out what it was that he wanted, and to do that he needed to get away.

'Your turn.'

Daniel looked down at a very harried and angry-look-ing lady dressed as an elf.

'What do you want written?'

'I haven't...' Daniel could feel the impatience in the people behind him. It had been more than a three-hour wait and he hadn't yet made up his mind.

And then he decided and took a little seat and told the lady what he wanted to be written.

She started typing on her mini-keyboard.

'That's it?' she checked.

'That's it,' Daniel agreed.

'Anything else?' she checked, clearly less than impressed with Daniel's attempt at expressing himself.

'No.'

'Well, I think you can do better than that.'

'I wasn't made aware that the letters got graded,' Daniel told her.

'The elves have all been trained—'

'Stop!' Daniel said. 'We both know you're not a real elf.'

She pursed her lips but after a brief standoff finally she hit 'send'.

'You can move down the line and watch your letter arrive.'

'Thank you.'

Daniel moved along the line and waited by the magic chute, scarcely able to believe he was doing this. He pressed cynical lips together as he thought of the computer and printer beneath the festive arrangement and then out it came—his letter to Holly.

He was asked to verify that it was indeed his letter and Daniel peered through a magnifying glass and read it.

Despite the fake elf's misgivings, Daniel worried that it actually said too much...but he nodded in agreement and then watched the glassblower work his magic.

It had cost a fortune.

It wasn't the money, or the time it took to make it, it was the fact that it was the closest he had come to sharing what was in his heart.

It was stay or go.

And staying felt harder.

CHAPTER EIGHT

CHRISTMAS EVE HAD always been special to Holly, whether or not she was working. The last-minute preparations, the excitement and anticipation and a certain sense of panic all seemed to combine to make it a truly magical day.

Last year, finding out that her mother was so unwell had had meant that it had been busy and fraught rather than exciting.

This year…

Holly looked around the bedroom and there was no sense of panic because everything was already done. Her presents were all wrapped and under the tree, last night she had gone and got petrol and now all she had to do was load up the car, drive to work, do her morning shift and wait for that once familiar, excited feeling to arrive.

Last night, for the first time, she had let herself cry properly over Daniel.

Determined to just let it all out so she didn't rot up everyone's Christmas, Holly had had a very good cry over a man who…

What?

She couldn't be angry because he had done nothing wrong. Daniel had been open and honest from the start. It was she who had taken it all too seriously and had kept looking for deeper meanings to everything. And so she had cried because she was simply sad that he was leaving.

Possibly he had already gone.

Half-heartedly she opened up number twenty-four on her Advent calendar and tried not to remember the time she and Daniel had done the same in this very bed.

It was a very nice-looking truffle, and when she bit into it there was a decadent shot of chocolate mousse.

Holly smiled because it was true—chocolate *always* helped.

A bit.

And there could be a chance that she would still see Daniel. Maybe he'd stop by with her Secret Santa present today, Holly thought, because there had been nothing under the tree at work last night.

And then she stopped.

Holly just stopped with hoping and wishing that things could be different between herself and Daniel and decided that she was being greedy and asking for too much. Last year, despite a rather dire diagnosis, she had prayed for a Christmas miracle and that her mother would still be here next year.

Esther was.

And so Holly got out of bed and showered and pushed all dark thoughts aside and refused to give her favourite time of the year over to a man who refused to embrace it or even bother to celebrate it.

Holly pulled on black jeans and boots and a red jumper for the commute to work. Her hair was particularly wild this morning but she just ran her fingers through the curls and decided to tie it back once she got to work. Red lipstick might be a bit much for the emergency department but it went with red earrings that flashed and she *refused* to be miserable today.

It was Christmas Eve after all!

Daniel wasn't in the least miserable.

He woke early and found that he was still looking forward to his shift at The Primary.

Breakfast was coffee, along with the most amazing chocolate truffle that he had ever tasted. Once showered and dressed he went and got Holly's present from the cupboard where it sat beside Maddie's and also presents for both his father and Amelia.

It was looking a little more like Christmas in his flat than it ever usually did.

But even if he was in a good mood Daniel spent the drive to work worrying that the present he had got for Holly was far too much and she might end up reading more into it than there was.

Still, he wanted her to have it, even if it just served as a nice memory of the wonderful night they had spent.

It had meant something.

She finished at midday, Daniel knew. That meant he could give it to her on her way out.

But even so…

He'd play it by ear, Daniel decided as he parked in the staff car park and got out. He had a small satchel that held his laptop and things and he placed the decoration carefully in there and went to make his way over to Emergency.

'Daniel!' The shout went up almost as soon as he'd got out of his car. He'd know that voice anywhere and he turned to see Kay frantically waving and standing next to Holly.

'We need a hand,' Kay called out to him in urgent tones.

'Okay.' He nodded.

'Hurry!' Kay called, and Daniel moved faster, wondering if someone had fainted or, from the way Kay was urging him, been run over, or…

'What?' he asked when he got there to find that nothing seemed amiss.

'I don't think Holly should leave all her family's presents in the car in case they're pinched, so if you could help us to carry them in…'

'I thought someone was hurt!' Daniel scolded.

'Why would you think that?' Kay asked as she handed him several Christmassy-looking bags that were all crammed to the brim with gifts. 'I just don't want to be late.'

He and Holly smiled and it was the first time that they had shared a proper smile since, well, since that night and the morning after.

Things had been awkward between them but felt a little less so today.

'How's Paul?' he asked as they started to walk.

'Don't ask.' Kay shook her head but Daniel wasn't going to be fobbed off.

'I just did!'

Holly answered for Kay. 'They're going to try and get him off the ventilator this morning. If not, he'll have to go to Theatre for a tracheostomy. He's been very up and down but mainly down.'

'It's been more than three weeks,' Kay sighed.

And both Holly and Daniel looked ahead because, yes, it had been a little more than three weeks since their night together also.

Hope was fading for all concerned.

'We'll put them in my office.' Kay suggested.

'Okay.' Holly nodded. 'I'll drop these off and then go back for the last lot.'

'There's more?' Daniel checked.

'Yep.'

'Give me those,' he said to Holly, unable to believe just how many presents she had. 'Go back and get the rest.'

Holly passed all her bags and parcels to him and Daniel staggered inside. Kay dropped the few she was carrying by her desk and then dashed off to grab a quick drink before handover, and Daniel realised that he suddenly had a chance to hide the decoration he had bought for the Secret Santa.

He went into his satchel and took out her gift.

It was too much, Daniel knew, and would cause loads of gossip if she opened it in front of everyone as she would surely know, straight away, that it was from him.

Yet he wanted her to have it and he wanted her to know how he felt.

But only once he had gone.

And now he could see the way to do just that, and so he slipped it into a bag that had a picture of a smiling snowman on it. So Holly! he thought as he headed for the staffroom.

'Did you bring your Secret Santa gift?' Kay checked, and Daniel pulled a face to indicate that he had forgotten.

'Oh, come on, Daniel,' Kay said. 'I'll see if I've got something you can put out.'

There was time for only a very quick drink but they all took it.

'Morning,' Trevor said, placing a beautifully wrapped present under the fake Christmas tree in the staffroom.

'And a delicious, delicate chocolate mousse truffle morning it is,' Kay said, and everyone laughed.

Daniel included.

They actually made him laugh, Daniel thought.

They found the happy in the smallest things and then watered it till it grew.

'That Advent calendar should be illegal.' Daniel joined in the conversation. 'I've been to three discount stores now but they've all sold out.' He looked up to see that Holly had come in.

'We're all worried,' she said.

'Worried? About what?'

'That the same work-experience student that made the ones on the fifteenth was let loose again and that the big day shall disappoint.'

'It never disappoints,' Kay said.

Holly, as she glanced under the Christmas tree and saw that Daniel hadn't added to the pile, rather thought that this year it might!

'So this is your last shift?' Kay asked Daniel as they all headed into the kitchen to drop off their mugs before their shift started. 'He's like that rock star...what's-his-name?'

'I have no idea,' Holly muttered as she rinsed her mug.

'The one who keeps doing his sell-out farewell tour and then a year later comes back and does it all over again.'

Kay allocated the staff and Holly was to work in the main section, which was where Daniel would mainly be, unless he had to go into Resus.

Holly was conflicted.

Though she had thought she wanted to see him, now that he was here it was proving hard.

Happy!

Holly kept reminding herself that it was Christmas Eve and that soon she'd be on the much-awaited and hard fought-for drive home!

Yay!

The patient who had just arrived, though, looked as grumpy as she felt.

'Leave me alone,' he told the paramedics as he was moved over onto the trolley. 'I don't want to be here!'

Holly had already gathered that.

Albert—he refused to give his surname or his date of birth—was homeless and had been found collapsed in a doorway. It was unclear how long he had been unconscious. The paramedics explained that the shopkeeper who had called for an ambulance had said he was used to him being there when he closed up at night.

He was usually awake by morning and told to move on.

They just hadn't been able to wake him this morning but he had sat up when the paramedics had arrived and insisted that he was fine. Albert had tried to get up and walk off but had been unable to do so and had finally agreed to come to hospital and be seen.

He was cantankerous, and very, very unkempt, with wild white hair and sore, cracked skin, and he refused to get undressed. More worrying than his appearance was a deep cough and a tinge of purple to his lips and tongue.

Holly checked his oxygen saturation, which was rather low so she slipped on some nasal prongs to deliver a low dose of oxygen as she took his temperature.

'You've got a fever.'

He nodded.

'Let me help get you into a gown so that the doctor can examine you.'

'I don't want you cutting my clothes.' He was coughing and wheezing but finally he allowed Holly to start removing layer upon layer of clothes.

First a coat, then a jumper, beneath that a jacket and then another shirt.

Kay came in and helped with his boots and bottom half.

It was always a bit of a feat to undress the homeless, especially in winter.

Soon, though, it was all bagged into two large plastic bags that Holly put under his trolley. Albert held onto a small leather bag and refused when Holly offered to lock it up in the hospital safe for him.

'You're not touching this!'

So Holly didn't.

And neither did she get very far with all the questions that needed to be asked and forms that needed to be filled in. He didn't want to reveal even his surname, let alone his next of kin.

'Is there anyone I can let know you are here?' Holly asked.

He gave a derisive laugh.

'Do you have any medical history that we need to know about?'

Albert didn't answer, and neither did he let Holly put in an IV or take bloods. All he wanted to do was to be left alone to sleep. Soon enough Daniel came into examine him.

Albert was more responsive to Daniel's questions than he had been to Holly's and he did let him listen to his chest.

'How long have you had this cough for?'

'It's been bad for a couple of days.'

'You've got quite a high temperature,' Daniel commented, and Albert nodded.

'I've had that since last night,' Albert said. 'I got the

shakes and I couldn't get warm but I think I was burning up.'

'Okay,' Daniel said, and he helped him lie back on the pillows and had a feel of his stomach, and though he tried to talk to him Albert didn't really communicate.

'I'm going to take some blood and then get an IV started,' Daniel said. 'We'll get a chest X-ray…' He went through it all but Albert just lay back. 'You can have some breakfast while you're waiting to go around, it's a bit of a wait.'

'I don't want breakfast.'

'Well, a cup of tea…'

'I don't want anything.'

Daniel could see that he was markedly dehydrated. The IV he was putting in would take care of that but he was more concerned with his lethargy.

'Is there anything else going on, Albert?'

'Everything's fine!' Albert's response was sarcastic and Holly watched as instead of leaving Daniel remained.

'How long have you been on the streets?'

'Long enough,' Albert said, but then he opened up a little. He had lived rough, on and off, for eighteen years. 'Sometimes I stay at a hostel and I was at a halfway house once for a few weeks but it didn't work out.'

He relied on several charities and soup kitchens for some meals and had to beg for help with the rest and he didn't want to see a social worker.

'I just want my chest sorted out and then I'll be gone.'

'How old are you, Albert?' Daniel asked, and though he had refused to answer Holly, now he did.

'Seventy-two.'

'And winter's barely got going,' Daniel said, and Holly saw Albert close his eyes at the thought of the prospect of another winter living rough but then he rallied and gave a shrug.

'It's not so bad.'

'Really?' Daniel checked, but Albert didn't answer. He just lay on his back and stared up at the ceiling as Daniel took some bloods and an IV was commenced.

'Would you like some breakfast?' Holly offered again once Daniel had gone, but again Albert shook his head.

'Leave me alone.'

The wait for X-Ray was a long one but finally he was back in the unit and sure enough he had lower lobe pneumonia along with a few more chronic issues.

He was started on antibiotics and as Holly added them to his IV she tried to engage him.

Albert was having none of it.

'I'm going to call the kitchen and see if they can send you something hot to eat,' Holly said, removing the untouched sandwiches that she had put out for him. 'I'll be back soon to do your obs.'

Daniel came in just as Holly left.

'She's a chirpy little thing, isn't she?' Albert grumbled.

'You could say that,' Daniel agreed. 'The admitting doctors will be down to see you, though it may be a while, but you're going to need to stay in.'

Often patients like Albert declined admission or set a very strict timeline for treatment, such as a few hours, but Albert nodded.

If anything, he seemed relieved that he would be staying in.

'How are you doing?' Daniel asked.

'Still coughing.'

'You shall be for a while,' Daniel said. 'I meant, apart from your chest?'

'I'm just…' Daniel waited patiently and finally Albert elaborated. 'I'm tired.'

It was as if everything was summed up in that short statement and Daniel knew he was hearing the very truth.

Tired of being sick.

Tired of a hard life on the streets.

And now that he had admitted just how tired he was it was almost as if he had given up because he lay back defeated.

'Albert, while you're waiting to be seen, I'm going to call the duty social worker.'

'What's she going to do?'

'Perhaps she can get the ball rolling on some accommodation for when you're discharged.'

'I'm not going to another of those hostels. There are too many rules.'

'Albert, why won't you let us help you?'

'Because I don't want your help.'

Daniel wasn't so sure that was true.

'So do you want me to ring the social worker?' he checked.

'Call her if you want to.' Albert shrugged. 'I don't know what she's going to be able to do, though.'

Daniel called the duty social worker from the nurses' station, where the radio was playing Christmas carols and there was a plate of star-shaped gingerbread out. Most of the nurses were now wearing tinsel, but for Daniel it all felt a long way from Christmas.

Actually, it felt like every Christmas he had known.

'Nora!' Daniel looked up as a flushed-faced Nora came in.

'I'm looking for Kay,' she said, and then promptly burst into tears.

He paged Kay, who was dealing with a domestic violence incident, and led a teary Nora around to Kay's office.

'Nora…' Kay rushed in.

'He's talking!' Nora said through her tears. 'He knows where he is and everything.'

Daniel blinked.

He had been absolutely sure that Paul must have died and from Kay's gaping mouth she must have been thinking the same. But it would seem instead that Nora had been holding things in all these weeks and now that the news was good she could finally allow some of her emotions out.

'They're thrilled with him,' she sobbed.

Daniel left them to it.

Who would have thought?

Not he.

He walked past the cubicle and there was Albert, just lying there dozing, but he opened his eyes as Daniel approached.

'I spoke with the social worker. Now that she knows you're being admitted—'

'She'll see me on the ward.' Albert knew the drill and finished Daniel's sentence for him.

Daniel nodded. With public holidays and a very heavy workload at this time of the year, they both knew it might take a while for Albert to be seen.

'You'll be here over Christmas,' Daniel told him. 'Is there anyone you'd like us to inform?'

'I doubt they'd want to know.'

It was an opening and the first hint of the life that Albert had left behind.

'Have you ever been in touch with your family?'

'No.' Albert shook his head. 'Well, I used to send a card to Emily, my great-niece, she's also my god-daughter, but

I wasn't well one year and I didn't manage to post it, then it seemed too late by the next.'

Daniel could see how it had happened. Oh, their lives were different in many ways but he could easily see how a couple of years of no contact might then make it hard to get back in touch.

And to know if you would even be welcome if you did.

'How old is she?' Daniel asked.

'Emily?' Albert checked, and Daniel nodded. 'She was two the last time I saw her. She'd be twenty now, I doubt she'd even know my name.'

'What about her parents?'

'Dianne is her mother,' Albert explained. 'She was my late sister's daughter. She's a chirpy thing too, like your young nurse. Dianne was good to me. Everyone took sides during the divorce but she always stayed back from doing that. I wasn't well.' He tapped the side of his head to indicate mental-health issues. 'Dianne always invited me over for Christmas but I'd always mess it up and start a row.'

'Why?'

'So that I could leave,' Albert admitted. 'I was embarrassed. I used to be a geography teacher. I missed out on head of department...they said I wasn't up to the responsibility but instead of proving them wrong, I proved them right and walked out. My wife had had enough by then and, looking back, I can't blame her. I lost my marriage, my job, everything really...' He shook his head. 'It's history.'

'I thought you said you taught geography.'

The silly joke made Albert smile but then Daniel watched as a very independent but very lonely man gave in then and started to cry.

It was very sad to watch but Daniel did so, and pulled

out some paper hand cloths from the dispenser so that Albert could blow his nose.

Holly came in to the sound of his tears but saw that Daniel was in there and left.

'Have you ever spoken with your wife?' Daniel asked when Albert had finished.

'I was admitted to hospital once when the divorce wasn't yet through,' Albert said. 'They called her but she told them that she wanted nothing more to do with me. I can't blame her for that.'

Daniel knew that the social worker would go through it all with Albert but that could be a few days away and, Daniel guessed, by then Albert could well have taken up his things and gone.

'Have you thought of calling your niece?' Daniel asked.

'Every day,' Albert admitted, and he went into the small bag that he would not let go of and took out a clear plastic bag. On it was a piece of paper and in very neat handwriting there was a number and his niece's full name and address. 'I don't know what to say if I call.'

Neither did Daniel.

Nearly two decades on, what did you say?

'They might have moved...' Daniel said as he looked at the address, but Albert shook his head.

'They're still there,' Albert said.

'How do you know?'

'Sometimes I walk past. There's a "For Sale" sign up, though. They shan't be there for long.'

It was now or never.

'Do you want me to try and call for you?' Daniel offered.

He rather hoped that Albert would shake his head. Daniel really did, because he didn't want to walk back into the cubicle and have to tell Albert that his family had terminated the call, as often happened in situations like these.

There was a lot of hurt on both sides, no doubt.

But instead Albert nodded. 'I'd like that,' he said. 'Please.'

Daniel took a few more details and as he walked out, Holly was walking toward him, carrying a tray. Her hair was piled up high and her smile was bright, if a bit forced, when she saw him. 'I got the canteen to send Albert up an early lunch.'

'Good,' Daniel said. 'I'm just about to call his niece, they haven't been in touch for eighteen years. I think Albert's hoping to resume contact.'

He watched as her smile faded. Holly would know only too well that the chances of this call ending well weren't great.

Daniel held the cubicle curtain open for Holly and she walked in with the tray. 'I've got a nice potato and leek soup for you, Albert, and it actually smells rather amazing.'

'You have it, then.'

Holly arranged the tray on a table and pushed it towards him but Albert wasn't interested. Instead, he lay back on the pillows and closed his eyes and wondered what the doctor would say when he returned.

Daniel wasn't hopeful.

He dialled the number that Albert had given him. It had been many years and given the little history Albert had told him Daniel wasn't sure that he'd be speaking to the right person, let alone that the call would be welcome, or that anyone would even pick up.

Someone did. 'Hi!'

'Hello,' Daniel responded to the cheery voice. 'I was wondering if I could speak with Dianne Eames.'

'She's not here at the moment.' The voice was that of a young woman and she sounded busy. 'Who's calling?'

'It's Dr Daniel Chandler from the accident and emergency department at The Primary Hospital.'

That tended to get a response!

'One moment...' She must have covered the phone but Daniel heard the young woman call for her mother and a few moments later another woman came to the phone.

'Dianne Eames speaking.'

She sounded brusque and impatient but, Daniel knew, that was often the way to cover fear.

'Is everything okay with Vince?' she asked.

'We had a patient admitted to us this morning. Albert Marlesford...'

There was a long stretch of silence.

'How is he?'

Daniel had to think for a moment before answering. 'He's been admitted with pneumonia. But, I'm not sure if you're aware, he's been living on the streets for some time.'

'Yes, I'm more than aware. That was his choice.'

'I understand that.'

'We tried to keep in touch with him, he used to send the odd card or letter and I'd go out looking for him...' There was a tense, inward breath that was followed by the sound of tears. 'He always managed to mess up Christmas every year, you could guarantee it!'

Given that it was Christmas Eve, Daniel thought for a moment that the message was clear—Albert wouldn't be messing up this one—but it would seem he had misinterpreted, Daniel realised, as Dianne continued to speak.

'Now he's managed another. I guess there won't be turkey at the table tomorrow.'

'Sorry?'

'I was just on my way to pick it up but that can wait… He's at The Primary, you say…'

It was then that Daniel realised that Dianne was saying that she was on her way in. That, even after eighteen years of no contact, Albert's niece would drop everything, even plans for tomorrow's dinner, to come and see him on Christmas Eve.

'Dianne,' Daniel said. 'To be honest, I think by the time you've got your turkey he might be a little more ready to receive visitors.' He decided it might be better for Albert if he explained things now. 'It might be nicer for him to be a bit more presentable when you meet.'

'He was always too proud for his own good,' Dianne said, and then thought for a moment. 'Can you tell him that I'll be in to see him this afternoon…? Hold on a moment.' Daniel waited and there was the sound of chatter in the background. 'Can you let him know that Emily will be in to see him too?'

She gave Daniel her mobile number and asked that she be called immediately if there was any change.

And that was it.

The phone call ended but instead of going immediately to tell Albert, Daniel sat for a long moment staring at the phone.

He had expected a cool reception, even to have the phone hung up on him, or at best to be bombarded with questions. Dianne hadn't required an immediate update on all the missing years, all she had needed to know was where Albert was, to be there for him.

Daniel walked over to his cubicle and saw that Holly was still in there, trying to persuade him to at least try and have a little something to eat, but Albert ignored her and simply closed his eyes.

'I just spoke with Dianne,' Daniel said, and he saw that Albert's eyes remained closed, no doubt bracing himself for rejection. 'She's going to come in a bit later with Emily.'

Then Albert's eyes opened.

'She said that?' Albert checked, and Daniel nodded and he watched as Albert's face broke into a smile.

'She was just on her way to pick up the turkey but she offered to come straight in…'

It was then that Albert started fretting. 'I can't see her looking like this….' How he looked was one of the many reasons that Albert hadn't knocked on his niece's door. 'I smell…'

'We can sort all that, Albert.' Holly spoke then. 'In fact, you get an early Christmas present!'

There was always stash of clothes in Emergency and Kay kept them in the same cupboard that she kept Christmas gifts. The clothes came mainly in the form of donations from staff and fundraisers and they were very valued, especially in situations such as this.

As well as clothes for Christmas, Kay ensured there were always presents, for the children, for the overnight patients, for people such as Albert, and she shopped throughout the year just for situations such as this.

Holly went into the dark storeroom and turned on the light. First she went through the men's clothes and found some smart navy pyjamas that looked large enough for Albert. They weren't new, but they were very neat, and the colour wasn't faded and all the buttons were on. Then she went through the wrapped gifts—they were separate barrels for men, women and children, and the gifts were also labelled by age.

On the shelf was a stash of chocolate stockings, already wrapped for anyone who might have been forgotten, but there were more pressing things than that needed for Albert today.

His early present was soap, deodorant and a comb.

As well as a wash Holly gave him a tidy-up shave with eyebrows and ears thrown in!

'Well, look at you!' Kay said as Holly prepared to move Albert up to the ward. 'You're looking grand.'

'I'm feeling it,' Albert said.

Okay, he was still rather rough around the edges and Kay looked at his feet, which were peeking out from the blanket. They would be attended to by the podiatrist at a later stage but for now he got an extra present of fluffy socks and he was certainly ready to meet his niece and great-niece again.

Holly smiled as she walked into the acute medical unit. It was far more elaborately decorated than Emergency—in fact, they had won the competition for Best Decorations.

Emergency hadn't even placed.

'Good morning, Albert,' a cheerful male nurse said. 'Actually, it's almost afternoon. You're just in time for lunch.'

'Good,' Albert huffed. 'I'm starving.'

'Have they been keeping you hungry down there?' The nurse smiled at Holly, who rolled her eyes. Her whole morning had been spent trying to get Albert to eat. 'We've put you in a four-bedded ward...' He gave directions to Holly. 'Bay Six.'

Bay Six had three other gentleman in it. Two were asleep but one nodded and said hello to Albert, who gave a cheery wave back.

'Thank you,' Albert said, once she had him settled in bed. 'Are you working over Christmas?'

'I'm just about to finish,' Holly said. 'Though I'll be back tomorrow night.'

'Well, thank you again.'

It was the nicest note to end her shift on. It was just so lovely to see Albert tucked up in bed and knowing that he'd be taken care of over Christmas. Holly made her way down to Emergency rather quickly. It was already after midday and she still had to get all her parcels out of Kay's office.

She would not be saying goodbye to Daniel, Holly had already decided. She had said it too many times, and on each occasion it hurt a little more. Anyway, he was busy with a patient and that suited Holly just fine. She loaded up the gifts and chatted to Kay, who was taking a quick break in her office.

'Have a wonderful Christmas, Holly,' Kay said. 'Now, don't go breaking your neck to get here by nine tomorrow night. I can stay back for an hour or so.'

'I should be fine.' Holly smiled. She had her presents piled up on a wheelchair and was ready to make a quick exit.

There was just one more thing, Kay reminded her.

'Did you get your present from under the tree?'

There hadn't been one there for her on her coffee break and Holly had tried to pretend that it didn't matter.

'Oh!' Holly feigned surprise, as if it was the furthest thing from her mind. 'I'll go now.'

She left the wheelchair with Kay and headed round to the staffroom and tried not to get excited but, unlike on her coffee break when she'd last checked, there was now a present under the tree.

But it was in the shape of a Christmas stocking but, worse, it was the wrapped in the same paper as the ones in the storeroom.

Holly knew with a sinking feeling that, not wanting her to receive nothing, Kay had stepped in.

Deep down she had known full well that Daniel would forget.

Yet she had hoped he wouldn't.

And even now, as she opened the little attached card, she hoped for something that might indicate she was more than an afterthought.

That was all she was, Holly realised as she read the writing.

Holly Jacobs
Happy Christmas

Daniel could not have cared less if he'd tried to.

Don't cry here, Holly told herself, just make it out to the car. And so she came out of the staffroom and walked around to the department wearing a big smile and added her parcel to the pile on the wheel chair.

'What did you get?' Kay asked as Holly walked past her office.

'A chocolate stocking.'

'That's nice.' Kay smiled.

Had she not known that it was from Kay's secret stash then it might have been a perfectly nice gift.

But instead of nice it spoke volumes to Holly.

Holly said her goodbyes and headed off but as she came out of Emergency and to the main hospital entrance she was just in time to see Daniel walking back from wherever he had been.

'Have a great Christmas, Holly.'

'And you.'

And this was goodbye, Daniel knew.

He was staying just long enough to see Maddie for Christmas and sort out the tenants but then he would be gone.

And he was not coming back here again.

This was hurting him too.

'It's been great working with you,' Daniel said.

Seriously? Holly thought.

We had sex in my hall and that's the best you can do?

She pushed the wheelchair and kept on walking but then turned around and Daniel did too and they stared at each other. She could not believe he would just let her walk away so easily, that their final goodbye was a thank you for being a good colleague.

And so, when she should have left it at that, Holly revealed a little of what she held inside. 'A chocolate stocking?'

'Sorry?'

'You couldn't even be bothered to go to the gift shop. Instead, you had to get something from the store cupboard to give to me. I think I deserved a bit more than that!'

For a moment he stood there but then, remembering the rules she had told him about Secret Santa, Daniel frowned.

'How did you know it was from me?'

'Because...' Holly said, and then wished that she'd never started this.

Oh, she wished, how she wished that she'd never swapped around their names in the first place.

An incredulous smile spread over his face and he

pointed to her as realisation dawned. 'You rigged Secret Santa.'

'I did not! I was organising it so I had to know who got—'

'Liar,' Daniel broke in. 'You rigged it. Why would you do that?'

'Because...' Holly said for the second time, only this time she continued to speak. Actually, this time she made an already bad situation worse! 'I was hoping to find out how you felt.'

'Felt?'

'About us,' Holly said.

'Us?'

'Not *us*, in that sense,' she hurriedly amended. 'Just that it felt like more than a one-night stand.'

She should be shot on the spot for admitting it, Holly knew, she should take her heart right off her sleeve and pop it back in her chest.

Holly couldn't roll like that with him, though. Somehow with Daniel she was her honest worst.

'What do you mean by more?' Daniel asked.

Holly decided that silence really was her best defence now.

More meant more!

She had glimpsed *them*.

Oh, she would work on her New Year's resolutions and become all aloof and sophisticated next year, but there was still a few days until then.

'Holly,' he calmly stated. 'We had a great night. Can't you just enjoy it for what it was?'

There was a chill coming up the corridor as the automatic doors slid open and closed. The floor was wet as people trudged in with wet shoes and dripping umbrellas and romance was, for Holly, officially dead.

'Enjoy your gap year,' Holly said.

'Gap year?'

'Isn't that what it is?' Holly jeered. Well, she attempted a jeer, but she wasn't very good at being mean. 'Isn't that what teenagers do when they want to sort themselves out?'

Daniel, on the other hand, was very good at being mean and he thought of her love of winter weddings and the dreamy look that came over her at times. He was standing looking at a woman who would rig Secret Santa to find out how he *felt*. And, far from telling her that he was feeling far too much of late, instead Daniel's words tumbled out on a sneer. 'Say hi to him for me.'

'Who?'

'Mr Holly,' Daniel said, and basically accused her of being on husband watch. 'Clearly that's what you're looking for. It was supposed to be a bit of fun.'

Fun!

And with that word he did Holly a huge favour, for he snapped any lingering hope that remained, like an icy twig in the park.

'Well, have a *fun* Christmas,' Holly said, and did her best, with a rickety wheelchair piled high with gifts, to stalk off.

And he let her go.

Daniel watched her walk towards the car park and told himself that he was well shot of some stalker who would rig Secret Santa and a woman who looked for deeper meaning in everything...

Then as he walked back into the department and as the world carried on around him, he regretted how they had ended.

Yes, there was another gift for her that she would find

perhaps later tonight, but there would be no chance of them speaking by then.

He couldn't even drop by her flat after his shift to apologise as she was heading straight to her parents'.

Daniel was very aware that most of his thirty-two Christmases had been ruined somehow and now he'd just gone and ruined Holly's.

'Let it go,' he said under his breath, and picked up a patient file.

He couldn't let it go, though.

'Where are you going?' Kay asked as he put down the file and went to walk off.

'I'll be back in a few moments.'

Yes, he really should have let it go, Daniel thought as he strode through the car park. It was freezing outside and pouring with rain and he was just wearing scrubs and no doubt he'd already missed her.

But he hadn't.

There was Holly, sitting in the driver's seat of her car, and she was hunched over the steering wheel and in floods of tears.

'Holly…' He knocked on the window and she looked up and in horror saw who it was, and got back to clutching the steering wheel and started crying some more.

It felt to Holy like humiliation heaped on humiliation, especially when he chose to be nice and came around the other side and climbed into the passenger seat.

She heard his sigh, felt his awkwardness and smelt the delicious scent of him.

'I am not crying about you.' Holly told him the truth, or part of it—for she was not solely crying about him, more the utter disaster of her Christmas Eve. 'My car won't start…' She turned the key to show that this time she wasn't lying and it emitted a terrible sound.

'Don't flood the engine…' he warned, as it choked and gasped its last.

'There's a lot that needs fixing,' Holly said. 'I've been putting it off.'

She knew she couldn't complain about her car breaking down. It was terribly old and had been on its last legs for the last six months but it had always seen her safely home.

Till now.

'I have to get home, though…' She was seriously panicking—the trains were a disaster on Christmas Eve and she had no idea how she'd manage getting all the presents home. 'I can't miss it. I'll call a taxi…'

'Holly…' Daniel just didn't get it. Yes, he was aware that he had little family to speak of but Holly was at the other extreme. If she had five kids waiting for their mother he might understand more. 'These things happen. A taxi, if you can even get one to agree to take you, would cost a small fortune. As well as that you'd then have to get back for tomorrow night and there are no trains on Christmas Day.'

'I can borrow my mum's car to get back.'

'Can't you just miss it?'

'We're not all like you,' Holly said. It was far easier to carry on being mean. 'Some of us want to be with our family at Christmas.' And then she stopped gripping the steering wheel and leant back as the need to score points faded and the truth came in. 'My mum's not very well…'

She'd told him that, Daniel remembered. She just hadn't revealed how sick her mother was.

Now she did.

'Why didn't you tell Kay?'

'She knows,' Holly said. 'Last year I had both Christmas and New Year off. Mum's actually doing better lately. This was supposed to be the real happy Christmas after the fake happy Christmas last year. To tell the truth, it's all a bit strained at home, Mum's become rather too used to getting her own way.' Holly took a breath. 'She's going to have to understand that these things happen...'

'Will she, though?'

'Probably not.' Holly actually smiled and then wiped all the tears away with the sleeve of her coat and looked over to where he sat and saw that he was wearing only thin scrubs and that his hair was all wet from the rain.

'Why did you come out?' Holly asked him. 'Did I forget to sign something?'

'No. I came out because I hated that we ended things on a row.'

'So do I.'

'I think we can both do better than that,' Daniel said. 'Why don't I drive you home? I don't finish till four but—'

'I can't ask you to do that.'

'You didn't ask,' he pointed out.

'It's Christmas Eve...' Holly flailed, yet he was calm.

'Hence the emergency.'

And it was an emergency, at least it was to Holly.

'How far away do you live?' Daniel asked.

'Three hours on a good day. Four if it's...' she looked out of the window and saw the sheets of rain and factored in the Christmas traffic. 'It might even be five.'

'That's okay, but I won't stay,' he warned.

'I know.'

'Just let's get you home.'

'Thank you.'

'Do we have to carry all the presents back into the department?' Daniel asked, and Holly laughed.

'No.'

It was decided that they would lock them up in his rather more secure car and Holly would take the underground home.

'I'll come and pick you up as soon as I finish.'

'Thanks.'

'Go and eat some chocolate,' Daniel said.

'Oh, I shall.' She held up the blasted chocolate stocking and they both shared a smile. 'I've got plenty after all.'

Holly, as she headed for home, was thrilled with the thought of a few more hours with him because Daniel was right…

They deserved better than to end it on a row.

CHAPTER NINE

DANIEL WORKED THROUGH the afternoon and at two he took a call from the acute medical unit.

'What time did Albert Marlesford's family say that they'd be here?'

'His niece had some shopping to do,' Daniel explained.

'I told him that she must be busy and to stop fretting.'

Daniel ended the call and told his cynical self to be quiet.

Of course Dianne would be in, he had spoken to her himself.

He was worried for the old boy, though.

'Shouldn't you be off?' Kay checked a while later, and Daniel glanced at the time.

'I should be and I am,' Daniel said. 'And this time it's for good. It's been an absolutely pleasure to work with you Kay.'

It really had been.

So much so that once he'd got his head sorted out, Daniel was wondering if, maybe a year or so from now, he'd be back—and not as a locum. But there was too much going on in his mind right now to voice very tentative thoughts.

And neither would it be fair to Holly to say he was considering returning someday.

'Don't forget your present,' Kay reminded him.

He went to the tree and there was a little parcel wrapped in silver with a curly bow. If Holly had rigged the Secret Santa so that he would get her name then presumably she had chosen a present for him.

He checked the attached card and saw her loopy handwriting.

'Open it,' Kay said.

'Later.'

He didn't go straight to the car; instead, he took his cynical self up to the acute medical unit and found that Albert's relatives still hadn't arrived.

Albert was comfortable, they said.

Sleeping.

And that was surely better than the streets but for a moment there Daniel had entered a world where families reunited.

After that he walked out to the car. It was already starting to get dark and he really should press on. Yet he sat for a moment in the driver's seat and wondered what she had bought and what had been written on the card but, rather than find out now, Daniel put it in his glove box. This journey had the potential to be awkward enough, without finding out that she'd bought him a little Holly & Daniel snow globe or...

Well, he didn't possess much imagination in the romantic Christmas present department. Still, he would guess that if she was *that* upset about the stocking, well, there was going to be something rather special for him in that silver parcel.

He'd open it tomorrow, Daniel decided. He'd open it when she was safely home.

Safely, because he liked her.

More than he cared to admit to himself and certainly more than he dared to admit to Holly.

Of course she was confused, because so too was he. For the best part of a year Daniel had been planning for this trip and desperate to get away.

Now, though, it felt as if there were more and more reasons to stay.

Daniel pulled up outside her flat and did his best not to recall chasing her up the concrete stairs, and as he knocked on the door he tried not to remember them falling through it.

'Come in.' Holly beamed.

'I'd better not,' Daniel said. He really, given what had taken place there, didn't want to stand in the hall! 'The traffic sounds pretty bad.'

'Of course…' She was a little flustered. 'I'll be one moment.'

He stood on the doorstep and then realised that Holly was on the telephone and so, rather than being like his father who would sit in the car, pressing on the horn until everyone came out, he stepped in and waved a hand as if to say to take her time.

Holly headed into her bedroom, which was really her living room. She had the television on, he could see, though the sound was turned down.

'We're just leaving now,' he heard Holly saying. 'No, don't worry about that. I'll see you shortly.' Then another pause. 'Mum, I really do have to go. Daniel's already doing me a huge favour.' She came to the bedroom door and rolled her eyes. Clearly her mother thought there was a lot that had to be discussed between now and three hours' time when Holly would be there.

'Yes, I've got the cheese,' Holly said.

So, rather than drumming his fingers and appearing impatient, Daniel went through to a small lounge room and took a seat and listened to the neighbours shouting.

'Sorry about that,' Holly said as she came through to the rather cold lounge. 'The logistics of Christmas in my family. Honestly…' She blew out a breath and picked up a coat from the chair. 'I'm ready.'

'I'm not,' Daniel admitted. 'I'd love a drink.'

'Sure.' Holly said. 'Coffee?'

'Please.'

He followed her into the kitchen.

'Do you want something to eat?'

And usually he would say no, but he hadn't had lunch and, given that he had no intention of stopping on the drive to her home, it would be a long time until he'd be eating again.

'Thanks.'

She made toasted sandwiches. Turkey, Brie and cranberry.

'It's Christmas after all.'

They smelt delicious.

'Now I can see the end of my movie.'

It wasn't a plan to get him into the bedroom, Daniel knew, given that she practically lived there.

And so she flicked the television back on and it was one of those stupid movies that ran every Christmas.

'Holly,' Daniel said, 'even I know the ending.'

She just smiled and sat on the edge of the bed to eat her own toasted sandwiches while Daniel took a seat on a small chair, though, rather disconcerting for him was this sudden wish to lie down and open a bottle of wine and watch the movie and…

…spend Christmas in bed.

'I love this bit.' She turned up the sound on the movie

as they ate and even Daniel laughed, because it was cheesy and funny and it was just very, very nice to be here.

'Did Albert's family come and visit him?'

'Albert?' Daniel checked, and then shook his head. 'How would I know?'

'I thought they might have popped into Emergency, or that you might have…' She gave him a smile. 'I bet they're having a good old catch-up right now.'

Daniel didn't return her smile; instead, he stood.

'Come on, we'd better go.'

The traffic was hell and the car inched its way through the streets but finally they hit the motorway.

Then the car stopped inching its way.

It just sat in gridlocked traffic as both pretended not to notice it was now after six.

'What are your plans for tomorrow?' asked Holly, just trying to be polite.

'No definite plans,' Daniel said.

'Will you see your family?'

'I'll pop in for ten minutes.'

He briefly turned and saw her rapid blink and saw the wrestle as she tried not to judge.

'Things are a bit complicated at home,' he said, when usually he offered no reason.

Thankfully the traffic eased a little and for the next hour they made if not good then reasonable time.

The phone rang out in the car, making her jump as it came over the speakers, and she glanced at the dash.

Dad.

Daniel didn't answer the call.

Then five minutes later it happened again and she could feel the tension in him.

There were signs for a service station and guessing

he might want to speak to his father without having it broadcast over the speakers for her to hear Holly asked if they could stop.

'Holly…' He glanced at the time on the dashboard. 'We need to push on.'

'And I need the loo.'

He gritted his teeth as they pulled into the service station and Holly got out. 'Do you want anything?' she offered.

'To get there this year. Just hurry.'

He watched her disappear into the building and then realising he could call his father Daniel did so. He kept an eye out for Holly as he was connected and they briefly spoke.

'Amelia's trying to sort out numbers for dinner…'

Daniel let out a silent mirthless laugh. From the way his father described it Amelia was counting out potatoes and fretting as to whether she had enough, when, in truth, she'd just give the number expected for dinner to the maid.

And as he sat there he could well recall coming home from boarding school where Christmas preparations had been in full swing to a house where there were none.

His father had often worked and no matter how nice the nanny was, she would far rather be on the phone to her own family on Christmas Day than entertaining him.

And he remembered with clarity the loneliness of Christmas and he was so over the pretence and the farce of it all.

'I shan't be there for dinner,' he told his father. 'I'll drop by with Maddie's present but I really can't stay for long.'

'We'll be going to the club in the afternoon…'

Daniel opened his mouth to say something, but wasn't

sure it was his place. At least his father made some effort
now, at least, for Christmas he tried to be home.

'When do you fly?'

'I still haven't booked,' Daniel admitted.

He didn't know if he wanted to go.

Holly was right.

Thirty-two was pretty old to be taking a gap year.

He was running and a little like Albert he was suddenly tired. 'I'll see you tomorrow,' Daniel said.

'Maddie wants to speak to you.'

'Tell Maddie I'll see her tomorrow,' Daniel told his
father, because he could see Holly making her way back
to the car. 'I have to go.'

Despite his telling Holly to hurry, she had taken the
time to stop for refreshments and he had to reach out and
open the door as she was carrying two take-away cups.

'Christmas coffee!' Holly smiled, handing him one of
the cups and then climbing in.

'You find the Christmas in everything.'

'I do.

He took a sip and pulled a face. 'What the hell is this?'

'Coffee and cinnamon, I think,' Holly said. 'And
maybe a bit of nutmeg?' Then she got to the real reason
she had taken so long. 'Did you call him?

And one of the reasons she irked him and one of the
reasons he liked her more than she knew was because
of moments like this—Holly had done the polite thing,
Daniel now realised. Guessing that he might not want
her around while he spoke with his father, she had made
a polite excuse to leave.

Then she had ruined her tact by asking if he had called
him!

'Yes,' Daniel said. 'He just wanted to check on numbers for dinner.'

'Are you going?'

'No,' Daniel said as they again hit the motorway.

'I'm sure he'd love it if you came along…'

Daniel said nothing and Holly could sense he'd prefer it if she didn't either.

'I'll leave it,' she offered.

'Please do.'

He stared at the car registration in front of him and then at the wall of traffic ahead and, of course, Holly simply could not leave it.

'But surely at Christmas…'

'Holly.' Daniel turned. 'I didn't offer you a lift home to indulge in a cosy chat about my family situation. I don't need your take on it.'

'Friends talk…' Holly started, and then gave in. Who had even said they were friends?

She didn't even have his phone number and he had never asked for hers.

'I wonder when it will stop raining,' Holly said, and Daniel rolled his eyes at her attempt at conversation. 'Is that banal enough for you? We can talk like strangers at a bus stop.'

'Holly…'

'I mean, it's not as if we're even friends. You couldn't even be bothered to introduce me to your ex.'

He knew she was referring to Amelia.

'She's not my ex.'

Holly rolled her eyes. 'An old one-night stand, then.'

'I've never slept with her.'

'I don't believe you.'

'You don't have to believe me, Holly.' God, she had a nerve. 'I don't have to explain myself to you.'

He wanted to, though.

It had been excruciating in the department store and

it had been that way for Holly too and no doubt why she had decided to walk off.

'I know it was awkward for you at the shop…'

'It was awkward long before that,' Holly sighed. 'Maddie called three times when you were in the shower. Was she your date the other day?' When he didn't answer she stared out of the passenger window. 'Honestly, Daniel, I don't know how you juggle them all.'

Then again, he hadn't attempted to juggle or hide, Holly thought, he'd just listened to his messages while she'd sat there, pulling on her boots.

'Amelia, the woman you met that day is my stepmum.'

To her credit, Holly said nothing, not even a little shocked gasp. She just turned back to look at him.

'That date I had last week was with my sister, Maddie.'

'Maddie's your sister?'

'Yes, and she's five.'

'Why didn't you just say?'

'Because I find it awkward. When we're out everyone assumes that she's mine.'

'Is that why you're still here?' Holly asked, and looked at him.

'Yes, she wanted me to see her in the nativity play and she's getting upset about me going away.'

'You'd be like a rock star to her.'

Daniel nodded. 'It's not all one-way, she's actually very good company. We go to the movies and things but I don't really go over to the house.'

'Because you don't get on with your dad?' Holly frowned. 'Surely you can get past that for her sake?'

And then his phone rang again and she glanced at the dash.

Maddie.

'What's she doing up this late?' Daniel asked, though more to himself.

'It's Christmas Eve.' Holly answered anyway! 'She's probably excited.'

When he answered the call, though, Maddie sounded a little strained.

'Is Father Christmas real?' she asked him. 'Thomas said it's all made up.'

'Thomas?' Daniel checked.

'He was Joseph in the nativity play.'

'The one with no teeth?' Daniel checked, and Maddie started to laugh. 'The one who nearly dropped the baby? I wouldn't be paying too much attention to him.'

'So there is a Father Christmas?'

'Yes.' He could say that because for all Amelia's faults she would make sure there were presents under the tree for her daughter. 'So you can stop worrying and go to bed and I'll see you tomorrow.'

'For dinner?'

'Not for dinner, I'm...' He could feel Holly's ears on elastic as she pretended not to listen and he couldn't even come up with an excuse. 'I'll see you tomorrow.'

'Why can't you just go for dinner?' Holly said once the call had ended. 'I mean, how hard could it be?'

'Holly, my father didn't even celebrate Christmas until he married Amelia. I used to sit at home with the nanny on her phone the entire day to her family overseas while he went to work.'

She knew she was hearing the truth, there was something in his voice that told her that Christmas had always been hell.

'Not all families are perfect, Holly!'

She could hear the dig and she stared ahead.

'My family's not perfect, Daniel.'

'Well, they come close.' Daniel mimicked her voice when she'd spoken about her birthday. '"My parents always make sure that both are celebrated!"' He reverted to his bitterness. 'Of course they do.'

'Not always.' And she stared ahead at the traffic and she told him a truth, and this time it was Holly who was more speaking to herself. 'They forgot my birthday once.'

CHAPTER TEN

'WHEN YOU SAY "FORGOT…"?'

'They forgot completely,' Holly said.

'Tell me.'

'No.' Holly shook her head. 'You've just admitted that you basically had no Christmas at all growing up, so it seems a bit shallow to be upset about missing out on one birthday.'

'How old were you?' Daniel asked.

'I was six, turning seven.'

So not a whole lot older than Maddie was now, and he could just imagine the hurt it would cause his little sister.

'Tell me,' he said, and his voice was kind and she found that she wanted to.

Silly, that some silly childhood memory could make her eyes burn all these years later.

'Usually we had birthday cake for breakfast on Christmas Day and I opened my presents and then we'd all go through to the lounge and Christmas Day would start. We still do that, though we have champagne now too. It was just one year…' Her voice trailed off as she recalled her confusion when they'd gone straight through to the lounge. And how she'd tried not to cry as she'd opened her presents. 'I kept thinking they were just pretending that they'd forgotten and then I realised they actually had.

Now I look back I can see it had been a difficult year for my mum. My Uncle Harry had been in hospital—he'll be there tomorrow… Drunkle Harry.'

Daniel smiled.

'And Adam, my brother, had been sick with bronchiolitis.'

'When did they remember?'

'When I went to bed. Mum came in to say goodnight.'

'Were you crying?'

'No, I had my nervous smile on!' Holly said, and they both laughed but then both fell silent.

She stared out of the window, recalling that odd day, and she knew that the tears in her eyes had little to do with some long-ago memory.

It was a little like how Daniel made her feel now.

As if something that was so terribly important to her meant very little to him.

If she hadn't pushed that envelope under his nose, if Kay hadn't prompted him, she'd be minus a chocolate stocking now.

Exactly!

And while, yes, he'd come out to make up for their row, if her car hadn't broken down they'd have already gone their separate ways by now.

Soon she would be forgotten.

Finally his chirpy passenger was silent and Daniel got the peace he had craved, except he rather missed her incessant chatter.

The traffic was barely moving and to fill the silence he turned the radio on and listened to the carols.

Another half a mile, another half an hour.

And still Holly said nothing.

She took out some Christmas cards from her bag and

started to write them but after a couple she gave in and put them in the door pocket. She was tired of being peppy and ensuring that everyone was happy.

Blue lights were flashing up the hard shoulder, though it was the police and fire brigade that were passing them, rather than ambulances.

'Have a look on your phone,' Daniel said, 'and see what's happening.'

'A lorry has lost its load,' Holly said.

'We might need to think about getting off at the next exit.'

'We can't,' Holly said as she went through the traffic updates. 'There's flash flooding and the exit is closed.'

And she expected a hiss of frustration from Daniel but instead he gave a soft laugh. 'Of course it is.' He looked ahead. 'We might have to find somewhere to stay the night.'

'I'm really sorry for messing up your Christmas,' Holly said.

'There was no Christmas to mess up.'

'Oh, that's right, it's just another day.'

She simply could not get how she could be so crazy about someone who cared so little about the things that mattered to her and she actually told him so.

'I'm glad that we're not going anywhere,' Holly said.

'It might start moving.'

'I'm not talking about the traffic,' Holly admitted, and raised the awkward subject in the hope of clearing the air. 'I'm talking about my mythical us.'

Daniel smiled.

'You'd buy me shoes or something for Christmas.'

'I would,' Daniel said, and then frowned. 'Don't women like shoes?'

'Not the flat work ones that you'd get for me. No, it

would be a combined Christmas and birthday present that I'd get from you and one of those horrible cheap cards.'

'I don't do cards.'

'Exactly!' Holly said, and then she sighed. 'I'm sorry I didn't stick to my end of the deal. I always knew I'd be lousy at one-night stands. I really need to loosen up.'

'Then do.'

'It's easier said than done.'

'It is easy, though,' Daniel told her. 'Just think of sex as fun.'

He'd used the F-word again but now it made her smile. 'How?'

'You just don't go looking for a deeper meaning in everything, just, as they say, enjoy the ride.'

'Ha-ha.'

'So what did you get me for Christmas?' Daniel asked, because he really was curious to know.

'Didn't you even open it?'

'Nope.'

'Then you can find out tomorrow. What did you get for Maddie?'

'The necklace you didn't like,' Daniel said.

'I didn't know then that she was five! She'll love it.'

'I hope so. And she'll find out tomorrow that she's adopted an elephant.'

'What did you get for your father?'

'A book.'

'Amelia?'

'A diary.'

Holly screwed up her nose.

'We don't get on.'

'Have you ever tried?'

'Once,' Daniel said. 'Not at first, though. My father and I fell out when he started dating Amelia. I didn't approve of the age difference. I found it embarrassing actually, and it was clear to me she was just there for the money. Still, once Maddie was born I decided to make more effort...'

'Because you realised they were in love?'

'No, Polly,' Daniel said, and turned and smiled. 'Because Amelia is as shallow as my father is distant and I wanted someone to actually be present for the child.'

The traffic was at a complete standstill. She could see the red brake lights snaking for miles into the distance and the car moved forward about a hand space every five minutes or so.

'I worry about Maddie,' he admitted. 'She's being raised by nannies and neither of them could be bothered to show up for her nativity play.' Daniel gripped the wheel. 'He just doesn't get it.'

'Have you spoken to him?'

Daniel said nothing.

Well, he had been about to give a derisive laugh and say something like 'As if that's going to change anything,' but instead he stayed silent as he thought some more about doing just that.

Again.

'I tried to when she was born,' Daniel admitted. 'It probably wasn't the best time. I had just turned down a surgical position in favour of Emergency. He told me that just as I clearly didn't want career advice from him, likewise he didn't need parenting advice.'

'It sounds like he does.'

The Christmas carols were still playing on the radio, all happy and jolly, and it was Holly who turned it off.

'Thanks.'

Daniel actually appreciated it.

'Why are you leaving?' Holly asked. 'It sounds like you want to be there for your sister.'

'I do,' he agreed. 'But I can't be.'

He knew she didn't understand so he decided to explain. After all, there was no chance of her ever meeting Amelia. 'I really tried to put aside my doubts about the marriage. Last year my father was working and I took Maddie and Amelia to a pantomime and I did all the big-brother stuff. Then Amelia said she wanted to decorate Maddie's room as a surprise and could I help pick out some paper...'

'What did you say?' Holly asked, and her antennae were up.

He could almost see them rising out of her fluffy dark hair and homing in, and, Daniel thought, for someone so sweet she was also rather shrewd.

'I said, no, that there were interior designers for all that and I chalked it up as odd but...' He held out his hand and made a wavy sign that said that the jury had remained out about the small incident but it had seemed odd at the time.

Holly nodded to show she agreed with his take on things.

'Then last Christmas I was invited over, as I have been for the past couple of years. I generally go for dinner, and for Maddie's birthdays and things. Her family were there and Amelia was a bit tense and hitting the mulled wine and then brandy, and then...'

'What happened?'

'I fell asleep on the sofa and while I was gone her family went home, Maddie went for a sleep and my father went to his club. I woke up and she was sitting beside where I lay and she said she was miserable and that though the money was lovely and everything he was old and she wanted young and, well, he'd never have to find out...'

Oh! She wanted to open the car door and get out onto the freezing motorway just to cool her cheeks.

'We didn't do anything.'

'I never asked.'

'Well, just so you know. Anyway, I don't really need you to believe me.' Actually, he did. 'Even if I'd wanted to, which I didn't, there would have been serious technical issues.'

'So, what did you say to her?'

'Not much.' Daniel sat silent for a moment as he recalled it. 'I told her it wouldn't be happening and got my jacket and went home. Since then I do my best to stay away.'

'I see.'

'Until September this year I worked at the same hospital as my father so it was pretty easy to find out what was going on and to only go over if Amelia was away. She goes on a lot of trips,' Daniel explained. 'I actually hadn't seen her since that day until the department store.'

'Okay, you're forgiven for not introducing me.'

He turned and she was wearing a smile, though not a nervous one.

'Embarrassing, isn't it?' he said.

'For her, I guess,' Holly said. 'Did you tell your father?'

'Good God, no!' Daniel sounded shocked at the very thought. 'I think I have to just accept that I'm not very good at family Christmases.'

'Oh, I don't know about that,' Holly said. 'You didn't do anything wrong, your father doesn't know and your little sister's none the wiser. I'd say you handled it all rather well.'

Daniel gave a small laugh.

No one knew, and certainly he hadn't envisaged telling anyone, but now that he had he felt lighter.

Holly, though, was grumbling as she again checked her phone for a traffic report.

'I'm starting to think I wasn't meant to get home for Christmas.'

'So is everyone else who is stuck in the jam,' Daniel said, and then he was practical, 'We can get off the motorway at the next available exit and try and find somewhere to stay the night or we can press on.'

It was long after ten p.m. A three-hour trip had already turned into six.

'I don't want to ruin your Christmas,' Holly started, and then thought about the long drive home he would have tomorrow. 'I've already ruined it.'

'Holly.' Daniel looked over and but Holly didn't look back, she was till reading the road report on her phone as if staring at it might make things change.

Her Christmas earrings had almost stopped flashing. Like the black box missing in a plane they still emitted the occasional hopeful bleep that Christmas cheer could still be found.

And they were right to hope, for Daniel found himself telling her something truly real...

'This is the nicest Christmas I've ever had.'

CHAPTER ELEVEN

'I NEED TO go to the loo.'

He had guessed she might because she'd kept crossing and uncrossing her legs.

'You went at the service station.'

'And then I drank both of the coffees.'

People were actually pulling over to sort out the essentials but there was no way Holly would be joining them.

Tonight, when she looked back on it, would be embarrassing enough as it was, without her pale moon rising.

'I think it's time we gave in,' Daniel conceded.

Another exit was coming up and it was now or never.

As they inched towards the exit Holly started ringing around local motels and bed and breakfasts from the list that came up on her phone.

'No room at the inn.' She sighed, because it would seem half of their fellow commuters had beaten them to it.

'No *rooms*,' Daniel pointed out, because Holly was trying to find two. 'The first one said that they had a double room.' He saw her jaw tense at the prospect of the two of them and one double bed. 'I've been driving for six hours, having worked all day,' Daniel said. 'I'm tired and I'm hungry. I can assure you that you could get up and pole dance and I wouldn't notice. Still, if you want, you can have the sofa.'

'What if there isn't one?'

'Then you can have the floor.'

'You're such a gentleman.'

'No, Holly, I'm not.'

With little choice Holly rang back and secured the room and a short while later the car pulled into a bed and breakfast. By now she was past caring if the presents got pinched and so thankfully didn't suggest they haul everything inside.

And he was very pleased that the snowman bag remained safely locked in the car.

Daniel did the checking in and Holly dashed to the loo and then returned to his side, pleased to find that the formalities were over. Daniel was talking to a woman whom he introduced as Mrs Barrett.

No, the formalities were not over!

She proceeded to repeat to Holly all the rules she had just told Daniel.

'No noise after midnight.'

'We really just want to crash…' Holly agreed.

'No parties in the room.'

'Honestly,' Holly said.

'Just let her finish,' Daniel broke in, and it became clear he had tried to hurry Mrs Barrett along a few moments before but to no avail.

There were to be no showers after midnight, clothes were to be worn between the bathroom and bedroom, and shoes were to be taken off and carried up the stairs and not left in the hall and…

'You need to sign the register every time you enter and leave,' Mrs Barrett informed Holly as she handed her a pen.

They took off their shoes and were led up some very creaky stairs.

'Breakfast is between seven and nine, no latecomers.'

'We'll be gone by seven,' Daniel said. 'Is there anywhere we can call to get pizza or...?'

'No.' Mrs Barrett shook her head and no helpful suggestions ensued.

'I'm starving,' Daniel mouthed to Holly, and she laughed.

'Here...' Mrs Barrett inserted a key and pushed open a door, and it was like entering a time slip because nothing in this room could have changed in thirty or so years. It was all crinoline and purple and there were little doilies on every available surface.

And there was no sofa!

'How much do I owe you?' Holly asked once they were alone.

'It's my treat,' Daniel said, and smiled a black smile because, really, this was far from the Ritz. 'Holly, I *have* to eat something.'

'I've got some cheeses in the car in a cool bag,' Holly said. 'And some chocolate...'

'We can have a picnic.'

'Oh, and I got my father some Scotch for Christmas, I'm sure he won't mind. I'll go,' Holly said, 'I know where everything is.'

'No, I'll go,' Daniel said, and picked up his keys. There was no way he wanted her going through the bags.

Daniel went back down and spoke with Mrs Barrett and he even managed a wry smile as she asked him to sign out.

He went to the car and found the cool bag and a present that was clearly a bottle of Scotch and then went back up to the room, threw himself on the bed and stretched out.

'Finally.'

Clearly he would not be giving up the bed!

'I had to sign in and out just to go to the car.'

There were two glasses on a little table with a jug of water and Holly poured them both a measure of Scotch and started to plate up the cheese.

Daniel headed off and had a shower and came back wearing only his underwear.

'You're supposed to be dressed when you come out of the bathroom,' Holly reminded him.

'Well, I would have had I had a change of clothes.'

Soon she was sitting on the floor as Daniel hung off the bed and they ate and drank and chatted and laughed.

It was nice.

More than that, it was the nicest Christmas Eve she had ever spent because, cheese and Scotch aside, Daniel was one of her favourite things, especially when he was half-naked.

He asked a bit about her family.

'Do you get on with your brother?' Daniel asked, and Holly nodded. 'Stupid question—you get on with everyone.'

'Not everyone.' And because he'd asked about her family, now she asked about his. 'Do you remember your mum?'

'A bit.' He nodded. 'She was the one who always made the effort at Christmas and things...'

'What was it like after she died?'

'I went to boarding school,' Daniel said. 'And, to be honest, I preferred being there than at home. It was miserable.'

'Maybe he was grieving?'

'Maybe,' Daniel said. He'd never really thought of it like that. 'I went to Rupert's one Christmas.'

'The one you were best man for?' Holly asked, and Daniel nodded.

'He's a good friend. When I was all set to boycott my father's wedding he talked me round. I guess that I went helps keep things, at least outwardly, civilised.'

'What was Christmas like at Rupert's?'

He shrugged. 'They were all really into Christmas, a bit like your family, I guess.'

'Did you enjoy it?'

'Not really,' Daniel admitted. 'I guess it just showed more clearly all that was missing in mine. I think things are very different for Maddie, though. Not perfect, of course, but a lot better.'

And he knew too that things were better still for Maddie when he was around.

'If you want a shower then you'd better go now,' Daniel glanced at the time. 'It's close to midnight.'

Holly headed out to the shower and had a very quick one and then realised she'd forgotten her pyjamas. She got exactly what Daniel meant about putting on old clothes so she wrapped herself in a towel and legged it back to the bedroom, but as she stepped in she saw that it was in darkness except for a candle.

'Happy birthday, Holly.'

'You remembered!'

'I did.'

'I'd actually forgotten that it was my birthday.'

'No, you hadn't.'

'I honestly had,' Holly said. 'Aren't you going to sing?'

'Nope.'

She knelt down and blew out her candle and found out that it was held in a little piece of carrot cake with orange and cream cheese frosting.

'I got it from Mrs Barrett when I went down for the

cheese,' Daniel explained. 'She warned me again that there were to be no parties after midnight.'

'We'll be quiet, then.'

'You can eat the frosting.'

Holly did and Daniel knelt down too and he had the cake, but one wasn't the same without the other and for that reason *only* they shared a little kiss.

They both tasted perfect.

It was just a simple kiss but both fought the urge to rip off each other's towel.

'Thank you,' Holly said, trying to pretend she wasn't turned on, 'for making it such a lovely birthday.'

'I haven't finished yet.' He got up and turned on the bedside light. 'You've got to open your present.'

'Present?'

'Yes.'

Her present was on the bed and wrapped in lilac tissues from a box that, incidentally, had a purple knitted cover over it.

The bedroom really was a treasure trove of nylon and knits.

'Oh, my!' Holly said when she opened it. Her present was a lovely leather wallet. A little used perhaps, but, actually, it was something of his, and while Holly was a little confused, she still said the right thing for appearances' sake.

'I can't take your wallet.'

'It's more what's inside that is yours,' he told her. 'Open it up.'

There was some cash.

'Count it.'

There wasn't very much, a couple of notes and some coins, and he made a little pile on the bedside table.

'Can you get your hair done for that?' Daniel asked.

'Er, no.'

'Your nails?'

'No.' Holly laughed at the very notion. He really didn't have a clue.

'I'm trying to be thoughtful,' Daniel chided her mirth. 'Could you maybe get a nail polish?'

'Indeed I could.' Holly beamed. 'I could get two, in fact.'

'Well, then, you can do your nails on me.'

'Thank you.'

'Keep looking.'

'There's nothing else...' Holly said, and then her voice trailed off when her fingers found something shiny and silver and she went to hand his wallet back to him. 'You didn't empty it out properly.'

'I did.'

'No.' Holly shook her head. 'You didn't.' She took out a condom. 'You're such a slut, Daniel. You forgot to take this out.'

'No, Holly, I didn't.'

Her cheeks were on fire as he continued to speak.

'One night, just for you...'

'That's such a generous present,' Holly said. 'So self-less.'

'I know. I can be nice like that at times.'

'I mean, you'd have sex with me just because it's my birthday...'

'Not just sex,' Daniel said. 'This would be just-for-Holly sex.'

'So you won't enjoy it?'

'That's not you for you to concern yourself with. Your wish, or rather your birthday wish, would be my command.'

'Just some fun?' Holly checked.

'Exactly!'

'I don't think so.' She shook her head. 'I thought you said that even if I was naked and dancing…'

'I meant it when I said it.' Daniel broke in. 'But that got me thinking about just that…'

'No.'

'Well, the offer is there, just tear the edge off that little wrapper and I'll appear!'

He got into bed.

And she put on tartan pyjama bottoms and a little top that were fine for home but not exactly Daniel Chandler worthy and climbed into bed beside him.

She lay on her back more than a little miffed by his gift offer but also intrigued at the concept of her wish being his command. 'You could be skiing down a mountain one minute and then diving head-first between my legs the next…'

'I'm not a genie, Holly.' He pulled her into his lovely, warm body. 'The gift offer expires at seven a.m. *Then* it's Christmas.'

'Why would you rot things up now?' she asked. 'It's taken three weeks to be talking and it would take us straight back to awkward again.'

'But it wouldn't,' Daniel said. 'I'd just be showing you how to loosen up. You say tomato…'

Holly frowned. 'I don't get it.'

'You call it making love, whereas I…'

'I don't call it making love.'

'You think of it as such.'

'Not really,' Holly said. 'Maybe a bit.'

He was right.

Oh, she wished Daniel wasn't. That she could just take out her heart and leave it on charge overnight, just as she had done with her phone. Yes, she wished she could say,

Go for it Daniel, have wicked sex with me all night and I shan't hurt when you leave me in the morning.

But she didn't work like that.

'The offer's there.'

'Noted.'

Because he clearly had no conscience, Daniel was soon asleep, whereas Holly lay there, listening to the sound of rain against the window and his heavy breathing.

His leg came over hers, but he wasn't making a move, it was just that he was tall and the bed was small.

And once she felt him harden and Holly lay there all nervous and tense and awaiting his pounce.

He didn't.

It was already the best birthday she had ever had!

CHAPTER TWELVE

Christmas morning

IT WAS COLD.

Not just cold, it was freezing.

So freezing that in sleep in they had rolled into the dint in the bed and wrapped themselves around each other, and for Daniel, who didn't really do the wrapped around you type of thing, or rather didn't usually, he woke for the second time with her in his arms and facing away from him.

She had on a little strappy top and pyjama bottoms yet his hand had found its way to her stomach and he went to remove it. His intent was to roll on his back so she didn't feel him hard against her, but then his hand chose to linger and then she stirred and it was a little too late for that.

Actually, it wasn't.

He could still roll onto his back now and then roll out of bed.

They could be up and packed and out of here and heading for her home.

Or he could kiss her shoulder as he had wanted to that morning all those weeks ago.

His hand was lightly stroking her stomach and he could feel that she was trying to keep her breathing even.

So too was he.

'Happy birthday, Holly.'

'Thank you.'

He was breathing through his nostrils in that delicious turned-on, decision-making way. Resisting and yet wanting.

She looked at the clock and saw it was just before seven.

And then everything went black because she closed her eyes to the feel of his mouth and the deep kiss that met her shoulder.

It was a slow, sensual kiss and his tongue was warm on her cold, bare skin and his hand slipped up her top and found her breast.

He toyed with her nipple and then rubbed her breast with his palm and his mouth moved up her neck to her ear so she could both hear and feel his ragged breathing.

Holly pressed her bottom back into him, just because she wanted more of the feel of him hard and turned on.

And Daniel too needed more because he slid the top up over her head, discarded it and then went back to her neck. He loved the feel of her now naked back against his chest.

Now his hand slid down further down and he listened to the throaty moans she made as he stroked her clitoris and delivered little volts of pleasure that had her thighs grip his hand.

And it was all about her yet he stopped just long enough that they both kicked off their bottoms halves. His free hand moved under her torso so he could play with her other breast.

He moved his hand down, sliding his fingers inside her. She could feel him nudging between her thighs, wet, warm and hard.

'Oh, God,' he said, but just quietly and not to her, and for a moment she wondered why. Then she understood, for he knew, even before Holly did, that she was about to come.

It was so intense that she brought her knees up.

There, the sensible part of him warned as she came to his hand. *Leave it there. Feel that bliss on your fingers and then smile and say Happy Birthday.*

It wasn't enough, though.

For either of them.

Her lovely birthday 'gift' hadn't left her sated, it had just made her hungry for more. She turned in his arms and they found each other's mouths briefly before he moved down to kiss her breasts, one by delicious one, tasting them for the first time.

Oh, that mouth, Holly thought as her fingers tangled in his hair. She wished he had two of them so he could keep kissing her breasts while also taking her mouth. His head followed the upward guide of her hand and their mouths met again in a kiss unplanned. Deep, slow and sensual, their tongues mingled and then their mouths parted in private focus as he entered her.

She moaned at the bliss of the slow long strokes that had her wrap one leg around him as they moved together.

They were kissing intensely, stopping only to stare into each other's eyes before kissing again. It was so real, so raw.

Daniel got up on his forearms just to watch her and she pressed her palms into his chest.

The tight, slick grip of her had Daniel revelling in the sensations and then the demand of his pace increased.

The shift in him started to tip her. Even when he had

taken her standing, fast and rough, he had been in measured control.

But now neither had hold of themselves, they were lost in each other. His hand came over her mouth and the sound of her affirmations were silenced. He felt the stretch of her smile on his palm as she realised the noises she'd been making. Daniel would usually have revelled in that but there was something about the simple sound of them, slick and in tune, intensely moving together that enraptured him. He forgot to smile, or to do anything other than focus hard…on her.

His breathing was ragged and hard in her ear as he pulled her deeper into oblivion.

Holly dug her fingers into taut buttocks and the fire low in his spine shot forward.

Her reward for silence? The deep moan of his release.

Heat met perfect heat and though she gripped and tightened and drew him in, as he shot into her, she also unfurled, for she opened herself up to him.

Those last thrusts were exquisite, those deep kisses, while still dizzy, were the most intense expression she had ever known. They coiled with each other, caressed each other, and their lips did not know how to part.

Until they did…

CHAPTER THIRTEEN

THEY LAY AFTERWARDS, both a little stunned by what had taken place.

She had never known just how beautiful sex could be and Daniel had done all he could not to find out.

The only sound now was the rain and they lay on their backs, idly holding hands as their breathing slowed down, and Holly knew, with absolute clarity, the moment he regretted it.

His hand let go of hers and raked through his hair. The sound then was one of tense silence.

'We didn't—' he started.

'I *was* there, Daniel,' Holly interrupted. She didn't need to be told that they hadn't used a condom.

He nodded, only it wasn't contraception that was troubling him, it was the closeness, the absolute abandon that he had never felt with another.

He couldn't pretend that they hadn't just crossed the line.

And neither could Holly.

Had he tied a red ribbon around it last night and shouted *Surprise!* well, maybe she could have chalked it down to experience, albeit a new one.

This, though, felt like she had just handed over her soul, only for it to be promptly handed back.

'Are you on the Pill?'

There were many ways this question could be asked, Holly thought. A necessary way, like a doctor. The hopeful way of a lover wanting to pounce.

Or the Daniel way—please, God, tell me you are.

She didn't answer and he got up and sat on the edge of the bed, reaching for his jeans.

'Yes, I'm on the Pill,' she finally said, just to put him out of his obvious misery.

Daniel nodded but said nothing.

And she stopped trying.

It was quite a feat for Holly, but she just stopped trying to pretend that this was okay and didn't even bother to wish him a happy Christmas, she just pulled on her pyjamas and headed out to get ready.

Daniel pulled on his jeans, loathing his own silence.

And just like the last time there were repercussions.

Big ones.

He was staring down the barrel of a future but he couldn't get a clear shot for all the obstacles that were in the way.

Hell, he couldn't even promise to be there for his sister when she needed him to stay.

'I'm ready.'

Holly stood at the door, but of course it wasn't that easy. They'd made quite a mess last night. He threw the remnants of their picnic in the bin and she packed up a few things.

And they were done.

'Do you want this?' He held up the bottle of Scotch and she took it in almost a snatch.

And whereas they should have been lingering in bed and then heading down for breakfast, instead they were signing the guest register to Mrs Barrett's disapproving eyes when Holly had to put down the bottle to pick up the pen!

They drove in strained silence on a now clear motorway.

Holly's earrings had stopped flashing and, from his reaction to the morning's events, all hope for them was gone.

'It's left here,' Holly said, even though his phone told them to take a right. 'It's just a bit quicker.'

The village looked gorgeous and they passed a pretty old pub and she already missed the lazy weekend afternoons the mythical 'us' could have spent there.

Had the closeness between them not completely gone.

Had he had the guts to follow his heart.

'Do you want to come in for breakfast?' Holly offered, even though she knew the answer.

'No.'

'Why?' Holly asked, because she needed to hear it.

Daniel stared out at the sleety street and there were times when you really did have to be cruel to be kind and so he gave Holly her answer. 'Because it would mean something to you. Because in Holly's world when the guy she's just slept with comes to her parents' it means something more.'

And she could say, no, it's just breakfast and my mother would never expect me to let you drop me off and not invite you to come in.

But that would be a lie.

If Daniel came in then so too would hope.

'You're right.'

'I can't play happy families, Holly.'

'You don't even want to try.'

'No.' Because over and over it had failed to work out.

'I'm going to go,' Daniel said, 'and you're going to go in and have a wonderful Christmas with your family.'

He got out of the car and started to unload her bags.

'You're not going to change your mind, are you?'

'No.'

'Are you going to go to your father's?'

'I'll drop off the presents and then I'm going to go home and catch up on some sleep.'

And it hurt that he'd rather get back on the motorway and spend Christmas alone than come in and spend Christmas with her.

'I don't know what to say,' Holly admitted.

She should leave it there really, given him a wave and show what a good detached lover she could be.

That wasn't her, though, and so, just as he climbed back into his car to leave, Holly spoke.

'I don't get you.'

'Holly, let's not do this.'

'No, let's.' Holly's smile was black. 'You see, Daniel, I don't think you're an utter bastard. A bit of one perhaps but if you really thought I was going to go and get stupid ideas about us from sex, you'd never have got into that crinoline bed last night. I think you'd have slept on the floor, or even in the car, rather than hurt me. And I also believe if a quick shag was what you'd wanted this morning, then for my sake you'd have managed to resist.' And then she said it. 'But it wasn't a quick shag.'

'Oh, that's right, we made love.'

He could be as sarcastic and derisive as he chose to be, but, as she'd said this morning, Holly had been there too.

And she could point that out to him, but the war was won and Daniel was the victor.

'I'm done,' Holly said. 'I really am. I've made enough of a fool of myself over you. And I'm not going to say thank you for the lift because the truth is I wish you'd never come out to the car park yesterday.'

'I came out because I didn't want us to end on a row.'

'Do you know what?' Holly retorted. 'It would have been far easier on me if it had.'

She staggered off under the weight of presents and this time she didn't turn around.

Her mother must have been peeking out of the window though because the door opened before she had to work out how to knock.

'Hi, darling, where's your friend?'

'He's not coming in.'

'Oh! But surely—'

'Mum!' Holly said. 'Please.'

If it wasn't Christmas Day she would love to run to her old room fling herself on her bed and cry but, of course, she couldn't.

Instead, she took her bags into the lounge and placed them beside the tree.

And she kept on hoping, so much so that she half expected a knock on the door and for Daniel to say he'd changed his mind, and maybe he'd stay for breakfast.

Instead, with all the bags by the tree, she stood and walked to the window, just in time to see him drive off.

And that was it, Holly knew.

She was never going to see him again.

They were done.

There was no time to process it, though.

Breakfast, as was traditional in the Jacobs family, was birthday cake. Holly blew out her candles and opened her birthday present from her parents and it was a gorgeous pair of earrings.

She took out her cheap Christmas ones that had now

completely stopped flashing and replaced them with her lovely new silver ones.

Then it was champagne with orange juice, though Holly just had orange juice because she was working tonight.

It was smiles and happy all round and Holly joined in, even if she felt as if a part of her had died.

Adam loved his necklace and in turn she loved the travel wallet he had bought, and they traded their gifts with a smile.

Then relatives started to descend and there were parsnips to peel and stuffing to make and then Drunkle Harry and co. arrived.

'I'll take up your coats,' Holly said.

She went up to her old bedroom and took a breath.

'Holly?'

She turned around as her mother came in and saw that she was holding a snowman bag.

'Is everything okay?'

'Of course it is.' Holly smiled her brightest smile but at the last moment it wavered and Holly was appalled with herself when a tear slipped out and she quickly wiped it away.

'Holly?'

She shook her head, because she was simply not able to talk about Daniel without breaking down.

'Is it your friend that wouldn't come in?' Esther checked, and Holly nodded.

'I don't want to talk about it now,' Holly said, and her voice was all shaky. 'I don't want to start crying and ruin Christmas.'

'I seem to remember saying that just over a year ago,' Esther said. 'I sat in the doctor's and I wanted one more perfect Christmas…'

'And we did.'

'Holly, it was awful. Your dad kept slipping out to cry, I burnt the turkey. Harry got so drunk...'

Holly started to laugh. 'It was still a good Christmas.'

'It turned out to be,' Esther agreed.

In the end they'd all had loads to drink and watched a sad film, which had been a good excuse to cry and just relax and stop pretending they were brave.

'You know, I remember when I forgot your birthday...' They just sat there on Holly's old bed and chalked up all the Christmas fails.

'You remembered it that evening,' Holly said. 'And I got a puppy out of it.'

'You did,' Esther sighed. 'Please tell me what's going on, Holly'

And Holly was about to point out that they could do this another time, but then her mum's hand came over hers.

'I know I've been difficult lately,' Esther said. 'But I can still be here for you.'

It had indeed been a long year, one where at times Holly had felt like she'd lost her mum, but it would seem that she was back now.

It was the best gift to have a cuddle from her mum instead of the other way around.

'The guy who gave me the lift home,' Holly said. 'Daniel. I like him a lot, well, I more than like him. I think he feels a bit the same yet he says we're going nowhere. In fact, he's heading overseas...' She gave a pale smile. 'He couldn't make it any clearer that's he's not interested in anything long term but...'

'You still want more.'

'Yes,' Holly said. 'I've never really felt this way before about anyone, not even close.' The one time she had, it hadn't been reciprocated. 'It's probably for the best, we'd never have worked out. I don't think he has a romantic bone in his body and he's not into Christmas. He's hardly even seeing his family, he just wants to go home to bed…' She shook her head as if to clear it. 'I can't believe I've fallen for someone who'd rather sleep his way through Christmas Day than be with his family.' Holly stood, even though her mum still sat there. 'Come on, we'd better go down.'

'You missed a present,' Esther said, and took a box out of the snowman bag.

'From who?' Holly frowned.

'I don't know,' Esther said. 'I was clearing the paper away when I found it. You brought it with you.'

'No.'

It was a silver box covered in fake snow with a silver bow, and it looked terribly like the ones she had seen in the department store. In fact, it looked a lot like the gift she had been considering getting Daniel.

It couldn't be.

Surely?

She looked at the name on the card.

To Holly
   I hope you have the wonderful Christmas that
you deserve.
   Secret Santa

Holly tried not to get her hopes up but her hands were shaking as she undid the bow.

It *had* to be from him.

She gasped as she saw a glass ball decorated with her name in silver, and delicate outlines of holly in jewelled green.

What captivated her, though, was the tiny silver envelope inside the glass that had her name on.

'Who's it from?' Esther asked.

'Him.'

'I thought you said he wasn't romantic.'

'He's not.'

'And that he wasn't into Christmas.'

'He isn't.'

Except Daniel had given her the most beautiful, romantic, Christmassy gift in the world.

It was actually the perfect gift, Holly thought as she held it up and the ball spun round, catching the light, but right now it was the letter inside that entranced her.

When would he have put it in her bag? Holly wondered. While they were at the bed and breakfast? But, no, he must have had it before that and then she realised it must have been when they had dragged her parcels in from the car.

When he'd thought she would never see him again.

Oh, it was so much better than a chocolate stocking!

And *so-o-o* much more frustrating!

'I don't see the point,' her father said as Holly hung it on the tree. 'Why would you go to the bother of writing a note that the other person isn't going to read?'

'I'm not sure,' Holly admitted.

'It's like those fire alarms,' mused Drunkle Harry. 'In case of emergency, break the glass.'

'There won't be any emergencies, Uncle Harry.' Holly smiled. 'He probably regrets buying it now. He told me he doesn't want me. I shan't be seeing him again.'

CHAPTER FOURTEEN

HE WAS THE FOOL. Daniel knew it.

As he watched Holly walk to her house in his rear-view mirror, that was exactly how he felt. She was buckling under the weight of presents, and then the door opened and her mother dashed out to help.

He could see her mother's bright silk scarf tied around her head and her slender body and guessed, rightly, it would have been one hell of a year for the family.

And he wanted to go in, to the warmth, to the laughter and fun.

He just didn't know how.

Christmas had always been a let-down.

A huge one.

The build-up would start and it had taken years for him to work out that the promise never came true.

And he was right not to go in, he knew, because it wouldn't be a friend dropping in for Christmas.

Holly was the big one.

The one to whom you promised things like for ever. And those were promises he felt in no position to give, so he started the engine and drove away.

The roads felt empty. Probably because most people were already where they wanted to be.

He pulled into the service station, the one opposite

but identical to the one where they had stopped last night and bought cinnamon and nutmeg coffee and went back to the car and drank it.

Really, Holly had ruined coffee for ever because, though it tasted as bad as it had last night, there was a certain warmth to it, this pleasantness.

He opened the glove box and looked at his gift from Holly, and the ridiculous thing was that he half hoped for a Daniel & Holly snowglobe and some crazy declaration of her love.

He read the card.

To Daniel
From Secret Santa

There wasn't even a kiss!

Well, he guessed there would be something more meaningful inside the wrapping. He opened it slowly and then frowned as a tube of lip balm fell into his palm.

A lip balm?

An expensive lip balm perhaps, but even so…

And then he realised it was Holly's attempt at being bland. Holly doing what he had told her to do and not be so serious about things.

Yet suddenly he was.

He watched as an elderly woman got out of a car and walked towards another. And some children got out and ran to her.

It must be their turn to have granny for Christmas.

Perhaps the families weren't speaking, Daniel pondered, because no one in either car waved to the other.

Yet the kids and the granny were all smiling.

They were somehow making it work.

He thought of Holly, sitting crying, contemplating a

taxi, simply desperate to get home. And he thought of his mother and all the Christmases she'd missed out on.

There were families fighting to be together, longing to be with each other, and there he was, running from his.

He was tired of running.

His phone started to ring; it was Maddie, of course, wanting to know how long it would be till he got there.

'About an hour, I think.'

'Have you got me a present?'

'Maybe.' Daniel smiled.

And then it was a case of please, please, please, could he stay for Christmas dinner.

He was about to say no but then he thought of what Holly had said—that it was embarrassing for Amelia, rather than him.

He could do dinner surely?

'Yes,' he said, and was almost deafened by her squeal. 'I'll see you soon, Maddie. Happy Christmas.'

He loathed that he hadn't been able to make it a happy Christmas for the woman who mattered to him the most.

And so, what was the second-best thing he could do?

He pinched one of Holly's cards from the door pocket and wrote one out for Maddie. Then he drove to his rather odd family and took out the bag that held presents and knocked at the door.

'Daniel!' His father greeted him with a handshake.

Despite the hurts of the past and the hurts of this morning, this Christmas *was* still somehow special. Something had changed in Daniel.

'I love it!' Maddie opened the tiny package and took out a silver neck chain with a little elephant charm with crystal eyes and then she read a certificate that said she'd adopted an elephant. 'Look, Daddy!'

Professor Chandler frowned and put on his glasses

to read the certificate. 'She's adopted an elephant?' He frowned. 'For Christmas?'

He had no idea, Daniel thought.

None.

Yet at least he was trying harder than he had when Daniel had been small because when Maddie whispered in her father's ear, he actually listened and then stood. 'We'll be back in a moment.'

That left Daniel and Amelia and she flushed an unflattering shade of puce and attempted to voice what was on her mind. 'About what happened last year...'

'Nothing happened,' Daniel said. 'And nothing ever shall. Let's just leave it there and focus on Maddie.'

Done.

And he turned as the reason he was here walked into the lounge carrying a very large box that was terribly, and therefore beautifully, wrapped by her.

'I chose this,' Maddie said. 'Jessica said you might not want it as you're travelling but we can keep it here for you when you've gone! You're going to love it.'

Intrigued, Daniel peeled back the wrapper on a very large box and then he gave a very delighted smile, especially at the thought of Jessica trying to dissuade Maddie from her purchase. It was a pink plastic popcorn-maker, with a happy picture of mother and daughter and mountains of popcorn on the box.

'I do love it,' Daniel said, and saw that it even came with a little bag of popping corn.

'You really like it?' Maddie checked, and when Daniel nodded she turned to her father. 'See! I told you.'

'You did indeed,' Professor Chandler agreed. 'Maddie, why don't you get Daniel his other present from under the tree?'

It was a wallet.

A very nice leather one and far from bland it made him smile, given where his had disappeared to last night!

'Thank you.'

And so to dinner.

Amelia declined wine, Daniel noted, and so did he, which he was very glad about given that as Christmas pudding was served his phone rang.

'They'll be wanting me to do a shift,' Daniel said when he saw who it was.

'Tell them fat chance,' his father suggested.

Except he said yes, but only because it was a night shift at The Primary and it was where Holly would be.

Perhaps he could make this a happier Christmas after all.

Or completely spoil it for her?

'I'll need to take food in,' Daniel said, because knowing that lot they would turn it into a party.

'You can take the popcorn machine in.' Maddie smiled.

'I'll see if there's anything nice you can take in,' their father said, and stood.

'Popcorn *is* nice!' Maddie insisted.

'Of course it is,' Marcus said, and he smiled at Daniel over her head. 'So nice that there might not be enough to go around.'

He had mellowed, Daniel realised as he followed his father into a very spacious kitchen, lined with all the mod-cons, all sparkling from lack of use.

Maybe he could, as Holly had suggested, try talking to him.

'There's some pâté and potted…' Marcus said, as he rummaged through the large basket of goodies.

'Dad,' Daniel interrupted. 'I went and saw Maddie perform in her nativity play.'

'I heard that you did. There's probably a ham in the fridge…'

'Dad!' Daniel couldn't give a damn about the ham. 'You should have been there.'

'Oh, come on, Daniel, do you really expect me to cancel surgery because—?'

'Yes,' Daniel said, and then he said it again. 'Yes!' he urged. 'When Maddie's a teenager she might want nothing to do with you but right now she does. You need to be there for the things that matter to her.'

Daniel watched as his father stood there, not cross at the discussion, more confused. 'You've got a secretary.' Daniel thought of Iris. 'I actually looked after one of your old ones the other day. Iris Morrison.'

'She was very efficient.'

'And very under-utilised. She would have loved to factor in your home life. Why don't you go through the calendar and mark out some days for the coming year, like Maddie's birthday and things, and have your secretary organise your schedule around that?'

'I could do that.' Marcus nodded.

He simply accepted the advice and it was then that Daniel realised that sometimes people simply needed to be told. Sometimes the cleverest of people needed help with what others considered the simplest of things.

And so, while they were on the subject, Daniel pushed on. 'And instead of three hours at the club this afternoon, why not take her for ten minutes to the park?'

'She likes the club, there's a playroom there.'

'No, Dad.' Daniel shook his head. 'She hates it.'

'Did you?'

And he could score some points here, Daniel knew,

he could stick the boot in and bring up, oh, so many, many things.

But it was Christmas.

And, more than that, this discussion wasn't about him. It was about a wary-looking little girl who now stood at the kitchen door. 'What are you two talking about?'

Daniel looked at his father, who stared back at his son for a moment and then turned to his daughter. 'I was just saying to your brother that we might go for a walk to the park after dinner if he wanted to come.'

'The park?' Maddie checked. 'The one with swings?'

'Yes.'

'And are you coming?' Maddie asked her brother as Amelia came in.

'I can't,' Daniel said. 'I need to go home and get some sleep and Holly will be back from her family soon...' He shamelessly borrowed Holly, but even if not physically present, by God, it had helped to have her sort of by his side today.

'Holly?' Amelia frowned.

'You met her in the department store the other week.'

'Sounds serious,' his father said, because if it was running into weeks for his son, then it must be.

They had worked at the same hospital after all and word got around!

'It's starting to look that way,' Daniel agreed.

It had actually been starting to look that way for quite some time now but he'd been doing his best not to see what had been right there under his nose.

Yes, try as he might not to be, he was still his father's son.

Though that might not be such a bad thing, Daniel realised, because even a rather old leopard could change its spots.

With a hefty nudge, of course.

As he was about to leave he gave Maddie the card he had written for her in the car.

'What does "ten school pick-ups" mean?' she asked.

'That you've got ten treats next year, though not all in a row.'

'But you're going away.'

'No,' Daniel said. 'I'm not. I might go on holiday, of course, but I'm not leaving you for a whole year…'

And maybe it made no sense to some, she was his half-sister after all, but as her little arms wrapped around his neck, staying close made perfect sense to Daniel.

Maddie was his sister and for her he would be here.

It was a good Christmas.

A great one even, for, as he climbed into the car with his pink plastic popcorn-maker, he watched as his father stood outside, with his daughter hanging off his hand, ready to go to the park.

It was the first time that his father had waved him goodbye.

Ever.

And, because it was Christmas, Daniel tooted and waved back as he drove off.

They looked almost like a normal family!

CHAPTER FIFTEEN

THE MOTORWAY BEHAVED and the drive was made so much easier in her mother's car. Holly had said that she would return it in a couple of days but was seeing in the New Year in London.

With friends and bubbles. She was going to keep all her resolutions this year—one being to be more sophisticated in her love life, and so never make such a fool of herself again with men.

Hell, and if she was ever to have a one-night stand again, she would call the shots—she would climb out of bed, get dressed and walk off without a word. The thought made Holy smirk.

Next year, though.

Right now she knew she had to feel this pain. She had Daniel's present swathed in bubble wrap on the passenger seat and she knew that this year Boxing Day would more like Box of Tissues Day!

Holly got to the hospital and parked, then unloaded all the food her mother had prepared for the night staff. There was rather a lot! She staggered again through the car park and was under the bright lights of the ambulance bay when she heard her name being called.

'Holly!'

A gruff voice had her turn around and she saw a little group standing around a wheelchair.

Holly made her way over, and as she did so a delighted smile split her face. There was Albert, sitting in the wheelchair with a drip attached to a pole and wearing a heavy Christmas jumper and a woolly hat.

She hardly recognised him.

'What are you doing, sitting out here with pneumonia?' Holly both scolded and smiled as she spoke.

'The nurses on the ward said the same,' Albert admitted, 'but it's too stuffy up there.'

'He wanted to come out for some air,' the elder woman explained. 'I'm Dianne, his niece.'

'It's lovely to meet you.'

'This is Emily,' Albert proudly introduced his family. 'She's both my great-niece and god-daughter. They brought me in some Christmas dinner and Emily has made me these.' He opened a tin and showed some beautifully decorated mince pies. 'Take one for your break,' Albert offered.

'I think Holly's got enough food to be going on with,' Dianne said when she saw Holly hesitate.

Usually she didn't accept food from patients and Dianne was right, more mince pies were the very last thing she needed. But, Holly guessed, it must be rather nice for Albert who had spent the last years begging to have food to give some.

'I'll have it on my break,' Holly said. 'If you could just…'

Dianne laughed and selected a pie and added it to the mountain of food that Holly carried.

'I'd better get inside,' she said to the little family. 'Happy Christmas!'

'And to you, Holly.'

'You made it.' Kay beamed as Holly came in. 'And you're early!'

'Someone can go home,' Holly offered, because the staff had done the same for her on the Christmas party night.

'Well, I'll send Anna home. Laura isn't getting here till later so I'm hanging around till then. I have to say, though, for Christmas night it's pretty quiet. Maybe, for once, everyone's behaving.'

Holly had worked a couple and maybe there were jinxing themselves by admitting it, but it actually was quiet. Christmas night was often the busiest with feuding families as well as too much food and alcohol combined. Also there was sometimes the very sick who had held on for that special day.

But, yes, tonight was quiet—at least it was in Emergency, though Kay soon told her that it was otherwise elsewhere.

'Theatre is busy and Maternity is steaming.'

'Who's on tonight?' Holly asked, and they glanced up at the doctors' board and saw that Daniel Chandler was down to work in Emergency tonight.

'We've got...' Kay frowned. 'That can't be right, he's left.'

'No,' Anna called out. 'We had to ring everyone but Daniel agreed to work it.'

And Holly blinked.

She couldn't do this.

She could not keep saying goodbye.

Or, worse than that, she could not keep getting her hopes up because that was what she repeatedly did.

Well, not any more, they were done.

No way would Boxing Day be spent in his bed.

Two-Strikes-and-You're-Out Dr Chandler.

He came in then, carrying boxes and food and with a mince pie on top of it all. Unshaven and gorgeous, he gave her a smile.

'Take your stuff around to the staffroom,' Kay told them, though for Holly it was a rather awkward walk.

'I see you have a mince pie.' Holly said, determined to keep this about the patients rather than them. 'Is that one of Albert's?'

'It is,' Daniel said, and told her he'd been outside chatting with them too. 'The family's moving to the country and apparently there's a little cottage on the grounds. Albert and Dianne both happily admit they'd kill each other under the same roof, but if he has the cottage he can have his privacy and they can keep an eye—'

'He's going to live there?'

'Yep,' Daniel said as they arrived at the staffroom and started to unload all the food. 'Great, isn't it?'

It truly was.

'Why have you brought in a popcorn-maker?' Holly asked.

'Don't you like popcorn?'

'I love popcorn.'

'Then I shall make you some later.'

Holly said nothing, she just headed to the changing room and arrived at the nurses' station a few minutes later in her scrubs and wearng her Christmas earrings.

Everyone was gathered, even Daniel.

'Happy birthday, Holly...' the call went up!

Kay went into her bottomless bag and pulled out a parcel. 'That's from all of us. We were going to do you a cake but...'

'I've had a lot of cake today!'

'We'll do cake next year,' Kay said. 'For your thirtieth.'

Holly groaned. 'Please, don't remind me! Anyway, I'm not working next year, I'm putting in my request now.'

'Did your mother tell you to do that?' Kay asked.

'I shan't be at my mother's on my thirtieth.' Holly smiled sweetly. 'I'll be getting drunk and having anonymous sex with a stranger.'

Kay puffed out her cheeks and tutted but everyone else laughed, even Daniel, and she was proud of herself indeed.

She would get over him.

Holly just had to get through tonight.

She opened her present and found it was a gorgeous jumper that she'd seen online a while ago. She had shown it to Anna, but it hadn't been available in her size.

Yes, she had very good friends.

She read her card and even Nora had taken the time to sign it.

'How's Paul?' Holly asked.

'He's fantastic. He even remembered where he'd hidden Nora's present.' Kay beamed. 'It was in with the lentils.'

'Well, thank God he came out of his coma to remember.'

'It's an eternity ring. No doubt she'll be down later to show it off to all the night staff…' And then her voice trailed off and she looked at Daniel. 'Are you wearing lip gloss?' Kay frowned.

'I am.'

'I can't keep up these days, I have to admit. Men wearing make-up…'

'I like it,' Daniel said. 'It keeps my lips soft, supple and kissable.'

There was something different about him that Holly couldn't put her finger on.

He wasn't at all aloof, he was lighter, funnier and now a part of the team, but it was more than that.

It was as if Daniel had become Daniel.

And, even more so, she wanted him.

CHAPTER SIXTEEN

'HAPPY CHRISTMAS, HOLLY.'

With just an hour left of the big day, and only a couple of patients trickling through, he found her standing at the nurses' station, pulling up some antibiotics that weren't even due yet, and he said what he wished he had said this morning.

Holly was very glad that he hadn't wished her a happy Christmas then, only because she'd have flung it back at him and said he'd ruined it.

Twenty-three hours into Christmas Day she was ready to hear it.

'Thank you.' She smiled. 'And to you.'

It *had* been a happy Christmas, Holly thought as she tapped the little air bubbles out of the syringe.

Despite the tears to come and the hurt yet to heal, it had still somehow managed to be the best Christmas and birthday she'd ever known.

'Was Santa good to you?' he asked.

'He was,' Holly said, wishing he would leave her alone, because it was hard to chat and play friends, but she tried. 'And Secret Santa was *very* good to me.' She looked into those absolute navy eyes, and there was still no silver, no little aqua dots, and she knew she loved him. 'Though he went way over budget...'

'Count yourself lucky. I got a lip balm.'

'The crème de la crème of lip balms,' Holly corrected him.

'Was I to think of you when I applied it?' Daniel asked, and it was he now who looked for a deeper meaning.

'No.' She shook her head. 'It was my I-am-so-over-you present. A bit nicer than I'd have got for others but certainly not in the chocolate stocking category.'

'What's wrong with a chocolate stocking?' Kay asked as she bustled in to get her bag and finally go home.

'Nothing,' Holly said.

In fact, a chocolate stocking was a whole lot less confusing than Daniel, and his romantic gifts and come-to-bed eyes, followed by the silent treatment the morning after.

Aaggh!

She wanted to scream but she didn't and no way, *no way* would she ask what was in the letter.

'Did you get any presents, Daniel?' Kay asked.

'I got a wallet from my father and stepmother,' Daniel said, 'and a popcorn-maker from my sister. We had a good day.'

'You stayed for dinner?' Holly frowned.

'I did.'

'Don't you get on?' Kay asked.

'Not really,' Daniel said. 'Though it's my stepmum that's the problem at the moment. Still, I do have a young sister...'

'How old is she?'

'Five,' Daniel said.

'And so how old is your stepmother?' Kay exclaimed in her less-than-tactful way.

'Twenty-seven.'

'Dear God!' Kay was stunned. 'That would be hard.'

'Actually,' Daniel said, picking up a file for the next patient, 'it's not. Much to Amelia's disappointment.'

Holly and Kay looked at each other as Daniel went to walk off. Holly could not believe he was finally being open about it, and as for Kay...

No, she wasn't subtle and she was also very, very shrewd.

'Did she come on to you, Daniel?'

Holly held her breath, wondering what his reaction would be.

'Last year.' Daniel nodded.

'And did you respond in kind?'

'Kay!' Holly admonished. Kay just went too far at times and Daniel clearly agreed because he turned around.

'No, I did not!' Daniel was all snobby and angry but it would seem Kay wasn't being nosey, she was just being very, very honest.

'I did!' She went purple in the face. 'Why do you think I work every Christmas? I'm trying to keep away from Eamon's twin?'

She was Irish, she was funny and it *was* Christmas night.

'One year his fecking mother made the same jumper and gave it to them for Christmas and so they were both wearing it...'

Holly watched a smile inch over Daniel's face as Kay proceeded to tell her story in the way only the Irish could.

'Well, I had everyone at the Christmas table, they were all getting on with their starters, and, given I had to get things ready, I ate mine quickly. I went into the kitchen to sort out the main course. I was taking the foil off the turkey and then Eamon came up behind me and he pinched my bottom and then we had a kiss, as you do...'

'Indeed,' Daniel said.

'It was quite a kiss actually,' Kay elaborated, 'but I told him that I needed to get on with dinner and that I'd deal with him better later and I gave it a little squeeze...'

And Holly laughed as Daniel's eyes popped a little.

'Then I walked through with the turkey and there was Eamon, sitting where I'd left him, and his brother was walking behind me... I knew I'd just got off with my husband's twin.'

They laughed so much!

Just laughed and laughed because somehow all families had their dramas and tales, all families were a little crazy.

Especially at Christmas.

'Did you tell Eamon?' Holly asked, when she had remembered how to breathe.

'Of course not,' Kay said. 'I mean...' She stopped talking in mid-sentence and looked over Holly's shoulder, and Kay's expression was so stunned that both Daniel and Holly turned around to see what had halted Kay in her tracks. 'Louise!'

It was Kay's daughter, accompanied by a very nervous-looking young man whose arm she was clinging onto.

'I was going to call you from Maternity...' Louise started to explain to her mother and then stopped as clearly another contraction hit. 'I don't think I'm going to get there.'

And Kay, the most competent, the most experienced, the utter glue of the department and, Holly guessed, her family too, just stood there not moving, like a tree in the middle of a field.

'Come on, Holly.' It was Daniel who moved.

He went over, shook the man's hand and found out his name—Gilbert—and then he guided Louise into a cubicle and Holly followed them all in. 'Let's help you up onto the trolley...' Daniel started, but Louise held onto the metal edges for dear life and started to bear down.

'Why don't we let the maternity department know?' Daniel suggested.

'I just have,' Kay said. She was present now, though not fully recovered from the shock of her daughter's arrival, but her voice was very deliberately steady and calm. 'They'll send someone just as soon as they're able to.'

Kay had brought in a delivery pack and Holly and Daniel were getting Louise up onto the gurney as she spoke on. 'They're very busy up there and, given we've got a registrar and,' she added, 'I'm also a midwife...'

'We'll be fine,' Daniel said in his composed, deep voice just as he had the night Paul had come in.

And he was calm, though not so aloof now, for he gave Kay's shoulder a little squeeze.

It was everything that was needed now.

CHAPTER SEVENTEEN

'WE'LL BE MORE than fine,' Kay said as she rallied. 'Now, Louise—' she was as direct as ever '—do you want me to wait outside? Just say if it's awkward for you to have your mother here.'

'*No-o-o-o!*' Louise shouted as another contraction took over and she clutched both her mother and her partner's arms and bore down.

Holly was very quickly opening up the delivery pack.

This baby really was in a hurry to be born!

'When did the contractions start?' Holly asked.

'Only an hour or so ago,' Gilbert answered. 'Though she's felt a bit off all day.'

'Why didn't you say when I called?' Kay asked.

'She didn't want you to worry, given how busy it is at Christmas,' Gilbert said, 'and we thought it would take ages.' He was trying to take in the speed of it all.

So was Holly—the head was almost out.

'Louise,' Daniel said. 'A big push, please.'

He was very polite as he made his request and Louise went from red to purple as she complied and then she made a request of her own. 'Can my mum deliver my baby?' she asked.

'I think that would be rather wonderful,' Daniel agreed.

When Kay came round, Holly watched as Daniel gave Kay's shoulder not one squeeze but two.

The first was to say, *I'm here beside you*, because for Kay this was the most important delivery of her life.

The second squeeze told her that she'd got this all under control—a midwife, a mother, a fabulous nurse, Kay was about to deliver her own grandchild.

And she coached her daughter well and soon a little head with dark hair was out and, with this push, the baby would be here.

'Oh…' Kay guided her grandbaby out into the world and delivered the vigorous bundle up onto Louise's stomach.

Daniel was there so he could step in if Kay became overwhelmed but it was simply a very beautiful birth.

'A girl,' Louise cried. 'Gilbert, we've got a little girl!'

He was a very proud father and Daniel handed Gilbert the scissors so he could cut the cord as the tiny little girl started to cry.

Holly was close to tears herself.

All births were beautiful but this one felt especially so.

And yet Holly felt sad.

'You have a visitor…' Laura popped her head around the curtain.

Eamon was there to take his wife home and when Louise called for him to come and meet his granddaughter he got the surprise of his life.

Holly knew she couldn't hold it together any more and when the midwife arrived from Maternity she slipped out and went and hid in the dark small theatre to let a few tears trickle out.

She had never felt so happy and sad at the same time.

She not only loved him, she really *liked* Daniel too,

and she didn't want him to be gone. She didn't *want* to have to get over him!

So she sat and decided to have a little Holly pity party and for ten minutes she sat there, but just as she was going to sneak out to sort out her face she heard his voice.

'Holly?'

She was too tired to even jump.

He didn't turn on the lights and she didn't turn her face to where he stood at the door.

'You have a namesake—they're going to call the baby Holly.'

'That's nice.'

'You forgot to do something today and so did I.'

He turned on the big bright lights then and he politely ignored that her mascara was down to her chin as he held up two Advent calendars.

'There's still five minutes left of Christmas.'

Even chocolate couldn't help with the way she felt, but Holly gave a thin smile and took her calendar and went to open the double doors.

'What do you think it might be?' Daniel asked, but Holly didn't answer. It was the last chocolate, the last special day, the last of them.

'A chocolate-covered gold leaf star?' he suggested. 'Or a little white chocolate dove filled...'

Oh, dear, just as he was getting the hang of Christmas the master chocolatier failed him. It was another little ball with red and green sticking out and a dusting of icing sugar.

'I think this must be why they ended up in the discount store,' Holly said.

They had come this far with their Advent calendars and so were sort of duty bound to eat them really. Even as they opened their mouths and dropped the chocolates in, both hoped they were wrong and that this time it would taste delicious.

It didn't.

'I hate glacé cherries.' Holly pulled a face and swallowed the bitter chocolate.

'And me,' Daniel said as he did the same. 'I think the chocolate's burnt!'

Then they looked at each other and, though she smiled, it was a sad one.

He loathed that he had hurt her.

Really hurt her, he knew, because they *had* made love this morning, and he had been an utter bastard afterwards.

'Don't you want to know what's in the letter?' Daniel asked.

'I'm going to smash it in the morning and find out,' Holly said, and they both smiled at the vision of her angrily taking a hammer to that blasted ball.

But then she started to cry.

'Go away,' she said.

'I can't,' Daniel said. 'Holly, I've been trying to leave for weeks but I can't. You've got me working Christmas, and adopting elephants and lining up in department stores for three hours just to get the perfect gift.'

'Three hours?'

'Which was plenty of time to change my mind, but I didn't,' Daniel said. 'I'm even arguing with elves...'

'Why were you arguing with elves?'

'I don't think my letter was effusive enough for them and, please, when you smash the decoration, bear in mind—'

'We both know I'm not going to smash it.' Holly sighed, but then she frowned. 'Bear in mind what?'

'That it was written before we…' He really struggled with the next two words. 'Made love.'

She smiled at her small victory.

'I shall bear it in mind!' Holly agreed. 'So what does it say?'

'I can't tell you. Elf rules.'

Holly rolled her eyes.

'Actually, if you guess correctly, I'll tell you so.'

'I don't want to guess.'

'What do you *think* the note might say?' Daniel insisted.

And so Holly thought for a moment and she smiled before delivering another little victory. 'I think it says "Are you on the Pill?"'

Daniel also smiled at her vindictive reference to that morning. 'I'm going to love rowing with you.'

And she could have sworn her earrings flashed, or was it hope that darted past her heart as he made reference to a future *us*.

Stop it, she told herself.

'What would you *like* the letter to say?' Daniel pushed.

And she knew what she'd like it to say, but she diluted it down, of course. 'That you like me a lot.'

'Correct,' Daniel said in sarcastic response. 'I got the little elves to write, "Dear Holly, I like you a lot." What would you *really* like it to say?'

'Don't,' Holly said, 'because I'll get all carried away and then…'

'You can get carried away, Holly. What would you like the letter to say?'

And she would be sophisticated next year.

'That you love me?' She said it as a question but it was the truth—it was what she wanted the letter to say.

She had no pride left and the emotional desert that was Daniel would just have to deal with it.

He gave a small snort at her soppy response. 'We've slept together twice, Holly.'

'I know.' She worried her bottom lip. 'It's embarrassing really…'

'What is? Your devotion to me?'

Holly nodded.

'I like it.' He grinned. 'Next guess?'

'No.' She shook her head. 'I don't like this game.'

His mouth gaped open and for the second time in their short history he pointed at her. Caught! 'You wanted it to say "Marry me"!'

'No, I didn't.'

'Holly, I don't hold out much hope for us if we're already reduced to lying. Did you or did you not hope it said that?'

'In very abstract wild dreams, possibly, while knowing of course it didn't say that…'

She had to know what it said.

'I'm going to go out to the car now and smash it!'

She was.

Holly was through being led down some emotional garden path by Daniel.

It was four minutes to midnight and with any luck that stupid ball would be history soon.

'Holly.' Daniel caught her arm as she went to go. 'Perhaps I should tell you that, for an inordinate sum, you can purchase a duplicate letter.'

'Oh.'

He opened his new wallet and instead of a condom nestled in the corner there was another shiny silver package and in the teeniest letters she saw her name.

It was rather tricky to open, but finally Holly got the letter out and she stared at the tiny squiggles.

'I can't read it.'

This was torture!

He went into a drawer and took out the magnifying glasses used for the most delicate suturing and she put them on and the tiny words came into clear view.

Dearest Holly,

I can only say this from a distance and only once I'm safely gone.

Sorry for being so contrary. You truly didn't deserve it. I want you to know that I've been cold and held back because, in truth, if I ever was going to settle down, and if there ever was that one person, then it would be you.

Daniel xxx

'The elf didn't approve,' Daniel said.

'Well, I do.'

As he took the magnifying glasses off her a part of her didn't want him to, she just wanted to stare at his words. But as the world came back to normal size she stared instead at him.

Into those absolute navy eyes that she had fallen in love with on sight.

And now she could admit it, not just to herself but to him.

'I love you.'

She'd never said it before, well, to her family and the dog and things, but not in the way she said it now.

'I know,' Daniel said. 'And I can't believe that I didn't want you to. I can't believe that I kept trying to avoid hearing those words. But *you're* the reason I couldn't leave and the reason I want to stay...'

Oh, there was work, and there was his sister, but his world had only fallen into place when she had entered it.

Life had started to get better the day Holly had arrived and it had made him not want to leave.

'It's you,' Daniel told her. 'And if you'll have me, and we hurry, you might get that winter wedding.'

'You mean it?'

'I more than mean it,' Daniel said. 'I've even chosen the location. We're getting married in a castle.'

Later he would tell her about a family holiday and happy memories and miniature castles and motorways on Christmas mornings and all of those things, but right now there was but one thing to be said.

'I love you, Holly.'

He said the words that he never had to any other and then he lowered his mouth to hers.

It was a soft and delicious kiss and it tasted of glacé cherries with a faint trace of bitter, burnt chocolate.

And it was wonderful.

* * * * *

If you enjoyed this story, check out these other great reads from Carol Marinelli

SEDUCED BY THE SHEIKH SURGEON
SEDUCED BY THE HEART SURGEON

THE SHEIKH'S BABY SCANDAL
DI SIONE'S INNOCENT CONQUEST

All available now!

THE ARMY DOC'S
BABY BOMBSHELL

BY
SUE MacKAY

MILLS
BOON®

Published in Great Britain 2016
By Mills & Boon, an imprint of HarperCollins*Publishers*
1 London Bridge Street, London, SE1 9GF

© 2016 Sue MacKay

ISBN: 978-0-263-91528-0

Dear Reader,

This is my twentieth book and I couldn't be happier. When my first book sold I was in awe of the whole process and felt stunned to have made it that far. Now I still feel the same. Not one story has been straightforward—as in I've never believed the process has got any easier. My stories come from the heart, and therefore I feel each and every one of them.

I thank you all for picking up and reading my stories. Without you I'd be wasting my time.

This one came out of the blue. It started with the idea of secret babies and war doctors. That's all. And yet here is a story that screamed out to be written.

When Sophie first sees Cooper she's smitten—but she isn't following through, right…? Throw in a bomb, casualties, surgeries and, hey, what comes next when you're up close to the hunkiest man you've ever seen? The result of which is a baby. It's what happens after this that is the real story. We can all be smitten and have a wonderful time, but it's the way we deal with the consequences that is life-changing.

Read the story to find out how Cooper and Sophie deal with them, and let me know what you think of their journey: sue.mackay56@yahoo.com or suemackay.co.nz.

Cheers!

Sue

This one's for my man,
for always supporting me even when the writing
turns to custard. And to my girl, her partner and their
two beautiful children because they are special.

Also to the Blenheim girls,
without whom I'd go bonkers more often than I
already do. Iona King, Barb Deleo, Louisa George,
Deborah Shattock, Nadine Taylor and Kate David.
You guys rock, and are so special. The best move
I ever made was to the Marlborough district,
where I hooked up with you.

To Laura,
the most helpful, wonderful editor I could wish for.

I love you all.

Hugs,

Sue

Books by Sue MacKay

Mills & Boon Medical Romance

Doctors to Daddies
A Father for Her Baby
The Midwife's Son

A Family This Christmas
The Family She Needs
Midwife…to Mum!
Reunited…in Paris!
A December to Remember
Breaking All Their Rules
Dr White's Baby Wish

Visit the Author Profile page
at millsandboon.co.uk for more titles.

CHAPTER ONE

'WOULD YOU LOOK at that? Sex in hard boots will do it for me every time.' The female sergeant at Captain Sophie Ingram's side ogled Captain Daniels striding across the dusty compound in their direction.

He *was* drop-dead gorgeous, Sophie admitted to herself as she tried to ignore the spark of arousal low in her body. A sensation she needed to shove aside. Working in Afghanistan was not the right time or place for liaisons. On a disappointed sigh, she told the military nurse, 'I'm off sex, hunk or no hunk available.'

Kelly's jaw dropped. 'You're kidding, right?'

'Not at all.'

'I mean, look at him,' Kelly spluttered.

She did. He *was* built.

The Kiwi captain, who'd arrived in camp late last night, widened his eyes as his gaze cruised over her. That delectable mouth lifted at one corner. Guess that meant he'd heard her blunt statement.

So what? It was best put out there. Saved time and misunderstanding. He could think what he liked. She wouldn't be hanging onto his every word in the hope of scoring during the three days he was in camp, helping out in the army hospital. Her last sexual experience had been something she didn't want to remember—or repeat—and had started her considering celibacy. Except it seemed some parts of her body hadn't got that message if the tightening in her belly and beyond was any indication.

'Captain Ingram?' The overly confident man stood in front of her, his hand outstretched in a friendly, yet provocative, manner.

Sophie nodded. 'Yes.' She took his hand to shake it but ignored the challenge staring out at her from the deepest pewter eyes she'd ever encountered. Neither would she acknowledge the rising tempo of her arousal. Sex was off the menu for the duration of her posting, no matter what. In her first weeks here a certain officer—now back home, thank goodness—had wooed her, then shown exactly what he thought the role of female personnel really was. Degrading didn't come close. Joining the army for an adventure was one thing, being treated disrespectfully was another. She'd since seen enough other liaisons end messily to know sex was best avoided on tour.

But she groaned. Captain Daniels with his dark, cropped hair and knowing eyes would tempt her every time. 'Welcome to Bamiyan NZ base.'

His eyebrow lifted in an ironic fashion. 'This is my third—'

The air exploded. The rock-hard ground heaved upward, shoving Sophie's feet up to her throat. Then she was airborne, her arms flailing uselessly, her head whipping back and forth. Slam. She hit the ground, landing on her back, the air punched out of her lungs, her limbs spread in all directions.

Stones pelted her. Dust filled her eyes and mouth. Breathing became impossible. *Whizz. Bang.* The air around her was alive, splintering as objects sped past her. Bullets? Fear gripped her. Who was firing at *her*? A heavy weight crashed over her, pinning her down. A human weight. What was happening? What had caused that explosion? Her heart beat so fast it was going to detonate out of her chest. Her ribcage rose higher and higher as she strained to fill her lungs with something purer than sand and dust. Her airway hurt. Her head hurt. Every single thing hurt.

'Stay down,' a deep, dark voice snapped.

She daren't open her eyes to see who the man protecting her with his body was. Gulp. Cough. Dust scratched the back of her throat. Strong arms were on either side of her vulnerable head. Muscular legs held down her softer ones. The one and only Captain Daniels.

Around them the gunfire was sharp and loud, and dangerous. Then suddenly it stopped. But the shouting and yelling continued. Orders were barked. Screams curdled her blood. Racing footsteps slapped the ground. Fear flew up her throat, filled her mouth. Was this *it*? The end? Lying on a piece of dry, barren dirt in some place she'd barely heard of growing up in lush green New Zealand? No way. She'd fight to the last, would not die lying here defenceless and useless. Flattening her hands on the ground, she tensed, ready to push upward, to remove her human shield.

'Easy.' That voice was right beside her ear, lifting the hairs on the back of her neck. Almost seductive—if she hadn't been terrified for her life.

Sophie squirmed, felt the muscles covering her body tighten.

'Easy,' he repeated a little desperately.

'Let me up.' She'd aimed for nonchalant, got light and squeaky. Damn. She was a soldier, supposed to be fearless. A little bit, anyway.

'Wait.'

Sophie needed to know what was going on. Apart from

flying bullets and a bomb exploding. Needed to assess the situation, see if she could move, find shelter, help someone. As a doctor she'd be required in the hospital unit. Squinting, she looked around to see if it was safe to move. And came eyeball to eyeball with Cooper Daniels.

Her heart stopped its wild pounding, stopped trying to bash its way out of her chest. Went completely still. Her lungs gave up trying to inhale as that intense grey gaze bored right into her, deep into places no one had been before. Places where she hid the vulnerability that directed her life. Shock ripped through her. Every muscle in her body seemed to twitch, tighten, loosen. Had she died? Been taken out by one of those bullets?

'Captains, move. Now. Sir. Ma'am.' Someone, somewhere above them, roared in a strained shout, 'Get up off the ground. We've got you both covered.'

I'm definitely alive. Sophie pushed at Cooper, desperate to get away from him, to find safety, to regain her composure and see what needed to be done. There'd be casualties for sure.

The weight lifted from her body, a hand snatched at hers, hauled her upright in one swift, clumsy jerk. 'Run towards the officers' quarters,' Cooper yelled in her ear as he tightened his grip on her hand. 'The hospital's a target.'

She ran, trusting him completely. But even as she ran she looked around, and gasped. Where the ground had been flat moments ago there was now a deep crater. An enormous dust cloud hovered above, blocking the sun's intense heat. Otherwise everything looked weirdly normal—apart from the troops stationed on the perimeter, facing outwards with machine guns at the ready.

Forget normal. A body lay against the wall of the

hospital block. Sophie shouted, 'Kelly,' and veered left around the destruction, aiming for the nurse.

Cooper pulled at her, tried to prevent her going in that direction. 'Wait. It's more exposed that way. Snipers will see you.'

Sophie got it. And wasn't having a bar of it. She paused to lock her gaze on him, her heart rate steady, her lungs finally doing their job. 'We need to get to Sergeant Brooks ASAP. Move her to safety.' She had no idea where the calmness now taking over came from, but she was in control, able to do something for someone, and not be a victim being protected by this man.

His eyes widened and he shook his head as though to get rid of something. 'You're right. Let's go.'

'Kelly was standing beside me when that bomb went off,' she muttered as they reached the nurse sprawled with blood pouring from a head wound and her legs at odd angles to her body. Dropping to her knees, Sophie reached to find a pulse, holding her breath as she tried to find any sign of life. Dread rose, and she quickly swallowed on it. Now was the time to step up and be professional; not let emotions override everything else. 'Come on, Kelly. Don't do this to me.'

A faint throb under her fingertip. 'Yes.' She slumped with relief. Her friend didn't deserve to die. Sophie kept her finger in place for a few more beats, to be absolutely sure, and looked at Cooper, who was crouched beside her, gently probing Kelly's head. 'She's alive. Get a stretcher out here. We're going into surgery.' Those legs looked in need of some serious work, as did the head injury. Blood also seeped into the ground from under Kelly's right shoulder. They'd have to do a thorough assessment but she wasn't hanging around out here for some sniper to pick them off.

'Yes, Captain.' Cooper was on his feet and racing towards the hospital unit, now all business, the challenging male no longer visible. Neither was the captain, aka general surgeon. He was just one of the battalion, doing the job of an orderly because she'd told him to. Impressive.

The man who'd thrown himself over her to protect her from those bullets. Very impressive. Sophie bit down on the flare of yearning and astonishment suddenly touching her again in that place she'd thought so well hidden. What was it about him that exposed her weak side far too easily?

'Captain Ingram, we've got two casualties from the other side of the perimeter,' a soldier called above the noise of troops clearing the area and checking on one another. 'They've been taken into the medical unit for assessment. That unit's now clear of danger.'

Nothing, nobody was ever completely out of danger, but she'd keep that gem to herself. Glancing up, she acknowledged the young man who was on his first stint overseas with the NZ Army and sometimes dropped into the hospital to talk or read to patients.

'Thank you, Corporal.' His face was chalk white. 'Did you sustain any injuries, George?'

'No, Captain.'

'Right. Captain Daniels is bringing a stretcher so we can shift Sergeant Nurse Brooks. I'd like you to help with moving her.' Shifting Kelly without doing more damage to her broken body was going to be a nightmare. Even if the unconscious woman couldn't feel a thing, Sophie knew *she'd* wince at every single movement. She hated inflicting any pain whatsoever on someone. Her fellow surgeons often gave her grief about that, pointing out that any surgery was followed by some degree of pain.

'Yes, Ma'am.'

Cooper skidded to a halt by their patient and lowered the stretcher carefully, as close as possible to her body. 'It's chaos inside. Injuries all over the place.'

Sophie swore quietly. Why? Who? How could anyone do this to another human being?

Get real, her inner voice snarled. *You're in a war zone. This is what you're here for.*

She knew all that, but reality sucked, brought everything into focus in full colour. On a ragged indrawn breath, she began organising the removal of Kelly from the hot, dusty outdoors and into the relative safety of the medical unit.

'I'll be operating with you,' Cooper informed her as they carried the laden stretcher towards the theatre section.

Sophie glanced at him. 'Surely you're needed elsewhere.'

'Orders. Kelly's the worst off by far.' Then he added, sotto voce, 'If you don't count the two deceased.'

Sophie's stomach dropped. She'd been refusing to consider some of the soldiers might've been killed. 'Do we know who they are?'

'Not yet.' Cooper locked his eyes on her. 'If you want to go find out I can take over here.'

She shook her head. 'No. Getting Kelly stable so we can evacuate her is more important.'

'I agree.' He gave her a smile that blew her heart rate into disarray again.

Suddenly Sophie felt light-headed, swaying on her feet as she stared at the floor. Reaching out for balance, her hand found Cooper's shirt sleeve and gripped tight.

'You okay?' he asked, concern flooding his voice.

Dropping her hand as though it had been scalded, she growled, 'Guess it's the shock catching up.'

'It does that.'

She was showing her inexperience in conflict situations. The past two months had been relatively quiet on the war front—near this base anyway. She'd been kept busy with small surgeries but nothing like this. Reaching Kelly, she started appraising the injuries more thoroughly.

'Multiple fractures of both legs and the pelvis. As well as that dislocated shoulder and fractured skull.' Sophie straightened up from the bed Kelly lay on, and looked at Cooper. 'She needs an orthopaedic surgeon,' which they didn't have. 'How much experience have you got in that field?'

'Enough to do the basics, but the sooner we can get her back to Darwin the better.' Cooper looked glum. 'It's going to be touch and go for her.'

'Right. Let's scrub up and do what we can.' Sophie looked around the ordered chaos, saw the commanding medical officer on the far side of the room and made a beeline for him to explain the situation.

'We've got two others needing evacuation back to Australia too,' she was told. 'A flight's being arranged for two hundred hours. Do what you can in the meantime.'

At the sink Sophie scrubbed and scrubbed her fingers, her palms, the backs of her hands. Sand and dirt and blood stained her skin and had got beneath her nails. Anger at what had happened had her compressing her mouth to hold back a torrent of expletives that'd do no good for anybody. But how could people attack others like that? Used to fixing people, making them better, it was impossible to comprehend the opposite. Her muscles quivered, whether in rage or shock she wasn't sure, but she needed to get them under control if she was going to be any use to her friend.

'Easy.' Cooper's word of the day, apparently. A firm hand gripped her shoulder briefly. 'Save the anger for later.'

Turning, she locked her eyes on those grey ones she was coming to recognise as special, or was that the man behind them? 'There's plenty of it, believe me.'

He nodded and dropped his hand to his side. 'I know. It gets me going every time.'

'Yet you keep coming back.' She'd heard that Captain Daniels was on his third tour of duty over here. Then she saw the gleam in his gaze and knew he'd picked up on the fact she'd taken note of details about him. Telling him she hadn't gone out of her way to ask anyone would only stroke his ego further so she spun away to dry her hands before holding them out to the assistant to put gloves on for her.

This whole sexual distraction was ludicrous when they were in the middle of an emergency. 'Do we even know if the attack is completely finished?' she asked no one in particular.

'Apparently so,' Cooper replied as he began scrubbing up, a smug look on his face.

He could get over whatever was causing that. They had surgery to perform, which left no room for anything else. Sexual tension included.

Uncountable hours later Sophie smothered a yawn as she leaned back against the outside wall of their little hospital and watched Kelly being transferred to the medic truck that would take her to the airfield. 'Thank goodness she's survived her first round of surgery,' she murmured to herself, suddenly wanting to hear her voice in the rare stillness of the night.

'She's got a long way to go yet.' Cooper loomed up beside her.

So much for talking to herself. 'I'm worried about her left leg. I suspect she's in for an amputation despite everything we did.'

'That patella wasn't broken, it was pulverised,' Cooper agreed.

'Kelly's a fitness freak, runs marathons for fun.' Not any more. Or not for a long time and after a lot of hard rehab. Tears threatened. 'It's so darned unfair.'

'That's war.' His tone brooked no argument and suggested she needed to get used to the idea.

'I know. But I'm hurting for a friend. Okay?' Sophie straightened her back, hauled her shoulder off the wall, took a step away. She'd had enough of Mr Confidence, didn't need reminding why she was here.

'Don't go. Not yet.' Cooper's voice was low and, strangely, almost pleading.

She hesitated. Going inside where everyone was still talking and crying and laughing as they finally came down off the high caused by shock over the attack and continual hours of urgent surgery turned her cold. But staying here, talking to Cooper Daniels, held more danger, and she'd had her fill of that already. 'Think I'll go to my bunk.'

'I'll walk you across the compound.' When she opened her mouth to say no he talked over her. 'We don't have to talk. I'd like your company for a few minutes, that's all.'

There were no arguments to that. None that she could find without sounding like she was making a run for it to put space between them. Anyway, she suddenly felt in need of company too. Talk about being all over the place. 'Sure.' She stepped away to put space between them and rammed her hands into the pockets of her fatigues. Then tripped on a small rock.

Cooper caught her, held her until she righted herself. Left his hand on her elbow as they slowly made their way through the throng of personnel wandering almost aimlessly back and forth on the parade ground they were crossing.

Out of the blue came the need to keep Cooper with her. His hand was reassuring against her unease. Leaning into him, absorbing the warmth of being with someone as tension held her in its grip, was a tonic.

Thump. She jerked around, staring into the night, seeing nothing more than she'd been gazing at a moment earlier.

'It's okay. Some clown tossed a metal bucket at the fence.' Cooper slipped his arm over her shoulders, drew her in closer.

'I thought…'

'Yeah. Me too.'

'Have you ever experienced anything like what went down here?' She'd known signing up to the army, even as a medic, had its dangers, but this was the first time she'd been confronted with the truth of living and working as an army officer in Afghanistan. She needed to toughen up and put it behind her, not let every little sound or bang have her leaping out of her skin.

Tension tightened the muscles in the arm draped across her shoulders. 'Once. Near Kabul.'

'Why do you keep coming back?' She'd signed up for one year and now she wondered how she'd make it through without turning into a freaked-out wreck.

'Army orders.'

So he wasn't up for personal conversation. 'Of course.' She pulled away, put distance between them again. Wrapping her arms around her body, she stared ahead at the officers' quarters. Lights blazed out over the compound and the idea of going inside to be surrounded by her colleagues became repugnant.

'Want to keep walking for a bit?' So he could mind-read. Probably as well as he could twist a dislocated clavicle back into place, as he'd done for Kelly. Or as easily as he had most upright females drooling over him without a word.

Including her, she realised. He had to be the most sexy, gorgeous, mouth-watering man she'd met in a long time. Had she drooled when Kelly had pointed him out? Couldn't have or he wouldn't have come over to see her, dribble on the chin being highly unattractive.

'I'll take that as a yes, then.'

Huh? Oh, right. Unused to women not gushing out answers to his questions? 'I won't be able to sleep. My head's spinning and my body aches from being tossed through the air.'

'That was some landing you made.'

'Didn't you get thrown down?' she asked, suddenly remembering how quickly he'd seemed to be with her, covering her as bullets had flown past. 'Thank you for protecting me. That was incredibly brave.'

'Honestly? It's something I did without considering the consequences. You looked vulnerable and I just fell over you.'

Sophie sighed. 'That's how brave people act. They don't weigh up the consequences. Wasn't it random how the three of us standing together ended up in different places? Kelly copped the worst of the explosion and was thrown in the opposite direction from us. We're relatively unscathed.'

'Be grateful. We were needed in Theatre afterwards.'

'True.' They were heading behind the officers' quarters into comparative quiet and some darkness. Sophie looked around, saw no one in the shadows, and stopped. 'Maybe I should go back.'

'Afraid to be with me?' That earlier challenge was back, deepening the huskiness in his voice.

'Not at all,' she snapped, even as awareness of him teased her. He was large; tall and broad. It would be so easy to lay her head on that chest and wrap her arms around his waist. She knew she'd feel safe for as long as she held onto him. Shock made her gasp.

But she didn't pull away from that tiny touch of his hand brushing against her thigh as he waited to see what she'd do. She couldn't move. Hell, she didn't even want to. Right this moment she needed him. Needed reassurance that she'd survived her first bombing alive and well. Needed to get close to another human, to share the horror and the recovery from the shock. Wanted more than to be held. Wanted to feel alive in his arms.

'Sophie?' Cooper growled.

She stepped closer, so near her breasts brushed his chest. Her nipples pebbled, throbbing with longing, echoing the sensations moistening her at the apex of her legs. She had never wanted a man so badly. Never. The afternoon's attack definitely had a lot to answer for. 'Cooper,' she whispered in reply. 'Please take me.'

'Are you sure?' he asked, the softness of his voice surprising her.

'Absolutely,' she told him fiercely. 'Absolutely.' Now. Not in five minutes. Now. She leaned closer, spreading the length of her body up the length of his. She immediately felt his hardness, knew his reciprocating need in an instant. Winding her arms around his neck, she raised her mouth to capture his.

Cooper took over. His hands spanned her waist, pulling her firmly against his body, so close they'd become one. His tongue pushed through to taste her, delving deep, taking charge.

Sophie lost herself in his kiss, his scent, his strength. Her hands grappled with tugging his shirt free. The need to touch his skin, to feel his heat against her palms was urgent. So urgent she slid her hands beneath the waistband of his fatigues, her fingers seeking that throbbing heat pressing into her belly. Wrapping her hands around him, she heard his groan by her ear.

'Sophie, you are driving me over the edge too fast.'

'I want fast.' Huh? Who was this wanton woman in her skin?

Cooper obliged, shoving at her trousers until they slid to her thighs, and then he cupped her.

All the air in her lungs whooshed across her lips as his finger found her hot, moist pulse. One slide of that finger and she was clinging to him, losing all sense of reality. Or was this reality? Another slide and her legs were trembling, losing the ability to hold her upright.

So she wrapped them around Cooper, holding herself over that wondrous finger, ready for his next muscle-tightening touch. But instead Cooper slid two fingers inside her and a scream flew up her throat, caught by his mouth. Since when had she become a screamer?

And then for the second time in twenty-four hours her world exploded. Shock waves hit her. Her body was racked with spasms, her head tipped backwards, and she was only vaguely aware of where she was. Again Cooper's strong body was plastered to hers, only this time it was her weight on him, her legs around his body. Then he moved to lift her higher and she was feeling him enter her, inch by excruciating inch until he filled her.

Then he withdrew to plunge in deep again. And again. And again.

Sophie completely lost her mind as her body responded to Cooper's. All she knew was she'd died and gone to some wondrous place she'd never experienced. All energy drained from her as her response overtook her.

And afterwards somehow she made it back to her bunk and slept the sleep of the completely sated.

CHAPTER TWO

Seven and a half months later...

COOPER SWIPED AT his forehead. The Aussie heat was re-
lentless. Darwin did not come cold. Not even cool. And
this was winter. Two hours since the troop carrier had
touched down and he'd already had enough, felt in need
of a cold shower despite showering and changing into
clean clothes less than thirty minutes ago.

He entered the Australian Army's busy medical unit
and looked around for her. Sophie Ingram. No doubt she'd
be another reason for a cold shower as soon as he set
eyes on her. He'd never been able to exorcise the woman
completely from his brain. One night, one hot act, and
she now ruled his thought processes far too often. Face
it, once was one time too many. But the times that really
bugged him were those in the middle of the night when
he was tossing and turning in desperate need of sleep.
She'd sneak in, reminding him of her amazing body and
that off-the-scale sex they'd shared. Only once, and yet it
had been the best he'd experienced in a life of experience.

There. Leaning over a table in the far corner, reading
a file, seemingly oblivious to the hustle going on around
her. The breath stalled in his lungs as he drank in the
sight of that tall, slight figure with perfect butt curves

that even fatigues did nothing to hide. Or was that his memory filling in the details? Her coppery brown hair hung in a long ponytail down her spine. He hadn't had a chance to run his hands through that silk, hadn't kissed her as often as he'd have liked. Both things he'd regretted even when the opportunity hadn't been there. If he had, would he still be feeling there was so much more to be enjoyed? It wasn't as if he wanted anything other than a rerun of that one act. If it didn't happen it wouldn't be the end of the world, but there was no harm in finding out if she was willing while he was here.

Sophie looked as cool as an iced beer as she straightened to turn side on to place the file in a tray.

Cooper gasped, the air exploding out of his lungs. His head spun so fast he closed his eyes tight in an attempt to stop it, to remain upright. Opening them again, the picture was exactly the same. He went hot, then cold, hot again. *Thud, thud, thud* slammed his heart. He swallowed—hard—but the sourness remained in his mouth. His hands clenched at his sides as he stared at the sexy woman he'd come to see with the idea of having a meal somewhere off base, hopefully followed by an evening in the sack. He had not come to be delivered a hand grenade that the pin had been pulled from.

'Cooper?' She was coming towards him, colour spilling into her cheeks. No longer cool. Shocked. Surprised. No. Make that uneasy. Which made perfect sense given the situation. She said, 'I heard you were stopping off for a couple of days on your way home.'

He fought the urge to back away. A coward he was not, but this was…enormous. Wrong word. He could even be wrong about what he saw. No, not about that, but about his role in the situation.

'I've just flown in from the east, landed a couple of hours ago.'

Her eyes widened. So she'd picked up on the fact he hadn't wasted any time dropping in on her.

'I heard you were still here and thought I'd say hello.' *Getting yourself in deeper, bud.*

She'd reached him and stood staring, hands on hips, caution darkening those emerald eyes that had haunted him in the deep of the night. Her voice wavered as she said, 'This is my last week here before I'm shipped back home to finish my contract in Auckland.'

She was going to Auckland? So was he. The day after tomorrow. Auckland was big. They'd never cross paths. *Coward.* That's what phones were for. Contacting people. 'I guess you're looking forward to that. The heat must be playing havoc with you.' He nodded abruptly at her very pregnant belly.

She's carrying a baby. He bit down on the expletives spewing across his tongue. Dread was cranking up from deep within. He had an awful feeling about this. A dreadful sensation that his world was rolling sideways and would never be the same again.

Sophie rubbed her lower back while her gaze was fixed on some spot behind him. 'Yes, the heat's exhausting, but it's more that I want to be home before this baby makes her entrance.' Now both her hands moved onto her belly in a protective gesture, as though she was afraid of, or warding off, something. *Or someone.*

Him? His reaction? He strove to be calm, barely held onto the question hovering on the tip of his tongue. When he thought it safe to open his mouth he asked, 'You don't want a little Aussie?' Who cared? Avoiding asking what he desperately needed to know and yet was afraid to find out was only stalling, not solving a thing.

'I'd prefer to be with my friends.'

Friends, not family. Showed how little he knew about her. 'How far along are you?' His breath caught in the back of his throat as he waited for her answer. It had been over seven months since the bombing in Bamiyan, since they'd found solace in each other's bodies. Was the baby his? If it was, why hadn't she told him about it? But why should she? What would she want from him? Apparently nothing, if it was his. There'd been no contact from her since that night, which in itself was unusual in his experience of women. If the baby wasn't his, then whose?

Sophie lifted her head, her chin jutting out as she said quietly, firmly, 'Seven and a half months. She's yours.'

He reeled back on his heels. Her direct reply knocked the air out of him and had his stomach sucking in on itself. It was one thing to wonder if he was the father; completely different to learn he actually was. Again heat flooded him. 'I see.'

Huh? I do?

Goosebumps lifted his skin. According to this woman he'd spent barely half a dozen hours with in total he'd made her pregnant. Should he believe her without question? Just accept her word for it without DNA testing? They'd had sex once. Once. What were the odds? How could he trust her to be telling the truth when he knew next to nothing about her?

Sophie was standing tall, her arms now at her sides, her hands fisted, her chin jutting out further, her eyes daring him to challenge her statement.

And just like that he knew she hadn't lied, wasn't trying to tie him into anything he didn't want. The tension left him. Then it was back, gripping him harder, tightening the muscles in his gut, his legs, his arms.

I don't want to be a father.

Did Sophie want to be a mother? Obviously she did or she'd have terminated the pregnancy, wouldn't she? She didn't know he never intended being a parent, or getting into a long-term relationship. That he played the field because he was just like his father, an expert at moving on from woman to woman. Where was the relief? Why wasn't he falling over backwards in gratitude for her not involving him in this baby's life? But now she had. There was no avoiding it. 'We need to talk.'

'Why?'

'Don't play games, Sophie. I'd like to know more about this baby, and how you're keeping. What I can do for you.' There. Responsibility kicked in even before he'd thought things through. Thanks to his dad for another lesson he'd learned well. As long as it didn't backfire on him.

'That's easy. Baby and I are healthy, and there's absolutely nothing I expect from you.' Despite her determined attitude, a flicker of doubt crossed that intense gaze, and her fists clenched tighter.

Unease rattled him. She did want something. Despite her statement to the contrary, there were things she'd want from him. He'd do the right thing. Stand by her and the baby. But that was the beginning and end of it. He wouldn't be tied down. Not for the sake of a child. It wouldn't work. He and Sophie didn't know anything about each other.

You know the sex can be out of this world.

One great bonk in extenuating circumstances didn't make a long-lasting relationship. Anyway, it probably wouldn't be the same again. Want to put that theory to the test? Yeah, he did. But wasn't going to now.

Another thing against further involvement was that he didn't do love. Didn't believe in it. He'd got this far without it. One too many times watching his father's latest girlfriend pack her bags and leave when he'd been a boy had taught him that getting involved with anyone led to nothing but anguish. It'd hurt every time, watching them walk away after he'd become close and begun to think they might be there as he grew up. Sometimes it had broken him. At first he'd had to learn not to cry, then he'd learned to be stoic, and finally gruff and rude. Love wasn't anything like it was cracked up to be. Not even the mother of his unborn child was getting a look in. Telling Sophie any of that wasn't happening, though he still needed to talk to her. 'What time are you taking a break?' he snapped, louder than he'd intended.

Sophie stared at him as though searching for something.

He only hoped he could provide whatever it was. All the more reason to go somewhere private before she said anything. 'Well?'

Looking around the busy room, where heads had lifted at his question, she shrugged, which set his teeth on edge. 'I can go to lunch any time I like. Despite how it looks I don't exactly get rushed off my feet. Unless there's a forced march in the wind,' she added with a tentative smile.

'Then you get queues of soldiers with all sorts of maladies that show no symptoms.' He wanted to smile back but was all out of them right now. 'Seen it all too often.' That caution on Sophie's face was unexpected, given how she'd thrown herself at him in Bamiyan, and again underlined how little he knew her. It also softened his stance the smallest of bits.

Toughen up. Don't go all soft over this. A baby, huh? A huge responsibility even if he only kept to the outskirts of the child's life. But…he was going to be a dad.

I am not ready for this. Will never be ready. This changes everything.

He and Sophie were now tied together in some way for ever. He turned for the entrance, his legs tensing, ready to run, hard and fast, as far away as possible, to outrun this crazy situation.

The only thing holding him back was that he'd always taken his responsibilities seriously.

Haven't been dealt this hand before.

True. It was as terrifying as that bomb in Bamiyan, and the consequences were going to last a lot longer. He had another mark to step up to, one he was not prepared for and had absolutely no idea how to manage.

'We need somewhere quiet for this discussion.' Sophie probably had similar concerns. Her sympathetic tone felt like a caress even if the intent of her words was a harsh reminder of what was ahead.

How could she remain so calm? He could hate her for that. No, not fair. She'd had months to prepare for today. And his anger was directed at the shock she'd delivered, not at her personally. But she should've told him. Then he'd have been prepared. A shudder rocked him. Really? Would he ever be able to look back at this moment and say it was a good thing to have happened? His hands clenched. Not likely.

'Is there somewhere we won't be interrupted?' Cooper demanded. There were a few personnel on this base he knew and would enjoy catching up with—some other time. His best mate would have to wait too. Right now he wanted this upcoming conversation done and dusted in one sitting, though he somehow doubted it was ever going to finish, that there'd always be things to discuss about their child. Their daughter. Sophie had said, *she's* yours. Oh, hell. A wee girl. His throat clogged. His daughter.

This would take some getting used to. If he even wanted to, and right now he didn't. How could a guy whose mother had committed suicide when he was six and a father who'd had an endless stream of women moving through their lives grasp the basics of good parenting?

'We could go to my quarters.' Then Sophie hesitated. 'No, we'll go off base. There's a place a couple of kilometres south where I can get a sandwich and you can have whatever you might want.'

An ice-cold beer would go down just fine about now. Sweat was rolling down his back. From the temperature or his turmoil, he wasn't sure. Probably both. 'You got a car?'

She nodded. 'I do.'

'Let's go.' The idea of that beer had his mouth watering, while the idea of talking about the baby and their future wasn't doing his stomach any favours, instead causing a tightness he couldn't loosen. So much for a quick visit and maybe a bit of sex. Sometimes life threw curveballs. Big suckers. He needed to learn how to catch them without doing any damage.

Sophie drove as fast as legally possible. Which said a lot about her state of mind. Lately she'd become ultra-cautious about a lot of things, like she was afraid to create further havoc in her life. But Cooper's sudden appearance in the medical unit had floored her. Knowing he was turning up had done nothing to prepare her for the sight of this man. None of her memories of that hot body had been exaggerated. No wonder she'd thrown herself at him in Bamiyan. But would she have if the situation hadn't been so explosive? Ha. She had to ask that when Cooper was involved?

She should've told him the moment she'd found out she was pregnant, but what would've been the point? She didn't want him thinking he had to become a part of her life. It wasn't as though they knew each other or were in love. Getting hitched or involved in any way whatsoever with a man because she was pregnant was not on the agenda. Marriage had never been something she wanted, and pregnancy hadn't changed her mind. She could support her own child, didn't need to do someone else's washing or clean up after him for the rest of her life so that her daughter could see her father every day.

Three days ago when Alistair had told her Cooper was coming he'd given her a chance to prepare what to say, yet her mind had remained blank.

She got on well with the lieutenant colonel, had managed to ignore the fact he was Cooper's close friend until now. She suspected he'd guessed who the father of her baby was right from the moment she said she'd met Cooper in Bamiyan at the time of the attack. He'd have done the sums. Was that why he looked out for her, made her life as easy as possible? Because of his friend?

The sooner they got to Harry's Place the sooner she could tell Cooper the little there was to say and then she could get away from his brooding presence. At least he hadn't erupted when she'd said the baby was his. He'd come close at one point but had managed to haul the brakes on his temper. Told her something about the man, didn't it? Controlled under fire. But of course she'd seen that before, knew how he reacted when being attacked.

'I don't suppose this rust bucket runs to air-conditioning?' Cooper looked decidedly uncomfortable as he tried to move his large body in the not-so-large car.

'See that handle? It's for the window.'

His sigh was filled with frustration, and probably had nothing to do with their mode of transport. 'I figured.'

Then use it. 'The tyres are near new, and the motor

hums. It's all I need.' It wasn't as though she took it on trips out into the desert or across state.

His head tipped back against the skewed head rest. He seemed to be drawing a deep, calming breath. 'Whatever possessed you to buy it in the first place? There must've been better vehicles available in town,' he snapped. The deep breathing was apparently a fail.

She ignored the temper and its cause. Plenty of time to talk about their baby once they got to Harry's Place. 'It's a hand-me-down that goes from medical officer to medical officer.' When his eyebrows rose she explained, liking the safer subject. 'A couple of years back some guy bought it and when he was shipped out he handed it to the incoming medic, said he wouldn't get much for it if he sold it and as most medics are never here for long it might as well become a fixture.'

For a moment Cooper was quiet and she hoped that was the end of any conversation. Silence was better than questions she found herself looking for barbs in.

But no. That was wishful thinking. 'How long have you got to run on your contract with the army?'

'Ten weeks, but I'm only going to be on call for those weeks. I don't expect to be called up. What about you?'

'I'm done. For this contract anyway.'

'You're going to sign up again?' She didn't know how she felt about that. It wasn't as though they would want to spend time together, yet he was the father of her baby. Despite her own reservations about Cooper, her daughter deserved to know her dad, to spend time with him. It would never be her fault her parents weren't together, and therefore she shouldn't suffer the consequences.

The irony had her pressing her lips together. She'd grown up having it rammed down her throat with monotonous regularity that *she* was the only reason her parents had married. Mum had been pregnant so they'd done the right thing and tied the knot. Unfortunately they hadn't liked each other and the numerous arguments had been monumental, always ending with the blame landing firmly at Sophie's feet. They'd certainly put her off getting hitched. Why bother when she was happy and free? Becoming trapped and miserable would be a rerun of her childhood. So—no tying the knot in her future. Unless she found a man she loved unconditionally and who returned the sentiment. As she hadn't been looking, she didn't know if such a beast existed.

'I think I'm over the military.' Cooper stared ahead as he answered her question.

'What next, then?'

'Hospital contract.'

'Where?' she persisted.

'Auckland.'

So he wasn't just visiting, he was stopping. Guess she should be glad they'd be in the same city. Shouldn't she? That depended on lots of things. 'That's where you come from?' When he nodded abruptly she commented, 'You're not happy with my questions.' It was like pulling teeth.

'Not particularly.'

Fair enough. 'But I know next to nothing about you.'

'That's how I like it,' he snapped.

With all his relationships? Or just the one involving her that he'd have to adjust to? Could be he thought she was working out how much she could ask for child support. She contemplated letting him stew for a while, then realised how bitchy that was. Not so long ago he'd been sucker-punched with most men's worst nightmare. Her memories of the day she'd learned about the baby were still sharp, and that had been months ago. Shock followed by excitement, followed by fear. Those emotions still rocked her some days. 'For what it's worth, I have no intention of demanding money from you to raise my daughter.'

'Our daughter.'

Kapow! So he'd accepted the fact he was a father. Or had he? Was this just a hiccup as he processed everything? Her head spun. It seemed too easy. Far too easy to be true. What was the catch? When no answers came to mind she focused on driving safely and getting to Harry's Place in one piece.

Wonder of wonders, there was a parking space right outside the main entrance. With her usual efficiency— baby brain on hold for once—she backed into it and turned off the engine.

Our daughter.

The knob came off the handle as she wound hard to close her window. 'Stupid car. Something's always falling off.' Opening the door to allow some air flow through, she couldn't stop her mind running away on her.

My baby. Our baby.

A knot formed in her gut, dread cramping her muscles. 'I don't expect *anything* of you.'

'I'm starting to get the picture. Why didn't you contact me about this? Apart from wanting nothing of me, wasn't I entitled to know?' His hand waved between them, sort of in the direction of her extended belly. As though he was struggling with the whole concept after all. Which made more sense and was a lot closer to the reaction she'd expected.

The heat was building up rapidly and making her feel very light-headed. Shoving out of the car, she slammed the door, leant against it until her balance returned. Stepping onto the pavement, she told him, 'It's not like we knew each other.' It was hard not to yell at him, to ram her words in his face.

'Which gave you the right to decide I shouldn't have anything to do with my child?' The pewter of his eyes was now cold steel. His mouth had become a flat line that dragged his face down, making her realise it was the first time she'd seen him without a hint of a smile softening his expression. No, that wasn't right. He'd looked stunned and shocked when he'd first seen her in the medical unit. No smile then either.

'I always intended telling you after the birth.' Her cheeks were getting hotter by the second, and not from the heat slamming up from the pavement.

'Why not before?' He stepped up beside her, dwarfing her with his size as he glared down at her.

'It's personal. Private.' She so did not want Cooper hanging around for midwife appointments and examinations. No, thank you.

'That's it? Personal? Private?' When she continued to watch him, he snapped, 'It took two to tango in the first place. You can't just kick me into touch and then haul me back as it suits you.'

She gasped. She wasn't doing that. 'It's not like that. I wanted this time to myself to get used to the fact my life's changed irrevocably.' She couldn't tell him that every time she'd thought of emailing him vivid memories of being piggy in the middle of her parents' disastrous marriage rolled in, and had her shutting down her good intentions. She'd been afraid to include Cooper in case her daughter had to grow up with the same pressures. Bad enough she knew next to nothing about good parenting, let alone adding Cooper to the mix. Tossing the hand grenade back at him, she asked, 'What could you have done these past months?'

'Supported you.'

How? Money? Marriage? They were in the army, unable to move to be with someone even if they wanted to. She shuddered. 'I don't need that from you.' Her friends would be there for her if—when—she asked. Her head spun. Happened a lot lately. The sun pounded her from above. Then the ground was rushing up to meet her.

'Hey, easy.' Strong arms wrapped around her, held her safe. Too safe. She liked these arms, remembered them holding her as they'd...made a baby.

Sophie struggled to free herself of Cooper. This was another reason she hadn't wanted him on the scene throughout her pregnancy. There'd been days when she'd gone into panic mode, wondering what on earth she was doing, going through with the pregnancy. But it wasn't like there'd been any alternative. She'd never have an abortion. But the thought of raising a child was frightening. On those bad days she'd been vulnerable, and if Cooper had been around she might've clung to him, relative stranger or not. There was something about him that could easily undermine her resolve to go it alone and that was dangerous—for the three of them.

Cooper kept his hand on her waist, and began walking her inside. 'Let's get out of this sun. It's debilitating.'

'It sure is.'

So are the spikes of heat in my blood brought on by your touch.

Her knees felt as firm as a piece of string, and her breathing was shallow.

Sex in hard boots.

Kelly's words from that fateful day ricocheted around her skull. There'd been an instant attraction back then, one she'd fully intended ignoring. Seemed bombs could blow up more than the earth and buildings and people.

All thoughts of staying clear of Cooper had gone AWOL when she'd leapt into his arms behind the accommodation block. Now he was with her, doing the same job to her internally as the sun was doing externally. Pregnancy had made her emotional, and this was just another example. Less than seven weeks to go and then she'd again be in charge of her hormones and everything they upset. Fingers crossed.

First there was a conversation to be had. How could she have got pregnant to a man she'd known a few hours and never seen again? A man she knew zilch about— being a sexy hunk didn't count. Except that's what had got her into this situation in the first place.

'Are you looking forward to becoming a mum?' Cooper asked as he sat down opposite her at a small table inside, after ordering their drinks and some sandwiches.

Sophie nodded slowly. 'I am now.' When she'd first seen the blue line on the stick she'd gone into denial. Being a mother had not been on her to-do list. That had ideas on it like climbing the Sydney Harbour Bridge, hiking in Greece, going to Iceland to see the Northern Lights. This…her hand touched her belly…was something she'd thought she'd consider later if and when she found the right man. Or if her biological clock switched on.

'But not in the beginning.' Cooper was studying her too intently for comfort. Looking for what? A history of madness or irresponsibility?

'I've never been inclined to settle down.' Too many things to see and do in this world to want to disappear behind a picket fence. Except that theory had slapped her across the face recently. Avoiding life was no longer an option. But Cooper wasn't going to take advantage of these uncertainties. 'Now I'm ready.' Despite the panic that occasionally overwhelmed her, she could say, *Bring it on*. She couldn't wait to meet her daughter.

Their daughter.

Eek, but this was awkward.

Thankfully her phone rang just then. Ignoring Cooper's scowl of disapproval, she answered. 'Yes, Corporal?'

'Captain, can you come back? One of the Unimogs went off a bank during the exercise and they're bringing the men in to be checked over.'

Instantly Sophie was on her feet. 'Any reports of serious casualties?'

At her question Cooper also stood up. 'I'm available if needed,' he said quietly.

'So far only two probable fractures have been reported, but we're to see all the personnel who were on board,' the corporal informed her. 'ETA is thirteen hundred hours.'

Less than an hour away. She had to head back and make ready for the soldiers. It was a lucky escape from the conversation she wasn't ready for. 'I'm on my way.' Sliding her phone into a pocket, she turned to Cooper. 'A Unimog tipped off a bank. So far we've got a couple of likely fractures. The rest of the crew is to be given the once-over. I've got the staff to cover it.'

'In other words, you don't need me.' Was that disappointment behind his question?

'I'd have thought after a long-haul flight you wouldn't want to work.'

'You were expecting me, weren't you?'

'Yes.' She turned to the guy behind the counter. 'Can you put my sandwich in a bag? I've got to go.'

'No problem, Sophie. How's that baby doing?'

'Like a gymnast training for the Olympics.' She grinned, then saw Cooper scowling again. Didn't he like her being friendly to the locals? Tough, he was out of luck. She did friendly. Plus guys like the one behind the counter had been a part of her life for the last few months. Cooper hadn't.

The baby kicked hard.

She sucked in a breath. Her hand automatically went to the spot and rubbed gently. It was as though the baby knew her dad was here and needed to remind Sophie he'd been a part of her life ever since Bamiyan.

Cooper was staring at her hand, his throat working hard. Awe filled his eyes and softened his mouth.

'You want to feel the movement?' she asked before she had put her brain in gear.

'No.'

Relief speared her, quickly followed by disappointment. Of course he didn't, stupid. 'Fine.' She turned away.

'Sophie? I'm still getting my head around all this.'

'Sure. I understand.'

I think.

She probably wasn't being fair. The guy would be tired from that flight squashed in the back of the transport plane with a load of other men. Throw in the shock of learning about the baby and he was allowed time to accept everything, wasn't he? 'Just trying to involve you a little bit.' She turned for the exit.

'Um, can I touch? Feel her?' The new look in his eyes held hope and excitement, and stopped short her sudden need to step away from him and run.

As if running was an option with a barrel sticking out from her stomach. 'Here.' On an indrawn breath she reached for his hand and placed it where her baby was kicking. She ignored the spike of warmth that stole up her arm from where she touched him, and the sense of rightness having his hand on her belly gave her. Because it wasn't right. Never would be. They didn't belong together and this was a very intimate moment. Even if they were standing in a café full of strangers.

When ignoring Cooper proved impossible she gave in and leaned closer, breathed in his scent. Hot male with a hint of musk. Her tongue lapped her lips. This was crazy. They'd spent less time together than most people had with their dentist and yet now they were having a child and her hormones were in a spin every time he came within breathing distance.

'Wow...' Awe drew out that single word and filled his eyes so that they glittered with amazement.

Danger.

The warning flashed into Sophie's brain.

He's not going to walk away and leave you to get on with having your baby. He's hooked. Whether he knows it or not.

Pushing at his hand, she stepped backwards. 'I need to get back to base.'

'I'm coming with you.' Cooper's tone told her not to argue. He changed his moods rapidly and often. Something to remember. Now all that amazement had gone; filed away, no doubt for him to take out at his leisure.

Which worried her. Yes, he was the father. Yes, she wanted him to be a part of their daughter's life. No, he was not welcome at the birth, or any midwife sessions beforehand. He was most definitely not going to take part in deciding where she'd live, or how many hours a week she'd work, or how to bring up her daughter. Those were her decisions to make.

But there was no avoiding the fact they were inextricably tied together for the rest of their lives.

'Can't you find something to entertain yourself in town for the rest of the afternoon?' she asked, even knowing his answer. Being crammed into the car together again made her throat dry and her head spin. Cooper frightened her. Simply by demanding his rights he could destroy her independence, which was her safe haven.

'I'm coming with you, Sophie.' He already had her door open and was waiting patiently for her to clamber in, an activity no longer done with ease now that she had an enormous stomach to squeeze behind the steering wheel. 'Maybe I should drive,' he said as he watched her awkward movements.

'No way,' she shouted, and grabbed the door to slam it shut. It was so tempting to throw the car into gear and race away, leaving him on the roadside. Childish, yes. Would it relieve some of the tension tightening her muscles? Absolutely.

Cooper must've seen something in her expression because he was around the car and sliding into the passenger seat even before the key was in the ignition. Worse, he grinned at her. 'Didn't know you had a temper.'

Which cranked her *temper* higher. 'There's a lot you don't know, Captain, and I intend keeping it that way.' The car jerked onto the road as she touched the accelerator.

A hand covered her thigh, squeezed lightly. 'Easy, Sophie. Let's take this one step at a time. First being to get back to base in one piece.'

Boy. Did he know how to wind her up or what? Her first reaction was to slam on the brakes and kick him out. Literally. Her second was to slam on the brakes and ask nicely if he'd mind getting out. Finally she wound down her window for much-needed air and drove carefully, and silently, back to work. But her teeth were clenched, and her jaw ached by the time she got there.

Why had she had sex with this man in the first place?

Sex in hard boots.

CHAPTER THREE

COOPER COULDN'T CONCENTRATE. On anything. Sophie. Baby. Both had stomped through his mind, destroying his renowned ease with most things.

She'd relented and made him part of the team to examine the men from the Unimog. He'd managed to be thorough and professional, but he was glad he'd been assigned the cases where the men said they were okay except for bruising. A matter of verification before signing them off that even he could manage while dealing with the bewilderment swamping him since Sophie's announcement about the baby.

'Get dressed, soldier,' Cooper told the musclebound specimen standing before him. 'You're in good shape.'

'Yes, Sir.' The guy might've answered him but his focus was on the woman on the other side of the room.

Sophie was busy, reading an X-ray plate of one of the less fortunate men's ribs and talking on the phone. She hung up. 'Three fractures on your right side, Corporal. With those, along with the torn ligaments in the same site, you're going to be very sore.'

Downplaying the pain earned her a grin. 'Yes, Ma'am.' He could've had his arm sawn off and he'd be happy as long as Sophie was dealing to him. It was no secret the soldiers adored her. Each and every one of them had eyes for no one else, even those in pain.

Cooper sighed. They weren't on their own. He struggled to keep his eyes away from her. She was gorgeous. Not only physically but in her style, her kindness to everyone without being overpowering, her quietness. The first time they'd been together he hadn't noticed any of these characteristics. There'd been too much going on with bombs and bullets and sex.

'Are you finished with patients, Captain Daniels?' Sophie had crossed the room to stand in front of him.

'The last soldier has gone. A few bruises to grizzle about is his lot.'

'Thank goodness we didn't get anything too serious, broken bones notwithstanding.' She was doing that belly-rubbing thing again.

'Are you aware how often you do that?' he asked thoughtlessly, and got a shy smile in return.

'Probably not. It's almost a habit.'

A cute, caring habit. 'I admit feeling the baby kick against my hand was…' A life-changing moment. Another one. The second in a matter of hours. Seemed anything to do with Sophie Ingram happened fast. Like that night in Bamiyan. Though that had made some kind of sense, given the attack and how they'd had to fight their own fears in order to help others so the moment they'd relaxed all hell had broken loose between them.

But the moment he'd seen Sophie today his world had tipped sideways. That was before he'd noticed her pregnancy. Everything he believed in as far as women and relationships went had been suspended while he'd struggled to get his head around the fact he was responsible for that bump Sophie carried so beautifully, if not a little awkwardly at times.

When she'd placed his hand on her belly and he'd felt his daughter kick, he'd known the baby was real and not just an idea to grapple with. Scary. What he hadn't counted on was the awe that had gripped him and the instant connection with the baby—and therefore with Sophie.

Forget scary. Try terrifying.

What was he going to do? Walk away? Man up? Find a middle line that worked for both of them? *The three of them*, growled a pesky voice in his head, reminding him he hadn't really got the hang of all this yet. He wouldn't be walking away. That much he did know. He wanted to. No point denying that. But he wouldn't.

'Captain Daniels?' A corporal stood beside Sophie. 'Lieutenant Colonel Shuker requests your presence.'

'Thank you, Corporal. Can you tell me where I'll find him?' Yay, someone to talk to who had nothing to do with his dilemma.

But as he followed the soldier across the parade ground his elation deflated quicker than it had risen. Alistair Shuker, aka 'List' to his mates, was going to ask him what his plans were for the future. He was going to wave that Australian Army contract under his nose and tease him with money and a soft posting.

'Coop, good to see you, man.' List punched him lightly on the shoulder. 'How was the flight?'

'Rough, hot and boring.' Cooper returned the punch and studied his friend. They'd been together on some hairy forays in joint exercises with their respective armies. List was a man a guy could rely on to get them out of a tight spot. He was also the only man who knew him well. They'd done a lot of talking in the deep of the night while waiting for situations to go down in Afghanistan. Too much. There was nothing List didn't know about him, and vice versa. Except that was wrong. There was one snippet of information List had no idea about. One Cooper wasn't about to share.

'That why you disappeared off base with our lovely doctor? Needed a cold drink? Or great company?' List was watching him so closely he had to be able to count his whiskers even though he'd shaved that morning.

Uh-oh. Did he know about the baby after all? As in who the father was? Had known before him? Cooper shivered. He didn't like the idea. Not one little bit. The baby had nothing to do with anyone else except him and Sophie. 'You're friends with Sophie?' And that idea made him squirm with something alien—jealousy. A nasty reaction he was ashamed to admit and yet found hard to squash. Why be jealous when he had no intention of settling down with any woman? Not even an auburn-haired, svelte beauty, who right now probably needed someone in her life to support her.

'Everyone's friends with Sophie. People adore her. No one wants to see her hurt.' The warning couldn't be louder—or clearer.

All the emotions of the day balled into anger and he took it out on List. 'Don't threaten me, *mate*. Whatever's going on in that head of yours is way off the mark, so shut up. If you haven't got anything better to say then I'm heading over to the mess where hopefully I'll get some peace and quiet.' And the very cold beer he'd missed out on at Harry's Place due to Sophie being called back. His blood was boiling as he spun around to head for the door.

'Coop, stop right there.' List wasn't quite pulling rank. The words were those of a commanding officer but the tone was that of a friend. Being a New Zealand officer didn't quite let Cooper walk away in a huff from an Australian counterpart.

As much as Cooper wanted to storm off, he knew his reaction wasn't only about his friend but a combination of everything that'd gone down since landing in Darwin. Stopping his retreat, he slowly turned round. 'You wanted to talk about me signing up with your lot?'

Keep off the taboo topic, mate.

He was subjected to a long and deep perusal before List finally shrugged and sat down. 'Yes.' He nodded at the vacant chair on the other side of his desk. 'You thought about it?'

Cooper elected to remain standing, still on edge. 'A lot.'

'And?'

'I admit to not knowing what I want to do. I'm sort over soldiering, and yet going back to Civvy Street seems too tame.' Restless didn't begin to describe him. There had to be a lot more out there waiting for him, but what? Something was missing in his life. That much he got. What, how, where and why were yet to be answered. A challenge of some sort might fix whatever it was that ailed him.

A baby had to be up there as one of the biggest challenges possible.

List leaned back in his chair and placed his feet on the desk. 'Sit down, man. It's me you're talking to.'

'Yeah, I know.' All too well. As quickly as it had risen, all the tension grabbing him evaporated. This was his best pal, the guy who knew far too much about him for him to be getting antsy. Cooper dropped onto the chair and propped his feet on the opposite end of the desk, rank forgotten for now. 'So how's life treating you?'

'Can't complain.' List grinned. 'Back on the mainland where it's relatively safe, lots of women hanging around, my folks just down the road.'

'I forgot you came from these parts.'

'Born and bred Northern Territory guy. Mum and dad still live in the house I grew up in.'

'I can't begin to imagine what that's like.' Cooper again felt a spurt of jealousy. What was wrong with him today? Never before had he thought other people, especially his pal, were better off than him. While his father was constantly on the move with work and women, never settling down with anyone for more than a year at most, Cooper felt he didn't have a home as such, but he'd got used to that. Dad always had his back and that meant a lot. He accepted that's how it was for him and that he was happier doing the same as his father than trying to be someone else. Stopping in one place with one woman for the rest of his life? He shivered. Not something he knew much about, and would probably screw up if he even tried.

Sophie sneaked into his head. Rubbing his palm where he'd felt the baby kick, he remembered the wonder that'd filled him at the thought *his* baby was in there. Not just a baby—his baby. What was he going to do now?

'You should try settling down some place,' List commented dryly. 'You never know. You might like owning a home, not a house. Having a family to come back to at the end of the day or a tour of duty.'

His house was just fine, thanks very much. 'Says the man who plays the field even harder than I do.' He'd ignore the barb List had delivered.

Or so he thought. 'Sure I do, but I'm looking, man. I want the wife and kids, the whole nine yards of snotty noses and nappies. The football in the back yard. The romantic nights under the stars when the kids are asleep in bed.'

Cooper rubbed his hands over his head. 'Thought I knew you. When did you get so staid?'

His pal laughed. 'When the plane landed here six months ago. I climbed down onto home turf and knew I was ready to settle down. I've had enough running around with the boys and not having anyone special to come home to after a particularly messy tour.'

'You're going to quit the army? And you're aiming to convince me to join up with your lot?'

'Don't put words in my mouth. I'm merely trying to get you to think things through clearly, make the right decisions with all the facts.'

There was that nudge again. This time like a bulldozer. List did know something about him and Sophie. He'd swear it. But he wasn't going to ask. A barrage of questions would follow. Questions he had yet to work out the answers to. 'Is there any other way?' he asked acerbically. Then shrugged. 'Up for a beer when you're done here?' Thinking could be highly overrated and right now he'd had more than his share of it. 'I could do with a distraction—and something cold and wet.'

And I do not want any innuendo about Sophie.

'Let's go. I'm not even meant to be here today, only came on so as I could give you a hard time.'

'Got my uses, then.' Cooper followed his mate out into the glaring sun, looking forward to catching up properly with him.

'How close are you to Sophie?' List tossed over his shoulder.

Cancel that. He should never have suggested a beer. 'Who says I am?' What had Sophie told List?

'No one. The fact that she was the first person you went to see on arrival speaks volumes. Usually it's me you're plaguing with your presence.'

Why hadn't he thought of that? 'There's no hiding anything from you, is there?'

List smirked. 'Don't forget it. One last thing and then I'll shut up.'

List didn't do shutting up very well, but what could he say? 'Go on.'

'I'd like to swap you onto the same flight out as Sophie's taking early next week. It's a long haul back to Auckland and I'd hate for something to happen and there be no medic to help.'

Worry lifted bumps on Cooper's skin. 'Is she having problems?' Please, anything but that.

'A couple of short bouts of sharp pain. She calls them some funny name, says they're false labour pains, but I don't know. Seems strange to me.'

The worry backed off. 'Braxton Hicks contractions. They're quite normal.' He could still leave on his planned flight.

'That's them. Normal, eh? Fair enough, but I'd still like you on that plane.'

'She'll be fine.'

And I'll be at home, getting on with my next career move.

'And if she's not? What if she goes into labour between here and NZ?'

There'd be people to help her, to deliver the baby and take care of them. 'I'll be on that flight.'

Stretching out on her bunk twenty-four hours later, Sophie put her hands over her stomach and stared up at the ceiling. The heat had drained the energy out of her once again.

Kick.

'You take your toll too, little one.' Little one. Soon

she'd have to decide on a name. There was a list in her drawer. Lots of names she liked but none that grabbed her. It wasn't as easy to choose as she'd have believed. A name was for life. She didn't want anything that could be shortened into an awful nickname, or something odd that might get her girl teased, but she didn't want plain and ordinary either. Her friends on base were constantly teasing her about her inability to make up her mind. Said it was a prime example of baby brain in someone who usually knew exactly what she wanted.

But then this whole pregnancy thing had been a brain mess. It shouldn't have happened in the first place, and would probably keep her celibate for a lot longer than she'd planned on.

Could just buy condoms by the ton.

Yep. That'd work.

Ha. She was only weeks away from becoming a mother. There wasn't going to be time for having fun with men. Junior here would need all her attention, and any spare time would be taken up with work. If she could find a part-time position after baby arrived. She had to. How else would they live? Babies didn't come free, and she wanted the best for hers. A cosy home—read a tiny but cheery flat. A loving mother—read one who'd never blame her daughter for holding her back from her career.

Somehow she'd find the balance between parenting and working, because one wouldn't happen without the other.

Knock, knock. 'Sophie?'

Cooper. The last person she wanted to see right now. But not acknowledging him mightn't work. He appeared to be the kind of man who'd walk right on in, and that would only make her look stupid. Struggling up off the bed, she reached to tug the door wide. 'Yes?'

Oh, but he looked good. More than good. Make that breathtaking. His white T-shirt accentuated his biceps and as for those pecs... Her cheeks reddened. They were out of this world. If she'd had to make a mistake then she'd made it with a seriously built guy. Her glance slid lower, took in the knee-length shorts that sat snugly on his slim hips.

'Sophie, can we spend some time together?'

'We worked in the same room all day.' She'd deliberately kept any conversation focused on patients or upcoming health programmes. Last night she'd seen him leave base with Alistair so had relaxed about eating in the mess, knowing he wouldn't suddenly appear at her side, full of awkward questions.

'I'd like to get to know you a little better,' he insisted.

Why so reasonable? At least she could argue with the angry version. 'It's hard to find privacy around here.' Did she really want to be alone with him when all she could think about was the outstanding features of that body his clothes did nothing to hide? A body she'd seen little of yet had known intimately.

'We could go somewhere there's air-conditioning,' he said with a tempting smile.

She made up her mind, hoping she wouldn't regret it. 'Air-con will get me every time. It's stuffy in here.' Learning more about Cooper couldn't hurt. As long as she kept it all in perspective and didn't start thinking they could have a future together. She hadn't forgotten his reputation as a playboy. Or her mum and dad's style of parenting. Which was what her baby would have if they got together. Very off-putting for her as well.

'I do have another idea. Want to go for a swim? I hear there's a nature park not far away that's safe from crocs. We could take a picnic.'

She knew exactly where he meant. 'You'd risk going that far in my car?' What would she use for a swimsuit?

Cooper swung some keys from his finger. 'Air con, remember?'

'Who have you stolen that off?'

'List.' She must've gaped at him because he explained, 'Alistair.'

'Of course.' Alistair would lend his vehicle to his mate.

Cooper jiggled the keys at her. 'Your choice. Swim or bar. Which is it to be?'

As her skin was moist with sweat due to the soaring temperatures and the additional weight she carried the idea of slipping into cold water was impossible to let pass. 'I'll change into an old shirt and some shorts.'

'Bring warmer clothes for later in case it gets chilly. I'll go get a couple of things and meet you back here in ten.'

The heat wouldn't cool down that much, and neither would she. Sophie watched him stride away, those long, muscular legs giving her heart palpitations. How could anyone be so perfect?

Aha, that's physically.

What about his personality? Couldn't be perfect as well. Probably not, but so far she hadn't found anything to make her dislike him or even be wary of him. Right now she didn't care. She was too busy enjoying the view.

Cooper waved over his shoulder at her without turning round. So he knew she was ogling him. Ego. He was so used to women falling all over him it would never occur otherwise.

Didn't help that she'd proven him right.

The water was cool and immediately brought down the heat that had plagued her all day. 'This is bliss.'

She was glad she'd come. Forget looking like a beached whale. For the first time in ages she was comfortable in the hot northern state. Auckland could be warm and muggy, but never did the temperatures reach the thirties. Which had to be a plus for when she got home.

'You're happy?' Water splashed over her as Cooper dropped down beside her.

'Very.' She sighed her pleasure.

'You're easily pleased.'

Sometimes. 'Where did you do your training?'

He went with the change of subject. 'Auckland. Qualified as a surgeon four years ago and signed up for a short stint with the army straight away. You?'

'Otago.' She'd been in a hurry to get away from home. Nothing to keep her there. 'I was four years behind you.'

'Why did you sign up for the military?'

'I love travelling and they were wanting surgeons for places I'd never been and was unlikely to visit on my own.' Travelling kept her focused and didn't allow time for the doubts and insecurities to creep in. If she didn't stay in one place for long she wasn't in danger of getting close to people.

'You wanted to see Afghanistan?'

'Why not?' It hadn't been her first pick but she'd signed up for an adventure. Not the army's fault she'd got more than she'd bargained for. 'Thank goodness it was only a twelve-month contract.' She shuddered as vivid memories of that attack in Bamiyan struck.

'Got more than you bargained for?'

'I still have nightmares about that bomb blast. Do you?'

'Often.' Cooper traced a finger over her chin. 'There are some good memories about what followed.'

Sophie's head jerked back. She had those memories too. But that had been then, while now was a whole new deal. 'I was incredibly naïve to think nothing would happen while I was there.'

I'm thinking bombs, not babies.

'I reckon every soldier who signs up is guilty of that. By the way, have you heard how Kelly's doing?'

'Really well, despite losing her leg.' They talked regularly. 'She's planning on returning to nursing on a part-time basis as soon as she gets the hang of her prosthesis. She's fallen in love with one of the medics who evacuated her to Darwin, and they've set up house together in Perth.'

'The strange twists of fate.'

Yeah. Look what fate had done for her. 'It's stopped me in my tracks, and made me reassess what's important. Before Bamiyan my life was all about surgery and travel. Now I've got someone else to think about.'

And I still have no idea what I'm doing.

'Are you going to continue working after the baby's born?'

'I'm hoping for part time at first.' The money she'd saved while in the army would see her through till the New Year if she was careful.

'You'll employ a nanny?'

She blew air over her lips. 'Not sure yet. I don't like that idea, but I do have to earn a living.'

Cooper pushed away and began swimming. His arms cut through the water, his strength pulling him along quickly and efficiently. What had she said? It was the truth. She didn't have a wealthy family to fall back on. She didn't have any sort of family to turn to really. Mum and Dad wouldn't want a bar of her and her baby, which was why she hadn't found the courage to tell them they were about to become grandparents. She couldn't face their scorn at having made the same mistake they had. But there was a difference. She wasn't getting married for the sake of her reputation, as her parents had done.

Sophie flipped onto her back to float on the current, but the bulge that was her belly poked up at the sky and she immediately dropped back onto her feet. Sinking until the water reached her chin she relaxed into the coolness and pushed aside all her doubts for another day. It was strange how that now she'd told Cooper about the baby everything else she'd been avoiding was filling her head. Finding somewhere to live, getting furniture, baby clothes and a bassinet. Then there was telling her parents about the mistake she'd made with Cooper. Time was running out and once she was home there would be no excuse for not sorting everything out. Including the doubts and fears that followed her into sleep every night.

'Can I see you when we get back to Auckland?' Cooper appeared from behind her.

She'd been so tied up in her own thoughts she hadn't heard him splashing through the water. 'I did say I wouldn't stop you from having a part in the baby's life.' Even with his now slightly longer hair plastered to his skull he looked good. Too darned good for her heart rate, which had risen too high in a blink.

'Just checking.'

'Cooper, if I say something like that I mean it and am not going to retract it.'

He nodded slowly. 'It's weird, being brought together over something so important with someone I know next to nothing about. Allow me the odd left-field question. I'm sure you've got plenty of your own.'

'Here's one.' But not so left field. Her T-shirt clung to her outline like a second, wrinkled skin, and left nothing to the imagination. 'Will you refrain from staring at me as I waddle out of the water and wrap a towel around my waist?' Except she didn't have a waist any more.

He should've laughed at that. He didn't. Instead, he put an arm around her and began walking them towards the water's edge. 'Don't talk like that. You're beautiful and your pregnancy makes you glow: it does not make you ugly or fat or ungainly. It suits you. Please, believe me.'

How could she not when he sounded so sincere? Looked at her like she *was* beautiful? Special even. Tears sprang to her eyes. 'You say the nicest things.'

Damn you.

But of course he did. He was a playboy. A charmer. But… She'd swear his words were genuine. Not meant just to stroke her ego and win him a few brownie points. She was vulnerable at the moment. Doing this on her own was bound to make her susceptible to whatever Cooper said. Wasn't it?

Actually, no, she didn't believe that. She was strong, and, despite baby hormones tearing into things, she was managing just fine—if she didn't think about everything that could go wrong before, during and after the birth. After would be a lifetime. A lifetime of hoping she got her role as a parent right, never hurt her girl, never let her down, loved her unconditionally. How could she do that when she'd never experienced it? One thing she knew for certain—she'd never needed a man to tell her she was beautiful before, and she wasn't starting now. She'd accept Cooper's compliment for what it was, and enjoy it. 'Thanks.'

'I mean every word.'

A warm glow that had nothing to do with the sun made her skin tingle. Could be that it might help, having him around occasionally. He'd lift her spirits on the down days.

Cooper flicked a blanket out over the grass and opened a chilly bag to produce cold water for her and a beer for him. 'We've got chicken and focaccia for dinner. Basic but the best I could find in that small grocery shop down the road from the base. I didn't want to waste time going into town. You might've changed your mind about coming out with me before I got back.'

'Once the idea of a swim was lodged in my mind nothing would've stopped me coming.'

'My fatal charm had nothing to do with it, then?' He grinned at her like he couldn't care less what she thought.

Grinning back, she said, 'Nope.' This easy banter between them was good, and fun, and helped her relax a little bit more. Wrapping her towel around her, she tucked it under her breasts and ignored the steady gaze Cooper directed at her. Ignored the urgent need cranking up in the pit of her belly, tightening muscles that hadn't had a workout for more than seven months. Sinking down onto the blanket, she stretched her legs out, leaned back on her elbows to look upward and tried to ignore how he was gazing at the baby bump with something like dread in his expression.

'It will all work out, Cooper.'

'You think?' Thankfully he shrugged into a shirt.

'I hope,' she said with a rueful smile, missing the view but hoping her internal heat would cool now.

'You have doubts?'

'Who doesn't at this stage?' He didn't need to know what hers were. He'd probably hightail it out of the country without a backward glance. Despite common sense and the self-preservation she usually relied on, she wanted to spend time with him.

Cooper threw her a curveball. 'What does it feel like to be carrying a baby?'

Where to start? 'Awkward. Cumbersome. Wonderful. Exciting. Frightening.' Ouch. Why tell him that? He'd have a multitude of questions, along with doubts about her ability to be a good mother.

Cooper parked his butt beside her and reached for one of her hands, wrapped it in his larger one, making her feel delicate. 'Tell me about frightening.'

Her heart lurched. She shouldn't have said that word but he had an uncanny knack of making her say things she never intended to. If only she had the strength to pull her hand free and forget the yearning his touch evoked. 'Oh, you know. Am I going to be a good mother? How will I handle the birth? All the usual things expectant mothers apparently think about.'

'Why wouldn't you be a great mum?' His thumb stroked the back of her hand.

This was the problem with knowing nothing about each other. She had to expose herself, her vulnerabilities as well as her needs and concerns. But not all of them, or with any depth. 'I didn't have great role models growing up.'

'That could be a benefit. You'll be determined to do better, not make whatever mistakes your parents made with you.' He sounded so sure of himself, so at ease with it all. And so right.

Which annoyed her. 'Easy to say if you've had the perfect upbringing.'

'Does that even happen?' he growled, and moved to put space between them, leaving her hand cold. Delving into the bag, he passed her some crisps. 'Here.'

Seemed like she'd touched a taboo subject. He'd wanted to know about her life, so he should be prepared to reciprocate with details about his. They'd come out for some time together and she didn't want to spoil it with an argument. Her annoyance backed off too easily as she munched on a handful of crisps. It wasn't often she got off base for some fun. Fun with a man she'd never quite got over, and knew would always hold a special place in her heart for giving her a child.

While devouring bulging triangles of focaccia and chicken, they talked about things that had nothing to do with the baby—army life, their medical careers, travel. For the first time since that blue line had appeared on the stick Sophie felt completely at ease and was just thinking she could do this every day for the rest of her time in Darwin when Cooper blew the evening apart.

'Sophie.' His voice was husky and thick. 'I've been thinking. Let's get married. I can support you if you want to be a full-time mum. That way I'd always be a part of our daughter's life and you wouldn't have to take all the responsibility. What do you think?'

CHAPTER FOUR

'MARRY YOU?' *BUT...* 'I can't.' *But...* Sophie spluttered water over her front. They didn't know each other. There was certainly no love between them. *But...*

Cooper looked startled. 'Can't? You're not already married?'

Sophie shoved awkwardly to her feet as hurt lanced her. 'How dare you? You think I'd have had sex with you if I was married? Even in the circumstances you believe I'd be unfaithful? Thanks a million, buster.' She was shouting and couldn't care less that people on the other side of the grove were staring. Cooper had handed her the biggest insult he could find. Then her stomach tightened, sending pains shooting in all directions. 'Ah.' She wrapped her arms around her belly and held her breath. This hurt, big time.

'You okay?' Cooper had risen to his feet too. 'Sophie, talk to me.'

Breathe. One. Two. Three. Another Braxton Hicks contraction. Fingers crossed. She wasn't ready for the real deal. Way too soon. The pain in her belly softened, backed off. But not the hurt Cooper had inflicted. She snapped her head up and glared at him. 'No, I'm *not* okay.'

'Easy.'

'That's all you ever say when things get heated. Easy. I'm telling you I am not going easy on you. Not after that bombshell you just delivered.'

'Which one?' His hands gripped his hips. Under his T-shirt his chest was rising and falling rapidly, like he'd run a marathon. But his gaze softened as it settled on her belly.

He was seriously disrupting all her carefully laid plans. No wonder she hadn't wanted him in on the pregnancy until after the birth. 'Both.'

'Tell me why we can't…' he flicked fingers in the air '…get married. It makes a lot of sense. We're having a child and she deserves a family to grow up in.'

'She'll have one. Mummy in one house, Daddy in another.' That sounded awful, but not as awful as Mummy and Daddy screaming that they hated each other and their daughter was the only reason they lived under the same roof. 'That's the way it's going to be. No argument.' Her lungs expelled air so fast her head spun.

Go away, Cooper.

'I don't get any say in this?' Cooper's voice was deceptively calm; that chest still moving too quickly being the giveaway to his real emotions.

Shaking her head at him, she said, 'About getting married, no.'

Why did that tug at her heart? Going solo wasn't how she'd ever envisioned raising a child, but that didn't mean she'd grab the first offer that came along. Sexy hunk making the offer or not. Sex in hard boots or not. Which made it difficult not to give in to Cooper when he turned those winning smiles on her. She fell for them every time, but so far, thank goodness, she hadn't made any major mistakes since he'd turned up on her patch yesterday.

'So we agree to live in the same city at least?' He ground out the question.

'We haven't agreed to anything yet,' she snapped back. Where had the usual calm, happy Sophie gone? 'I'm going home to Auckland. You say you might be stopping there, or you might be going back overseas with the army. Where would you want me living if you choose to do that, huh? I'm not following you around military bases.' As if.

Calm down, girl. This is not the way to solve the differences between us.

What was the right way? Seemed they got on just fine if they kept off the subject of their child, but the moment anything to do with her and her future arose they were at loggerheads. 'Cooper...' She tried for a reconciliatory tone. It wasn't easy. 'Thank you for asking me but I will not do this for our child's sake. That's no way to start a marriage. I am open to discussions on where I live and how to raise our daughter.'

How come he was suddenly talking marriage? Alistair had warned her in an offhand way about his friend's reputation of love 'em and leave 'em. Would he be faithful when there was no love between them? And, seriously, why should he be? Another reason to stick to her guns. 'Why get hitched at all?' she asked.

Uncertainty flickered through his eyes briefly and then he was in control again. 'It's the right thing to do.'

Oh, no, it's not. Believe me.

'No one gets married because they're having a baby any more.'

'Maybe they should. I'm thinking about our child here, and how it's going to affect her, living in a single-parent family.'

'It's not uncommon these days. Not by a long shot.'

If only she'd lived with one parent and visited the other she might be making a better job of her own life. Following through on his comment, she said, 'You don't really want to be married. Why should you? It would cramp your style.' When his mouth tightened she continued. 'We're all but strangers to each other. The worst possible grounds for settling down together, don't you think?'

He barked a laugh. 'To think the first time I propose I'm having to justify myself.' His fingers whitened as his grip tightened. There'd an interesting line of bruises on his hips later. 'What would make you reconsider your decision?'

'Nothing.' When he stared at her as though she'd hurt him deeply she relented. 'It's not about you. I was the only reason my parents married and I've paid for it all my life.'

The hurt dulled a little. 'That's sad.'

'It was downright cruel.' She bit on her bottom lip to prevent any more unnecessary words spilling out. She also held her breath in an attempt to hold back the tears that threatened. She never cried about her childhood. Never. The back of her hand came away from her face wet. Maybe it was time she did. Oh, sure. That would solve a whole heap of problems.

'It doesn't have to be like that between us and our girl.'

A sledgehammer might work better. 'Cooper. Listen to me. You haven't thought this through. Getting married will cramp your lifestyle so much you'll soon become frustrated and angry and want out. Then who pays? Our daughter for one.'

And me for another.

Her mouth dropped open.

Why would I care? It's not as though I love him. I mightn't have been able to forget him but that's because I'm carrying his child. I do not, could not love him.

'Sophie? You okay?' The man totally wrecking her day stood in front of her, concern plastered all over his face.

Blink. 'Yes.' Blink. *No.*

Sure, he's hot and gorgeous and even fun to be around when he's not talking about our futures, but live with him as his wife? Not likely, sunshine.

'You've gone pale.' He was studying her thoroughly. When her hand automatically rubbed her stomach his eyes dropped to watch. 'You're not having another pain?'

She shook her head. 'Let's go back to base. I'm tired.'

Annoyance replaced his concern, but he didn't argue, just began packing up their picnic. 'Fine.'

Being tired was quite normal these days for Sophie. But being bemused by the thought Cooper might mean something to her was new. How could he after so little time together? It didn't make sense but, then, none of this did. Admittedly she'd feel a little less irresponsible if she could believe she had some feelings for him. Getting pregnant by a complete stranger did not sit well when she knew how much pain an unwanted pregnancy caused those involved. Justifying it by acknowledging she might've felt something for him that night would lighten the guilt. Sometimes she wondered what she was going to say when her daughter asked about her father. Hardly going to build confidence in her when her mother told her it had been a brief encounter of the sexual kind that had carried no other meaning than to satisfy an urge brought on by a bomb exploding metres from them.

But if Cooper hung around and became a part of his girl's life then no explanations would be necessary. Would they?

The silence was thick enough to cut as Cooper drove back to the base. He was stunned at his offer of marriage.

Where had that come from? Getting married would be totally wrong. It went against everything he believed in. He'd never stay in a relationship for long, even one involving a marriage certificate. He was his father's son in that respect. *Unfair.* True. Dad had never left his wife, just all the women that had come afterwards. Mum had opted to leave them—by tying a noose around her neck and hanging herself from the garage rafter.

He shivered as the hated memory slapped him. Dad's hoarse shout coming from the garage. *Mandy, don't leave me.* Was that why his dad never settled for long? He'd often wondered but had never asked. Too much hurt to be raised if he did.

Yet none of that explained why the moment Sophie had turned him down he'd hurt bad. Really bad. No one had ever turned him down for anything quite so abruptly, and his proposal had been serious, a handing over of part of himself. Her reply had been a hot lance spearing him. He hadn't planned on asking her, hadn't given it much thought except to toss the idea aside as ludicrous. Still, the words had spilled out. Gratitude should be his response to Sophie's answer. It wasn't. 'Now what?'

'We swap contact details.'

He hadn't realised he'd spoken out loud. 'You know we're on the same military flight out of here on Monday?'

'I thought you were going tomorrow.' Was that dread in her voice?

Please, no. He didn't want her keeping him at a distance. 'List changed my arrangements.'

'You're telling me you didn't have any say in the matter? You're in different armies.'

'He can be bossy at times.' Now was not the time to tell Sophie that List was concerned about her, and it especially was not the moment to be saying he agreed. That

Braxton Hicks contraction had been sharp and hard, had turned her face white and her eyes wary. He wanted to be with her on the flight in case she had more or, worse, went into early labour. He did not want other men on that plane delivering their baby.

Sophie huffed something like a strangled laugh. 'You're not telling me anything new.' Then she gasped. 'He's not done that so I've got a doctor on hand? He's been nagging at me to stay here until after the birth.'

Bang on, Sophie girl. 'You got it.' But not all of it. He'd already figured that List was interfering, pushing them together as much as possible.

'Fingers crossed I won't be needing you. I'm sorry if Alistair has put you out.'

He wasn't exactly up to speed on delivering babies so couldn't argue with Sophie on that one. 'I prefer the arrangements anyway. No stopping in Sydney on that flight, just straight through to Whenuapai. Home sweet home.' Five days late meant less time getting his house sorted before taking up the temporary position at Auckland Hospital he'd signed up for while sorting out what he was really going to do.

'Have you got your own place?' she asked wistfully.

'A house in Parnell. My dad house-sat for me this trip.' And supposedly met the next great love of his life while there. Cooper's teeth slid back and forth, grinding hard. When was Dad going to learn that none of the women he thought he'd fallen in love with were right for him?

'I've got to make appointments to look at apartments to rent as soon as I get home.' She nibbled at a fingernail. 'I've never cared too much about where I lived before.'

But apparently now she did. That spoke volumes about her determination to do things right for her baby. 'Where will you go until you find somewhere suitable?'

He reached across and gently tugged her hand away from her mouth. 'Don't do that. You'll regret it in the morning.' Her nails were always immaculate, resplendent in shockingly bright shades that she'd changed twice in the time he'd been here. He preferred the red to yesterday's orange.

Sophie turned her head to stare out at the passing scenery. 'I could go to my parents'.'

Her lack of enthusiasm for that idea dripped off each word. Who could blame her? After her brief revelation about her childhood he certainly couldn't. 'They'll welcome you?'

'I guess.' Then she straightened up in her seat and turned to face him. 'Of course they will. It'd only be a temporary arrangement.'

An idea was slowly creeping into his mind. An idea that needed thinking through, required looking at from all angles before he spilled it out to Sophie. He wasn't going to blurt it out like he'd done with that marriage suggestion. Once was stupid, twice was really dumb.

But... 'You could stay with me. My house is big enough that we wouldn't be tripping over each other,' he blurted.

Damn it, Sophie. What have you done to me? I go and say the craziest things without any consideration to the consequences when I'm around you. I've never acted so impulsively in my life. Not since I was eight and told Dad's live-in girlfriend number two that I loved her and that I wanted her to stay with us for ever. That she could be my mother if she wanted.

Again silence reigned. Sophie hadn't answered and seemed to be intent on the passing scenery, dry and boring as it was. Might be for the best. Like his marriage offer—if she didn't say yes to moving in with him then he didn't have to worry about anything. Didn't have to consider that they'd be sharing his space, which wouldn't be straightforward given his reaction to her whenever they were together. She was easily the most tantalising woman he'd known. Even now his blood heated and they weren't exactly cosy with each other. His groin had been aching since arriving yesterday, and that had started before he'd set eyes on her. Anticipation had a lot to answer for. Yeah, he still wanted her, needed to make love with her again. Maybe then he'd get past this annoying niggle.

Because that's what she was to him. A persistent itch. To think he'd invited her to stay with him.

Sophie's carrying my baby.

Which gave him responsibilities, if nothing else. He'd stepped up and offered some solutions for the future, and she wasn't barrelling him over with her acceptances. Still, he had to help her in every way possible, whether she liked it or not. There were a lot of things he could do to make life easier for her as she settled into becoming a mother. Whether he liked it or not.

He'd spent his adult life playing the field with women, but he'd never been a brute or deliberately hurtful, and now he would not walk away from Sophie. Her point about a loveless marriage was valid, and in some ways he was thankful for her turning him down. It was all for the best. He wasn't the kind of guy who'd be able to live like a monk for the rest of his life, and if Sophie kept him at arm's length it could get tricky. It was doubtful that Sophie would want to stay clear of men either, but he doubted he'd be her first pick. She'd been hot for him that night in Bamiyan, had pretty much thrown herself at him. No denying he'd been ready and waiting to catch her, though. But here in Darwin she'd been a lot more circumspect around him.

Cooper pulled up outside the barracks and hauled on the handbrake. 'You've gone awfully quiet. You okay?'

'You keep knocking me sideways. First marriage, now the offer of staying with you. I never expected any of that. Thank you. Please don't think I'm ungrateful. I just happen to be a pig-headed woman who puts her independence before anything else. Except my baby, something I'm only just realising.' She finally smiled at him.

The warmth went straight to his heart, and any problems he might've thought up about sharing his home with her dissolved. 'I wouldn't take that away from you. I start at the hospital in a few days and won't be around the house very much anyway.'

Sophie shook her head at him. 'I intend finding my own place. Your home would always be yours. I wouldn't be able to change things or spread out all over the show as I'm exceptionally good at doing.' There was that smile again. 'Definitely not a tidy creature, me.'

'Don't write my suggestion off so quickly. You've got a few days before we fly out of here. Think about it.' Next he'd be begging. Did he want her living with him so badly? No. But the idea of her in a poky flat in some rank suburb was equally unbearable. She'd be comfortable in his place. He'd be able to get to know her and most likely get over the things about her that were bugging him. Living under the same roof wouldn't only show the good aspects of her character but the not-so-good ones, the things he'd struggle to put up with day in, day out. Likewise for Sophie about him.

'Cooper, you're warring with yourself, so how can I take what you say as the right thing to do? You may be trying to persuade me your way is right but you're not sure about it. It's there in your eyes every time you try to convince me you've got the perfect solution.'

Already she could read him. He found her a smile. 'Can you see that I don't give up easily when it's important to me?'

'Saw that seven months ago, pal.' She was laughing at him.

Cooper reached to draw her into his arms and held her against his chest where she fitted perfectly. His breath hitched at the back of his throat and for a moment he couldn't utter a word, so he just enjoyed the moment. What would she do if he kissed her? It would be a risk to find out. He didn't want her rejecting him completely. Not when they were having a baby.

Finally he managed, 'Crazy woman. I'm starting to really like you.' Liking her was okay. Anything stronger wouldn't work, but as that was as implausible as flying to Saturn he was safe.

'Now, there's a novel idea,' she quipped as she snuggled closer.

He swallowed hard and lowered his chin to the top of her head, breathed deep to absorb the scent of sunscreen and flowers, and relaxed against her. Felt her breasts rising and falling softly, not hard points pressing against him like last time he'd held her. Her short breaths against his shirt, her hands on his chest, everything about her made him feel complete. She took away some of the doubts that had been niggling him since he'd first seen that baby bump. Whatever the difficulties ahead, they'd manage, would sort out how to go about raising a child between them in less-than-perfect circumstances. He wasn't worried on that score. He also wasn't giving up trying to convince her to move into his house. Not yet. Though he should be. Because becoming a father still didn't sit easily with him. And having a woman on his patch permanently had him in a hot sweat of the worst kind. Yet—this was Sophie. The one woman he'd never forgotten; remembered her body as hot satin in his hands that night that had led to this situation.

Sophie pulled back, smoothed her already smooth shirt over her breasts. Then she locked her eyes on him and drew in a deep breath. 'I've got something to show you. Can you wait here?' It must be important, going by the way she held herself.

'Of course.' Glad of the distraction, he switched the ignition off and got out to open her door. Leaning back against the car, he watched her walk slowly into the building. Exhaustion tugged her shoulders downward and made her head droop. What was so important that she had to show him tonight? His mind came up blank, so he stopped trying to work it out and waited for her to return.

Then she was back, handing him a large envelope. 'This is yours to keep. If you want,' she added with uncertainty.

Which only intrigued him more. 'What is it?'

'Take a look. I kept a copy for you.'

He opened the tab and shook the contents out into his hand. One sheet of heavy paper. A photo. No, a scan. His mouth dried. His heart went into overdrive, sending his blood thudding around his body. His hand shook as he held the picture out to study. 'Our baby?' he croaked.

Sophie stepped closer. 'Yes. Look, there are her legs, and one arm. Isn't that amazing?'

He was incapable of speech. His chin jerked downward once, abruptly. Wow. His daughter. Amazing didn't begin to describe the overwhelming love for this tiny being flattening him. It filled his heart. It would be easier to chop his arm off than to walk away now. He was a goner. Over a baby. A baby he hadn't met yet. Who'd have thought?

'Gorgeous, huh?' An arm slid around his waist. Sophie. She must feel exactly as he did. Smitten.

He blinked as tears threatened to spill down his face. 'Yeah. Gorgeous.' And still downright terrifying. And so not what he'd wanted for his life, but he would not, could not give up now.

'Stop fighting it.' Sophie grinned up at him before stretching to place a soft kiss on his mouth. 'Goodnight, Cooper. Sleep well.' Then she walked inside, closing the door behind her.

He wasn't going to sleep. Not tonight. Staring at the scan, he shook his head at the enormity of what had befallen him. Yesterday he'd thought it'd take a long time to accept his upcoming fatherhood. He'd never factored in the love, the instant need to protect, the expectations of watching her grow up that were gripping him. He hadn't had a clue. Not one.

Sliding into the car, Cooper drove slowly across to the accommodation block he was staying in, barely taking his eyes off that photo long enough to see where he was going.

Sleep well, Sophie had said. Not likely. He was going to put the scan back in the envelope and store it safely in his bag, then he'd go for a run. Pound the road and try to settle the beating in his chest and find some reason for all the turmoil going on in his head.

CHAPTER FIVE

AFTER TAKING FOR ever to go to sleep, Sophie was woken by banging on her door and someone calling out. 'Captain, wake up. You're needed in the medical hut.'

Two-twenty in the morning. Must be urgent. 'Coming.' Rolling out of bed, she grimaced. Her back ached. Her head was full of cotton wool. And the baby was dancing nonstop. As for the thoughts about her baby's father that had followed her right into sleep, she was about ready to forget she'd ever met him if it meant some peace. The pillow beneath her hand was wet. Her cheeks below her eyes were puffy. She'd been crying? In her sleep? Never.

Shrugging into a shirt and pulling up her fatigue trousers, she opened the door. 'Hey, Simone, what's the problem?'

'Some of the guys have been in a brawl with civilians,' Simone told her. 'Down at McGregor's Bar.'

'So we've got drunks to contend with.' Great. 'Where did I put my boots?' She looked all around her room, came up empty-handed.

'Want me to look?' Simone grinned.

'Go ahead. Oh, no, there they are.' Feeling unsteady, she held onto the bed end as she leaned down to pull the offending boots out from under a chair.

Simone was at her elbow immediately. 'Are you all right?'

'Must've leapt out of bed too fast.'

'Captain Daniels is already at the unit, trying to quieten some of the noisier of the idiots.' The nurse was not known for her patience with soldiers who'd overindulged and got themselves into trouble.

'Who asked Coop—Captain Daniels to lend a hand?' That grin widened. 'Your friend Cooper?'

'That one.' Of course everyone on base would know she and Cooper had spent a few hours together.

'Seems he was out running when he came across the guys fighting with two locals outside the pub. Pulverising them was his summation. Something about the soldiers defending a young woman.'

Why was Cooper running in the middle of the night? Sophie shut her door and led the way outside. 'The police involved?'

'Our MPs and the state troopers. The troopers have taken the civilians to their hospital. We've got our morons to deal to.'

'Maybe not morons if they were looking out for a woman.' Any male who could go past a woman, or any one, in trouble wasn't worthy of being called a man. Unlike Cooper. Even now she could feel his body covering hers in that dirt as the air had exploded around them.

'Huh,' grunted Simone.

'Nothing too serious reported in the way of injuries, though we have a minor knife wound and a couple of black eyes,' Cooper informed Sophie the moment she stepped inside the medical unit and noted the four men waiting to be checked over. 'Noisy but not drunk,' he added.

Two MPs were trying to hold one of the men upright but he seemed determined not to use his legs for some reason.

'Wonderful,' she muttered.

I got up for this?

'I told Simone not to bother you but she wouldn't listen.' Cooper was peeved about something. Being ignored by her nurse probably. Well, Simone was never going to look at him twice. He was a male.

The noise level was rising. Standing to attention, she yelled in her best parade-ground voice, 'Soldiers, quiet.'

The room instantly became silent. Sheepish men in various states of disarray froze on the spot.

'Stand up straight. Including you.' She nodded at the man the MPs were holding. She didn't lower the decibels. Only one way to treat the soldiers when they were in this state, and that was to remind them who and what they were. Pointing to a table, she snapped, 'Form a line over there.'

'Want me to take the stab wound?' Cooper asked into the quiet.

Sophie nodded. 'All yours. Simone, who's next?'

Simone led a man across and pushed him onto a chair. 'Sergeant Dexter took a direct hit in the eye and another on the back of the head, Captain.'

Sergeants were supposed to prevent their men getting into trouble, not be in the thick of it. Unless he'd been trying to stop the fight. 'What happened, Sergeant?'

'Looking out for my men, Captain.' His mouth was a flat line.

'I meant your injuries.'

'Took a fist in the face, twice. Hit the back of my head on the kerb when I went down, ma'am.'

Sophie tilted the man's head forward and examined the wound at the back. The bleeding had stopped. 'I'm going to put some stitches in here.'

'Thank you, ma'am.'

'How's your vision? Any blurriness?'

He shook his head and winced. 'No, ma'am.'

This was not the time to be brave, but Sophie knew better than to say so. He had a reputation to uphold in front of his men. She held out a penlight torch. 'Hold this for me.'

His reaction was swift and firm.

'Good. Headache?'

'No.' Again he winced.

'Care to rethink your answer?' She stared at him for a long moment but got nothing back. His head would be thumping. Male pride could be plain stupid. 'Sergeant, you've taken a hard hit on your skull, which could've shaken your brain, resulting in a concussion.'

'I understand.'

She'd give him a concussion herself if he didn't start answering her questions honestly. Retrieving the torch, she shone it into the corner of his good eye. The man blinked rapidly. 'Sure there's no fogginess in your sight? Or your head?'

'I can see you clearly.'

Guess that was something. 'What about the other side of the room? Can you read the top line on the notice-board?'

One side of his mouth lifted in a wry smile. 'Staff rosters for August.'

She gave up. Being stubborn was something she understood all too well. 'I want you to come and see me the moment you feel any nausea, have blurred vision or a strong headache. Understand?' When he nodded, she continued. 'About this other eye…'

It was swollen shut. Not a lot she could do until the swelling went down. After cleaning his grazed cheek and forehead with disinfectant in case he got an infection, she picked up a needle and syringe. 'I'm giving you a local anaesthetic so I can suture the back of your head. Ready?'

The sergeant turned whiter. 'Yes.'

Within minutes she'd finished and was tugging her gloves off to toss in the bin. Then she unlocked the drugs cabinet and put a few antibiotic tablets in a bottle. 'Here you go. One every twelve hours until they're finished. And some analgesics.'

Reluctantly he took them, and quickly shoved them in his pocket. 'Thank you, ma'am.' And he was gone.

Shaking her head, she called, 'Who's next?'

'Bruised ribs and a punch to the gut,' Simone informed her as she nodded to a lance corporal to approach.

'I'll check those ribs,' Sophie said. He might need an X-ray. Pressing carefully over the reddened, swollen area, she judged the lad's reactions and with what she could feel decided he'd been lucky. 'Take it easy for the next couple days.'

Cooper was finishing up suturing a corporal's knife wound, and glanced up as Sophie approached. 'This man won't be holding a rifle for a few days. The knife went nearly through to the other side at one place.'

A commotion at the unit's door had Sophie whipping around to see what was going on. The room spun. Grabbing at the nearby table, she held on until her head returned to normal.

'Sophie? Captain Ingram?' Cooper was before her, reaching for her arms.

She stepped back on shaky legs. 'I'm fine, Captain.' There was no air in the room. Her feet were leaden. 'I'm fine,' she repeated more forcefully.

'I'll see what the racket is about.' His lips were tight and his eyes were shooting daggers in her direction.

Just then an MP and a soldier pushed inside, the sergeant she'd released held between them, his head lolling forward.

'Put him on the bed,' she ordered as she focused on work and not the pounding behind her eyes. 'What happened?'

Someone told her, 'He was halfway back to his quarters when he dropped. Out cold, he is.'

Cooper lifted the man's legs and helped manoeuvre him onto the bed. 'This the guy who hit his head on the kerb?' he asked her.

Nodding, she picked up the sergeant's arm to check his pulse. 'Concussion for sure. He was denying any symptoms, and I couldn't nail any, apart from his obvious headache. I want him sent into the city hospital for a scan. Simone?'

'Onto it,' was the reply.

Silly man. Why did he let pride get in the way of receiving the correct treatment? Even if she hadn't foreseen him losing consciousness she'd have been better prepared to treat his symptoms.

Cooper nudged her shoulder lightly with his. 'You did your best.'

'Pulse is low.' She raised the eyelid on the man's good eye. No one home.

'Respiration rate is low,' Cooper commented.

It felt good having him working beside her. 'He's coming round. Sergeant, can you hear me?'

The sergeant's eyes opened briefly.

Thank goodness. It was a start in the right direction. 'You blacked out. We're going to send you for a scan.' She spoke slowly and clearly.

He opened his eyes for a little longer.

'That knock on your head is more serious than I first

thought.' Not that she'd had much to go on. 'Has your headache got worse?'

He nodded once, then put his hand up to his mouth.

'Bucket,' Cooper called loudly.

Simone returned to say the ambulance was backing up to the door.

Since Cooper was dealing with her patient Sophie filled out a form for the hospital ED. 'Simone, I want you accompanying him after we've finished checking him over.'

'No problem.'

Fifteen minutes later the unit was quiet, empty of everyone except Sophie and Cooper, who was putting the kettle on to boil.

'Want a cup of tea? Or hot milk?' he asked.

Sinking onto a stool, she felt shattered. So not up to speed. The heat and her pregnancy were taking their toll. 'I made a mistake not insisting he tell me his symptoms.'

'I heard some of your conversation. He was never going to admit things in front of his men.' Cooper dropped teabags into two mugs. 'Tea it is.'

'I should've known to take him into another room.'

'He should've known to talk to you. Are you on parade at zero seven hundred?'

The thought made her feel even more tired. 'Yes.' Four more days to go. 'Never thought I'd say this but I'm looking forward to stopping work, and I haven't even been busy in here.' She glanced at the stack of notes from their earlier patients. 'Most of the time, at any rate.'

'You could ask to be stood down.'

She raised one eye brow at him in reply.

'I figured,' was Cooper's only comment.

While she drank her tea she cruised the internet for places to rent in Auckland.

'Can't that wait?' Cooper asked with his usual bluntness.

'The sooner I set up appointments the sooner I'll find somewhere and can get my mess sorted.'

'There is an alternative, Sophie. You can bunk down at my place for a few days if you're still determined to find your own place.' He was frustrated with her. It showed in his tone and the tightness of the hand holding his mug.

It was more than she needed right now. Shutting down the laptop, she took her tea and headed for the door. 'See you after parade.'

'Attention,' shouted the sergeant leading the parade.

Boots slapped the tarmac as rows of soldiers stood straighter than straight.

Cooper was to the side of the ground, standing at attention but not part of any unit. Sophie was at the front of the medical corps, eyes to the front. She hadn't said a word to him over a hurried breakfast in the canteen. Exhaustion had rippled off her like heat waves in the desert. Her fatigues needed straightening and her hair could do with being tied tighter but far be it for him to point that out. Someone on the parade ground would do it and cop her wrath for their effort.

List stood at the front, ready to talk to the troops. He glanced Cooper's way, and then at Sophie. A frown appeared on his brow, and he dipped his head at Sophie.

What? Cooper's gaze returned to her. She seemed to be struggling to stay upright, swaying on her feet. Her chin was pushed forward as though she was willing herself to stand erect. As he made to step out and head to her she slumped in a heap.

Cooper ran. 'Sophie.' Instantly dropping to his knees, he reached for her, felt for a pulse. It was slow but at least it was there.

Simone had been standing two away and was as quick to reach her as he'd been. 'Sophie, what's happening? Did you faint?'

'Let's get you inside out of this heat. I need to check your BP.' Low blood pressure would explain what had happened. Might explain a few incidents where she'd appeared to lose focus briefly. Like when she'd lost her balance outside Harry's on the day he'd arrived. It made Cooper think he was on the right track.

Sophie flopped against him, blinking and trying to rub her head. 'What happened?'

Cooper held her gently and looked up to growl at the man next in line. 'Get a stretcher. Now.'

'Yes, sir.'

'Sophie, can you hear me?'

'Yes. I'm fine.'

'You're not fine. When did you last have your BP checked?'

Simone answered for her. 'I did it two weeks ago. It was normal.'

'Two weeks and you haven't had a reading since?' No wonder he needed to keep an eye on her. She wasn't doing a good job of looking after herself. 'What about blood sugar?'

'Shouldn't we talk about this inside?' Simone glared at him before tilting her head towards nearby troops. 'Sir.'

List appeared, saving him having to answer. Simone was right. 'Captain Ingram? Are you all right?'

She nodded. 'I'm fine. Please continue with the parade. With your permission, Sir, I'll go to the medical unit.'

'Permission granted,' List snapped. Then he leaned

down and said quietly, 'Take the morning off, Sophie. You've got to look after yourself.'

Whatever she'd been about to say was forgotten, instead her eyes widening as the soldier arrived with a stretcher. 'That had better not be for me. I'll walk, thank you very much.' Instantly she struggled to stand up.

Cooper put a restraining hand on her arm. 'No, you don't. You've just taken a tumble, and before you say a word, think about the baby.'

The look she sent him should've frozen him to the spot for eternity. At least she sank back down to the ground and muttered, 'All right.'

Cooper sighed. She had landed on her knees and tipped forward but had gone sideways just before her baby tummy could hit the ground. Still, he wanted to check her over, make sure Sophie and the baby were fine. And find the cause of these light-headed incidents she was having. This definitely wasn't the first, and he doubted it'd be the last until they knew more.

Above them List pressed his lips together, no doubt smothering a smile at Sophie's reluctant concession to Cooper's order. 'Right, soldiers.' He nodded to Simone and the soldier who'd brought the stretcher. 'Take Captain Ingram inside.'

Cooper felt for the two as they reached down to lift the stretcher once Sophie had slid across onto it. She had plenty more of those icy glares and wasn't worried about sharing them around.

List leaned close to murmur, 'Go with her. Make sure she's all right.' Then he marched back to the front of the parade.

Cooper muttered, 'Try and stop me, mate,' and strode after the stretcher bearers. Now the fun would really start.

Except Sophie surprised him. 'I'm feeling stupid.

There've been a few times when I've experienced light-headedness but I put it down to the heat and lack of sleep. What sort of doctor does that make me? It's not a good start to motherhood, is it?' Her eyes lifted to him, imploring him to go easy on her.

She didn't have to ask. He wasn't about to rip into her, only wanted to make sure she and baby were safe. The sadness and worry blinking out of those green eyes hit him hard. She wasn't as confident as she made out. Yet she insisted on going it alone. Not on his watch she wasn't. Not now, not ever. They were in this together. Even if not living under the same roof, he'd make absolutely certain he was always there for her. 'I heard doctors usually made the worst mothers, always thinking of all the horrific things that can go wrong. It's cool that you're not like that.'

Suspicion clouded her eyes. 'You don't think I'm too casual?'

'No, Sophie, I don't. You look fit and healthy. I haven't seen you do anything you shouldn't, like go jogging in the heat or drink alcohol. Our baby is in perfect hands.'

She gasped.

So did Simone.

Cooper slapped a hand on his forehead. 'Sorry.' He'd forgotten they weren't alone. 'I shouldn't have said that.'

Simone was smiling as she looked at Sophie. 'Don't worry. I know nothing.' Then she leaned over to give Sophie a hug. 'Knew you were more than friends.'

Sophie looked surprised. 'Actually, we're not. Not really.'

Time he was out of there. Partaking in a discussion with the hard-nosed sergeant about their relationship was not happening. 'I'll get the sphygmomanometer and phlebotomy kit.' And some air that wasn't laced with Sophie scent and filled with words he wanted to refute. They weren't friends, not in the true sense of the word, yet he wanted to be. More than anything. He wanted to be able to spend time with Sophie and say anything he liked, help her without wondering how she'd interpret his actions. At the moment they were leery of each other, and he was past putting up with that.

Neither woman tried to stop him going, but when he returned with the equipment needed to take a BP reading and some bloods to send to the lab Sophie was on her own, looking glum.

'Hey, you're doing fine.' Cooper ran a hand over her shoulder.

Tears glittered out of the eyes she raised to him. 'You think? I'm feeling so hopeless.'

Pressure built in his chest, and the need to be there for her expanded further. This wasn't just about his responsibility towards her and the baby. This was about that friendship they didn't have yet. 'There's not a hopeless bone in your body.'

'I'd say thanks but, really, you don't know me at all.'

'I know you're stubborn, kind, fun, sexy...' Now, why had he added that? Friends and sex were a mismatch. Except sex had led to them being tied together with a child. Now the friendship had to start. Which meant sex was off the list. 'Did I mention annoying and adorable?'

Now she looked disappointed. 'It's been said before: you're a charmer.'

He'd meant every word and hadn't been trying to get his own way about anything. He'd been wanting to make her relax and stop fretting about how she was coping. That wasn't good for her or the infant. 'Let's find out what's going on.' He held up the BP cuff.

Holding out her arm, she told him, 'You can't do a glucose test. I ate breakfast.'

'We'll start with a non-fasting and if that's even slightly raised we'll follow up with a fasting blood tomorrow.' No more stalling.

Sophie sagged, her chin hitting her sternum. 'Get on with it.' There was no strength in her words, just defeat.

That unsettled him further. He preferred the fighting, stubborn Sophie to this one. Watching the monitor until it beeped, he felt out of his depth. Sure, reading BPs and taking bloods was basic medicine, but cheering up his patient when he was so involved was more complicated than he'd expected. And he was about to add to her gloom. 'BP's too low.'

'I figured.' She shook her head. 'Gestational diabetes is looking more likely by the minute.'

'They don't necessarily go hand in hand,' he argued.

'I know.' She held her arm out again and watched quietly while he drew some blood.

Three hours later Cooper found Sophie munching on a healthy salad and reading files in her office. 'Your glucose is a little too high.'

'So tomorrow I'd do a glucose tolerance test. Can we start early? I get hungry all the time.'

'I'll take the fasting sample twelve hours after your dinner tonight.' And fingers crossed the final results would be normal.

They weren't. 'I've got gestational diabetes.' Sophie put the phone down the following afternoon and stared at Cooper.

'I was hoping otherwise.' But he wasn't surprised at the result.

'You and me both. Guess I'm off the ice cream.'

'They can relax in the canteen. There'll be enough left to go round everyone from now on.'

Her smile was tired. 'Home is looking better and better all the time.'

Home meant a lot to do, if what he'd gleaned from their conversations was true. 'You made those appointments for viewing properties yet?'

'I've got four lined up the day after we touch down.'

Of course she had. Tired she may be, inefficient she wasn't. 'Anything that really excites you?' Would it be wrong to hope not? He might've got off the hook when she'd turned down his offer to live with him for a while, but more and more the need to be there with her for these weeks leading up to the birth was dominating his thoughts. She needed pampering. He was going to pamper Sophie? Yep, and why not?

'Yes, all of them,' she replied in the flattest voice he'd heard in a long time.

'Better than nothing you like.'

She didn't answer.

CHAPTER SIX

THE TEMPERATURES FINALLY *EASED*, for which Sophie was grateful. The heat had been all-consuming. By the time she boarded the air force plane bound for home she was almost sorry to be leaving.

'Thanks for everything you've done for me,' she told Alistair as she stepped up to kiss his cheek. 'You've been a pal.'

He wrapped her in a bear hug. 'Keep me posted on junior, and take care of yourself. I want a photo as soon as she arrives.'

'You'll get one.'

She was surprised to see his eyes glistening before he turned away to Cooper and said, 'Hey, man.'

Sophie watched them do the man hug and thump on the back thing, and almost laughed out loud. Guys. These two were close. She'd been a part of their camaraderie over the past few days, going with them to the pub for dinner twice. Theirs was an easy friendship grown out of hard times during active duty. She'd have liked that with someone. The closest friend she'd made in the army was Kelly, and she'd missed her every day since she'd been evacuated from Bamiyan.

'Come on, let's get on board the tin can.' Cooper took her elbow.

Sophie promptly pulled free. 'I'm not an invalid,' she said, but there was no annoyance in her words. She seemed to have run out of steam since her collapse on parade. Learning about the diabetes had knocked her sideways too, and made her ultra-careful about everything she ate.

'But you are proud.' Cooper grinned. 'Don't want anyone to see you being helped up that ramp, do you?'

She glanced across the shimmering tarmac to the plane. 'It's not Everest.' Not quite. When she got home she was not going to go for power walks ever again. Neither would she do press-ups or sit-ups or take up running once her baby was born. She was so over exercise. Though she did quite like her sculpted figure—if it was still there.

The aircraft interior was stifling. Sweat prickled her back instantly. 'Can you leave the ramp open on the flight?' she asked the young girl overseeing the last crates being loaded.

'No, Captain. That would be dangerous.'

'Fair enough.' She laughed and turned away from the serious face staring at her as though she was crazy.

Cooper led the way to two empty bucket seats. 'These'll do. I'll stow our rucksacks.'

Kick. Laying her hand on the spot, she rubbed. *Kick. We're going home, sweetheart.*

Home. A foreign word in her vocabulary. Home was apparently where the heart was. So whatever flat or apartment she rented, her heart would be there for her baby. She hadn't experienced making a home for herself, had usually rented a room in a house filled with colleagues and got on with working until the next trip. As for furniture and kitchen utensils, there was a lot of shopping coming up.

It wasn't easy lowering her butt all the way down to the seat almost on the floor.

'Hey.' Cooper was there, holding her elbow to prevent her from sprawling on her face.

'Thanks.' *Kick, kick.* 'I think little miss is aware we're off on an adventure. She's not letting me forget her.' As long as she didn't decide to make her grand entrance in mid-air. Shoving aside that fear, she asked herself if that would make her daughter an Australian or a Kiwi.

'What's causing that confused look on your face?' Cooper asked.

'When did you last deliver a baby?' Why had she asked? It wasn't what she'd been thinking at all, and she didn't really want to know the answer if Cooper hadn't delivered for a long time.

'A while ago.' He still sounded confident, but he'd been a surgeon for four years and surgeons always sounded confident.

'Define a while.'

'Sophie, are you having pains? We can get off now, but you'll have to be quick. We're due to take off in five.' He started to get out of his seat.

'Easy,' she gave back to him. 'Just passing the time with inane conversation.' But all her fingers were crossed. Having a baby on the plane, surrounded with air force personnel, was not her idea of fun. Probably wasn't Cooper's either, she realised as she shifted her butt to get comfortable.

Behave, little one.

Cooper held his breath all the way across Australia and the Tasman Sea, not letting it out until the west coast of New Zealand came into sight. Even if the ridiculous happened and Sophie started labour now they'd be on the ground within a very short time and there'd an ambulance and midwives and a hospital in case their baby needed special attention.

But even as those thoughts zipped through his head he couldn't help wondering what it would be like to be there when his daughter was delivered. He crossed his fingers he wasn't tempting fate. Sophie would hate to have her baby thirty thousand feet up in the air surrounded with people she'd never met before. She'd also intimated she wasn't having him anywhere close during the birth. Somehow he had to persuade her to change her mind.

Shock jerked him. Being at the birth would be very intimate. She'd told him a friend was planning on being there for her. That irked. He should be there. He'd got her pregnant, hadn't denied his role, so surely he could see it through to the end? The more Cooper thought about it the more he knew he had to be at the birth. Would it make her more comfortable with his presence if he promised to stay at the top end of the bed? He'd hold her hands and give her water, wipe her brow. Yeah, right. He'd never make a good nurse. But this was Sophie. A woman he was beginning to treasure: to care for as a special friend.

Friends didn't have the kind of hot sex he'd been imagining with Sophie every night in his room at Darwin.

'You'd finally relaxed, and now you're all tense again. What's up? Are we nearly home?' Sophie mumbled against his chest, where she'd been sleeping for the last couple of hours.

'There's land beneath us.' His arm had gone numb ages ago, but he hadn't moved in case he woke her. Those grey smudges under her eyes had been a dead giveaway. She was exhausted. Which meant she was in no shape to take a taxi home to her parents' and deal with explaining her situation. As far as he knew, they weren't expecting her, which could add to her problems, given there wasn't a strong bond between them all. Neither did they know they were about to become grandparents.

Nor did his father. Cooper was saving that for when they got together over a beer and played catch up. The old man would be okay with it. Might even be ecstatic. Then again he might roar with laughter and ask what Cooper had been thinking to get a woman pregnant. The straight answer was there hadn't been any thinking going on at the time.

Sophie sat up and stretched her legs in front of her. 'You heading for your house as soon as you're through quarantine?'

'That's the plan. What about you?'

'I'm staying on the base for the night.'

No way. What if she went into labour? She'd be alone, no friends, no midwife that she'd got to know. 'Why?'

'Easier. I'll head into the city for those appointments tomorrow and decide what I'm doing after that. Probably visit Mum and Dad, suss out their reaction.'

Cooper was shaking his head at her. 'You're coming home with me.'

'No, I'm not.' But there was no substance to her words, and hope had briefly flicked through her eyes.

'No argument. It's a done deal. One night, if that's all you want. Then you can sort things out and decide what you're doing. But today, after this long, uncomfortable flight, you need a hot shower and a decent meal and then a good night's uninterrupted sleep. Something that's not guaranteed on base.' Now he was sounding condescending. But he cared, all right? Someone needed to be looking out for Sophie, and at the moment he was the only person on hand.

'Put it like that and I'm finding it hard to turn you

down. One night only, right? That's the deal. I'll be out of your hair tomorrow.'

'If that's what you want.' It was for the best. They couldn't live under the same roof permanently. How could he bring a woman home knowing Sophie slept down the hall? If he wanted to, that was. Huh? Since when didn't he bring females home?

You haven't even looked at another woman since landing in Darwin and seeking out Sophie.

Get real. Sex had been non-existent since Sophie. Not even a casual hook-up. Opportunities had been endless. It had been his own interest that had been lacking. Captain Ingram had spoiled him for other women.

But that didn't mean he was making Sophie the centre of his attention. She might be gorgeous and fun, and pregnant with his child, but she wasn't the love of his life. Would never be. No one would. He enjoyed, preferred, being single and he wasn't prepared to give that up. Not even for Sophie and his child? Especially for them. They had the power to hold him down. Every decision he made would be tempered with what was best for them. While that wasn't so bad, his unreliability as a father and partner was.

He had a lot to be grateful to Sophie for. Turning him down had shocked him but she was right. They wouldn't be able to sustain an enjoyable relationship, platonic or otherwise, under the same roof for ever. It would certainly be unfair on their daughter.

His mother had opted to desert him by taking her own life, and while that was different it had set him to becoming independent, and he'd started closing his heart to loving with abandon. He and Dad had been lost without his mother, and he wasn't prepared to go through that again with anyone else, or inflict a similar loss on someone.

So thank you, Sophie, for being strong and turning me down.

The woman putting him through the wringer these days flicked him a tired smile. 'You sure there'll be hot water? Your dad won't have forgotten to leave it on?'

'If he has we'll pay him a visit.' Cooper dropped an arm over her shoulders and tucked her close. 'Everything will be just fine. You'll see.'

'I'm looking forward to it.'

He wasn't sure what she was looking forward to, but he was happy to be taking her to his place for the night. It felt kind of right. She belonged in his life now, she and the baby. Just how much had yet to be debated. But he didn't want them there as the complete family he'd never had.

Or did he? Cooper shivered. It wouldn't work, went against everything he'd believed about himself.

Sophie stretched and rubbed her aching back as she waited for the kettle to boil in Cooper's kitchen. Yesterday's flight, sitting in that seat that had done nothing to hold her properly, had taken its toll. As for sleeping through the night in cooler temperatures? Forget it. She'd tossed and turned for hours, sleeping fitfully when her eyes had finally closed.

Kick.

'Hey, little one. You didn't get much sleep either, did you?' She rubbed her belly. At least they were home. Her daughter would be born a Kiwi.

'I like it when you do that.'

She turned to find Cooper leaning against the door jamb, his hair a ruffled mess and stubble darkening his jaw. Now her stomach tightened for reasons other than her baby pushing on it. She still hadn't been able to get past the fact she found Cooper sexy and desirable. If only she wasn't so enormous she might contemplate leaping on him and having wild sex again.

Whoa. What was she thinking? Gripping the bench, she held on and waited for that dumb idea to disappear.

'You all right?' Cooper was right there, his hand on her upper arm, his eyes full of concern.

No, not at all. What would he think if he knew what had been going through her mind? Not once over the past few days had she seen desire or lust for her in his face. Which told her exactly what she needed to know, and must hold onto—he wasn't interested in her except as the concerned father of the baby she was carrying. 'Couldn't be better,' she lied, pulling away.

Cooper's pewter eyes locked on her. 'Really?' When she said nothing, he added, 'I don't think so.'

'I'm not going into labour if that's what you're thinking.'

'I wasn't. There was something in your eyes that makes me wonder what's going on in that sharp mind of yours.'

Wonder all you like.

But her cheeks were heating, giving her away. 'I'll have a shower.'

'What time's your first viewing appointment?' Cooper was still watching her closely.

All her skin was hot, not only on her face. There was an ache deep down, sending her blood racing and her heart thudding too loudly. He must be able to hear that. Aiming for the door, she threw over her shoulder, 'Ten o'clock in Newmarket.' Just up the road, but as it was bucketing down outside she wouldn't be walking.

'I'll be ready.'

That stopped her in her tracks. 'No need for you to come. I've ordered a taxi.'

Irritation tightened his usually tempting mouth. 'Cancel it.'

'I'm not in the army now.'

At least not where you can order me around.

'I'll drive you to all your appointments.' When she scowled at him he added, 'I've got nothing else on this morning.'

'Thought you were going to see your father and then check in with the hospital.'

He shrugged. 'Nothing that can't wait.'

Slapping her hands on her waist, or where her waist used to be, she growled, 'This is why I couldn't live here. You're so bossy and think you should have the upper hand all the time. Is this how you act when your charm doesn't work?'

He didn't say a word.

Which goaded her into saying, 'You think I can't cope? That I'm not up to looking out for myself? Next you'll be saying I can't raise my daughter on my own.'

Cooper was in front of her, in her face, instantly. 'Our daughter.'

True. But, 'Nothing's changed, Cooper. I am looking for an apartment to move into the moment it's available. I will not live with you for any longer than necessary.'

'So you're not moving in with your parents at the end of the day?'

She'd walked into that one. Losing her temper had been a mistake. 'Excuse me.' She stepped around him, careful not to let her stomach brush against him. She didn't trust her body not to get in a lather even when she was angry at him.

'Don't forget to cancel that taxi.'

Plenty of words spilled into her mind, but somehow she managed to hold onto them. Silence was best. Sometimes.

* * *

Sophie turned to the letting agent. 'How soon can I move in?' Judging by the stacks of packed cartons the current tenants were already on the move.

'A week from tomorrow.'

Her heart sank. A week living with Cooper. Or having to front up and ask her parents if she could stay with them. They'd say yes. That wasn't the issue. Being told over and over what a fool she'd turned out to be was. She hadn't learned anything from them, they'd say. Well, yes, she had. She wasn't getting married for the sake of it. A loveless marriage was never in her plans. But, then, neither had been having a baby. 'I'll take it.'

'You can't,' Cooper snapped from across the dog-kennel-sized lounge.

'Of course I can.' But she understood the shock on his face. The apartment was tiny, dark and in a less-than-desirable suburb. She was tired, and fed up with looking at places. 'It's available weeks sooner than the others I've looked at.' And it was affordable. She found a smile for the agent. 'Shall we do the paperwork?'

'I need a bond and a deposit on the first fortnight to hold it for you.' The woman dug through her bag for a key. 'I'll get the forms from my car.'

'Not a problem.' Tick. One job on her long list sorted. Tomorrow she'd start looking for furniture. Or should she buy a car first? Then she'd be independent of Cooper. She delved into her handbag for a credit card. An appointment with her new midwife came before anything else.

'Can we talk about this before you sign up?' Cooper parked his tidy backside against the bench next to her.

'No.' Why wasn't she feeling happy to have found somewhere to live? Probably something to do with it being an unexciting place. But she had to suck it up and make the most of everything. She was planning on staying put for the next year at least, and starting out miserable wouldn't be clever.

'Sophie. Are you sure? Can't we look at more places tomorrow?'

'There aren't any others. I went through the agencies' lists again this morning.' There'd been two she'd nearly asked to see but what would be the point? They were out of her price bracket and wandering around them would only increase her frustration level. *That* did not need any help. Not when she had Cooper driving her mad with need at the least convenient moments.

He didn't bother to hide his impatience. 'All right. What's wrong with the first one we saw?'

The steep rent. 'I didn't like it.' The large, sunny rooms, the modern kitchen, the small yard out the back, and the easy drive to the hospital once she went back to work: all added up to a perfect package. If she had loads in the bank.

'Sometimes I don't understand you.'

Neither do I.

'You're not meant to. Anyway, I'd swear I heard a sigh of relief when I turned it down.'

Guilt flushed his cheeks a light shade of pink. 'Even so, I'd prefer you there than here, if you still insist on finding your own place.'

So *that's* what all the less-than-helpful comments and questions at each apartment she'd viewed had been about. He'd been trying to deflect her from renting a property. Should've known. 'I get it that you want to help me—' *in ways that suit you and not me* '—and you can. By backing my decisions. If I get it wrong I'll even agree to you laughing and giving me some stick.' Lifting up onto her toes, she brushed a kiss across his mouth. 'Thank you for caring.' Whatever had precipitated that move she instantly regretted it while wanting more. Wanted to seal her lips on Cooper's, to savour him, breathe him in. To shut him up. To get a taste of what she'd known that wild night in Bamiyan.

Warning. Danger. This is Cooper.

She jerked backwards.

Hard, hot hands caught her around her middle, pulled her hungry body close to that chest she'd been ogling on and off all morning. Had he noticed? Did he understand she still wanted him? Even in her balloon-sized, less than desirable shape?

Stop with the questions. Make the most of being sprawled against him.

Good idea.

'Don't you ever forget I do care about you.' And then his mouth covered hers, possessed hers. Cooper took charge. As his tongue slid inside her mouth, the sensations caused by that hot thrust sent her mind into orbit so that all she was aware of was Cooper, holding onto him.

That hint of the outdoors that was his trademark scent. His full, masculine mouth. His firm muscles pressing against her softer ones. His erection pushing into her belly. Gulp. His erection. She moved against him, the long, hard length causing her lower muscles to contract with tension, with need, with memory.

'Oh, excuse me.' The woman was back.

Sophie leapt out of Cooper's arms, but he quickly caught her and held her in front of him. Hiding his reaction to her? Her face was flushed and no doubt her eyes would be slumberous with desire. Great. Now she'd probably have to find a new rental agent. 'S-sorry. We... It's just...' None of the woman's business.

'I understand,' the agent said, glancing at Cooper.

Any woman would, Sophie thought as she held out a shaking hand to take the forms from the amused woman. 'Let me fill these in and we can all get on our way.'

Before you decide I can't have the place.

'It's not too late to change your mind,' Cooper growled beside her ear, lifting the skin on the side of her neck in a delicious, tingling sensation.

It wasn't only her skin having a meltdown. All parts south of her baby bump were in disarray, hot and tight. Ready, willing and wanting. Why had she kissed Cooper? Why wouldn't she? It'd been a chaste touching of her lips on his, not a hot, deep kiss. No, not until he'd taken over and turned it into something off the radar. The man was so sexy it was impossible to ignore the feelings he evoked in her any longer.

And he wasn't even wearing boots of any kind.

'Have you changed your mind?' the woman asked, a hint of annoyance in her voice.

Sophie shook her head to clear the images of Cooper that had taken over her brain. 'No. I haven't,' she said, putting determination in her tone. She would not be side-tracked by anyone, least of all Cooper. She needed a home for her baby, and she needed it now so there was time to fit it out properly. Scribbling her signature across the bottom of each form placed in front of her, she waited for the calm to come at having achieved finding her future home.

But instead she found herself staring around the gloomy room, wondering what she was doing there. There was a good offer on the table if only she'd swallow her pride and take up the challenge. Cooper's house was all the things this place wasn't.

The agent was quick to put the signed papers in her bag. 'I'll be in touch when the current tenants have moved out.'

And that was that. 'I have somewhere to live,' she muttered as she sank into the front seat of Cooper's car.

'You already had somewhere if only you weren't so stubborn,' she was told sharply.

Couldn't argue with being stubborn. She'd warned him about that. 'You'll thank me for this later.'

Cooper said nothing as he drove away from the apartment.

Thank goodness, Sophie thought. She'd done enough talking to the agent that morning to last all day. Quiet was exactly what she wanted. Her hand hovered over her belly where the baby was also quiet. Too quiet? 'Baby?' Automatically her hand rubbed her tummy. Nothing. 'Move, will you?' The panic was rising in her chest, up her throat. 'Come on.'

'What's happening?' Cooper asked, already pulling off the road to stop the car. 'When did you last feel movement?'

'Not for a while.' When? She racked her brain. 'I don't know when. Before we got to the last apartment.'

'You're sure?' The worry in his eyes did nothing to allay her fears.

'No. I'm not. But she's lying very still now. She never stops moving for long. Cooper, what if…?'

'Don't go there.' His hand caught hers, squeezed gently. 'Easy, Sophie. I'm sure everything's all right. Can I try to feel some movement?'

'Yes.' She jerked her top up to expose her belly, and couldn't care less when Cooper's eyes widened. 'Hurry.'

His hand was cool on her skin, but his touch was so gentle she calmed a little. Until he stopped touching her and tugged her shirt down again. Taking both her hands in his, he said quietly, firmly, 'We should get this checked out to be on the safe side. Can you ring your midwife and tell her we're coming in?'

'I haven't made an appointment with one yet. We only got home yesterday.' The panic became a full-blown roar in her head. 'My baby. Something's wrong. I know it.'

Cooper pulled out into the traffic. 'Auckland Hospital's just down the road. We'll go to the ED.'

'Whatever. Just hurry.' Her hands clutched at her belly, while silently she begged the baby to kick as hard as she could. 'I don't care how much you hurt Mummy, I just have to know you're all right.'

Nothing.

She wanted to bang her stomach in the hope of jarring baby into action, but common sense won out—just. It wouldn't work, and might even give the baby a shock. If she was all right. 'Hurry up,' she yelled to Cooper.

He wasn't exactly going slowly, but right now a racing car at full throttle would be too slow. Too bad if there was a cop lurking in the area. If he tried to stop them he'd get an earful from her. Or he could escort them to the hospital, flashing lights and all.

'Hold on,' Cooper snapped as he took a corner too fast.

A glance at the speedo told her they weren't going as fast as it felt—or as she'd like. But there was nothing they could do in the heavy traffic except go with the flow. Of course there was no parking outside the emergency department. Murphy's Law was working overtime today.

'Let me out,' she all but shouted. 'You can find parking without me.'

'Okay, okay. Take it easy.' Cooper pulled up beside a parked car and flicked his hazard lights on.

She wanted to shout at him for using the 'easy' word but when she jerked her head around to argue with him she saw nothing but concern and worry looking back at her. Pulling the brake on her temper, she said, 'I'm try-ing, believe me.'

'I know.' His smile was strained, but the finger he ran down her cheek was gentle and soft, and made her heart tighten. 'Go on. I'll catch you up ASAP. Hang on. There's a car three spaces up pulling out. Quick, out you get.'

She gritted her teeth in exasperation as she struggled to extricate herself. Infuriating how moving wasn't the same as it used to be before baby. Baby. Her hand flattened on her stomach. Baby.

Please, don't let us be too late. Please let them find a heartbeat. Please, please, please.

Sophie shoved out of the car, lurched as she fought to keep her balance.

Cooper called after her, 'Be careful. I don't want you slipping in all that water covering the path. You'll hurt yourself and that won't do baby any favours.'

He sounded so sure baby was going to be all right, but she'd seen the worry shadowing his eyes, turning his cheeks pale. Despite everything she felt a moment of gratitude for his presence. If not for Cooper she'd still be back at the apartment, freaking out, not knowing what to do. 'Hurry.'

I need you.

Sophie ran.

Every second counted. Losing her baby was not an option.

'Hang in there, sweetheart. Mummy's getting you help.'

She skidded on the smooth concrete at the ED entrance. Teetered on one foot, regained her balance, her heart pounding.

Slow down.

She couldn't, beat the doors with her fist when they took for ever to slide open.

Bang-bang-bang.

The shots cracked through the air.

Sophie dropped to the ground hard, the air ripping out of her lungs, her shoulder taking the brunt of her fall. She cried out as pain snagged her. Rolling onto her side she curled up as tight as possible, making herself small so the shooter wouldn't have an easy target.

'Sophie,' Cooper shouted.

'Get down,' she yelled back. 'You'll be shot.'

'Sophie, it's all right.' He was there, kneeling beside her, reaching for her. 'There're no terrorists here.'

'Get down,' she repeated, stronger this time. 'There's gunfire.'

'No, Sophie, listen. That was a car backfiring. You're safe. We're safe. We're in Auckland. Not Bamiyan.'

'How can you be sure?' Her heart was thumping. How did he know no one wanted to kill them?

Cooper stood up and looked around. 'Nothing out of the ordinary going down, I promise.' He reached a hand down to her, ready to haul her to her feet. 'Do you think I'd risk your life if I had the tiniest suspicion everything wasn't all right?'

The fear backed off as she glanced left, then right. No one was running for their life. There were no shouts or screams. In fact, no one seemed worried about anything. Not even the small group gathering around them.

'Does the lady need this?' An orderly with an empty wheelchair paused beside them.

Starting to feel a little stupid, Sophie gripped Cooper's hand to pull herself upright. 'I'm fine. Just took a tumble. Thank you for your concern.'

'You're welcome,' the man said, before his gaze landed on her belly. 'You went down hard.'

'That's why I want to get her to a doctor. Now.' Cooper tucked her against his side. 'Ready?'

She nodded and took a step, wincing as her ankle protested. 'Think I pulled a muscle.' She tried again, tentatively this time, and was relieved to be able to stand on the foot. 'What an idiot. I seriously thought someone was firing at me.' Looking up at Cooper, she tried to explain, knowing he'd think she was a sandwich short of a picnic. 'For a moment there I was back in Bamiyan.'

'I figured. I've seen the same reaction in some of the guys after they've been in a battle. I'm just surprised it hasn't happened to you before.'

'It did once. But that was on base in Bamiyan. Thought I was over all that now.' Then her reason for being here slammed into her nightmare. 'The baby. I still can't feel any movement. I need to find out what's happening.' Or not happening. Sophie's heart slowed. This was turning out to be the day from hell.

Taking her hand in his, Cooper said, 'I'm with you all the way.'

Together they headed inside to the receptionist who'd stood up the moment they appeared. 'Are you all right?' she asked.

No. My baby's in trouble.

'I'm Sophie Ingram. My baby's stopped moving.' The words gushed out at about the same rate her heart was beating. She drew a breath, dug deep for calm. Felt dizzy instead. She grabbed at Cooper's arm for support, felt relief when he wound that strong arm around her again. She sank against him and drew from his strength.

'We need an urgent scan,' Cooper backed her up. 'It's been over an hour since Sophie felt the last movement.'

That long? Her heart slowed. Too long. Her knees knocked, and if Cooper hadn't been holding her she'd be in a heap on the floor. Again. 'Please, get me help,' she begged.

Within minutes Sophie heard the wonderful sound of the security door buzzing open, allowing them access to the emergency room.

A woman in blue scrubs approached. 'Hello, Sophie. I'm Dr Kate Wynn. I understand you haven't felt baby move for a while. How far along are you?'

As Sophie answered the doctor's questions they were led into a cubicle. She wanted to relax. This gripping tension would not be good for her baby. But her muscles were as tight as ever.

'You're doing great,' Cooper told her quietly.

'What if...?'

'Let's wait until we know what's going on before looking for the worst-case scenario,' he suggested with the tiniest of hitches in his voice.

'You're right.' But, but what if?

Kate told them, 'I'm getting a Doppler sent down so I can listen for a heartbeat. That way we'll know more about what's going on.'

Sophie wished she could feel half as relaxed and professional as Kate appeared, but today her doctoring persona had taken a hike. 'Hurry, please,' she whispered as Cooper helped her onto the bed.

'What's happened? You've got fresh grazes on your leg and arm.'

'Sophie slipped on the wet path outside.' At least he hadn't said she'd thrown herself on the ground and put her baby at risk of being hurt. 'I don't think she did any damage. We are both doctors,' he added with a grimace.

Being a doctor wasn't helping her baby right now. 'I'm fine, unless I've hurt my baby.'

Kate said, 'I doubt it. She's got a lot of protection surrounding her in there. Unless you landed belly first?'

'No.' One thing she'd done right. Twisting to land on her hip and shoulder had hurt her but protected her daughter.

The curtain opened to admit an orderly. 'One Doppler as required.'

'Right, let's get started.' Kate took the instrument and nodded to the orderly to leave.

Kick.

Sophie gasped. 'Oh. Ow! Do that again.'

Kate looked surprised. 'I haven't done anything yet.'

Kick.

Sophie spread her hands over her extended stomach. 'Cooper, put your hand there. She's alive and kicking harder than ever.'

His large hand slid under one of hers, and his eyes filled with relief and wonder. 'Go, girl.' His voice cracked and he stopped talking.

'Me? Or baby?' she teased through the tears now clogging her throat.

'I'll check baby's heart before giving you two a few minutes alone.' Kate smiled and said moments later, 'Listen to that. Nothing wrong with that heartbeat. Be back shortly for a full examination.' Putting the Doppler aside, she slipped out and closed the curtains tight behind her.

Cooper's hand splayed across Sophie's stomach was so large, and strong, yet gentle. So right. Like he was laying a claim on her.

What?

The question screamed into her head. It was not right. Cooper didn't have a place in her life, only that of her daughter's. But she couldn't push him away, liked the strength and warmth of his hand. Needed him at her side for now. Had needed him ever since she'd thought something was wrong with their baby. All her strength and determination to do everything properly had gone, leaving her like a jelly on the inside. But having Cooper at her side settled her jitters a little at least.

Reaching around his arm, she placed her hand over his. 'She's a busy girl in there. I'm never going to tell her to take a rest again.'

'You probably woke her up from a lovely sleep when you dived to the ground and now she's paying you back.' His smile was lopsided, filled with concern as he stared at her baby bump.

That concern would be for the baby, she acknowledged to herself. Not her. He had no reason to be worried about her. Apart from her crazy reaction to a car going past, that was. She wasn't important to him, wasn't the love of his life. Her shoulders slumped. If only they were in love and expecting their first child, together on all fronts. Not dodging around each other, trying to get along without too many arguments.

Thinking like that was dumb. She didn't love Cooper—never had, probably never would. Any feelings like that would be due to baby brain. Besides, it wouldn't work if she did. He wasn't going to fall in love with her, and a one-way relationship was as bad as her parents' hateful one.

'Right.' Cooper straightened up, stepped away from the bed. 'Let's get you sorted and then we can go home. You look whacked.'

Thanks for the compliment.

She snatched her shirt down over baby and growled, 'Tell Kate I'm ready.'

And stay out there so I don't have to see you get all excited when we get to hear baby's heartbeat again.

But she knew she could never do that. So much for keeping Cooper on the other side of the door every time she went to see the midwife. After this he was involved, and it would be petty to tell him otherwise.

Horror struck her. Did that mean he'd be there during the birth? She so wasn't ready for that.

'Let's go home,' Cooper said thirty minutes later.

Home. Yes. She needed that—somewhere to relax, unwind, forget the fears that had blitzed her today. 'Let's,' she agreed.

Then she stumbled. Home? With Cooper? No. She was going back to his house for a few days until she had her apartment fixed up. *That* would be home. Not Cooper's place.

'You okay?' he asked warily.

'Yes,' she snapped.

'I'll drop you off and head into the hospital. I need to touch base with the unit before I start.'

'I'll get a taxi.' When his eyebrows rose and his mouth tightened she added, 'I'll visit Mum and Dad.' Ask for a room.

'No, Sophie, You need to rest and put today's scare behind you, not go getting uptight about your parents.'

He was right. Of course. One more night at his house couldn't hurt. Could it?

CHAPTER SEVEN

COOPER STRODE DOWN the corridor towards the surgical unit, relieved to have left Sophie at home.

As long as she stayed there. Though he doubted she was in any hurry to see her parents. What really was going on in that family? The less Sophie told him about herself the more he wanted to know.

Talk about getting under his skin. He needed to put space between them. Needed to get back on track with being a support person for the mother of his child, no more, no less. Needed to remember he didn't do relationships of the close and personal kind, and to do so would be to the detriment of Sophie and the baby. And him.

What was he afraid of? That he'd take them in then send them packing when they got too close, and demanded more of him than he had to give? Turn Sophie into one of those women Dad had coming and going? She couldn't get close if he kept the barriers up. Couldn't hurt him if he didn't allow her in.

Under your skin already, remember?

Then there was the baby. A whole other story. He'd never walk away from his daughter. Which meant he'd never walk away from Sophie. He wouldn't feel incapable of looking after them and opt out for ever, as his mother had. The only thing he was incapable of was loving Sophie. Oh, and making up his mind about how far to press her to stay under his roof where he could do a better job of looking out for them.

When she'd dropped to the ground earlier his heart had stopped. Throw in her fears about the baby not moving and he'd come up with a dreadful scenario. Stroke or, worse, a fatal heart attack. His hands had been shaking as he'd touched her, reached to find a pulse. Even when he'd felt the steady thump, thump of blood pounding through her body it'd taken minutes for his panic to back off. He didn't want to lose Sophie. Not now. Not ever.

He wasn't making a lot of sense with this. Who would in the circumstances? If only Sophie would get out of his head, give him quiet time when he wasn't actually with her. But no. She was in there, tap-tapping away at his resolve to remain uninvolved, making him resent her for getting him in a lather over everything. She was forcing him to face up to his mother's suicide and how he hadn't forgiven her for deserting him.

If his mum had got help for her obsessive, compulsive excessive disorder his life would've been so different. All their lives would've been different. He might even be able to fall in love without thinking up a hundred reasons why that was bad for him and the other person involved.

Cooper stopped to stare out a window onto the motorway below. What if he stopped fighting this? Gave up and took things as they occurred? Dealt with imagined shootings and lack of kicks systematically? Helped Sophie move into that grot box of an apartment instead of trying to talk her out of it? Surely then he'd get past these feelings of need, of wanting to spend more time with her. Emotions that came from his desire to do the right thing, nothing else.

Get it? Nothing else.

'Cooper? That you?' a woman called from somewhere further down the corridor.

He recognised the sultry voice instantly. 'Svetlana, good to see you.' The last person he wanted right this minute.

She reached him and wrapped her arms around him. 'Where have you been? I've missed you.'

'Oh, you know. Offshore with the army.' He shrugged out of the hug. 'You're looking as lovely as ever.' Yuk. How crass. That speculative gleam in Svetlana's eyes needed a dose of cold reality fast, not encouragement. He knew how she operated, had been a willing participant in the past, but was not interested now.

Her smile widened and her tongue peeked out at the corner of her mouth. 'Army life has been good for you.' She squeezed his biceps.

Cooper took another step back. What had he seen in her? Uncomplicated sex. The only answer. They'd had some fun encounters, yet now he felt nothing, no frisson of excitement. Nothing. Just an image of Sophie shimmering in his mind. 'Can't complain.'

Svetlana followed, stepping closer, her cloying sweet perfume a thick cloud around her. 'Want to have some fun tonight, or one night this week?'

'Thanks, but I'm tied up all week.' *Come on.* 'In fact, I'm busy most of the time.'

She blinked rapidly. 'You haven't gone and got yourself all hooked up with a little wifey, now, have you?' Her smirk suggested she knew full well what his answer would be.

No, he hadn't. Wasn't ever likely to. But that didn't mean he was available for a quick romp either.

You always have been in the past.

Exactly. In the past. Not now. Not since—Sophie.

'Nice catching up, Svetlana.' He deliberately glanced at his watch. 'I'm running late for an appointment. See you around.'

Cooper strode away, feeling guilty for his abrupt dismissal but also relieved to be away from the woman. Unfortunately there'd be no avoiding her completely since her white coat with the stethoscope hanging from the pocket suggested she worked here. Obviously she still overdid wearing the gear even when not required so as to show who and what she was.

Unlike Dr Ingram. Happy to wear fatigues or shorts and T-shirt, Sophie preferred casual in her approach to doctoring. Until she was with a patient, and then everyone knew her role. That day in Bamiyan she'd taken charge of caring for Kelly, calm despite her shock, completely cognisant of the medical details despite the fear in her eyes. Everyone who had worked on Kelly had settled into doing their jobs quickly—all because of Sophie's professional and quiet manner.

Even him. For a moment after the explosion when the bullets had started to fly he'd been terrified for his life, and for that of the beautiful woman he'd met only minutes earlier. He'd leapt to cover her body, fearful of either of them taking a direct hit, and once they had been back on their feet the shakes had set in. If not for Sophie he might've run screaming for the hills. Okay, maybe not. But it would've taken him a lot longer to settle down enough to help the wounded without leaping into the air at every loud noise.

He turned into the surgical unit and went to find Shaun Langford, the head of department and former mentor from his years specialising right here.

'Hi, Cooper. We're looking forward to working with

you again,' a nurse told him, and the receptionist nodded in agreement.

'Thanks, ladies. It's good to be back.' It really was. So much so there was a spring in his step as he reached Shaun's office. He was coming home, back to a place he'd enjoyed, where people he'd liked still worked, where he knew his role and gave it his all. Yeah, could be he'd made the right decision for his future without being aware of it.

So career move sorted. That only left his personal life.

Sophie sat back on her heels to admire the stacks of carefully folded baby clothes on her bedroom floor. 'Not bad, if I say so myself.'

'Talking to yourself is not a good sign.'

Cooper. Her skin heated at the sound of that gravelly voice. 'You're home early.' There went her quiet time. Over the last two days she'd spent the afternoons pottering around his house, pretending she lived here, as in permanently, and loving every moment of it. Cooper had an eclectic collection of furniture that made her smile. There was endless redecorating required, yet it didn't matter. The house was warm and cosy, like no place she'd lived in before.

As for all those images of the good-looking hunk standing beside her right now, they'd be the bane of her life, appearing too easily, often doing her head in. She needed to be getting her A into G and making the apartment ready to move into, but it seemed too much of an effort. Staying with Cooper was the soft option. And more exciting. There was also a certain closeness between them in the way he took her BP every morning, noted what she ate. He'd soon drive her crazy with all the attention and then she'd leave.

If she could. The sense of belonging that wrapped

around her every time she came through the front door would be hard to walk away from. The essence of this house was Cooper. It said, *Take me as I am.* If that wasn't Cooper Daniels, then what was?

Right now he was reaching a hand down to help her up off her haunches. 'I haven't officially started yet.'

Pushing to her feet, not an easy or pretty manoeuvre these days, she said, 'So you go to the hospital first thing every day because I'm under your feet?' If he stayed at home she might've got to work on her list. Baby furniture was an urgent requirement. If baby made her appearance now she'd be sorely in need of just about everything. Except clothes.

His hand fell away from her elbow. 'Thought I'd go with you to the car yard, see if you can't find something half-decent to get around in.'

'That's not necessary.' She could find her own car—with the help of an Automobile Association mechanic. If she ever got around to arranging that.

'You don't want a car?' He was being deliberately obtuse.

She could be likewise, hopefully keep him a little distant. 'I'm aiming for a SUV.'

'Then let's go find you one.'

'No, Cooper. This is mine to do.' She was quite capable of finding her own vehicle, just not of doing it right away.

'Fine. Then let's go look at cots and beds and tables. At the moment your baby will be sleeping on the floor, and so will her mother.'

'Again, my problem.' Why was she being belligerent? Cooper was only trying to help. She should be pleased. In fact, why was she so reluctant to do any of the things she'd been busting to do while waiting in Darwin to come home? 'I did book an appointment with a midwife for to-morrow.' One thing off the list.

'What's up, Sophie?'

'Nothing. I bought clothes, nappies by the carton, and some cute little toys this morning.' Three hours in the mall had had her staggering under all the bags of good-ies. Not practical things but adorable baby things in every colour of the rainbow. They were all that interested her at the moment. So unlike her not to be charging through the stores, picking out what she needed and getting them delivered fast.

'You bought loads of all of those yesterday.' Amuse-ment lightened his eyes to that pewter shade she adored and turned her insides to mush.

'True.' There wasn't much space to move in this room, the floor being covered in bags from every baby outlet within a five-kilometre radius. 'Leave it, Cooper. I'm having fun.'

I am? Shopping till I drop, getting so many baby out-fits that most of them will never be worn, by this baby at least, is fun?

'Think about it. I haven't been near malls since I left New Zealand nearly eleven months ago. I didn't bother in Darwin, not needing much because I wore a uniform.'

'We're going out.' His amusement had vanished.

'To the car dealer or the furniture shops?' she called after him, letting annoyance flare up. It was easier to deal with his high-handed attitude that way, and it pushed aside the sudden yearning to rip their clothes off and make wild, passionate love.

He was back at the doorway. 'My baby is not sleep-ing on the floor. Neither is she going without a safe car to ride in. We'll start with the furniture.'

'There's nowhere to store it until I get the keys to the apartment.' Her desire was rapidly abating.

'Then we'll put it all in my third bedroom.'

'You're taking charge,' she growled. Though it made sense. Someone had to since her baby brain was obviously incapable. But she wasn't telling him that.

'Too right I am.'

'Who'd have thought there were so many choices?' Sophie muttered as she strolled down yet another aisle in the baby furniture warehouse. 'Here I'd been thinking a bassinet was just a bassinet.'

'You hadn't figured on choosing between turned, stained wood or plain, painted wood; between pink, blue, white or every other colour under the sun. Or one with a shelf at the bottom or not.' Cooper grinned at her. His mood had lifted since they'd arrived at the massive outlet. 'And that's only the actual bassinet. Which mattress and flounces do you like?'

But she was distracted. 'How about those cute bunnies to string across the top for baby to look at?'

'She's supposed to sleep in this thing, not lie awake, staring at plastic baubles.' His grin widened, and excitement crept into his eyes.

'Right, then we'll go for the basic, no-frills version.' Not likely, but she could pull his strings. That excitement was tightening her belly and turning this into an adventure.

'I'm having the classy, stained wood one, with that pink flounce that has elephants cavorting over it.'

'You're buying a bassinet?' That had not been part of today's excursion.

'Of course I am. Where else will baby sleep when she's

with me?' The excitement dimmed, and his mouth tightened. 'I need to duplicate everything you get.'

'She can't stay with you. I'll be breastfeeding.' Why hadn't that occurred to her? Of course Cooper would want his daughter to stay with him sometimes. She'd even suggested it. But that had been in the future, not until their daughter was on a bottle and no longer brand-new.

A warm hand descended on her shoulder. 'You're winding yourself up over nothing. I just want to be prepared for when my daughter does spend time with me.'

And she had promised he'd have input in her life, which meant the baby would stay with him. 'We'd better buy lots of feeding bottles, then.'

The tension instantly evaporated from his face. 'So let's really get into this. Two of everything.'

'Everything?' She choked as unexpected laughter rolled up her throat. 'You're serious, aren't you?'

'Yep.' The excitement was back, and she was glad. Then Cooper grinned. 'Starting with bassinets. I'm taking that one.' He tapped the one he'd nodded at earlier.

'But I like that one.' She laughed. 'Though not as keen on the elephants as the butterflies.'

'It's mine. I saw it first.' Then he locked his gaze on hers. 'Unless you really, really want it.'

She shook her head. 'It's yours. I've just seen another one I like better. Which baby bath do you think?'

'We need help here.' Cooper looked around for a shop assistant and soon had people following them, writing down everything they selected so that deliveries could be made to their respective homes next week.

But slowly Sophie's enthusiasm died. Why were they doing this? Sure, she needed to set up for her baby, but Cooper? He didn't need quite as many things as her. It was as though he intended having the baby living with him a lot, not for some weekends when he wasn't working.

'I see an in-depth discussion coming on.' Cooper nudged her as he slid his credit card back into his wallet after paying for everything, against her wishes. 'What's up? You not happy with me decking my house out for my daughter?'

She hadn't thought it through properly when she'd said she'd never prevent him being a part of their child's life. 'She's going to be living with me.'

'Most of the time, sure. I'm making her comfortable when she visits me, though.' His mouth tightened. 'You're not reneging on your promise of allowing me to be a part of her life?'

'No, I wouldn't do that. Never. Not after the way my parents treated me.' But... 'We need to draw up legal papers covering custody and what comes about in the event of something happening to me. Or you.' Sophie wanted to slap her forehead. She'd been very remiss not thinking about this sooner.

'You are right. We should see a lawyer.' Taking her elbow, he led her outside to his car. 'Talk about deflating the moment.'

'I'm sorry,' she snapped. 'Actually, no, I'm not. We were having fun when this is serious. We haven't thought everything through. There're so many legal ramifications about being parents it's terrifying. I've been completely irresponsible.'

'Don't go blaming yourself, Sophie. I admit none of this had occurred to me either. It would've, eventually.' His sigh was loud and despondent. 'Why today when I was enjoying myself?'

Her stance softened. 'Yeah, that was fun, wasn't it?'

Then she got wound up again. 'This goes to show how unprepared to be a good mother I am.'

'We're not going there. For now we agree we'll sort out the legal stuff ASAP. In the meantime let's go home.'

Home. Again that word sank into her like a ball of warmth. If only. 'Let's,' was all she said.

'How's the body? I bet you've got some major bruises after throwing yourself on the ground.'

'One or two.' She ached in a lot of places.

'You don't think you need to talk to someone about your reaction to a backfiring car?' A load of caution laced his question, like he wasn't sure of her reaction. 'I'm thinking of the baby and what harm you could cause her throwing yourself down like that. Once she's born she'll be more vulnerable if you're holding her.'

She'd presume he cared, and wasn't about to tell her she was incompetent to be his daughter's mother. She also got that he was only concerned about the baby. Fair enough. That's how she was supposed to want it. A timely reminder that she was still on her own. 'I saw the shrink in Darwin when I first got there, and was told I did not have PTSD, or if I did it was very mild.' Despite the annoyance winding up tight inside her, she conceded, 'But a second time after eight months is concerning.'

'Maybe you need to talk to someone again. Another opinion won't hurt.'

Did that count when it came to her ability to be a good mother? 'I'll look into it.'

'I know a good guy. We were in the army together one tour. I'll give him a ring tomorrow, get you an appointment.'

Forget annoyed. Anger burst out of her mouth. 'Stop bossing me around. I'll make my own arrangements, thank you very much.' She seethed. 'Who do you think you are? Telling me what to do, who to see, where to shop? It's got to stop. Now. I was perfectly capable of looking after myself before I met you. Nothing's changed.' She was yelling, but seriously? The guy needed a bash over the head.

'No problem. Just thought I could help, take some of the strain away from you.'

What strain? Babies were delivered every day and no one suffered badly. A yawn ripped through her. She was exhausted, and Cooper wasn't helping by adding pressure to her already mounting worries. But he was here, had given her a place to stay, and helped organise furniture delivery. Tears spilled down her cheeks. What a mess she was. At sixes and sevens over everything. Another yawn dragged at her. A tired mess.

Yet the moment she walked inside Cooper's house the tension plaguing her instantly fell away.

Yes, this house was a haven. A home. The kind of place she'd love to come back to at the end of a busy day, or stay put in on days her baby was grizzly.

Her hands splayed across her belly. This had to stop. It was imperative she move into her own place—fast. Turn the apartment into something as comforting as Cooper's home, without him there. Of course she'd delayed. She didn't know where to start, how to create a home that she and baby would be safe and secure in. She'd never known that for herself. Growing up, home had been the place where she'd slept and eaten and done her homework and listened to her parents arguing. Her bedroom the sanctuary she'd hidden in when the arguing had escalated into a full-scale war. Not once had she ever walked in the front door and sighed with contentment. As she did here. Talk about being in big trouble.

'Sophie? Are you all right? You're not having pains,

are you?' Cooper hovered over her, anxiety replacing the cool demeanour he'd shown since they'd talked about her supposed PTSD.

'I'm fine. No pains.' Just a crazy revelation that she had to deal with. She was not staying here permanently. Like to or not, she had to move on, set up her own life. Just as she'd planned since learning she was pregnant.

So get on with it.

'You'd tell me?' The anxiety hung between them.

'Yes.' Locking eyes with Cooper, she said with all the force she could muster, 'I will let you know the moment I think I'm in labour.' She couldn't keep him out of the picture on that score. When she'd gone into meltdown over the lack of movement from the baby Cooper had given her strength when she'd needed someone to cling to. She couldn't push him away over this.

'Good.' He tossed his car keys up in the air, snatched them and repeated the action. 'So tomorrow we'll find you a suitable car.' He wasn't easily diverted.

Something she'd be wise to remember. 'I'll do that in the morning.' While he was at the hospital.

He shook his head. 'Uh-uh. I'll do some research on the net while you tell me why you want an SUV instead of a car.'

'You can stop looking so smug. It doesn't suit you,' she growled, trying hard not to smile at him. He'd won and yet she couldn't find it in her to be cross. Not really. He had a way about him that made her feel more and more at ease. When he wasn't reminding her that there were lots more problems to add to her list than she had to tick off. Lawyers, a midwife, and now a psychologist had to be dealt with.

In the meantime, Cooper merely laughed and booted up his laptop.

* * *

'Three more ticks on my list,' Sophie sighed late the next afternoon. Things were starting to come together nicely. 'I like my new midwife. She's so enthusiastic.' When Cooper's eyebrows rose, she added, 'And professional, and competent.'

'What else is on that list?' Cooper asked as he drove through the rush-hour traffic in Newmarket on their way home from a car dealer. 'Apart from a vehicle, which it looks like we've got sorted now.'

'Dinner. Can we swing by the supermarket? I feel like pasta tonight.'

'What's with all this pasta? Seems you're always eating it. You're not of Italian extraction, are you?'

'Irish. Except I'm not fussed about spuds.' She smacked her lips, her stomach sitting up in anticipation. 'Can't go past the sauces that go with linguine, and then there's ravioli and the delicious fillings.'

'You been to Italy?'

Nodding, she explained, 'I spent four months there after completing my internship in London. I didn't want to leave.' Not only was the food divine, the men were just as mouth-watering. Though not as delectable as the man in the driver's seat beside her. Only the car's seat? Or was he driving her life now? He definitely played havoc with her focus, which should be entirely on preparing for the baby, not on kisses. Hot kisses that swamped her mind with memories of his body against her, diverting pictures that had her longing for more.

'Why didn't you stay on in Italy?'

'I couldn't get a work permit so I returned home and saved up for the next adventure, which was in Chile.'

'We're not going to eat Chilean food, then?'

'They eat a lot of potatoes. But having said that, I did

enjoy most things. Lots of seafood and meat. *Pastel do chocio* was my all-time favourite, sort of like a shepherd's pie. Haven't seen that in the supermarkets here.'

Cooper turned into the supermarket parking building. 'You might have to go back to Chile for that. From things you've said, it sounds as though you've done a lot of travelling. You got a thing against staying at home?'

More like a thing about staying still. 'My travelling days are on hold for a few years.'

'I suppose they are. But that's not what I asked.'

As a diversion she'd missed the gate. 'Travel's exciting and opens your eyes to so much more than we've grown up with here.' And it had kept her from spending time wondering if she'd ever be able to settle down in one place for long. Every time she thought about finding a place of her own she'd think about how uncomfortable her parents' home had been and known she'd had no idea how to make hers any different. Except that had bitten her on the backside this year. Settling down *was* her current goal.

As they walked inside Cooper mused, 'I haven't seen much of the world. Only the out-of-the-way and often inhospitable places the army sent me to.'

Sophie shivered. 'I'm over those. Not going back to dangerous areas again.'

'Cuts out quite a lot of the world at the moment. Hideous.' Cooper swung a shopping basket between them.

'There are definitely places to stay away from. I can't believe some of the things going on at the moment.' She paused, listening hard. Had she heard a cry? But nothing untoward reached her. Must've been imagining it. Snapping off a plastic bag, she began selecting tomatoes. 'Need some mushrooms too.'

'I'll get them.'

There it was again. A low cry, almost a groan. 'Something's not right.' Dropping the tomatoes in the basket, she headed for the next aisle.

'What have you heard?' Cooper was right with her, the empty mushroom bag still in his hand.

'Like someone's in pain.' She stared down the next aisle. Nothing out of the ordinary. Was her imagination overacting? No. There it was again. 'Hear that?' She headed for the next aisle and raced down it. Sitting the floor was a heavily pregnant girl, her face contorted with pain. Sophie reached for her hand. 'Hi. My name's Sophie. I'm a doctor. What's happening?'

'I think my baby's coming.' The young face scrunched up tight as a contraction gripped her.

The cry of pain that accompanied it cut through Sophie. 'Breathe deep, go with the pain, don't fight it.' She tried to remember everything she'd heard in antenatal classes in Darwin.

'Easy for you to say,' grunted the girl.

Cooper knelt on the other side of the distressed girl. 'Has anyone called an ambulance?' he asked the gathering onlookers.

'Yes,' replied an older woman dressed in the store's uniform. 'Just now.'

'Good. What's your name?' he asked the girl, adding, 'I'm Cooper, another doctor.'

'Melanie. It's coming,' she cried as another contraction caught her.

She might be right, Sophie conceded. Those contractions were very close. 'We need to examine her,' she said quietly so only Cooper heard. 'But it's hardly ideal here.'

'Not a lot of choice.' He stood up. 'Can you all give us a bit of privacy? Carry on with your shopping and leave us to help this girl.'

'I want some tinned corn for my fritters,' a woman said. 'If you can just step out of my way.'

Cooper sounded calm, too calm. 'Do you have to have it today?'

'It's my son's favourite dinner.'

'Make him something else,' Cooper snapped, no long holding onto his temper. 'This young lady's situation is more important.'

Sophie held onto a smile and concentrated on talking to Melanie. 'How far along are you?'

'Thirty-six weeks.'

Too early. Thirty-seven was considered safe. 'Cooper, we might need the paediatric ambulance.'

'Onto it.'

Sophie turned back to Melanie. 'Has your pregnancy been normal so far?'

She nodded. 'Blood pressure fine. No diabetes. Not even Braxton Hicks pains.'

Better than me, then.

'Have you called your...' Sophie paused to glance at Melanie's left hand '...partner?'

'He's busy.'

Really? Too busy to be here for Melanie and his baby? 'Want Cooper to talk to him?'

Melanie's face shut down. 'No.'

Something was definitely off key here, but it wasn't her place to ask questions that were obviously awkward. Not wanting to upset the younger woman any more, Sophie changed the subject slightly. 'Can I examine you?'

'Not with those people gawping at me.'

'Fair enough. Cooper?'

'Onto it.' Striding up to the nearest person still standing watching the fun, he said in a very firm tone, 'Move, sunshine. Out of this aisle. Now. And the rest of you. Where is the store manager?'

'Coming,' called a young man, scurrying towards them.

'Clear this lot out of here right now.' Did he just add under his breath, 'The guy's still wet behind the ears'?

Sophie felt her smile widen. Almost immediately they had the aisle to themselves. Cooper on the rampage was something to admire. His tone brooked no argument, like he was on the parade ground again.

'How's that?' she asked Melanie. 'We're alone.'

A contraction rippled through the girl and she didn't, or couldn't, hold back a scream.

Sophie reached for her nearest hand and held on. 'Breathe, in one, two, three, out one, two, three. And before you say anything, I'm pregnant too.'

Melanie's eyes popped open. 'So you know what this is like.'

Ah. Caught. 'No. My first time.' She squeezed Melanie's hand. 'Sorry. I'll shut up with the advice.'

'Do you want your baby?'

'Absolutely. Don't you?'

'No. Yes. I'm not ready.' Tears oozed slowly from the corners of Melanie's eyes. 'It's not fair.'

Sophie knew all about that, but it seemed she'd come to terms with her deal better than this young woman. 'I'd like to check what's going on. We're on our own now.' Where was that ambulance?

Cooper placed himself between them and the end of the aisle while Sophie took a discreet look. Melanie wasn't wrong. 'Your baby's very nearly here.'

'So I'm going to have him in the supermarket.' Her expression was wry. 'Guess that goes with everything else that's gone wrong.'

The rising and falling sound of an approaching siren reached them. 'You might get lucky and have the baby in the ambulance.'

Even before she'd finished saying that Melanie bent over her stomach, snatching for Sophie's hand as pain hit her.

Sophie used her free hand to rub Melanie's back. 'You're doing great.'

'So are you,' Cooper said from behind her. 'Like the pro you are.'

Warmth stole through her. 'Thanks.' Then she shook her head. 'Watch this space. It'll be very different when it's my turn.'

'I'll be there to rub your back. And hold your hand.'

She nodded. 'Yeah, you will be.' Decision made. She wouldn't go back on it. She'd need someone there and while a girlfriend had volunteered she knew it had to be Cooper with her. For the baby. And for him. He needed to be a part of the birth. It was his daughter she'd be bringing into the world and she wanted to be able to tell their child that Daddy had been there when she'd arrived.

A paramedic squatted down beside them. 'Hi, there. I've been told there's a baby in a hurry to make an appearance.'

'A big hurry,' Sophie told him. 'The baby's nearly here.'

'You're a doctor?'

She nodded. 'We've got minutes, so I don't know if you want to remove Melanie to the privacy of your ambulance or carry on here.' She had to hand over. It was how the system worked. But she could stick with Melanie. 'You want to try and make it out to the ambulance? There's a stretcher ready.'

'Ambulance,' Melanie grunted as she sucked in a breath and squeezed Sophie's hand. 'If there's time.'

There wasn't. Melanie's baby rushed into the world seconds later. The paramedic was instantly busy clearing the wee boy's air passage and checking his reflexes.

When the baby cried Melanie smiled and held her arms out. 'Can I hold him?'

Sophie let go the breath she'd been holding. This girl did want her baby. Whatever the situation she was facing, her baby was welcome despite her earlier denial. 'The paramedics need to take care of him for now. Let's get you onto that stretcher and shifted to the ambulance. You both need to go to hospital.'

'Will you come with me?' Melanie locked her eyes on Sophie. 'Please,' she begged. 'I don't want to be on my own.'

'Is there anyone I can call?'

The girl's head moved slowly from side to side. 'No. My parents have disowned me, and the baby's father doesn't want a bar of him.'

'Of course I'll come with you.' How could she not? Raising her eyes to Cooper, she was relieved to see his approval beaming out at her. When did she need Cooper's approval for anything? Worse, why did it feel so good? Just something else to worry about in the middle of the night.

CHAPTER EIGHT

'LET'S EAT OUT,' Cooper suggested on the phone three days later. 'There's a new Italian place just down the road.'

'That's cheating. You know I won't be able to pass on that.' But it would be fun to go out for a meal and relax, talk about things that had nothing to do with her new apartment that she'd spent the last two days scrubbing. She'd got the keys on Wednesday and should've moved in immediately. On closer inspection the place was a bit of a tip. The cold weather had also made the empty rooms uninviting.

'That's a yes, then.' He sounded exhausted.

'Are you sure you want to? I could cook eggs.'

'No eggs. Need a proper meal. We've been doing an appendectomy. I'll be home by seven.'

I'll be home by seven.

How domestic. Sophie hugged herself. Cooper had got to her in a big way. He didn't frighten her with easy comments like that one. Instead she was slowly being sucked into his life. Her barriers were coming down, one by one. To the point she almost wished she could say yes to his suggestion of living here permanently. This hesitation in everything she did at the moment was debilitating. All her life she'd leapt into things, be they work, travel or parties. She'd grabbed life with both hands and raced away. Filling empty voids was essential, kept her sane. If she dared to stop, there was a whole load of pain and rejection waiting to pounce and knock her to her knees. This past week she hadn't run anywhere and she was still standing. No wonder that apartment remained empty.

Kick.

'Hello, in there. I hope you're up to a night out, because that's what's happening as soon as your father gets home.'

Had she really just said that? As in sounding like they were a regular family doing everyday things together? She couldn't have. But she had.

Sophie sighed. Tomorrow she'd put in a big effort to finish getting the apartment ready, so she could move in.

But first she'd shower and put on an outfit that didn't look like a sack over baggy clown's pants. The red, scoop-necked top she'd purchased yesterday would go perfectly with her black, leg-hugging trousers. Yes, she'd spruce herself up for the evening. See if she didn't get a smile from Cooper.

Cooper couldn't believe the beautiful apparition that floated down the hallway towards him when he stepped inside his house. The exhaustion dragging him down vanished in a heartbeat and his body tightened with excitement.

Steady. Nothing's happening here.

'You're looking fabulous.' Sexy as all hell. Hot. Stunning.

She did a very unlike Sophie thing. She blushed. 'Th-thanks.'

He couldn't help himself. He reached for her, pulled her close, and the baby bump tapped him at waist level. 'I mean it. You're one beautiful lady.' She smelt so tempting. And all that shining hair that she'd left free of its usual tie-back needed his fingers running through it. Her eyes were wide and welcoming and...

Cooper placed his hands on each side of her head to tilt her to one side. All the better to kiss her. His lips covered hers and he inhaled as her mouth softened under his. It wasn't enough. His tongue slid into that warmth, tasted her. He didn't need to go out to dinner. He had all the deliciousness he needed right here.

Sophie sank against him, pressing their baby into him as she moulded her breasts against his chest. Lifting her arms, she slipped them over his shoulders to meet at the back of his neck. Warm. Soft. Caressing.

His knees threatened to buckle. He held her tighter, kissed her harder, loved her more.

What? He jerked his head back. Loved her more? As in he already loved her? Absolutely not. That wasn't possible. All he felt for Sophie was compassion, concern and friendship. Responsibility. Didn't he? What about the sexual attraction?

'Cooper?' She was blinking at him, surprise piercing him from her gaze. Hopefully hurt or anger wasn't mixed in there.

'Sorry.' He jammed his hand across his hair. 'I don't know what came over me.' Yeah, right. 'I couldn't help myself.' Pathetic.

'Oh.' Her knuckles pressed against her mouth. That delectable mouth he'd just kissed. It *was* a very kissable mouth. It distracted him when he wasn't concentrating. Not how this was meant to be. Not at all.

'Give me ten to shower and change, then we'll head out.'

He didn't wait for her response, suddenly afraid she'd say no, say she didn't want to go out with him. If she had any sense that's exactly what she should do. He didn't want that. Forget the love word that had shot into his kiss-hazed brain. He was attracted to Sophie. Attracted? Try totally wanted her, dreamt of her underneath his body, making out. She was hot, even with a baby on board. Or was that because of the baby bump? Did that make her even more desirable?

Whatever. Cooper snapped the shower faucet to hot and tugged his clothes off. Confusion reigned. He wanted Sophie. Yes. Glancing down, he swallowed a smile. Too obvious, man. One kiss and his manhood throbbed with need. One kiss? Give over. He'd been excited to see her even before he'd put the key in his front door. The shower should be set on cold, not hot.

He wanted Sophie to live in his house so he could step up and be a good dad and support person. Though how he'd manage that when he physically needed her so much he didn't know.

'I went and saw Melanie again today. Jacob is ready to go home tomorrow,' Sophie told him later as they waited for their meals. Seemed she was on top of things.

A groan filled his mouth. Bad description. 'Where's home?'

'She's renting a room in a house in Ponsonby. It doesn't sound nearly as good as the suburb's reputation would suggest.'

He hadn't been surprised to learn Sophie had taken an interest in the young woman who seemed to be on her own with her baby. 'How can she afford to rent?' How could her parents have kicked her out because she was pregnant? That was when their daughter would've needed them the most. His blood had boiled when Sophie had first told him how Melanie's father had given her five minutes to pack some belongings and one hundred dollars to start out on her new life, before slamming the door behind her.

'Social welfare are helping. But this is a girl who was doing well at school, had potential as a pro tennis player, and had lots of friends.' Sophie's eyes glittered. 'I seriously don't understand.'

'Me either.' He covered her hand with his. 'Everyone makes mistakes.' Yep, look at them.

Sophie must've been thinking the same. Her mouth lifted into a beautiful smile.

Using that word a lot tonight. But that was Sophie. Beautiful. He was about to tell her when their meals arrived. Saved by the lasagne. 'You as hungry as that plate suggests you need to be?'

'I am eating for two.'

'How do you know Junior likes pasta? She might hate it.'

'She's a mummy's girl. She'll like it.'

He grinned and finally relaxed totally. Why waste a night out with a stunning woman by being uptight and on edge about what next might come out of his mouth?

'What else did you do today, apart from visiting your new friend?'

'Had the furniture delivered and got the men to put it in the correct rooms. The apartment's starting to look a little bit like home.'

'You didn't shift anything yourself?' She could be so annoying with her independent streak. He'd told her half a dozen times that they'd get the furniture brought around tomorrow when he'd be there to help with the heavy lifting.

'Nope. Amazing how a pregnant tummy has men, even strangers, falling over backwards to help.'

Her grin caught him, made him forget to be disappointed at the fact he hadn't been the one to help her.

'Don't go. Stay with me. We can make it work.'

She gaped at him. 'We've had this discussion. Nothing's changed.'

Come on. Convince her this was the right thing to do. He reached for her hands, held them lightly in his. 'Sophie, this is important to me, to us. Definitely important for our baby.'

When she opened her mouth, he shook his head at her. 'Hear me out. I heard what you said about growing up with your parents at odds all the time, but it doesn't have to be like that with us. We'll make certain it won't. I believe that. We already like each other. Let's at least try. For our daughter's sake.'

Her cheeks whitened. 'Low blow, Cooper.'

'It wasn't meant to be. Believe me.' Drawing in a deep breath, he managed, 'Sophie, I'd like to marry you, share my home with you, bring up our child together under the same roof. I'm not asking for anything more than that.'

'Anything more?' she spluttered. 'That's more than enough. How do you honestly think this idea of yours would work out? Huh?'

'We'd have separate bedrooms.' His heart stuttered. Of course they would. How else could they manage? It had to be his manhood talking. His heart had no place in these negotiations. 'There are enough bedrooms, two bathrooms, and I'm sure we can work out ways to avoid spending too much time together in the rest of the house if that's how you—we—want it.' Sounded clinical if he was listening to himself, so he wouldn't. 'I want to be there for you and our daughter all the time. Not just have visiting rights when it suits you.'

'Back up. You want me to marry you. Sorry, but in

my book marriage is the whole deal, or not at all. I'm opting for not at all. We don't love each other. Or know each other very well. Us getting together would be a carbon copy of what I grew up in—a cold, loveless environment where everyone puts themselves first. No, thank you. I couldn't wait to get away when I grew up. I never want my child feeling that way. It's horrible.' She stuffed a spoonful of lasagne into her mouth and stared at him with a dare in her eyes. Challenging him to refute what she'd said.

'We wouldn't be blaming our child for being together.' But even as he said it he knew he was wrong. If they didn't get along someone would pay the price and that would most likely be their daughter, even if she wasn't blamed for their mistakes.

Sophie spooned up more food and said nothing.

Which annoyed him. 'Okay, you might have a point.' But he needed to be doing the right thing for Sophie and the baby. It was inherent in him. 'Your parents are still together, right?'

Her head dipped in acknowledgement.

'Have you ever wondered why when they apparently hated each other so much?' She'd kill him now. No doubt about it.

But Sophie appeared stunned. After a long moment she said, 'I guess they think it's too late to go it alone.'

It wasn't much of an answer but he suspected she had no idea. Would she spend time thinking about her parents' relationship and try to see it in a different light now? He was sorry he'd put that disturbed look in her eyes. He reached across the table to take her hand. 'I was six when my mother died.' Now, where had that come from? 'She took her own life.'

Sophie blinked, but still remained quiet.

Actually, he was glad he'd told her. It felt right to explain his background, and take the focus off Sophie for a while. 'She suffered from OCD. I didn't understand what that meant for years. I just thought she didn't love me so found a way to leave so I couldn't follow.'

Sophie turned her hand over and interlaced her fingers with his. 'Your dad didn't explain?'

Mandy, don't leave me.

'I don't think he knew what I was thinking. He was a wreck himself, shocked to the core. He loved Mum and never thought she was capable of doing anything so drastic.' It had taken years for him to learn that much—his dad always ran shy of talking about the difficult years when Mum had been off the wall with her disorder.

'You must've been so lost.'

That was exactly what he'd been. 'Yes.'

The tender look Sophie gave him filled him with yearning for all the things he'd denied himself for so long.

Jerking his hand free, he leaned back in his chair. 'My dad stepped up to the mark for me. I always knew I could rely on him.' Dad had made sure he'd had everything he'd needed in the material sense, and he'd loved him. No doubt there. But he'd needed a mother too. Except his mother apparently hadn't needed him. 'It's important to me to do the same.' To bring home women and introduce them as his next great love, and then later explain how it hadn't worked out? No. Absolutely not.

Then you're going to live a celibate life?

No. Absolutely not, but he wouldn't be making rash statements about women being there for his child either.

Shoving her plate aside, meal unfinished, Sophie said quietly, 'I'm sorry about your mother. It must've been dreadful. You're lucky your dad was there for you.' Her shoulders rose as her chest expanded. 'But don't you see what you've told me? Your father brought you up sin-glehandedly and you've done well. You and I can both bring up our child equally well without being joined by a piece of paper.'

'Not any old piece of paper.' Why wasn't he leaping with glee? Sophie had once again given him his free-dom. Yes, he'd be there for his daughter, but without all the other stuff that being married would bring. It was the perfect solution. So, start leaping.

His feet were stuck to the floor, his body not up to moving with joy. This had to be the most bewildering experience he'd had as an adult. He'd put himself out there to meet his obligations, and had been turned down more than once, which had given him back the lifestyle he'd always enjoyed. A life of fun and women, and tak-ing jobs anywhere he chose. The life he'd aimed for since he'd been a wee nipper. Yet now nothing felt right. Why? At the beginning of the week he'd applied for a perma-nent position at the hospital. But sorting out his personal life wasn't as easy to achieve.

Sophie stood up. 'I'll pass on coffee.'

As he waited for his credit-card payment to go through he studied the one woman capable of stirring his world with little or no effort just by being herself. Yes, she was beautiful, and that beauty was more than skin deep. The way she'd handled the birth of Jacob and his mother's distress had been little short of amazing, and now she visited Melanie every day to see how she was getting on. She cared, deep down, for people. Were strangers re-placements for family and friends? If that was true, his daughter would still be in good hands. So would he if he ever needed her help, or even just her company.

'Can you remove your card, sir?' the waitress asked.

'Sorry, daydreaming.' He slid the card into his wallet

and followed Sophie out to his car. Daydreaming about this woman who'd got his boxers in a twist. Unfortunately only mentally. He'd like nothing more than for her to be tugging them off his butt and dealing with him—after he'd sent her over the edge with an orgasm that would brand her as his.

Sex like they'd shared in Bamiyan. Off-the-scale sex. Typical. He was back to thinking about the physical with Sophie. Was that his problem? If they spent one hot night in the sack would all this turmoil disappear? There'd be no need to propose marriage, or suggest they share his home? Sex was the answer? If so, great. Bring it on. But he had a sinking feeling in his gut that he was so far off the mark he wasn't in for a good night's sleep this side of Christmas.

Rubbing her forehead, Sophie wished her headache away and snatched up the keys to the SUV Cooper had found for her yesterday. The mechanic had just given the all clear to buy it. 'Thanks, Graham. I'll head to the car lot and hand over the money.' A lot of money that would make a sizable hole in her savings. She'd spent more than she'd intended. Reliability and safety were top priorities, and Cooper had talked her into a newer model than she'd budgeted for. He'd offered to pay the extra, which had only got her back up and had her refusing his gesture.

She was doing a lot of that at the moment. Marriage. A home. And now money for the SUV. No one had ever made her so many kind offers before. In the end that's all his marriage proposals were. Kind. Generous. Considerate. Not binding in terms that would keep them together in a loving relationship. He didn't want a noose around his neck, and she had no doubt that's how he'd see her after a while.

Did *she* want that noose? It wouldn't be a snare if she loved Cooper. But it would be a one-way street and that she couldn't tolerate. Better to be in love and lonely but standing strong than to be wishful and despairing as her love got trampled on.

'Drop by any time if you need help attaching the baby seat.' Graham held the driver's door open for her to clamber in, bringing her back to reality and what she needed to do.

'Thanks.' What a kind man. He'd already gone out of his way to pick up the SUV for her. He'd had his office girl make her a mug of tea while she'd waited, and had filled in the change of ownership papers. Why couldn't she fall in love with a man like that? Not that she'd fallen in love with any man yet. Who was she kidding? Not even she was believing that line any more.

She had fallen for Cooper. It had happened when she hadn't been looking. Drip by drip, wearing down her resistance. What was there not to love about the guy? Throw in that he supported her and the baby already and she was toast.

But loving Cooper didn't mean marriage. He certainly didn't love her. His proposals had been all about obligations, nothing else. Cleverly worded, but obligations none the less. At least he had accepted he was the father and hadn't done a bunk. Not by a long shot. Better than she'd hoped for in those months before he'd found out.

The few kisses they'd shared had been devastating, undermining her every time. Sizzling. Demanding. Earth-shattering.

Her phone rang from somewhere in the depths of her handbag. Pulling over, she put the gear shift into park and finally managed to find the phone just as the ringing stopped. The number on the screen was familiar, and one she'd avoided for too long. Her mother. She'd avoided Cooper's left-field query about why her parents were still together too. The answer could tip her off balance. Her belly tightened. She couldn't put off telling her parents about the baby any longer. Might as well get it over with. Then she could get on with her real life.

Back on the road she changed direction to head for the harbour bridge and the north shore. Her heart began a heavy pounding and her mouth dried. At every major intersection she had to fight not to turn around and head back to Parnell and Cooper's house. Her safe haven. Whatever her parents had to say when they learned about her pregnancy, it wouldn't be good. Worse, they were going to be hurt she'd kept it to herself for so long.

Then she was turning into the street she'd grown up in and there was no more time for prevarication.

'Mum, you're looking different.' Sophie stood back from hugging her mother. It wasn't the hairstyle or the chic clothes. No changes there. But there was a subtle difference she couldn't put her finger on.

'*I'm* looking different?' Her mother's gaze was fixed on the baby bump.

That's it.

'You're smiling.' Truly? Warmly. At her. Or at her extended stomach.

'Oh, Sophie, you're pregnant. That's wonderful.' Wonder filled her mother's eyes.

And shocked Sophie to the core. Her world lurched and she had to put a hand on the wall for balance.

'Jack, get in here and see what Sophie's brought us.'

Pardon? 'I didn't know Dad was at home. What about work?' How could her mother be pleased about that? It didn't make sense. Her mother only relaxed around the house when he was at work.

'I'm fully retired as of…' Her father stopped in the doorway. 'You're pregnant.' He stated the obvious.

'Yes.' Now that everyone was aware of the impending baby Sophie's tight muscles relaxed, allowing her stomach to push further out. 'Phew, that's hard work.' Then she thought of the explosion that would surely come as her parents got to grips with the situation, and her stomach tightened again.

'Sit down, darling, and tell us everything. When is the baby due? Who's the father? Anyone we know? Where is he?' Her mother hadn't taken her eyes off Sophie's tummy once.

Everything? I don't think so. You also don't know anyone I'm friends with.

She sank onto the couch and immediately her mother sat beside her, again shocking her, while her father took the armchair opposite. 'I'm due in five weeks.'

'You're tiny for being so far along.'

'I don't feel small, Dad. The midwife doesn't think so either.'

'So you've got that organised already.' Her mother settled back against the cushions, looking like she was there for the long haul.

She'd fill them in on some of the details and get on her way. 'I met my midwife last week, a few days after I got back. I apologise for not coming to see you sooner but I've had to find somewhere to live, buy furniture, a vehicle, and a hundred other things.' In other words, she'd been too busy. It was the standard excuse in this family and everyone understood it for what it was—easier to stay away and avoid the arguments.

'You're here now. That's what's important.'

Huh? Was this a dream? Would she wake up soon and find she was still in her SUV about to descend upon her parents and this was all wishful thinking? Put there by Cooper's crazy suggestion that her parents might not dislike each other? 'I'm currently staying with a friend.' Get it over with. 'He's the baby's father. I'm dossing down at his place until my apartment's ready to move into, which looks like being the day after tomorrow.'

'You're not going to live with this man?' her dad growled. 'He doesn't intend taking full responsibility for you and the baby?'

'Jack, that's enough.'

That's more like it. 'I'm not moving in with him. My choice. Not his.' If anyone should understand it would be her parents.

'He wants you with him?' her dad asked.

No, not really. He only thinks he does. 'Cooper's proposed and I've declined.' Before either parent could rant about that, she added, 'He's also suggested I live permanently in his house, if not as his partner then as a friend, so as he can be there for the baby. Again I said no.' Sophie sat back and waited for the eruption.

All she got from her mother was, 'You've always known your own mind. If this is what you think is right then we're behind you all the way.'

Her dad added, 'As long as you understand how hard it's going to be on your own with a baby.'

Things were getting stranger and stranger. Her father agreeing with her mother? Over something she'd done? They were even smiling at each other. How weird was that? 'Um, are you both all right?'

Do you like each other?

'Yes, darling. Why wouldn't we be?' her mother asked.

'You've brought us the most wonderful news. We didn't expect to become grandparents for a long time, with you so busy dashing off to exotic places around the world or working your tail off at the hospital.'

Dad said all that without a scowl.

Suddenly Sophie started laughing. This really was a dream. Had to be. There was no other explanation.

'Sophie? What's so funny?' Her mother looked worried.

She had no idea. Not really. Spluttering as she tried to control her hysteria, she managed, 'It's just baby brain.'

'It was totally odd,' Sophie told Cooper that night. 'I was with Mum and Dad for a couple of hours and not once did they as much as glare at each other, let alone give me a hard time. It was as though they like each other.'

'Maybe they do.' He looked smug.

'How's that possible after thirty-four years of disliking one another?' Why now? Because she didn't live with them any more? Couldn't be. She'd left years ago. Sophie shook her head. 'I *think* they were my parents.'

Cooper grinned. 'You want to get DNA done on them?'

It wasn't funny. It hurt. 'They seemed happy together, and that's an alien word in their relationship.' Or was that only when the three of them had been together? Her stomach sucked in on itself. She'd known she was the problem with their marriage, and now that she'd gone they were starting to find each other again. Ouch.

'Maybe they've woken up to the fact they've wasted a lot of years arguing, and now it's time to enjoy life together.'

'That would be too easy to accept.' But she wanted to. She was done with the pain her parents could inflict. Would love to let it all go and move on. Move on instead of racing away as though chased by an angry bull.

Cooper placed his hands on her shoulders. 'Give it a try. Take what they offer and forgive them for the past.'

Her eyes filled. 'Forgive them?' She choked. 'After a lifetime of pretending everything was fine? Of bearing the brunt of their unhappiness?' She shuddered.

'Yes, Sophie, exactly that.' Cooper's eyes were locked on hers. 'What's to lose?'

'My reasons for everything I do.' Gulp. She'd like to let it all go, she really would. But how?

'Our baby replaces that, surely?'

Hot tears spilled down her cheeks and she let them. 'Yes,' she whispered. Her daughter was her reason for living. Undeniable. She'd put her life on the line for her. Click, click went her spine. 'You're right. Thank you.'

For telling me how you see it.

Cooper's lips brushed her forehead. 'I'm here for you. Always.'

'Dad asked me to move home. As in he meant every word and was genuinely disappointed when I said no.' Which had blown her theory out of the water. Was it possible her mum and dad had fallen in love? Had the attraction that had resulted in her birth always been there but overshadowed by the responsibilities thrust on them by their upright, rigid families?

Cooper's face tightened. 'Nice to know I'm not the only one being turned down at the moment.'

Sophie waved a finger at him. 'I've done the right thing for all of us.'

I think. But then I am suffering from baby brain a lot. Could be I've got everything wrong. Even the bit about not loving Cooper.

Huh? No. She loved the man. No doubts. And that's where it stopped. She'd be strong, take this new twist in her life on her own, work it out day by day.

Everything was so complicated these days. What happened to just being a surgeon who worked hard to save money to go on exotic trips? *That* woman knew exactly what she wanted from life and didn't get sidetracked by cute little dresses with teddy bears romping all over them. Or by men built for sex. Or by a man with the biggest heart she'd come across, and a body she wanted to spend more time up close and personal with. A man who'd offered her more than she was able to deal with, was afraid to accept in case her heart was stomped on.

A man who'd just steered her in a completely different direction from any she'd gone in before.

Her blood moved faster as a thread of excitement sprang to life in her veins. She was going to be a mother— a loving, caring, happy mother. She would not bring her own childhood into this relationship with her daughter.

She would not argue and fight with Cooper when things didn't go her way.

She'd embrace her love for him and hope that it would set her free.

CHAPTER NINE

'TELL ME MORE about your childhood,' Cooper urged. After her revelation about her parents he wanted to know why Sophie felt so adamant about not marrying. Their lack of love, or inability to show it, didn't seem reason enough for Sophie to avoid marriage.

'What's to tell?'

Everything. He'd start slowly, ease his way around to the big questions—if he got the chance. 'You've never mentioned siblings. I take it you're an only child.'

'Mum and Dad didn't want me. Why would they have had more kids?'

The pain in her blunt reply churned his gut. He obviously hadn't understood how deep her anguish went. It had been wrong of her parents to have been so unloving. How could anyone not love Sophie?

He'd been busy in Theatre most of the day, yet all he'd been able to think about was how he needed to get home to see what Sophie had been doing. Had she done too much heavy lifting or moved some of that furniture by herself? Knowing she wouldn't hesitate worried him, yet the moment he'd walked in his front door all the tension had gone. Just like that. He'd come *home*. Home was where Sophie was. So he'd be without a home very shortly.

'Do *you* want more children?' The question popped out.

Her eyes widened. 'Let me get used to this baby first.'

'I always wanted a sister when I was growing up. Thought I'd have someone to share my thoughts about Dad's girlfriends with. But that probably wouldn't have worked out anyway, boys and girls seeing these things differently.'

Her chin lifted. Her eyes fixed on him. Sizing him up? Or deciding how much to say? Finally, 'I wanted a sister so that someone would love me and not blame me for everything.'

'Someone to share the blame.' Sophie's eyes returned to normal size, the green beginning to sparkle. 'I think I would like another child in a couple of years. But I'm getting ahead of myself.'

'You might be, at that.' Cooper's gut squeezed tight. He didn't want to think of her having other children. Unless he was the father. What a strange picture that brought to mind. Two people, unmarried, not living under the same roof, having more than one child together. Not right. Neither was Sophie having this one on her own. He had to be there, be a part of their child's life all the time, not every second weekend.

Her shoulders lifted in an eloquent shrug. Then, thankfully, her mouth tipped upward in a cheeky smile. 'Relax. It's not happening—unless we're in the same place and a bomb goes off.'

'You need a bomb to fire you up into a wildly hot woman?' he asked before putting his brain into gear.

Her cheeks flushed an endearing shade of red. 'Only to leap into a complete stranger's arms.'

'For the record, we'd known each other five hours.'

'Exactly. Strangers.' She was looking everywhere but at him, that red shade deepening.

'I don't regret a moment of that amazing time.' A very short encounter he'd never forgotten. The surge of longing, the heat of her body around his, the intense release. The calm that had followed. 'Do you?'

Her hand patted her belly as her brow furrowed. When she looked directly at him it was as though he'd been hit with a stun gun. 'Me neither. Not at all,' Sophie whispered.

'Because you got a baby out of it?' His heart paused, his lungs holding onto the last breath he'd taken.

Coppery hair slid across her shoulders as she shook her head. 'That was a bonus.'

Not a regret. Neither was making love, if he'd interpreted correctly. The air hissed over his lips. His heart got back to normal, though still a little loud. 'I thought you were hot the moment I first saw you standing with Kelly.'

Surprise widened her eyes again. 'Sex in hard boots.'

'What?'

'You strode towards us like you owned the world, all lean, hard muscle and completely at ease with yourself. A man used to getting his own way.'

'You labelled me sex in hard boots?' Laughter was building up inside him. He'd never have guessed. 'I always believed if it hadn't been for the high level of tension we were feeling brought on by the bombs and bullets I'd never have got close enough to make love to you.' She hadn't been putting it out there to him.

'Kelly said it first and I couldn't deny she was right. Later, I knew it for a fact.'

She wasn't being coy about that night. Neither had she been at the time, throwing herself into his arms and wrapping those legs around him.

Cooper stood and crossed to lean down so that his face was close to hers. His arms were either side of her head, his hands splayed on the back of the couch she sat on with her legs tucked under her butt. 'You were sex in fatigues. Those boring old army outfits should've been banned from your wardrobe.' He'd never thought any woman looked great in them until he'd seen Sophie that day.

Tilting her head back, she locked her eyes on him. Amazing how bright that green was. Like highly polished emeralds. Her tongue did a quick lap of those full lips he'd taken a fancy to. *They're only lips.* Hot ones.

'I've still got a set somewhere.' She grinned.

'Are you suggesting we get dressed up?' To get undressed in a hurry if past experience with Sophie was anything to go by.

She leaned closer, her mouth brushing his. 'No.'

Cooper pushed nearer, his mouth on hers. Kissing Sophie was rapidly becoming his favourite pastime, and he'd happily take it further if she was willing. The edginess he'd felt from the moment he'd seen her in Darwin had got more intense over the weeks since. His manhood often ached with longing for her, keeping him awake for hours every night. 'I want you,' he whispered, afraid she'd leap up and go lock herself in her room. Not that she'd been backing off with their kiss.

Sophie placed her hands around his neck, pulled him down over her, her lips not leaving his mouth. Her legs straightened out and somehow she was nearly on her back. Actions were speaking louder than any words she might've said.

Cooper followed through, lying beside her, not quite covering her body, cautious of knocking that baby bump too hard. His hands sought her bare skin, sliding under the blouse and up to those heavy breasts. When his fingers found her nipples she drew a quick breath.

'Oh, yes, more,' she groaned.

Happy to oblige he slid further down to place his mouth over one tight nipple and ran his tongue back and forth until Sophie's back arched under him and her hands gripped his head. Holding him there. A groan poured through him as every part of his body tensed in sweet anticipation.

'We need to shift,' Sophie murmured by his ear.

Really? 'Not far,' he replied between licks.

'Easier if I'm on top.'

'No problem.' With Sophie in his arms he flipped them over. Immediately she straddled him, her moist centre touching, teasing, tempting him.

I've died and gone some place out of this world.

His hands roamed the stretched skin of her tummy and his lips trailed kisses down over the wondrous baby bump. Then Sophie was gripping him, rubbing against his body slowly, and he was lost.

Sophie woke smiling. Her body ached pleasurably. Her muscles were loose, sated for the first time in a long time. In more than eight months. That first time hadn't been enough.

Cooper's arm lay across what used to be her waist, and his regular breathing touched the back of her neck, making her warm and cosy. Happy even. She was with Cooper, in his bed, and she didn't want to be anywhere else. Everything was right in her world. Waking up next to this man was new to her. To do it again would be wonderful. After another night like the one they'd just shared. To do it every night would be incredible—and impossible. Reality would hover outside the door, ready to pounce if she got too complacent.

Kick, kick.

'Ouch.' Talk about a timely reminder.

Kick.

'You're hurting Mummy.' Though to be fair, baby would've been bounced around at times throughout the night.

'Good morning, beautiful.' Cooper propped on one elbow to lean over her. 'How's our girl? We didn't wear her out, did we?'

Sophie took his hand and placed it where the baby was doing her morning warm-up routine. 'I wish.'

'Whoa. She's really going for it.'

'Have you thought of names for her?' Asking about names had never been on her list of things to discuss with Cooper. It should've been. No names that she'd first written down were making her smile.

Taking her chin between those fingers she remembered doing amazing things to her body during the night, Cooper forced her to turn so he could eyeball her expression. 'Thank you for asking. There are a couple I like but didn't think you'd want my input.'

She hadn't for a long time. But after all they'd shared over the past ten hours it was time to let go some of the fear of sharing that kept her alone. Besides, she was moving on now. If she and Cooper could spend a night together like the one she'd just woken from, then there was a lot more they could do together. The only reason they weren't was that she was still holding back, tying down her independence because to let any of it go terrified her. Her independence had been born of necessity, a way to survive the brutal onslaught of her parents' tirades. It had been the light she'd focused on, the future she needed to escape to. Despite deciding to let go of the past, it wasn't happening so easily. There were habits to break here. 'I said I'd never stop you having a part in baby's life. That includes choosing a name for her.'

He nodded, so she continued. 'I've got a list that's getting shorter by the day. I keep thinking I'll find something better. What names have you chosen?'

'Lily and Emma.'

'Lily. I like it.' Emma was on her list, but not Lily. 'Lily Ingram. That works.'

'So does Lily Daniels.'

Sophie winced. 'Ingram-Daniels. Bit of a mouthful.'

Cooper sat up. 'We know how to fix the problem. My offer's still on the table.'

A chill lifted the skin on her arms. They could share a night of mind-blowing sex. They could even agree on a first name for their child. But they would never agree about marriage. Rolling over awkwardly, she stood up from the bed, and immediately felt at a disadvantage as Cooper's gaze cruised her big, extended body. It was one thing to make love with him, but to stand here while he studied her was too much. Snatching up a pillow to hold against her, she headed for the door. 'I need to shower.'

'You are very beautiful, Sophie. Don't hide from me.'

She hesitated. Cooper hadn't watched her growing slowly, inch by inch over the months. He was getting the full-blown picture and not cringing. That said a lot for the man. It also told her that she needed to put a stop to this before she got in too deep. They were not having an intimate relationship. Despite spending the night in his bed exploring each other's bodies. Despite the warmth expanding through her even now when her legs were tense, ready to run.

No more running, remember?

'Nothing's changed. I can't marry you.' Okay, so some things would take for ever to change.

'Are you sure that's because of how your parents treated you growing up?' Determination was lighting up in his eyes. 'Or is there a deeper reason?'

Sophie wasn't sure at all any more. But one thing she'd swear was that she would not marry a man who did not love her. Even looking forward, that was non-negotiable. 'Whatever the reasons, they're mine. You need to get it into your head once and for ever that we are not tying the knot.'

Not waiting for his reply, she headed for the bathroom. Cooper was capable of talking her into making decisions that were wrong for her. She had to be strong as she worked out her future. Had to hold out for what was important to her, because that was important for her child. She couldn't accept the first offer that came her way. Even if it came from the only man who'd managed to rattle her with his caring ways, his kindnesses and his humour.

Don't forget his determination to see something through.

Exactly. That was why she was taking a shower and not another round in bed.

The sex in hard boots image had a lot to do with her wanting more of him. Her lungs expelled overheated air. But it went further. Behind that stunning face and hard body was the man who had her longing for a life she'd never believed in.

It's not possible, no matter that you love him.

'Sophie?' Cooper called down the hall. 'If you're that certain, why did last night happen?'

A very good question, and one she had no answer for except, 'I like sex. I like you. Why not?'

Her flippant words would sting him, but this was about keeping the wall erected between them.

The first step towards that was to move into her apartment.

'Then rest assured it won't be happening again. Neither will I propose again.' His voice was heavy with pain, the words silent hits against her heart.

She'd done a number on him, and for that she was very sorry. His pain cramped her stomach. Guilt made her squirm. She should've gone about it in a softer, kinder way, but he never took notice of anything she said. Until now. Harsh words had made a difference. Sometimes the sledgehammer approach was all there was. He'd finally got the message. He'd said so. No marriage. No sex.

Life was looking up.

She sank against the bathroom wall and pressed her fist against her mouth. From the mirror desolation stared her in the face.

Cooper glared out through the rain at his overgrown lawns. What did people do on a Saturday afternoon in weather like this? He'd spent the morning at the hospital, visiting his patients, talking to them about their surgeries and when to expect they might go home.

He'd even had a coffee with Svetlana as a delaying tactic against coming back to this empty shell of a home. The instant they'd sat down in the cafeteria he'd regretted asking her to join him. She'd read his invitation differently from how he'd meant it, and turning her down again hadn't sat comfortably with him. He didn't like deliberately hurting anyone. But what was a man to do?

There was no excitement within these walls. Since Sophie had moved out, not even leaving behind one piece of clothing or a book for him to hold, the place was back to being a house, not a home. She'd made the difference. Had made it warm with her personality, vibrant with her enthusiasm for their impending baby. Typical. The moment he'd realised how much he'd had with her she'd done a bunk.

So go grovel. Ask her to come back.

It wouldn't work. When Sophie said no she meant no. Changing her mind was mission impossible. Besides, there were only so many times he could handle being turned down. When she'd said she liked having sex with him his body had sat up but his heart had slowed at the reminder they wouldn't be getting married.

It went to show that other parts of his body were wiser than his heart and brain. Sex with Sophie was hot and, apparently, uninvolved. The only kind of sex he'd ever gone for. Now that his heart had decided to get in on the act everything was skewed. But he'd soon quieten that down. Had to. No other way to survive life post-Sophie.

Couldn't she see he was only trying to do right by her and the baby? Grinding his teeth, he held back the oath threatening to emerge.

His phone vibrating in his pocket was a welcome distraction. 'Hey, Dad, how was your trip?' he asked.

'Hello, son. Queenstown's got to be the best place to visit in winter. We visited Arrowtown, went tobogganing on Coronet Peak without breaking a leg, and I won't mention the fabulous waterfront restaurants.'

We. Cooper sighed. *Here we go again.*

Dad had another young woman to trot out and about. At least *he* didn't go for ridiculously younger females. 'When did you get back?'

'Last night. Which is why I'm ringing. You at home, by any chance? Thought I'd drop by and catch up on what you've been doing.'

'Sure thing.' His afternoon wouldn't be so dull any more. Spending time with his father was never boring, even if it was sometimes uncomfortable, depending on his latest conquest.

'I'm bringing someone with me I'd like you to meet.'

Nothing new in that. 'I'll make sure there's a bottle of wine in the fridge.' Make that two. Might as well enjoy the afternoon and drown out thoughts of Sophie for a few hours.

'It's a pleasure to finally meet you, Cooper,' the woman his father had introduced as his 'special friend', Gillian, held out her hand.

Knock me down.

Cooper took the proffered hand, trying to hold his mouth from falling open. 'I have to say the same.' A special friend was nothing new. But Gillian was lovely in a completely different way from Dad's previous encounters. Dressed in simple black trousers with a blouse that didn't expose acres of flesh, she was refreshing. *And* she'd definitely left her thirties decades ago. 'Delighted.'

'I'm not staying long,' Gillian told him as she accepted a glass of wine. 'I need to hit the supermarket, and I'm sure you both have plenty to talk about without me butting in all the time.' She gave him a knowing wink before turning to his father. 'Don't forget to ask Cooper if that date suits him.'

His father smiled softly. 'Not likely to, am I?'

Something was up. Cooper's gut had begun churning and turning sour in an old familiar way. At thirty-eight years old his stomach should know it was wasting acid. Whatever his dad did he did, and that was that. The only hope he could come up with was that his father hadn't decided to sell up and invest his money in some offshore scam. Though that was highly unlikely, the old man being shrewd with his money, if not with women.

The churning continued, but Cooper refused to ask any questions. He knew they only brought answers he wouldn't like. He'd wait until his father came out with it.

Which he did before the front door had closed behind Gillian. 'We're getting married, son. Next month. Eighth of October, to be exact.'

Kapow! Dad was settling down. With a woman his own age, and who didn't look like she'd promise the earth and leave anyway. 'Dad.' He choked up. He spun a chair around and straddled the seat. The back rest was essential for his arms, which in turn held his head up.

'You'd never have guessed, would you?' If anyone wondered what a smile from ear to ear really looked like, they only had to look at his father right now.

'You care about Gillian that much?' Role reversal here. Not that his father had had the opportunity to quiz him about any particular woman becoming a permanent fixture in his life. *Sophie*. Yeah, right. No need for questions when she wasn't interested.

'Yes, I do. I want to give her everything. I want a proper relationship and I know I'll have it with Gillian.'

This could be good for the old man, who'd been lonely since his mother had left them. He was a man who didn't like his own company too much and filled the empty gaps with women. Until now completely unsuitable women.

A man just like me.

Gasp. Give over. Not true at all. Then why did he move around a lot? Join organisations like the army where time alone was a rarity? Because he wanted to give something of himself to his country. Sure. That came into it, but it was hardly his primary motivation.

'Cooper? Are you not happy for me?' His father sounded worried, annoyed even. 'I assure you Gillian is a wonderful woman, and you won't change my mind.'

'I'm thrilled. Seriously.' He stood and reached to wrap his arms around his father. 'I can see she's lovely.' Why had it taken this long for the old man to find someone more suited to him?

Stepping out of the hug, his father sat down and stretched his legs out. 'I just wish I'd met her twenty years ago.'

Cooper sprawled over the couch. 'Guess them's the breaks, eh?'

'You'll be at the wedding? It's going to be small, just Gillian's daughters and their husbands, and grandchildren, and you.'

'Try keeping me away.' For something as huge as this he was accepting it too easily. His stomach had returned to quiet mode, his arms no longer felt tingly and useless. 'I've always wanted this for you.' And thereby for himself. Then his tongue got away from him, which only went to show he hadn't quite accepted his father's news yet. 'You're not rushing this?'

His father beamed contentedly. 'Neither of us is getting any younger. There's a reason why that's a cliché.'

'Come to think of it, I haven't seen you so relaxed in years.' If ever. Which wrapped it up for Cooper. 'You're happy. I'm thrilled.'

'Yes, son, I am. Gillian makes me feel calm—about everything.' He raised an eyebrow. 'And we both know how stressed I usually get about anything and everything.'

'True.' Something he'd inherited to some extent but did better at controlling than Dad.

'It's not what she does but how she comports herself, dealing with situations in an orderly, quiet manner.'

'I know what you mean,' Cooper muttered.

'You do?'

'Yeah.' Shock rippled through him. 'I do.' Sophie did that for him. The first time had been when that bomb had blown their world apart. She'd got back on her feet and immediately began assessing the situation from a medical point of view, giving orders, saving lives. That calm ability to prioritise and make sure Kelly and the others had got the absolute best care while chaos had reigned around them had settled his pounding heart and put his fear on the backburner. He knew he'd looked in control, but internally he'd been a mess.

Since then there'd been other instances where a look or word from Sophie and his worry settled. 'I totally get you.'

'Who is she?' his dad asked, with a knowing gleam in his eye.

'Sophie.' Oh, hell. The baby. Reality clanged into his head. 'What date did you say you're getting married?'

'October the eighth. Is there a problem?' His dad's mouth tightened. 'I want you there.'

Cooper stood up and paced across the room. Turned, came towards his father. Be calm. How could he?

Sophie, where are you when I need you? I'm about set off another grenade.

His chest rose on an indrawn breath. Think of Sophie and how she calmed him.

Sophie.

'Dad.' His fingers rammed through his hair. 'How do you feel about becoming a grandfather?'

CHAPTER TEN

'HELLO, JACOB.' SOPHIE took Melanie's baby and held him close. 'How's my favourite wee man this morning?' Tears threatened. That had been happening a lot today. Baby brain? Confusion over her relationship with Cooper? Waking up alone in her cold apartment? All of the above and more.

'Grizzly, hungry and tired,' Jacob's mother retorted. 'But I wouldn't change a thing if it meant being without him.' Her face lit up with love.

Sophie sat on the second chair in the kitchenette of the tiny flat supplied by social welfare that Melanie had moved into with her help. 'I can't wait to hold my baby now.' Since Jacob's arrival the birth of her daughter had become very real. After talking with Melanie, so were the sleepless nights, the constant crying and disgusting nappies. None of which dampened her excitement. Bring it on. Bring her on.

'Counting down the days, are you?' Melanie asked, with a worried look at Jacob. 'I didn't do that. I was so afraid of the pain, as well as worrying what I'd do afterwards.'

I bet you were.

'I don't want her coming too early. But I'm so ready it's hard waiting.' She wouldn't wish health issues on her child just for the sake of a few days, but she'd had enough of carrying this bulge around.

'I had a visitor today,' Melanie said quietly. 'My mum.'

The mother who'd kicked her daughter out of her home months ago. 'How did that go?'

'She wants me to have Jacob adopted so I can get on with my life. She says I have no idea what it's going to be like, giving up everything for a child, and I'm going to regret it for the rest of my life.'

A chill slid up Sophie's spine. Hadn't her mother complained often about how she'd given up everything for her? How she'd had to stop her nursing training, how she'd married the wrong man, how her life had become dull and pointless. All because of her daughter.

Thanks, Mum.

'She won't budge on her stance?'

A fat tear slid down Melanie's face as she shook her head. 'I thought she loved me, but she won't listen to what I want. I'm supposed to make something of my life. Being a mother doesn't count.'

The bitterness appalled Sophie. But she also understood it—because she'd been there. Was sometimes still stuck there, but now she was slowly edging her way ahead. Listening to Melanie's tale only strengthened her resolve to do what was right for her baby and not what her heart wished. She'd been right to turn Cooper down about marriage and even about sharing his house. 'Don't let them beat you. You are strong, and on the days you don't think you can cope you've got my number.' She'd come to care a lot for this tough young woman in a very short time. 'We'll work our way through your problems.'

'Thanks for the *we*. It means a lot. Now, I'd better feed Jacob before he screams the roof down and the neighbours complain.'

He had become very vocal in the short time Sophie had been holding him. 'Hey, wee man, talk nicely to Mummy. She's the drinks trolley.' Standing up, she stretched and rubbed the small of her back. 'I'd better get cracking.' Cooper had asked if he could visit her on his way home from work.

Of course she'd said yes, because she hadn't found the strength to do otherwise. She missed him. Her apartment was cosy but nothing like Cooper's comfortable home where she'd loved curling up on the sofa with a book and coffee. She wanted to say that the difference was in the size of the apartment, but it wasn't. It was in the lack of Cooper's company. She'd enjoyed sharing a meal with him, and discussing surgery, and the army and life in general, in finding socks on the bathroom floor. Just knowing he lived there had put her at ease in a way she'd never experienced.

'You're looking tetchy.' Cooper grinned at her when she opened her front door to his knock. 'Will these cheer you up?' He held out a bunch of daffodils. 'First of the season, though it doesn't feel like spring today.'

A gust of cold wind underlined his words. Shivering, she took the bright yellow bundle. 'They're lovely.' Moisture dampened the corners of her eyes. Cooper had brought her flowers? He'd rung her each day since she'd moved out nearly a week ago, always friendly and chatty, always asked if there was anything she needed doing. Not once had he made a comment about them being together for the baby's sake. She didn't know this Cooper, and wasn't sure how to take him.

'I thought so.' He looked as pleased as he sounded.

'Come in so I can shut the not-so-spring-like weather out.' Heading into her small lounge, she suddenly stopped. 'I don't own a vase.'

'Not used to getting flowers, then?' He chuckled.

'Ego.' No, she wasn't. 'I'll put them in the coffee plunger.' It was the only tall, narrow container that came to mind. Put on shopping list one vase. Just in case. 'Want a wine?'

'Got bourbon, by any chance?'

Add bourbon to the list. 'Sorry. Since I'm not drinking I haven't filled the cupboard with spirits.' And she was saving on the dollars that had dwindled far too rapidly since returning from Darwin.

'Wine will be fine. Shall I get it while you're arranging those daffodils? Oh. Very classy.'

She'd pulled the paper from around the stalks and dropped the flowers into the plunger. 'There. Arranged.' She added water and placed the colourful bunch in the middle of her new table. 'They brighten the place up heaps.'

'How was your day? Did you see the midwife again?' He leaned that delectable butt against the bench, bottle in one hand, glass in the other.

'Yes, and all's good. My BP's hovering on borderline low but that's better than where it used to be.' Thank goodness. That had been scary.

'And your glucose?'

'No change.' She'd been meticulous in avoiding sugary foods from the moment she'd learned she had diabetes. No way was she hurting her baby, neither did she want the diabetes to continue after the birth. 'I paid Melanie a quick visit. Jacob's a treat. I'd swear he's growing already.'

'How's Melanie coping?'

'She's awesome with Jacob, considering she's only eighteen and on her own. Her mother's paid a visit, apparently pushing her to put the baby up for adoption.

Even said she knew a couple who'd take him.' At least her parents hadn't done that to her, though she might've been loved better if they had. She'd never know, and she didn't think the answer had been for her to be adopted out. They were *her* parents, and she did love them in an oddball kind of way. And since visiting them to drop her news in their laps she'd begun to think they might reciprocate that love after all.

'Sophie? You're looking sad when moments ago you were all smiles.'

'Why are some parents so assertive? What's wrong with asking Melanie what she wants and trying to help her achieve that?' Her own doubts flooded in, cooling her skin and making her shiver. What if she couldn't be the mother she hoped to be, the mother she'd have adored as she'd grown up?

'Come here.' Cooper wrapped his arms around her. 'You're going to be the best mum yet.'

She should pull away from this man, who was becoming very adept at reading her, but it felt so right being held by him, leaning against that hard body. She needed his strength today. Her own ability to stand strong had gone on holiday, leaving her prone to pointless tears. Even better, though, Cooper apparently believed in her. That was gold. Tipping her head back to look at him, she said, 'You sound so sure. Thank you. It makes a difference.'

'Only speaking the truth.'

Even when he didn't know her well. Breathing deeply, she pulled away before it became impossible to leave him. 'What have you been up to today?' She flipped the conversation onto him and away from all her insecurities. Enough of them for one day.

He picked up his glass, his soft, caring gaze still on

her. 'The usual follow-ups with patients, appointments with new ones, and an emergency gall-bladder operation.'

'That sounds like fun. I'm envious.'

'Fun is not the word I'd use, though, yes, I still get a kick out of performing surgery. Why the envy?'

'I'm bored.' More tears threatened, which was ridiculous. What was wrong with her to be acting like a spoilt brat? Looking around the apartment, the answer was obvious. 'Now that I've got everything ready here and have bought more clothes and toys than baby will ever use, I'm missing work.'

'You're restless. Find me a thirty-seven-week pregnant woman who isn't. When did you last perform an operation?'

'Two days before you turned up in Darwin. An appendectomy.' Serious work had been referred to the local hospital.

'Nothing too taxing, then.' He sipped his wine. 'Make the most of this time. I bet once the baby comes you won't have a moment to spare.'

'Yeah, yeah. I know all that. But I've never been one to sit around, and I've already had my fill of the malls.'

'And I was sure you're a female.' Cooper gave her one of his delectable smiles.

The kind that went straight to her libido. Damn him. Sex was not happening. Not now, not ever again. So a distraction was needed. 'Want to grab something to eat and take in a movie?'

As distractions went it worked—sort of. Sophie managed to tamp down her libido as she ate her burger and chips. It helped that while he ate his second burger Cooper annoyed her by pointing out that fast food was not healthy. Then the movie enthralled her and all thought of sex was forgotten.

Until she climbed into her lonely, cold bed and tried to go to sleep. Big fail. Wrapping her arms around herself to find some warmth, all she could think was what if Cooper had come in instead of dropping her off at the door? Would they have ended up in bed, making out? Would he now be kissing hot, slick trails over her breasts and down to where she throbbed with need? Would she have given in to her longing? Or would she have fought it, pushing him away once again?

You're never going to know.

Right now she had to snuggle tighter and forget Cooper. Forget she loved him, and focus on her own life and how everything was now about the baby. Starting with getting some sleep.

Not happening. Deep breathing didn't work. Swapping from her left side to her right was no better. Even when her body warmed, sleep remained elusive.

Rolling onto her back, she stared up at the dark ceiling.

Cooper brought me flowers.

The last time anyone had done that had been in her third year at med school and she'd been going out with one of her fellow students. It had been her twenty-third birthday and he'd taken her to dinner at his father's restaurant. That's when she'd understood he'd been far too serious about her and she'd pulled the plug on their relationship. Somehow she didn't think Cooper was about to walk away from her. Not when he'd proposed twice. She had done her darnedest to push him away, but it seemed he didn't know when to give up.

You're not being fair. If you don't want to settle down with Cooper then don't keep him on a string.

She hadn't known she was.

You went out with him tonight, didn't you? You accepted those flowers.

The warmth left her body. Had she been a bitch? Using Cooper when she was out of her depth with this pregnancy? As if anyone could keep him dangling. He was in charge of his own life. But one thing was true. She'd been unfair. All because she loved him, and at the moment needed his steady presence.

So why the flowers?

The doorbell rang as Sophie was just about to throw something at the wall in boredom. 'Coming,' she yelled in relief.

But when she yanked the door open and was confronted with two burly guys, leaning against what appeared to be a large chair wrapped in padded plastic wrap, disappointment tugged. 'I think you've got the wrong address.'

'Sophie Ingram? This isn't Apartment Three, The Willows?' One of the guys deliberately stared at the bronze three on her doorframe.

'Yes, but that's not mine.' Her finger stabbed in the direction of the chair.

The other guy tugged a packing slip from his pocket and read it. 'Yes, it is. Bought and signed for yesterday by a...' He squinted. 'Cooper Daniels.'

Her jaw dropped. Cooper had bought her a chair? Whatever for? She had two reasonably comfortable ones in her lounge and there was no room for another, even if she needed it.

A chair is bigger and says more than daffodils.

'You know this dude?' one of the men asked.

'Yes.'

I thought I did. But he's buying me things. Gifts. Hadn't expected that.

'You'd better come in.' She glanced at her doorway. 'How are you going to fit the chair through this gap?'

'No problem. We're instructed to put it in your bedroom.'

Clang. Her jaw was behaving badly this morning. 'My bedroom?' She'd be needing to knock a wall down to make space. 'I think you should put it in the lounge.'

'It says here that we've got to put the chair in your bedroom.' The guy squinted at the docket again and grinned. 'And that we're to take no notice of the lady if she insists otherwise.'

'You'll have to shift my bed,' she acquiesced.

'Not a problem.' Grin-face chuckled. 'You don't look in any state to be moving heavy furniture, if you don't mind me saying.'

Did she have a choice?

Just you wait, Cooper Daniels.

But after the men had managed to fit the chair into a corner of her room by manoeuvring the dresser to one side and the bed in another direction, and had gone away, she'd removed metres of plastic wrap to find a leather rocking chair that matched her furniture perfectly. No denying the gift was thoughtful and caring. Like Cooper. A nursing chair was exactly what she wanted and hadn't been able to justify spending money on.

'Last weekend I met someone whom I quite like,' Cooper told Sophie on Friday night when he turned up at her apartment after work.

Sophie's heart stopped. Cooper had met a woman? One he liked? What about…? Her? Their baby?

'Her name's Gillian and she's in love with my dad. They're getting married.'

Sophie's knees sagged in relief. Leaning against the table for strength, she said, 'Married? I'm glad you like her.' Phew. But she shouldn't have been worrying. If she wasn't marrying him then she had no right to be disgruntled.

Cooper pulled a chair out from the table. 'Sit down. You look ready to drop. Ah, not as in about to have the baby.'

Sinking onto the chair, she leaned her elbows on the table and lowered her chin into her shaky hands. 'Tell me more.'

And divert me from the shock of that sudden stab of jealousy.

Cooper twirled his bourbon glass between his finger and thumb. 'Dad started dating within a year of Mum's death. I guess he was lonely.' His throat worked as he sipped his drink. The silence stretched out between them. A shudder jerked through him. 'Dad had a succession of young women, none staying long. Though the second one did hang around for nearly a year and I thought at the time she might become my stepmum. It didn't happen.' He put his glass down with a bang. 'Anyway, this isn't about me. Gillian's close to Dad's age and they're in love. It's so odd seeing Dad tripping over himself to please her. Not that Gillian takes advantage. She's just as busy making him happy.'

Sophie wished she could have a drink too. Seemed everyone was fixing up their lives lately. Maybe there was hope for her one day.

Cooper continued, 'The thing is, I told Dad about the baby, and he and Gillian want to meet you. You're also invited to the wedding, though there's a problem there. It's on the same day as Junior is due.'

Sophie's head was whirling. 'Slow down. I can't keep up.' She didn't want to. This was too much. Cooper's father and soon-to-be wife wanted to meet her, presumably as grandparents-to-be. Why had she never considered this? Cooper had hardly ever mentioned his family so she'd not thought it through. It wasn't all bad. Not bad at all really. 'Our baby will have four grandparents.' A smile began lifting her mouth as her heart warmed. 'That's wonderful.'

'Agreed. Did you hear the rest of what I said?'

'No. Wait. The wedding date. It's the same as our girl's expected arrival.' Her buoyant mood sank. Naturally Cooper would want to attend his father's nuptials. Until this moment she hadn't realised how much she was depending on him being with her for the birth.

'How many babies arrive on their due date?' Cooper asked with a smile. 'Let's wait and see what happens. I am going to be there for the birth, Sophie. Our baby comes first.'

Hope flittered through her, to be followed by pain. 'I can't ask you to forego your father's wedding.'

'You didn't. I'm telling you. I am not missing my daughter's birth.' His smile was so soft and intoxicating it made her want to curl up on his lap.

So she remained on her chair and waited for this particular brain fade to settle back to normal.

'Feel like going round the corner for Thai?' he asked before she'd got herself under control.

Thai, Indian, burgers. She didn't care what she ate. She'd be with Cooper for another hour or so. The sigh that escaped her was full of excitement.

So much for restraint around this man.

* * *

Glad of the mask covering his lower face, Cooper relaxed into a smile as he began the final layer of sutures on Jason Mowbray's abdomen.

Last night Sophie's face had been a picture when she'd heard his father wanted to meet her. There'd been no doubts whatsoever about Dad becoming a grandfather—he'd embraced the whole situation in an instant. Sophie had been just as accepting of his father's place in her baby's life.

She'd kill him if she knew how hard he was trying to get her to rethink her stance on getting married. Getting her to meet his father and Gillian was all part of the plan.

The chair had been a huge hit. For a moment when she'd first rung after it'd been delivered, he'd wondered if he'd gone too far. He had been prepared to argue his case, which was that as the baby's father he was entitled to look out for the baby's mother. The argument hadn't eventuated, Sophie being ecstatic about the chair and forgetting to be annoyed at his interference.

Cooper dropped the suture needle into the kidney dish and straightened up, rubbing his lower back with one hand. 'Right, that's done.' Nodding at Becky, the anaesthetist, he added, 'Let's bring him round.'

'That tumour wasn't as large as you'd predicted,' the senior registrar on the other side of the table commented.

'Something to be thankful for.' Jason still had a rough time ahead, with chemo and radiation as soon as today's wounds healed. The guy was only thirty-five. Far too young to be dealing with cancer.

Cooper had seen it all before, often, and always wondered what was ahead for him. Life was unpredictable, was meant to be grabbed with both hands. He knew it.

Yet he'd been so restless for so long, not knowing what he wanted to be doing—to be grabbing.

You haven't been restless since landing in Darwin last month.

Because of Sophie. Yeah, he got it. Seeing that she and the baby wanted for nothing, were safe and cared for, was his focus at the moment.

There were more ways of proving to her that he could be a good father and ideal partner than by putting his future in her hands with marriage proposals. Empty proposals. If only he'd known his true feelings for her before putting them out there, he might've convinced her he meant it. Might've told her he loved her. He froze. His hands clenched. No, he would not have done that.

It had taken his father's comment about how Gillian calmed him, centred him, for *him* to realise Sophie did the same for him. She was the centre of his universe. He was still reeling with accepting what that meant. That he loved her—with every cell of his body. Now he had to show her. He wouldn't think about what he'd do if she never came round. Probably go back to the army and transfer offshore. No, he wouldn't. He had a daughter to factor into any moves he made now.

'Cooper? You all right?' Becky was peering at him with a worried look.

'Yes.' The bones in his fingers cracked as he unclenched them one by one. Couldn't be better. 'How's Jason doing?'

'Coming round slowly.'

As per normal, then. Air huffed from his lungs. Thank goodness. He still needed to know his patient had come through the anaesthesia before he fully relaxed after every procedure he performed. A leftover from the very first operation he'd performed as a consultant when the woman had had a fatal cardiac arrest as she'd been coming round. Not his fault and yet he'd carried the guilt ever since. 'Right, take him through to Recovery.'

Becky nudged him. 'Got time for a coffee before going to talk to Jason?'

He always tried to have a moment with his patients in Recovery, hopefully reassuring them as they fought their way through the post-anaesthetic haze. 'Put the kettle on. I'll grab my phone.'

Urgency drove him to his locker. He'd been out of communication for two and a half hours. What if Sophie needed him? The blood was racing around his body as he tapped the screen. No new messages. He sagged against the locker in relief.

'That baby's certainly got you in a twist.' Becky was shaking her head at him. 'Like all first-time dads.'

'That obvious, huh?' Hauling himself upright, he shoved the phone in his pocket and slammed the locker shut. 'There's less than three weeks to go. I'm going to be shattered by the time she does make an appearance.'

Becky just laughed. 'That's only the beginning.'

Not really. But she didn't know he wouldn't be dealing with the interrupted sleep, the midnight feeds and dirty nappies.

But the days were speeding past. By the time the baby arrived he hoped he'd have made inroads with getting closer to Sophie. He loved her. No argument. Winning her over was proving to be a hurdle.

Proposing for a third time was not an option. He couldn't take rejection again. Not when he finally understood how much he loved her. Hearing Sophie say no now would break his heart into so many pieces he doubted his ability to put them back together. He just had to continue spending time with her, helping her get prepared for the birth and doing the little things with the hope she'd begin to appreciate having him around.

'Here, get that into you.' A mug of murky coffee appeared before him.

A train whistle sounded from his pocket. *Sophie?* Coffee slopped on the floor as he fumbled for the phone. His ear hurt where the phone hit. 'Hello? Sophie? What's happening?'

'We're on.' A breathless gurgling sound followed her sentence.

'Are you laughing?' Couldn't be in labour, then.

'Sort of,' she gasped around a groan. A long groan that had nothing to do with laughter and everything to do with pain.

His stomach clenched, his jaw tightened. Sophie was in pain.

Sophie's in labour.

And he was here in the hospital, doing nothing to help her. 'Where are you?' The coffee mug hit the table. His scrubs flew across the room in the general direction of the laundry basket. 'I'm on my way.'

Erratic breathing came from the phone. 'Cooper.' His name was ground out. 'I need you. Now. At the maternity unit.'

'On my way.' Yeah. She needed him. He slumped forward. Was he up to speed with this? Could he help or would he be a hindrance?

'Cooper? Is the baby coming?' Becky was wiping up spilled coffee.

His head jerked. Pulling himself straight, he looked the anaesthetist in the eye. He was strong, he did not flinch at the first sign of trouble. He would be there with Sophie, for Sophie, all the way through the birth. 'Yes.

I've got to go. Can you see Jason, explain and tell him I'll be in to see him later?'

He didn't wait for her reply.

He barely waited for the traffic lights to turn green.

As for the lift up to the maternity unit? Forget it. He took the stairs two at a time.

'Which room?' he yelled as he charged towards reception. 'Sophie Ingram.'

'Right behind you.' A midwife chuckled.

The door banged against the wall as he tripped over his own feet and fell through it. 'Hey, Sophie, I'm here.'

'I think everyone on this floor is aware of that.'

Cooper stared at the woman standing by the window, looking for all the world completely relaxed, like she had nothing pressing to do. 'Why are you so calm?'

Because she's Sophie, that's why.

'You didn't sound composed on the phone.' Not at all.

'That's because—' Sophie gasped, leaned forward to wrap her arms around her belly, the muscles in her neck cording as a contraction seized her.

'Hey...' Cooper stepped up, wound his arms right around her. 'I'm here, sweetheart.' She was tense, her whole body contorted with pain. How could he take that away from her? Take the pain into his body for her?

She sank against him, her body now limp. 'That was the worst yet.'

Using his palm, he rubbed gentle circles over her back. 'When did you start labour?'

'About two hours ago. I couldn't find my phone to call you. It was in my bag all along.' When she lifted her head she gave him a watery smile. 'It's happening. Our baby's coming. I can't believe it.'

Cooper's heart crunched at the sight of her misty eyes

filled with awe. Leaning down, he brushed his lips across her mouth. 'You look beautiful.'

Those emerald orbs widened, and she gave him a sweet smile. 'You're delusional.'

Then the smile snapped off, the eyes tightened into slits and she was gripping his shoulders, hanging on grimly as her body took another hit.

'Remember to breathe.' The midwife appeared beside them. 'You're doing fine, Sophie.'

'There wasn't long between the last two contractions,' he noted.

The midwife nodded. 'I think this wee girl is in a bit of a hurry. Time for another examination, Sophie.'

Um, should he disappear for a few minutes? But he wanted to be with Sophie all the way. She shouldn't be on her own at all. The midwife didn't count as a special support person. He locked eyes with her. 'I can wait outside.'

Warmth stole through him when she shook her head. 'Not necessary. Stay and hold my hand.'

So calm. So Sophie.

Cooper wanted to retract those words later when Sophie cried out with pain and squeezed his hand to breaking point. All semblance of calm had taken a hike.

'You're doing great,' he told her as her body tensed under the power of another contraction.

'Huh. Like you'd know.'

'You've got me there.'

'Don't be smart. Shut up and hold me.'

Yes, ma'am.

Catching her around the waist, he tugged her gently so she was draped over him. Putting his hands to good use, he began softly massaging the knots in the muscles around her shoulders.

Knots that returned within minutes as another contraction took over.

Cooper started again. Stopped to hold her as she worked through the pain gripping and squeezing at her. Started massaging, stopped to hold, massage, hold. Time became a blur.

Until the midwife told Sophie, 'Time for another examination.'

Then he held Sophie's hand while they waited for the verdict.

'Baby's crowning. We're almost there. You're doing really well, Sophie.'

Cooper kissed the back of Sophie's hand. 'You're amazing.'

Emerald became sort of green-grey as Sophie's eyes turned misty. 'I'm glad you're here with me. With us.'

Who knew what colour *his* eyes were now? They were certainly wetter than normal, and his voice croaked as he said, 'We're a family.' One way or another.

Surprisingly he didn't get slapped for saying that. Instead, Sophie pulled his head down to kiss him. A full lips-on-lips kiss that spoke of happiness and love and exhaustion.

The kiss finished abruptly as Lily Ingram-Daniels rushed into the world, giving her mother one last, long grip of pain.

When Lily eventually obliged the midwife with a cry Sophie reached for her baby, all trace of pain gone from her face, replaced with love so strong and fierce Cooper had no doubt his daughter was in the very best of hands.

Cooper's body was racked with relief and love, with amazement and fear as he gazed at his daughter. He would love this wee girl for the rest of his life, would do anything to protect her and keep her happy. He feared what could happen to her and knew that was never going to leave him. He'd become a father.

Slashing his hand over his eyes and across his cheeks didn't stop the flood of tears, just as others streaked down Sophie's cheeks. If he hadn't loved her before this moment then he'd have fallen for her right now. Her sweat-slicked skin glistened, her damp hair clung to her face, and she was the most beautiful sight he'd ever seen. *They* were. Mother and daughter.

'She's got your colouring,' Sophie said without taking her eyes off her girl.

'As long as she's got your nature.' He grinned.

Then Sophie did look up at him. 'Sit on the bed.' She held her precious bundle out to him. 'Come on, Dad, meet your daughter properly.'

His knees buckled, depositing him beside Sophie with a thump. His arms were reaching for Lily even before he'd shuffled his butt further onto the bed. And then his arms were full of the sweetest, softest little girl he'd ever known. He stared at her, drinking in the cutest little nose, the few strands of dark hair, the clenched red fist that had pushed free of the blanket.

'Here.' Sophie leaned forward with a tissue to mop his face. 'You're going to drown her at this rate.'

The midwife cleared her throat. 'The paediatrician wants to see Lily to make sure everything's fine.'

Sophie's chin shot up as she asked, 'What are you concerned about?'

Cooper's heart stopped.

Please, no. Pick me, leave my daughter alone.

'Nothing's wrong. Around here it's routine to have babies checked over by any specialist who's hanging around the joint.'

Sophie sighed. 'That's good. Thank you.'

Cooper knew he was grinning like a loon but didn't care. 'Baby brain eh? And you thought it would be gone the moment little miss here put in an appearance.'

She whacked his arm softly. 'Thanks a lot.' Her eyes followed Lily as the midwife took her away. That perpetual smile faded.

'Hey…' He wrapped both her hands in his. 'Relax. She's going to be fine. So are you. Hopefully you'll get some sleep tonight.'

Her nose screwed up in annoyance. 'Whatever's best for baby, I know, but I'd prefer to be going home now.'

'You have to learn to feed Lily first.'

'Why, isn't it as easy as it looks?'

'You're asking me?' He grinned. It might be weeks before his mouth returned to normal. 'But I can hang around to keep you from getting bored.'

And watch over his girls.

CHAPTER ELEVEN

SOPHIE COULDN'T BELIEVE she'd fallen asleep. Not when her baby was in the crib right next to her bed. How could she not have stayed awake to watch over her? She pushed up onto an elbow and peered into the crib, marvelled at the sweet face and the tiny body wrapped in a blanket.

I produced that?

Pride filled her before worry took over.

I went to sleep. How could I?

'I've been keeping an eye on you both,' Cooper said softly from the other side of her hospital room.

Thank goodness someone had. 'How long have I been out?'

'An hour. And relax. You needed it. Lily's been sleeping the whole time but I think the nurse will be in shortly to watch you feed her.' He looked so at ease with all of this.

Sophie felt her heart lift as she studied him. 'I couldn't have done any of this on my own and there's no one else I'd have wanted there for the birth.' Not even her friend who had intended being her birthing partner.

'I wouldn't have missed it for anything.'

Unless she'd been an idiot and not allowed him in the room. But she hadn't. At least she'd had the sense to see he had every right to be there, and in return she'd had the best partner imaginable. 'You were awesome. Didn't know you could massage like that.' His hands on her back and shoulders had been firm, yet soft, as he'd worked out the knots in her muscles. He'd soothed and calmed with his hands and his quiet words of encouragement.

The wicked grin that lit up his face told her exactly what he was happy to oblige her with. 'You only have to ask.'

If she had the courage to do exactly that, she doubted she'd be able to hold out against him any longer. He might love his daughter, but he didn't love her, and that was the bottom line. 'Asking is not my strong point.'

'Don't I know it?' The grin didn't dim.

Neither did the tightening sensations low in her belly. That grin would get the man anything. Two days after giving birth and she wanted Cooper? She could want all she liked, but she wasn't getting him. Even if her body was ready—*no, body, you're not*—she would not give in to the heat that rose through her far too often whenever Cooper was near. Heck, he only had to look at her and she melted.

'You've gone quiet.' Finally he stopped grinning, his mouth tightening as he crossed to look down at his daughter. 'About this afternoon…'

They were going home. Pounding began behind her eyes. The fun was about to start. She'd have to manage without nurses popping in to check up on Lily, without help at the press of a button, no more grumpy little lady banging less-than-tasty meals down on the bedside table. 'I'm looking forward to it,' she fibbed.

'I'm taking you home with me.'

They'd agreed it would be best if Cooper picked them up rather than her trying to cope with a taxi. He'd even taken the latter half of the afternoon off work. 'I know…

Oh.' She finally heard what he'd really said. 'No, we're not going to your house. I've got the apartment ready.'

Her hands were enfolded in large warm ones. 'You can leave any time you like. But you've been so snug in here and my house is toasty warm. Not to mention I can cook dinner every night, save you having to worry about what to have.'

Her apartment was chilly, the heat pump never quite getting up to speed despite the fix-it man working on it twice. 'I can manage my own meals.' That's what can openers were for.

'I'll get up to change Lily's nappies during the night.'

'Sold.'

The grin returned. 'Should've said that first and saved myself the trouble of having to cook dinners.'

Cooper's house was as warm as Sophie's hospital room had been because he'd loaded up the log burner before going to pick her and Lily up. He'd made up the bed in the room she'd been using before she'd hightailed it to her apartment. He'd put a bassinet where it would be easy to reach. There was a change table and stacks of nappies and wipes and singlets and little bodysuits. All things he'd purchased last night after leaving the hospital. They'd come in useful whenever Lily was with him.

Sophie stared around, then choked up. 'You make everything seem so easy.'

'Happy to help.' *Tick.* Another point in his favour. He was probably making an idiot of himself, but how else could he entice her to move in permanently? His little bundle of joy flexed an arm, diverting his attention away from Sophie. His heart swelled.

Doubt trickled into Sophie's face.

'You're overthinking things again.' Cooper laid Lily

in the bassinet. 'One day at a time, okay?' He held his hand out, his mood suddenly serious. Wrong. Not serious. Vulnerable.

'You really want us here, don't you?' A pulse beat in her throat.

'Yeah, Sophie, I do.'

More than you can believe.

He'd do anything to change her mind about living alone, put as much energy into winning her over as he used to put into keeping women at a distance. Hard to believe he was the same man. Maybe he wasn't. All because of this wonderful woman.

'I love you,' said Sophie.

Cooper blinked one eye open. The lounge was in semi darkness and no one was standing by the couch he'd fallen asleep on. No Sophie. He must've dreamt those three little words. Because he wanted to hear them so much?

Soft warmth held his arm against the back of the couch. Glancing down, he took in the tiny dark head tucked against his chest. Of course. He'd taken Lily to change her after a feed.

When he'd returned with the baby to her bedroom Sophie had been comatose. Pulling the covers over her, he'd beaten a hasty retreat and settled here with Lily until such time as one or other female woke.

He hadn't meant to fall asleep. Guess the birth and a full operating schedule every day this past week had finally caught up. No wonder he'd imagined he'd heard Sophie saying the impossible.

His eyes drooped shut. Ping. He stared across the room to where he thought he'd heard something. 'Sophie?'

'Who else?'

His blood heated some more as the full effect of her smile touched him. If only that hadn't been a dream. 'Last time I saw you...' Her face had been soft and devoid of worry, her mouth curved upward and her cheeks flushed rosy pink. 'You looked so relaxed I couldn't wake you.'

'You should've. I don't have four surgeries scheduled for tomorrow. Or is it today?'

If only it was Saturday. The alarm wouldn't go off at six. His patients wouldn't be lying in wait after a sleepless night. His daughter and Sophie would be with him all day. 'What is the time?'

'Time I took over so you can go to bed and get a proper rest.' She was there, reaching down for their daughter, those full breasts spilling forward inside her pyjama top.

Sexy. Beautiful. But most of all a woman in love with her infant. If only she had enough for him as well. 'How long have you been watching us?'

The rosy pink in her cheeks intensified. 'I woke in the dark and panicked. Tore out here looking for Lily. Seeing you holding her like she's precious, even in your sleep: it's a picture I'll never forget.' She turned her head away.

Snatching at her hand, he brought her hand to his lips, brushed a soft kiss across her palm.

'Cooper.' Her voice sounded lower than normal, and strained. Slowly her head came round so she faced him, apprehension tightening her mouth.

Thud, thud inside his chest. She was going to drop a bombshell, he could see it in her eyes. He tried to deflect her. 'Go back to bed. I'll bring Lily to you when she wakes.' Coward.

'I— You—' She closed her eyes and drew a long, slow breath. Then she locked her gaze on him. 'I love you.'

What? Was he still asleep? The beating going on against his ribs told him, no, he was wide awake. That he'd heard the one thing he'd been wanting to hear for days. But he needed to be sure. 'I dreamt of you telling me that.'

Her smile was shy. 'It wasn't a dream. I did say it while you were lying there.'

He wanted to leap to his feet and punch the air, shout out the window, wake the whole street. He needed to hold Sophie, tell her his feelings. But he was holding his daughter. Without taking his eyes off Sophie, he slowly eased upright. 'You love me.'

The wonder filling him, wiping away all the doubts, was turning him into a puddle of love and desire.

Her eyes were wide, filled with worry. Where had his strong, brave woman gone? 'Yes,' she whispered. 'Yes.'

'Don't be afraid,' he said softly against the continuous thumping still going on in his chest. 'I needed to know that.'

'You did?' Her teeth were gnawing at her bottom lip.

Carefully placing Lily on the baby rug spread on the floor, he reached for Sophie's hand, tugged gently. 'Come here.'

The moment she lowered herself onto the couch he shuffled sideways so they were touching from shoulder to hip to thigh. With his free hand he took her chin to turn her to face him. Locking his eyes on hers, he told her the truth. 'No one has ever told me that before.'

'No one? What about your father?'

'Men in my family don't use the L word. The one and only time I told someone I loved her I was eight and she was twenty-eight. She left Dad the next day.'

'You don't say it, but you certainly show it. I've seen how much you care about me since you first learned we were pregnant.' The nibbling stopped. Hard to continue when those full lips were lifting into a smile. A smile that was quickly dampened with a stream of tears.

'I will always look out for my own.' A road block in his throat kept him from saying anything else.

'I don't want to be a responsibility. I want to be some-one you share your life with.'

His jaw slackened. The road block became thicker. And the knots in his gut loosened. 'That's what I want too.' He'd known it for weeks now, had probably felt it since the day their world had exploded in shrapnel, bullets and dirt. But he'd been afraid to voice it in case Sophie turned him down again. Coward. Love was worth laying his heart on the line for. He'd been wrong to deny himself. But... His lungs expanded on a new breath. Could he say the L word?

Unaware of what he was trying to say, Sophie contin-ued. 'I'm glad I told you. In fact, I'll tell you again. Coo-per Daniels, I, Sophie Ingram, love you from the bottom of my heart. And...' Her hand came between them, palm up. 'And I always will.'

Absolutely. 'And I love you, Sophie, most sexy, beau-tiful woman on the planet.' Go for it. Risk all to gain all. 'Mother of my child, filler of my dreams, I have to ask you. Will you marry me?'

The baby shrieked.

Sophie laughed.

And he held his breath.

'Bad timing, little one,' Sophie spluttered. 'Guess that's what a mother's life's all about.'

His lungs were about to burst.

Sophie?

Stunning emerald eyes locked on his as she leaned in close and trailed a soft kiss over his mouth. 'Yes,' she breathed. 'Yes for the first time you asked. Yes for the second, and definitely yes today.'

Lily shrieked again.

'There's no denying that,' Cooper said as he handed their daughter to her mother. 'Did I really say I loved you? And did you agree to marry me at last?' His head was spinning. It had taken thirty years to tell someone he loved them and this time the result was unbelievable. No, make that amazing, wonderful. Perfect.

'All of the above.' Sophie nestled the baby against her nipple and grinned at him. 'Didn't hurt a bit, did it?'

'No. Funnily enough, it didn't. I should've tried it years ago.'

Sophie's grin dipped.

'Only in practice to make me better at it.'

Her lips tipped upwards again.

'You are so easy to please.' He grinned back.

'Don't get complacent already.' Then she looked down at their daughter. 'You don't know how lucky you are, darling, having Mummy and Daddy together, and loving each other.'

Cooper's heart swelled. 'I'm the lucky one around here.' He'd found love, learned to give love, and all many years before his old man had. 'All because of you,' he whispered against Sophie's lips. Just before he claimed them in their most passionate kiss yet.

EPILOGUE

'MERRY CHRISTMAS, MY *LOVELIES.*' Cooper swept into their bedroom with coffees in one hand and two small gifts perfectly wrapped in Christmas paper and with red ribbons in the other.

Sophie pinched herself. The most gorgeous man on the planet—even with that ridiculous Santa's hat on his head—and he was hers. 'Enjoying your honeymoon, are you?'

Yesterday they'd married in the rose garden at the Auckland Domain with a small group consisting of their parents and friends there to support them and share in the special moment.

'You bet. Here, let me take little one while you open this.' Cooper swapped present for baby in one deft move. Leaning in, he kissed her softly. 'I so love you, Sophie Daniels.'

'And I you, Mr Sex-in-Hard-Boots.'

'Love it when you talk dirty.' He grinned and tickled his daughter's tummy. 'Guess what I've got Mummy for Christmas? A pair of hard boots for me to wear to bed.'

Sophie spluttered into her coffee. 'Just as well I bought you sexy red lace knickers, then. In my size, of course.'

'Open your present, will you?'

'Patience not being your strong point, I guess I can do that.'

'I have better strong points.' He grinned.

'Not in front of the children.' She grinned back and tore the paper off the small jewellery box. Flipping the lid, she gasped at the silver charm bracelet lying on white satin. 'It's beautiful.' She'd wanted one for so long, but had thought it pathetic to buy her own. Picking the bracelet up, she rubbed her fingers over the charms Cooper had added. 'Aw, shucks, a heart. You really can be romantic when you try.'

His hand tapped his heart. 'She wounds so easily.'

'And a baby's bootie. For Lily.' Tears clogged her throat until she looked at the third charm, and then laughter cleared the blockage. 'A work boot.'

'A *hard* work boot. Cool, eh?' He looked so pleased with himself. 'I had that one made specially.'

Sophie slipped the bracelet onto her wrist, her fingers lingering on the hard boot. 'It's beautiful. Thank you.' Then she leaned closer to thank him properly. Married kisses were just as exciting as previous ones.

Of course Lily interrupted, not liking to be left out of most things her parents were doing.

Cooper sighed. 'Yes, my girl, there's a present from Santa for you too, but I don't think it's going to distract you long enough for me to give your mother her real Christmas present.'

'Santa, you're a bad influence.' Sophie opened the second present and a similar, though smaller bracelet glittered at her. 'I'm glad you chose different charms.' Her heart filled with love for this man who'd become such an essential part of her during the last year. When she'd seen the New Year in at a party last January she'd no idea what was in store for her. Just went to show life was full of surprises. 'I'd better get up. Everyone will be arriving soon.'

'Melanie's already phoned. She's running late. Jacob's being difficult this morning.'

'We will hold off opening presents until they're here. My parents are always late anyway.' She reached for Cooper's hand. 'I can't believe we're having a real Christmas, as in family and friends and parcels and a big, eat-too-much lunch.'

'A proper one with parents, or grandparents, depending who you are.' His eyes were moist. 'Thank you. I never had this and thought I never would. I owe you for ever.'

Now Sophie's eyes filled, and she shook her head at her husband. 'No, you don't. We are not beholden to each other. Not when we love each other so much. Our daughter is so lucky to have us, and everything we can give her, like a perfect Christmas Day.'

'I'll go put that turkey in.'

'We're not eating for hours. It'll be dry.'

'Turkey's take hours, slow cooking and plenty of basting. Trust me, it will be perfect.'

Sophie laughed. 'I trust you with most things, but cooking the turkey?' She shook her head at him. 'I'm going to ring Gillian and ask her.' Darn, but that sounded like they were part of a family. Of course they were. That had brought it home to her, that was all. That was everything. There were people in her life she could ring and have inane conversations with about how to cook the turkey or what to do when Lily was grizzly. It had taken time but now she had the life she'd once dreamed of. Everything had come together. Sinking back into the pillow, she beamed at Cooper and Lily. 'Wow.'

'That's it? Wow?'

'Yeah. I am so happy.'

And when Cooper kissed her again she knew for real how lucky she was. Especially when Lily didn't interrupt this kiss. *Wow.*

* * * * *

If you enjoyed this story, check out these other great reads from Sue MacKay

DR WHITE'S BABY WISH
BREAKING ALL THEIR RULES
A DECEMBER TO REMEMBER
REUNITED...IN PARIS!

All available now!

MILLS & BOON®

MEDICAL ROMANCE™

THE ULTIMATE IN ROMANTIC MEDICAL DRAMA

A sneak peek at next month's titles...

In stores from 29th December 2016:

- **Falling for Her Wounded Hero** – Marion Lennox
  and **The Surgeon's Baby Surprise** – Charlotte Hawk

- **Santiago's Convenient Fiancée** – Annie O'Neil
  and **Alejandro's Sexy Secret** – Amy Ruttan

- **The Doctor's Diamond Proposal** – Annie Claydon
  and **Weekend with the Best Man** – Leah Martyn

Just can't wait?
Buy our books online a month before they hit the shops!
www.millsandboon.co.uk

Also available as eBooks.

MILLS & BOON®

EXCLUSIVE EXTRACT

Saoirse Murphy's proposal of a 'convenient'
arrangement with paramedic Santiago Valentino
soon ignites a very inconvenient passion...

Read on for a sneak preview of
SANTIAGO'S CONVENIENT FIANCÉE
by Annie O'Neil

Saoirse went up on tiptoe and kissed him.

From the moment her lips touched Santiago's she
didn't have a single lucid thought. Her brain all but
exploded in a vain attempt to unravel the quick-fire
sensations. Heat, passion, need, longing, sweet and tangy
all jumbled together in one beautiful confirmation that
his lips were every bit as kissable as she'd thought they
might be.

Snippets of what was actually happening were hitting
her in blips of delayed replay.

Her fingers tangled in his silky, soft hair. Santi's wide
hands tugged her in tight, right at the small of her back.
There was no doubting his body's response to her now.
The heated pleasure she felt when one of his hands
slipped under her T-shirt elicited an undiluted moan of
pleasure. He matched her move for move as if they had
been made for one another. Her body's reaction to his
felt akin to hitting all hundred watts her body was capable
of for the very first time.

She wanted more.

No.

She wanted it *all*. The whole package. The feelings. The pitter-patter of her heart. Knowing it was reciprocated. Being part of a shared love. Not some sham wedding so she wouldn't have to live in a country where her soul had all but shriveled up and died.

She felt Santi's kisses deepen and her will-power to shore up some sort of resistance to what was happening plummeted. This felt so *real*. And a little too close to everything she'd hoped for wrapped up in a too-good-to-be-true package. That sort of thing didn't happen to her. And it wasn't. She'd started it, Santi was just responding. She heard herself moan and with its escape her resolve to resist abandoned her completely.

Don't miss
SANTIAGO'S CONVENIENT FIANCÉE
by Annie O'Neill

Available January 2017
www.millsandboon.co.uk

MILLS & BOON®

Why shop at millsandboon.co.uk?

Each year, thousands of romance readers find their perfect read at millsandboon.co.uk. That's because we're passionate about bringing you the very best romantic fiction. Here are some of the advantages of shopping at www.millsandboon.co.uk:

* **Get new books first**—you'll be able to buy your favourite books one month before they hit the shops

* **Get exclusive discounts**—you'll also be able to buy our specially created monthly collections, with up to 50% off the RRP

* **Find your favourite authors**—latest news, interviews and new releases for all your favourite authors and series on our website, plus ideas for what to try next

* **Join in**—once you've bought your favourite books, don't forget to register with us to rate, review and join in the discussions

Visit **www.millsandboon.co.uk** for all this and more today!